D0925269

## UNCORRECTED PROOF FOR REVIEW
## PURPOSES ONLY – NOT FOR SALE

Content may change before release.
If quoting passages, please refer to the sales edition.

**Published by**
Isotopia Publishing

**Tentative Publication Details**
*(Sale date and price subject to change)*
On-sale date: February 8, 2022
Ebook Price: $5.99
Paperback Price: $19.99
Hardcover Price: $29.99

Ebook ISBN: 979-8-9853303-1-1
Paperback ISBN: 979-8-9853303-0-4
Hardcover ISBN: 979-8-9853303-2-8

**For publicity or to request additional
review copies, email:**
beth@bethcgreenberg.com

# THE QUEST FOR PSYCHE

## BETH C. GREENBERG

### A NOVEL

To Michelle—
Thanks so much for
bringing Cupid into
your heart!

ISOTOPIA
PUBLISHING

For anyoe and everyone
who wants to believe.

BOOKS BY
BETH C. GREENBERG

THE CUPID'S FALL SERIES:
*First Quiver*
*Into the Quiet*
*Quite the Pair*
*The Quest for Psyche*


*Isotopia,* by Jeff Greenberg
(prepared for publication by Beth Greenberg)

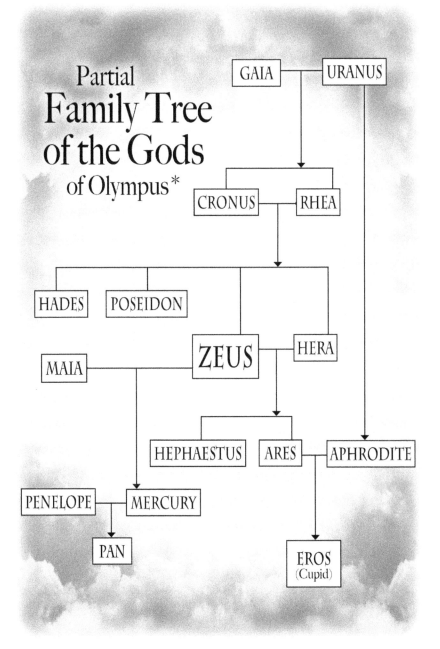

Partial
# Family Tree
# of the Gods
of Olympus*

GAIA — URANUS

CRONUS — RHEA

HADES    POSEIDON

**ZEUS** — HERA

MAIA

HEPHAESTUS    ARES — APHRODITE

PENELOPE — MERCURY

PAN

EROS
(Cupid)

*This chart reflects the names chosen by each
god/goddess after the Great Syncretism in the year 480.

A full cast of divine characters can be found at the back of the book.

She had not yet seen her destined husband. He came only in the hours of darkness and fled before the dawn of morning, but his accents were full of love, and inspired a like passion in her. She often begged him to stay and let her behold him, but he would not consent. On the contrary he charged her to make no attempt to see him, for it was his pleasure, for the best of reasons, to keep concealed.

"Why should you wish to behold me?" he said. "Have you any doubt of my love? Have you any wish ungratified? If you saw me, perhaps you would fear me, perhaps adore me, but all I ask of you is to love me. I would rather you would love me as an equal than adore me as a god."

—"THE TALE OF CUPID AND PSYCHE"

Translated from the Latin of Lucius Apuleius by Charles Stuttaford

# JUDICIOUS HONESTY

Nothing agitated Pan more than standing idly by—especially while Cupid was drowning in heartache across town. Punishment of a mischievous god was no laughing matter, and the God of Love had earned himself a doozy of a punishment—actually, *three* doozies and counting. Three burning, all-consuming, unrequited loves.

First came Mia, the sexy yoga instructor raising three young sons on her own. Next came Ruthie, the middle-aged writer of romance whose marriage was on the brink of collapse. And just when Cupid thought his torment couldn't get any worse, Aphrodite cursed her son's heart with a raging passion for his best friend Pan.

It wasn't Pan's fault Cupid was hopelessly in love with him or that Cupid was duty-bound to help Pan find true love with someone else, but that didn't make him feel any less lousy about it. The two old friends had been busy untangling their feelings when along came Professor Reed Scully, the genteel, intellectual, *straight* mortal Aphrodite had chosen as Pan's Right Love. Though they seemed the unlikeliest pair, Pan and Reed fell swiftly and thoroughly in love. Soon after, Cupid stopped communicating with both of them.

As Cupid's friend, Pan would have been inclined to let him slip off the radar to lick his wounds. But as Concierge to the Divine, Pan had an obligation to watch over Cupid until his ascent home to Mount Olympus. Radio silence was not an option.

Seeing that his partner needed help, Reed had gently offered up his plan, one that required Pan's trust and patience. Trusting Reed turned out to be astonishingly easy. The professor was the smartest, kindest person Pan had ever known, and he, too, had a sweet spot for Cupid.

Patience, however, would never be Pan's strong suit. He really, *really* hated waiting, and he did so now in typical god-of-the-wild fashion—pacing furiously. Trailing him back and forth across Reed's kitchen floor were the four shepherds that had so quickly grown attached to Pan, and if he were being honest, the feeling was mutual.

The phone in Pan's tense grip buzzed with Reed's incoming texts. He stopped dead in his tracks.

**Pizza delivered. Q promised to take your call. Good luck. I'll be in my car.**

*Good ol' Reed.* The meat lover's pizza had broken the ice. Now it was up to Pan.

He dialed Cupid's number and brought the phone to his ear. "C'mon, Q. Pick up, pick up, pick—"

"Hi."

Pan's heart jolted at the sound of his best friend's voice. "Hey!" The simple exchange was the first he and Cupid had spoken in days. Yesterday morning, Pan had sent an all-caps text demanding to know if Cupid was still on Earth. Cupid had sent back a thumbs-up emoji.

"Thanks for the Trojan pizza," said Cupid.

"Sorry for being sneaky, but we couldn't think of any other way to get you to talk to me."

"It's actually pretty delicious." The image of Cupid enjoying the pizza brought a half smile to Pan's face.

"Nothing better than a greasy pizza to cure a mai tai hangover," said Pan.

"*Mai tai?* That's oddly specific."

*Whoops.*

Cupid sighed loudly. "Cheri called you."

"She cares about you." That she did, and since both Cupid and Pan had slept with the bartender of the Stagecoach and they were all on good terms, Pan knew he could count on her to look out for Cupid.

"I didn't realize you had the whole town spying on me."

"You're still my responsibility, you know." Pan regretted the words even as they left his mouth.

"That's why you called? Because I'm your job?"

"Dammit, Q!" Pan's raised voice drew Margaux to his side, and Pan skimmed his hand along the Beauceron's back to soothe her. "No, that's not why I called. Can you just give me a chance, please?"

"I answered the phone, didn't I?"

Yes, he had, and Pan couldn't blow this opportunity. "You know I felt terrible about having to say you couldn't go to therapy." Pan could not imagine any scenario where the Divine Council would look favorably on Cupid blabbing to some mortal about his feelings.

"That makes two of us." Boy, Cupid wasn't making this easy on him.

"You can count Reed as three. He wouldn't let it go until he found a solution—which he did, of course." Pan couldn't keep the pride out of his voice.

"Reed? Why didn't he tell me about it himself when he brought the pizza?"

"He knew you would need to hear me say I'm okay with it first," Pan answered.

"Wait, you're okay with therapy now?"

"There's an app," Pan answered cautiously.

"Like a dating app?"

"Sort of, but instead of finding you a date, this app connects you with a mental health professional. Reed can explain all the details to you. The important thing is that the whole process can take place through a chat window. You and the therapist won't ever actually speak to each other—hence, less chance of accidental blurting."

Cupid huffed. "So you don't want me to be honest."

"I want you to be *judiciously* honest."

"What does that mean?"

"It means there's a way of telling the truth without spilling your last gut."

"*Hmph!* If what Reed said about confidentiality is true, we shouldn't have to worry about spilled guts."

"Yes, in theory," Pan said, "but there are certain details that would land us all in grave trouble with both the gods and the mortals, not the least of which is getting yourself committed to a lockdown unit of a psych hospital."

"I'm not an idiot, Pan."

"I know that." It was just that he was so goddamn honest.

"How is this person supposed to help me if I don't tell them everything?"

"Because at the end of the day, your problems are no different from the majority of humans walking around this planet: a shattered heart, an effed-up relationship with your mother, trust issues up the ying-yang. That ought to be plenty for you and your therapist to chew on."

"Great." Cupid went quiet.

"For what it's worth, Q, I think you should go for it."

"You do?"

"Yeah, I do. It's already been a whole week with no sign of your next Worthy—or has Aphrodite set your heart on someone new, and you've kept it from me?"

"Nope. It's still you," Cupid said with a sad sigh that felt like a hand squeezing Pan's heart.

"And who knows how much longer she'll keep your heart twisting over me? What if—" Pan couldn't say the words.

"What if *what*, Pan?"

Pan cringed. As long as he'd lived and as much as he'd seen, Pan would never be good at delivering crappy news. "What if *this* is your eternity?"

A soft, scared voice melted Pan's heart. "You really think I messed up that bad with you?"

"No! Hell, I can't figure out where you messed up at all, but we both know it's not what I think that matters."

"No," said Cupid. "I just never imagined Mother could leave me here forever with my heart in a million pieces."

"And she may not," Pan offered hopefully. "Your heart could be set on someone new any minute, and you'd be over me before you could say 'whiplash.' But still . . ." *Ugh.* There was no sugar-coating this, as much as Pan wished he could. "We have to believe your next breakup will be even worse, and worse again after that."

"I can't even imagine how," Cupid said with a groan.

"Probably not helpful to try. The point is, some coping skills and professional support could be really damn helpful, and Reed has convinced me this app is worth a try. The man conducted a scientific investigation that would put Apollo to shame."

"That was kind of him."

"That would be Reed." Pan stiffened his shoulders and pulled on his lover's affect like a favorite sweater. "I want to make damn sure Q doesn't end up at the hands of some quackadoodle who'll do more harm than good."

"That's what he said? Quackadoodle?" Pan could hear Cupid's grin.

"Yep. This from the PhD." Pan was beaming now. "Reed is ready and willing to share what he's learned with you. Just say the word, and I'll send him back upstairs."

"What? Where is he?"

"He's sitting in the parking lot outside your building." Pan chuckled.

"You're okay if Reed and I decide this without you?"

Hell no, Pan wasn't okay. He hated that Cupid couldn't stand being in his presence.

"Of course," Pan replied. "Whatever it takes."

"You know I would never want to cause any problems for you and Reed."

"Are you kidding? We wouldn't even be a 'we' without you."

"Let's not go there, Pan."

Pan hadn't planned on heading down this path, but he was on it now. "I should have been your easiest Worthy. I know who you are. I know why you're here. And I know"—his voice caught—"I know you love me."

"Pan, *please*." Cupid was straining to keep it together, too.

"Let me just get this out?" Pan waited for Cupid's sigh. "At first, I wanted to hold out hope it would be you and me. And then, I couldn't quite accept that I deserved to be a Worthy. And then, Reed . . ." Pan tipped his face toward the gods, who were surely still laughing. "I mean, *Reed.* What the fuck, right?"

"Right," Cupid echoed quietly.

"I was an ass, and I just needed to tell you I'm sorry for all the crap I put you through, and I love you and thank you for not giving up on me." Pan was weepy and sniffly and starting to feel ridiculous even if only the dogs could see him. "*Heh*. Look who's spilling his guts now."

Pan ugly-snorted, making them both crack up. They stayed on the phone together, laughing until they were spent.

"Thank you for this," Cupid said after the laughter trailed off. "And I plan to work really hard on myself so I can be around you without hurting so much."

"That's good, Q. I've missed you."

"Me too, Pan. So much."

Pan's heart split wide open. "Can we talk again soon?"

"Sure. This wasn't so bad." Still a lousy liar, but Pan had no desire to call him on it this time. "Bye, Pan."

"Take care, man."

Pan's heart was a little lighter as he tapped out his text to Reed: **Your turn**.

2

# WINGS

Cupid was in desperate need of a shower, but he barely had time to throw on a clean shirt before Reed arrived with a soft tap on the door.

"*Now* will you have a slice of pizza?" Cupid asked, grinning at the friend who had practically run out of his apartment earlier.

Reed smirked back. "Sure, if you have one to spare."

"Make yourself at home. I'm sorry, I don't have much to offer you to drink." In fact, the contents of Cupid's refrigerator consisted of four packets of ketchup, half a lime, and a quart of curdled milk.

"Water's fine." Reed was busy arranging his jacket and cane on the chair beside him when Cupid returned with the water, a clean plate, and a napkin. "Thank you. Your conversation with Pan went well?" Reed slid one of the two remaining slices onto his plate, then drew the pizza to his mouth.

"Probably as well as it could have. Thank you for whatever you did to convince him to reconsider therapy."

"Glad I could help. How much did Pan tell you about how this works?"

"He just mentioned an app. So, what do I do? Put up a pathetic-looking profile picture and hope someone feels sorry enough for me to swipe right?"

Reed smiled kindly. "Not quite. Basically, you enter some details about your situation, and they match you up with one of their online caregivers. Then, you and this person communicate by phone or email."

"Sounds easier than dating," Cupid said.

"Yes and no," Reed replied mysteriously. "Might I show you what I discovered?"

Reed waited, eyebrows cocked, for Cupid's nod before placing his phone on the table between them. "I've made a study of the various features of each of the apps—areas of expertise, anonymity of user, ease of navigation of the site—so as to narrow the field."

"And to weed out the *quackadoodles*."

Catching Cupid's amused grin, Reed grinned right back. "That too."

"And how many are in this narrow field?"

Lowering his chin, Reed peered over his glasses at Cupid. "One."

Cupid leaned in closer as Reed tapped on the app, a white butterfly with the word "Wings" in light purple. The dot over the *i* transformed into a tiny butterfly flapping its wings as the slogan appeared: *We give you back your wings.*

"My wings. *Huh.*" Cupid hadn't much thought about those wings since his descent, aside from the occasional flight Morpheus had sent him in dreams. There was much to be said for feeling solid ground beneath one's feet. "I'm not sure getting back my wings is going to improve my situation."

"Oh. *Right*," said Reed. "Most, uh, mortals—sorry, I'm still getting used to referring to myself that way—would hear 'wings' as a metaphor for freedom. In your case, the *actual* wings complicate the issue, but if you can set that aside for now . . .?" Again, Reed waited for Cupid's confirmation.

As Reed tapped and swiped and explained what he'd obviously spent much time studying, Cupid marveled at the comfort of being in Reed's company again and how much he'd missed their friendship. Reed's bright-eyed exhilaration had a way of spilling over, especially when he slipped into teaching mode.

"Now here's the real beauty of Wings, and why we believe it's perfect for you."

The "we" jolted Cupid like a strike of Zeus's lightning bolt—swift, unexpected, and devastating. Reed and Pan were the "we," the Right Love bond Cupid would forever remain outside of.

Reed had stopped talking. "Sorry, have I lost you?"

Lost seemed the perfect word to describe Cupid's state, not just now but through his whole, pitiful life. From Earth, Cupid could so plainly see how he had never fit in on Mount Olympus, how his bubble of privilege and his love-tipped arrows had distanced him from anyone who might have formed a genuine attachment. Only Pan had ever broken through, and Cupid had lost him twice, first to death and now to Love.

How did this misery end? An hour stretched out like a year before him. Eternity was unimaginable.

The room tilted like a dance floor with flashing lights. Cupid gripped the table with both hands.

"Q?" Reed's fingertips met Cupid's white knuckles, a tentative touch that drew Cupid's gaze. "Is this okay?"

Cupid nodded. Reed's touch didn't sting like Pan's.

"Look, this takes courage. I get that." Reed settled his palm gently over Cupid's fist. "The hardest part is taking that first step, allowing yourself that hope that you can feel good again. And you *can* feel good again."

Reed's expression held all the intensity of his own journey—the physical and emotional trauma of being shot at close range, the loss of the teaching job he loved so dearly, the grueling battle to regain use of his leg, and finally, acceptance.

"You were saying, about the beauty of this app?"

A warm smile broke across Reed's face. He tapped his phone where it said *Meet your therapist.* "Doctor Mariposa Rey. Impressive bio. Impeccable references. Rest assured, I have thoroughly vetted them all."

"Thank you, Reed. I—"

"Not at all." Reed waved his hand to stem the flow of Cupid's gratitude. "She has five years of experience with remote patient treatment, so she knows the milieu."

"Milieu?"

"Sorry," Reed said. "She's familiar with the online therapy environment. *And* she's the only practitioner, which makes Pan very happy."

Cupid understood that part well enough. "Only one person to worry about when I blurt."

"It is a consideration," Reed replied somewhat apologetically, "but it's all good. Dr. Rey *is* Wings. And if you'll indulge me in a moment of logophilia . . .?" Reed glanced up hopefully, wildfire dancing behind his eyes.

Cupid couldn't keep up with the man's vocabulary. No wonder Pan had started tossing around big words lately. "Sure?"

Reed chuckled. "I'm a serious word nerd, so I couldn't help but notice that the doctor's first name, Mariposa, is Spanish for butterfly—"

"Wings!"

"Yes, *and*," said Reed in his teacher voice, "*butterfly* is also the English translation of . . .?" Reed made a wheel of his hand and rolled his question at Cupid, whose heart started to pound as it had back at the Academy whenever the teachers caught him unprepared.

Cupid could only answer with a shrug.

Unlike the instructors on Mount Olympus, Reed didn't torture Cupid for the answer he didn't have. "Your friend and mine, *Psyche*." Reed regarded Cupid as if he'd just untied the Gordian Knot.

"Huh." Reed's word games felt a bit circular to Cupid, but he was happy Reed was enjoying his discovery. "You really think this Dr. Rey can give me a reason to get out of bed?"

Reed nodded. "I wouldn't be here if I didn't think so."

Cupid would have agreed to bloodletting if he'd thought there was a glimmer of hope. "Okay, I'll give it a try."

"Excellent! I'll stick around while you work through the registration process. Some of the assessment questions can be a little tricky."

"It's okay, Reed, you don't need to trouble yourself—"

"No trouble at all. I'll just . . . declutter a bit." He was already out of his chair, scooping up a pair of discarded socks. "Think how much better you'll feel when you can see your floor again."

Whatever gains Reed's tidying up made on Cupid's mood were lost again as Cupid worked through the disclaimers. He'd seen the phrasing before on dating apps—no guarantees *that*, not a substitution *for*, can't be responsible *if*—and each checked box chipped away at Cupid's optimism. The last warning stopped him cold.

*This app is not for you if you are in urgent crisis.*

Cupid had been in urgent crisis since he'd been tossed off the Mount. For three months now, the bliss of passionate love and the wrenching pain of heartbreak had thrown Cupid from one extreme to the other. This app *had* to work—he was fresh out of options.

The next section was easier. No history of severe mental illness, never hospitalized. He was nearly in the clear when another hurdle jumped in front of him: *This is not the right solution for you if you have thoughts of hurting yourself or others.*

"Reed?"

"What is it?" Seeing Cupid's stricken expression, Reed rushed to his side. "Oh. That day you came to Pan's for your arrow?"

Cupid nodded.

"Have you thought about hurting yourself again?"

"No." Cupid had focused on drowning his pain with a steady stream of alcohol, sex, and sleep. "I'm pretty sure I couldn't end myself even if I wanted to."

Reed gave Cupid's shoulder a squeeze. "Let's not get tripped up on this. What's next?"

A whole lot of words Cupid had never heard before. With the patience of Penelope, Reed helped Cupid distinguish anxiety from depression, trauma from grief. Cupid next filled out something called the DASS-21. By the time he finished the survey, Cupid was truly wretched. Who could ever love such a mess? Certainly not a good man like Reed.

"You did well," Reed said, patting Cupid on the back. "Hard part's over. Now all you have to do is fill out the emergency contact info and choose a screen name."

"What's the emergency contact for?"

"They need to have a person they can contact in case your therapist becomes concerned you might be a danger to yourself or someone else."

"Would you be my emergency contact, Reed?"

Reed registered surprise before swiftly masking his emotions. "I would be most honored."

"Good." Cupid typed in Reed's contact info. "Now, for my screen name . . . could I just have her call me Q?"

3

# TREASURE HUNT

Posey had just signed off a chat session with *anxiousaddie* when the "new registration submitted" notification popped up in the corner of her screen. Her prospective new patient would have already received an automated response with another warning to call 911 in the event of an emergency and a disclaimer carefully crafted by her lawyer, giving Posey a twenty-four-hour window to respond, but it was conscience, not liability law, that dictated her standard of care. When a cry for help found her inbox, Mariposa Rey answered.

Caution always tempered the thrill of a new venture, but Posey clicked on the "inquiries" tab with a receptive mind and heart. The new patient interview opened, and she scanned it with practiced eyes: thirty-three-year-old male, no history of mental illness, first time seeking help.

The anonymity of the wide, wondrous web had proven to be as much of a godsend for Posey as for the patient. While many of her colleagues rejected the notion of administering therapy through a screen, for Posey, it was the only way.

Screen name: *CallMeQ*. How one self-identified to an unseen therapist was always a significant data point, whether it gave away much—*cry4help, upsanddowns, getmeagun, headcase*—or held its secrets. *CallMeQ* struck Posey as conversational—informal, light, almost playful. A friendly introduction, an opening handshake—an encouraging sign, she thought.

Most likely, the Q stood for the man's first name, but it was possible he was identifying with a fictional character. Two came to mind—the gadget specialist of James Bond fame and the complicated life-form from the *Star Trek* series Posey would have to study further if he turned out to be the inspiration. In any event, the screen name did not throw up any red flags. Posey pulled a robust breath through her lungs, releasing the pressure valve on the vigilance she'd learned to bring to each initial encounter.

Phase two: the treasure hunt. Five years of experience as an online therapist had taught her how to climb inside the new patient interview, how to read the pages like a map to the psyche, where to dig for buried treasure. Mental illness could be a crafty hide-and-seek player, but Posey prided herself on her ability to root out the truth.

She squeezed the lever that raised her desk to match her standing height. This part was physical; she couldn't be still if she tried. The trick, Posey had discovered long ago, was to free her mind from the linear. By poking around the intake form as curiosities struck her, she could most efficiently juggle and realign the pixels until a picture clicked into focus.

Posey often started with the DASS-21, the quickest gauge of the severity of a respondent's emotional pain. As with any other data point, the DASS responses were only as valid as the self-reporter's perceptions, but in this case, perception was often the most accurate indicator.

Let's see how you're managing, Q.

Aha! *There* were the telltale signs: a pronounced lack of motivation and meaning, fairly typical symptoms of depression. One other concerning response among the anxiety indicators raised Posey's antennae, a high frequency rating for "I was aware of the action of my heart in the absence of physical exertion." Bouncing to statement four, a similar anxiety indicator related to breathing, Posey noted his response: "did not apply to me at all." Zero. *Huh.*

An outlier, perhaps? The inconsistency was worthy of a mental note, even if one of the answers turned out to be an errant click. A patient's "mistakes" were often instructive too.

Okay, I see your pain. Now, let's see if we can locate the source.

Posey liked to save the "What brings you here today?" for the initial chat rather than the intake form. That didn't mean there weren't markers—in some cases, blinking neon signs—embedded in her questionnaire. Considering Q's age and the fact that this was the first time his distress had brought him to therapy, Posey had a hunch the appeal for help was tied to an event. But what?

Scroll, scroll, and *boom!* Relationship issues, tagged high on the distress scale. Posey would have bet her license some heartbreak had triggered this episode, the poor son of a bitch. Six times out of ten, a breakup was the impetus for seeking out therapy. If that were the case, Posey was certainly qualified to offer coping strategies—more qualified than she would have wished on her worst enemy.

What other breadcrumbs have you dropped for me, hmm?

"Well, *hello,*" she said aloud to the last high score on the "family relationships" page.

Family dynamics had always fascinated Posey. Every individual was part of some unique tapestry of interwoven threads—child and parent, marriage, divorce, sibling rivalries, birth order,

Oedipus, Electra, family pets, what-have-you—and like it or not, every individual was affected by those relationships. Posey could feel that familiar itch starting at the edge of her brain: *I can help.*

A working hypothesis was forming as the clues swirled together: depression, relationship issues, family conflict. Attachment issues, perhaps?

And now, it was time for the read-through from start to end, taking time to digest Q's answers as a holistic package. Were there pieces that did not fit? Absolutely. But did she have a fair idea of what she was getting herself into, and did she reasonably believe she could help this man? *Yes and yes.*

Those two yeses would have been enough to green-light the application, but there was something else, too, something humming between the lines, speaking directly to her intuition. Posey was intrigued.

And the timing was right. The orientation phase required an investment of time and energy Posey could only spend on one new patient at a time. Her five current patients were all in the later phases of therapy—three in the throes of exploration, the other two nearing resolution. Her plate was clear for onboarding a new patient.

Her fingers hovered over the keyboard, tingling with the new challenge. Something—or maybe everything—about the application inspired Posey to warm up her boilerplate invitation to entice him to follow through. She left off the request for insurance information; if and when the time came for discussing fees, Posey would make sure money did not present a barrier.

*Thank you for reaching out to Wings today. I have reviewed your registration materials. I'm sorry you are experiencing these challenges right now, and I believe I can help you improve the quality of your life.*

If you would like to pursue treatment, we will begin with an introductory session in a private chat room that will only be open to the two of us. Please respond with three time slots that work for you, and I will find a place in my schedule to accommodate you. I sincerely hope we can "meet" very soon.

Best regards,
Dr. Mariposa Rey

4

# IN MOTION

If Aphrodite had forgotten her shortcomings as a mother, spying on the psychologist provided a harrowing reminder.

"Dear me, what have I *done?*" the Goddess lamented atop a string of curses ill-suited to her delicate, royal lips. Served her right, she supposed, for not consulting Ares before setting this plan in motion. She had no choice but to tell him now, and he'd be none too pleased she'd gone rogue.

Aphrodite returned her gaiascope to its stand and strode to her dressing room on quickened feet. Anticipating her lover's mood, Aphrodite donned her softest, rose-petal pink chiton, painted her cheeks to a demure blush, and spritzed her cleavage with the perfume he'd gifted her after their last "strategy meeting" in the War Room. She slathered her feet with her finest lotion until her heels were as smooth as silk and slipped into her lowest sandals. Ares always enjoyed a height advantage.

Before dashing from her chamber, she plucked the gaiascope from its mahogany stand and slipped it inside the travel satchel. This was no time to be without Earth-vision.

She ordered her chariot hitched as she darted through the baker's kitchen, snatching three freshly baked sugar cookies, Ares's favorite, from the cooling racks. She hadn't seen her husband in days, not since the awkward summit in their bedroom, and she did not seek Hephaestus now for goodbyes.

Sweeping her robes into the golden carriage, Aphrodite set her thoughts on Ares's palace. Her doves flapped their downy wings in perfect unison and lifted her into the sky.

She closed her eyes, concentrating on the rhythmic thrush of wings and the gentle breeze on her cheeks, but there was no peace to be found today. Her mind whirred in frantic circles, searching for the right words to assuage her lover's ego, and her pulse quickened to keep pace with her thoughts. One did not seek out the God of War without a battle plan, and he was not a god easily distracted, no matter how enticing the seductions.

"Give our boy a challenge," Heph had said, and with that, identified the narrow overlap of the highly diverse motivations of Ares, Aphrodite, Cupid, and himself: allow Cupid his own Right Love before bringing him home, but make him work for it. After days of stewing, Aphrodite had come to grips with what she had to do.

The stroke of brilliance, if she did say so, was engineering the meet through Reed, the perfect unwitting envoy. The soft-hearted classics professor had already proven himself a most effective operator as the third corner of Pan and Cupid's love triangle, and now he'd discovered the butterfly.

No less muddled of mind or heart, Aphrodite pulled the gaiascope from its pouch and gripped the burnished bronze handles lovingly forged to fit her palms, now slick with sweat and with good reason—her worst fear was playing out before her very eyes. The doctor's offer to help came too quickly; Cupid's response was even swifter.

"Not yet!" she exclaimed into her Earth-glass. "Slow down!"

The dappled doves, confused by the unusual order issuing forth from their mistress, slowed their wings but not in sync. The golden chariot bumped and strained to find equilibrium, jouncing its solitary passenger from side to side.

"No, no! Not you!" she cried out to her doves across their jeweled yoke. "Onward to Ares with haste!"

The chariot righted as the doves regained their harmony, cutting a path toward the God of War as straight and true as one of Cupid's arrows. Not for the first time that day, Aphrodite wondered at the wisdom of her heart's wishes.

5

# EAGERNESS

Not ten minutes after she responded to the new applicant, a notification chime alerted Posey to his response. *My schedule is entirely flexible. The sooner the better.*

Mixed news. An "entirely flexible" schedule could indicate unemployment, lack of routine, possibly a lack of discipline, or an absence of positive social interaction. On the other hand, the flexible schedule could be the sign of a highly driven self-starter, the current lack of motivation a completely opposite state from normal, which would explain his urgency to get started.

In any case, Posey appreciated his eagerness. It nearly matched her own.

There was much to be said for striking while the iron was hot, at least that's what Posey told herself when she returned his message with an unusual offer: *Shall we meet in the chat room in fifteen minutes?*

His "YES!" reply made her wish she could send back a smiley emoji, but she'd tightroped enough professional lines already. She wrote back with the log-in instructions, drew a Q on the front cover of a fresh composition notebook, and opened to the first page with a thrum of exhilaration that accompanied the most promising beginnings. Her favorite pen seemed to spew the words by itself, like the old Ouija board she and her sisters used to bring out at slumber parties. Facts first, as Posey had been trained, jotting down today's date, Q's age, gender, and mental health history before moving on to complaints, concerns, and topics she'd want to touch upon in the chat room.

So deep was Posey into her thoughts that the notification chime gave her a start. He'd entered the chat room. Posey clicked on the link to join him.

In the upper right corner of her screen sat the avatar she'd created when she established Wings: a female, heart-shaped face with honey-toned skin, almond-shaped eyes with caramel-colored centers, a thin, straight nose, round lips with a deep Cupid's bow, and wavy, shoulder-length, chestnut hair. Except for the fact that she usually wore her hair clipped back off her face, the digital composite was a surprisingly accurate likeness.

Next to Posey's avatar, a square containing a blank silhouette awaited *CallMeQ*'s customization. He would be receiving prompts for selecting facial features and hair right now. She hoped Q would engage. Anonymity was a gift bestowed by the internet, but a faceless name on a screen offered little warmth. The customized avatars were a nice compromise. Safely hidden behind cartoon versions of themselves, Posey found she and her patients could more quickly form a human connection in the chat room. She could never tell, obviously, how closely any of her patients' avatars matched their actual looks, but she was curious to see how closely Q's aligned with the image her subconscious had created from his intake materials.

Soon enough, the face appeared, and she had her answer—*close*.

An oval face with a skin tone one or two shades lighter than her own, a classic Greek nose, bright baby-blues, wavy, black hair, and a pair of lips that might have been the perfect mate to her own.

And so we meet, Q.

6

# FIRST CHAT

Doctor Rey's quick response pulled Cupid from his pacing circuit, one of several bad habits he'd picked up from Pan. Reed
had reminded Cupid it could be hours, even a full day, before
he might hear back from the therapist, but Cupid had rushed
through his shower just in case. He knew the doctor couldn't
see him through the screen, but the invigorating shower and
crisp, clean clothes—*thank you, Reed*—felt like exactly the fresh
start Cupid needed.

The Wings avatar creator threw him. *Please choose a face
shape from the options below.* How was Cupid to be an expert in a
face he'd only known for eighty-six days? He wished Reed had
stayed to help him with this part, too. He started with the hair
choices—easy—but he had to consult a mirror six separate times
while picking his skin tone, nose shape, the exact color blue for
his eyes. He wasn't sure he had the other pieces right until he
dropped the lips into the frame. *Cupid's bow,* no question about
that, he chuckled, and just like that, he was looking at himself.

**MR:** Hello, CallMeQ.

The message popped up on the screen next to the doctor's cartoon likeness. The matching Cupid's-bow lips on Dr. Rey's avatar made Cupid smile.

**Q:** Hello, Dr. Rey.
**MR:** Please call me Posey.
**Q:** Like the flower.

His mother loved posies, especially bright-pink ones.

**MR:** Yes. How would you like me to refer to you?
**Q:** Q is fine.
**MR:** Very nice to meet you, Q.
**Q:** You as well.
**MR:** I'd like to start by telling you a little bit about how this process works and give you a chance to ask me any questions you might have. Does that sound okay?
**Q:** Yes

Cupid would have tacked on a smile after his response, but he didn't see any emojis.

The doctor proceeded to type several messages filled with details Cupid had already learned online, but he watched the screen politely and dropped in an "okay" here and there to let her know he was paying attention.

**MR:** If we both decide we're a good match, I recommend a course of 3 sessions to start. In between our chats, I will probably ask you to keep a journal of your thoughts and feelings. Does that sound comfortable?

That did not sound comfortable.

**Q:** Will you be reading the journal?
**MR:** Only what you want to share with me.
**Q:** I guess that would be okay.
**MR:** That brings me to my last and most important point. Since we're communicating with words on a screen, it will be harder for me to judge your comfort level than if we were sitting in a room together. I am relying on you to respond as honestly as you're able and to let me know if you're experiencing any discomfort, and I will do the same. Can we hold ourselves to that standard?

Cupid wasn't sure about any of it—not the honesty, not the journal, not the thoughts and feelings—but he sensed that this app, this doctor, would be his best chance. He was so tired of feeling awful.

**Q:** Yes
**MR:** Excellent. Do you have any questions for me? Anything about our process or therapy in general?

He mostly just wanted to get on with it. In fact, just chatting with Posey had already brought him a glimmer of hope—though he supposed it might have been the clean underwear and not smelling like the dumpster behind the Stagecoach.

**Q:** Is it crazy I already feel a little bit better?

He felt foolish as soon as he hit send, but Posey's response eased him.

**MR:** Not at all. Making the decision to seek professional help is a powerful first step toward recovery. Sometimes, talking to a stranger who won't judge you can feel a lot safer than sharing with friends and family.

Considering Cupid's family, that wasn't saying much. As for his friends, Pan was clearly off-limits. Reed had quickly become a valued friend, but there were obvious boundaries. Mia and Ruthie didn't know the whole truth about him, and anyway, Ruthie was hundreds of miles away starting her new life.

**MR:** You're not alone, Q.

Posey's words leaped off the screen. *Alone* was exactly, profoundly, what he was. Now and into the indefinite future. His hands slid away from the keyboard. Tears stung his eyes.

*You're not alone.* Could he take those words inside his shattered heart? Maybe not yet, but they held him in their warm embrace, swirling around him like a caterpillar spinning its cocoon. The butterfly logo popped into his mind.

**MR:** Are you still with me?

How many times had Pan asked him that since his fall? Cupid wiped his eyes and started typing.

**Q:** Yes. Sorry. I was thinking about what you wrote.
**MR:** Processing is good. When you're ready, can you tell me what made you decide to seek therapy today?
**Q:** It's my heart. I've had a very rough breakup, and I can't seem to get past it.

**MR:** Heartbreak can be devastating. Do you recall when you first started feeling this way?

**Q:** Yes. Right after Mia. She was my first love.

**MR:** First loves often leave a heavy footprint on our hearts. How long ago did that relationship end?

**Q:** About two months ago.

**MR:** That's a long time to feel lousy. How long had you two been dating?

**Q:** About a week.

**MR:** I see. Do you want to tell me about Mia? If it's too painful, we don't have to talk about her.

**Q:** No, it's fine. Mia's great. She's an amazing mother to three great little boys. The baby was just starting to trust me when we were involved in a terrible car accident.

**MR:** Oh no! Was someone hurt?

**Q:** Yes, a truck driver was killed.

**MR:** I'm so sorry to hear it. That's terrible.

**Q:** It was awful. His brakes failed, and he ran a red light and caused an 8-car pileup.

**MR:** It sounds like a traumatic night. What about you and Mia and her boys? Everyone was okay?

**Q:** We were all fine. Mia wasn't in the accident. She was out on a date.

**MR:** With someone else?

**Q:** Yes

There was a longer pause than usual.

**MR:** Did you and Mia have an open relationship?

**Q:** I don't know what that means.

**MR:** It means the two of you had agreed to see other people while you were dating each other.

**Q:** Oh. We had agreed Mia would see other people.

**MR:** But not you?

**Q:** No, I couldn't. My heart was set on Mia.

**MR:** So you were okay with Mia seeing this other man the night of the accident?

**Q:** Not at all! That's why I went after her. Reese was going to break her heart, and I needed to let her know.

**MR:** You took Mia's boys to confront her while she was on a date with this Reese?

**Q:** I know that sounds bad. I didn't want to bring the boys to the restaurant with me, but I didn't have a choice. I was babysitting them at the time. Mia was very upset with me.

**MR:** I see. Would you say that decision is what caused your breakup?

In truth, their breakup came on their first date, in Mia's bed. Cupid pinched his eyes shut as the dizzying sequence of events replayed: the passionate lovemaking, his untimely declaration of love, Mia's horror, the deafening silence of her heartbeat. But it wasn't until he heard the drumbeats of Mia and Patrick's Right Love that Cupid's very last hope for some kind of divine override was dashed away.

**Q:** That was the night Mia met Patrick—the police officer in charge of the accident scene. I knew right away they were meant to be together. I had to let her go.

**MR:** They began a romantic relationship at the scene of the accident?

**Q:** No, not until the next morning.

The question brought a smile as Cupid recalled lugging armfuls of stuffed animals through the toy store aisles with the stiff and formal Lieutenant Goode, who was trying so very hard to win the boys' hearts—and, in turn, their mother's. Truth be told, the romantic gestures were Cupid's idea, but Patrick's heart was in the right place.

> **Q:** Anyway, Mia and the boys are happy, and that is all that counts.
> **MR:** And what about your happiness? You've been in pain for two months now?
> **Q:** Not the whole time. I got over Mia when I met Ruthie.
> **MR:** Who is Ruthie?
> **Q:** She's the woman I fell in love with after Mia.
> **MR:** May I ask how long after Mia?
> **Q:** It's hard to remember. I think it was 2 days.
> **MR:** You fell in love two days after you and Mia broke up?
> **Q:** It might have been 3 days.
> **MR:** What happened with Ruthie?
> **Q:** When I met her, she was having doubts about her marriage.
> **MR:** I see. Did you two have a physical relationship?

Remembering his promise, Cupid answered honestly though the memory still pained him.

> **Q:** Just the one time I tried to kiss her. It was a terrible slip. But pushing me away made Ruthie realize she wanted to save her marriage, so it worked out in the end.
> **MR:** For Ruthie.
> **Q:** And Zach. That's her husband.
> **MR:** So you sought out therapy after Ruthie broke your heart?
> **Q:** No. I'm here because Pan broke my heart.

**MR:** Who is Pan?

**Q:** Pan is my best friend.

**MR:** Your best friend broke your heart?

**Q:** Yes. I fell in love with Pan after Ruthie.

**MR:** Ah. How long after Ruthie?

**Q:** About a week.

**MR:** And what happened with Pan?

What didn't happen with Pan? But Cupid couldn't explore those memories, not yet.

**Q:** We tried to make it work, but he was meant to be with Reed.

**MR:** Pan is a man?

Oh, the different ways Cupid might have answered that question!

**Q:** Yes

**MR:** Do you mind if I ask about your sexual orientation?

**Q:** If you're going to ask me for a label, I don't have an answer. I just love who I love.

**MR:** Understood. Do you feel that "loving who you love" is problematic?

**Q:** You mean Mia, Ruthie, and Pan?

**MR:** Not specifically those individuals. Some people who identify within the LGBTQ community experience discrimination or violence because of their orientation. If that were the case, it would inform the way we craft your treatment plan.

**Q:** I don't think my problems have to do with any of that.

**MR:** Fair enough. Moving through your survey, I see you
have flagged family issues. I'd like to get some specifics if
that's okay?

Here was where doling out the truth would get really tricky.
He didn't want to hurt anymore, but he also didn't want to put
Pan in harm's way. Cupid took a deep, cleansing breath and
reminded himself to take his time with his answers.

Don't mention the Goddess of Love or the God of War . . .
or immortality.

**Q:** Sure
**MR:** Are your mother and father still alive?
**Q:** Yes
**MR:** Do you see them both on a regular basis?
**Q:** I live with my mother—or I did up until very recently.
I hardly ever see Father.
**MR:** Your father lives elsewhere?
**Q:** Yes. I've lived with my mother and stepfather as long as
I've been alive.
**MR:** So your parents have been divorced longer than 33 years?
**Q:** They were never married.
**MR:** Would you characterize their relationship as combative?

Right now, they were probably chasing each other around
Ares's compound naked. The visual made Cupid cringe, and he
failed to see how sharing it with Posey would "help inform his
treatment plan."

**Q:** The only thing I've heard them fight over is me.
**MR:** I see. And would you say you have a close relationship
with your mother?

The question made him swallow hard.

**Q:** Not anymore.
**MR:** Would you be able to pinpoint when that sense of
closeness changed?

Oh yes. Right at the exact moment she shoved him off
Mount Olympus.

**Q:** It was the day before I met Mia.
**MR:** The day after a rift with your mother, you fell in love for
the first time?
**Q:** Yes
**MR:** I see. Perhaps we can explore that a bit further?

Cupid was pondering his reply when another message
appeared on his screen.

**MR:** Oh dear! I've just noticed the time. I apologize, but I'm
afraid I have to end our conversation here for the time
being. Is there anything else I can answer for you about me
or the Wings model before we break?
**Q:** No, thank you.
**MR:** In that case, I'd like to review my notes and think about
whether this feels like a good therapeutic fit. I'd like you to
do the same. I'll be back in touch within 24 hours.
**Q:** I'll be here.

Never had Cupid uttered a truer statement, for where else
could he be? Stuck here in this dreaded limbo . . . but feeling,
miraculously, a little less alone.

# 7

# THE MOTHER'S PLIGHT

A flurry of activity in the front court of Ares's palace drew the God of War's attention from the gunfire at the Syrian border. The gaia wall cleared, suspending the view of the battlefield below to reveal a far more enticing scene just outside his window. A wide grin cut into his cheeks as he spied the cause of the commotion—an unannounced visit from one extremely agitated Goddess of Love.

Lately, nothing aroused Ares so thoroughly as the sight of Aphrodite—the more flustered, the better. Military skirmishes between foreign armies in faraway lands could only provide the God of War so much amusement. A good one-on-one conflict with a worthy adversary was the truest test of might, and the spoils of this war with Aphrodite were by far the sweetest he'd ever tasted. He flicked his tongue across his lips in anticipation of their first kiss of the day.

"Whatever has you so harried, Goddess?" he wondered aloud as he watched Aphrodite scramble out of her carriage. Oh, she was a hot mess, smoothing her mussed hair and disheveled robes while gesticulating frantically to the sentries. He could have interceded with no more than a wave inviting her upstairs, but he much preferred watching her grovel.

The urgent knock of his most trusted sentry came at the War Room door. "Beg pardon, sir!"

Ares played the scene to his fullest advantage, calling his answer through the closed door with carefully staged disdain. "What is the purpose of this intrusion?"

"The Goddess Aphrodite begs entrance. She says the matter involves your son and is of great urgency, and"—the voice grew more intimate—"the utmost privacy. How shall I answer, sir?"

Great urgency *and* utmost privacy? Ares could hardly have wished for a more tantalizing circumstance.

Challenging himself to keep her off-balance as long as possible, Ares inched open the heavy door. Aphrodite's dizzying perfume, thick with pheromones and the spices Ares had hand-picked himself from Apollo's apothecary, wafted into his nostrils and nearly wrenched his focus from the sentry. "Dismissed," Ares said curtly.

Only after the guard marched away did Ares turn his attention to Aphrodite. Robed in flesh tones, the flush of her regal cheekbones stood out like two ripe, red apples.

"Goddess." He dazzled her with his most charming smile but did not yield entry to his inner sanctum.

"Yassas."

My, my. Aren't we formal?

"You are looking particularly enticing this afternoon." Acknowledging her efforts was the very least he could do, and he did so with a lascivious gawp at her succulent breasts.

She blinked up at him through painted lashes, her sea-foam eyes rippling with nervous energy. Something was terribly wrong. He'd never wanted her more.

"To what do I owe the pleasure of your spontaneous visit?"

"I need you to see something," she said, frenetic gaze darting past him into the War Room.

Curiosity piqued, Ares invited her through the doorway. "By all means, come inside."

He could all but hear the wild flutter of her pulse as she squeezed past him, her nipple grazing his bare arm. He wasn't sure whether to award a point to her or himself.

"May I offer something to relax you? A glass of Athiri, perhaps?"

"Not now." She bolted to the gaia wall as if shot from a cannon, and Ares sped to her side. Worry creased her forehead as she summoned the view, what appeared to be a home office belonging to an unfamiliar female.

"What are we looking at?" he asked. "Who is that woman?"

Their view zoomed in on said woman and then closer still, to the pen moving across her page. SERIAL ROMANTIC, the woman wrote in all caps. OEDIPUS COMPLEX!! "Crap," said the woman, then slapped the notebook shut and held it down as if something terribly destructive might otherwise escape. It didn't surprise Ares to make out the letter Q on the cover.

A wretched groan issued forth from Aphrodite, and Ares turned to find her beautiful face marred with anguish. He cupped his lover's cheek and gently coaxed her gaze from the glass.

"Look at me, Goddess." A note of warning shot through his concern. "What's going on?"

Aphrodite met his steely gray stare with repentant doe eyes. "That woman is about to tell Cupid what an awful mother I am."

"Why would she do that?"

Aphrodite twisted away from his grip and threw a glance over her shoulder. The woman had left the notebook on the desk and walked into another room, which appeared to ease Aphrodite's tension for the moment, at least her earthbound tension. Around Ares, the goddess was as skittish as an impala at a leopard party.

"I don't even know where to begin."

He sure didn't like the sound of that. Whatever she'd done, Cupid was involved, and that meant she'd placed Ares's reputation on the line. The perfume and the carefully staged costume made sense now, a brazen deployment of the weapons in her artillery. He'd taught her well—too well, perhaps.

"I advise you to choose a beginning, and do it soon," he said evenly.

Composing herself somewhat, she grasped Ares's hands in her clammy palms and exhaled heavily. "Our son has sought out the services of a psychotherapist."

"To what end?" Ares asked, his jaw tightly clenched.

"The usual one, I suppose." When Ares glared without answering, Aphrodite added, "Looking for some way to ease his despair."

"You mean to say he was looking for a way to weasel out of facing the consequences of his actions." His hard words caused Aphrodite to flinch, but Ares couldn't find it in him to feel remorse.

"There's an argument to be made that by exploring therapy, he's owning up to his shortcomings."

If Ares clenched his teeth any harder, he'd shatter his molars. "Are you making that argument?"

A tear rolled down Aphrodite's cheek, and her mouth trembled with her reply. "No."

"So, the boy has made a grievous mistake, yet again. We'll deal with it as we have the others." He knew she wanted the boy home, but what did a few more days amount to? Grains of sand in the vast ocean of eternity? For the life of him, Ares could not figure out why she was behaving so dramatically. It wasn't like her at all.

"No," she said again, shaking her head emphatically. "This isn't like the other times. This isn't Cupid's mistake." A sob caught in her throat. "It's not a mistake at all. That's the problem."

"You're making no sense!" His patience was near its end. He didn't appreciate being kept in the dark, and Aphrodite well knew it.

"This is extremely difficult for me." Gathering up all the strength left inside her, the goddess steeled herself with one last sniffle. "And you're not making it any easier!"

The urge to guffaw came over him so powerfully, he had to bite the inside of his cheek to stifle it. If he'd learned anything about winning the heart of this fierce woman, he knew that laughing in her face would spoil any chance of lying with her again—*ever*. Eternity was a long damn time for a woman to hold a grudge, but this goddess could and would, if so provoked.

The moment of clarity brought to mind the most unlikely question of Ares's immortal life: *What would Hephaestus do?* Odder still, he received an answer.

Setting aside eons of military strategy and interpersonal conflict tactics and game theories accumulated throughout the broad swath of history, Ares swept his lover into a hug. "I'm sorry, my flower."

She melted into his body and wept.

"I'm here," he whispered again and again.

They rocked together as hot tears poured out of her and poured some more until he began to worry they might never stop—and still, he did not understand why she was so bereft.

She wriggled out of his arms, fingers wiping tears and snot from her swollen cheeks. "Don't look at me," she begged as she spun away. "I'm a wreck." It was the most beautiful he'd ever seen her.

"Come, my love." He drew his arm around her shoulders and led her to his bedchamber. "I'm going to make you some tea, and we are going to lift this awful burden off your chest." *And then, we are going to make the sweetest love.*

The waiting tested him. Even after the teapot whistled, Aphrodite still hadn't emerged from his bathroom. He tapped on the door just the once, asking if there was anything he could do for her. "Give me another minute," she'd pleaded, and he did.

She finally came out, holding a washcloth over her face, covering all but a sliver of her puffy, red eyes. He gave her the warmest smile he could muster, and though he could barely see her expression, he read gratitude in it. He poured them both a cup of tea and sipped his quietly while she situated herself at the table beside him.

She lowered the washcloth, revealing a grin. "You hate tea," she said.

His laughter rattled the teacup in his hand, causing the tea to slosh so dramatically against the sides, he had to set it down for fear of scalding them both. "I really do." He grasped her hand and drew it to his lap. "I thought it might relax you if I had some too."

She regarded him as if she'd never seen him before. He wasn't sure he recognized himself. "Thank you for that," she said quietly. "All of it."

He nodded, watched, and waited some more, not wanting to break this spell. He'd almost forgotten the circumstances that had brought them to this point—until Aphrodite released a loud sigh and reminded him. "That horrible woman is going to tell Cupid I am to blame for all of his problems, and he is going to believe her."

"Such is the mother's plight."

"Spoken like a man," she retorted.

"Why do you care what some horrible, random stranger tells him?"

"That's not some random stranger. *That* . . . is Cupid's Right Love."

"What? You chose a Worthy for him without discussing it with me?" He released her hand, and she slipped away.

"Before you get upset—"

"Too late," he said, regretting it instantly. Falling slave to one's emotions was not an attractive quality.

"Ares, please. Let me explain."

Anger would have easily won out if not for the bolt of insight still reverberating through his being. Channeling his inner Hephaestus, Ares clasped his hands in his lap. "I'm listening."

She matched his forced smile with one of her own. "I didn't just choose this woman. She has always been his Right Love. It's only now they're encountering each other for the first time."

"*Always?* His Right Love is an immortal? Who is she, and why doesn't she live here on the Mount with the rest of the gods?"

"Her *soul* is immortal, as all are. She has lived in every generation in a different mortal body of my choosing."

"Are you saying he could have found her at any point in the last three thousand years?"

"Technically, yes," said Aphrodite, "but they would have been incapable of loving each other."

"Your fail-safe." Ares marveled at Aphrodite's design: the archer of the love-tipped arrows could never fall in love.

"Yes. The fail-safe which I *suspended* in order to set the first curse of Love upon his heart."

"Cupid's punishment." Oh, what Ares had demanded of her! No wonder she'd dragged her feet.

"Yes. And once afflicted, his heart was fully consumed by Mia, then Ruthie, and now Pan . . . and it all could have ended right there if only he could have just ascended." A wail escaped her.

The hairs on the back of Ares's neck stood at attention, tiny little soldiers alerting the commander of danger. "What have you done?"

"You said it yourself. I couldn't call my son home with his heart all torn to pieces. He'd never have forgiven me. I had to give him a chance to find his Right Love, no matter how it wounds me."

He fashioned his expression into a gentle, supportive question mark, though his insides were more of a ramrod exclamation point. "And . . .?"

She sighed. "And I may have bumped the Wings app to make sure Reed would find her."

"You . . . bumped . . . the app?" Ares understood just enough to know he didn't begin to understand. "Translate, please."

"I influenced a number of internet users to manipulate the search ranking of Mariposa's site."

"I see," he replied, though all he saw, really, was that Aphrodite was far more devious than he'd given her credit for. "However did you know to do that?"

Her blush was real this time, not a trick of tinted powder. "Have you not taught me to stay one step ahead of my adversaries?"

He shook his head in awe. "I'm impressed." So impressed, he nearly forgot his anger over her unilateral action. "What's your next move?"

"My move?" A huff escaped her lips. "What can I do now but look on helplessly while this woman turns my son against me?"

"I don't understand why you would choose Cupid a mate who wishes to harm you."

"She's not out to harm me, personally," Aphrodite replied miserably. "The psychoanalyst is the natural enemy of the mother." And nothing, knew the God of War, united like a common enemy.

"Then why a psychoanalyst at all?" Ares was going to require a nap after all these mental gymnastics.

"That part is beyond my control. Like it or not, our son's perfect match is Psyche."

"*The* Psyche? Apuleius's story of Cupid and Psyche is not a fanciful tale?"

"It's a prophecy, albeit wildly outdated and grossly mischaracterized."

Ares stifled a smirk. If memory served, it was Aphrodite's vanity that set the story's events in motion. "Of course you were, love."

"Not that the truth is any more flattering," said Aphrodite. "I know I'm a horrible mother for keeping them apart all this time."

And here was Ares's great test. Could he master the urge to jump in and offer advice? It helped, he found, to press his lips tightly together.

"If I've loved my son with what *some* might describe as a stranglehold, it's because I alone knew the risk if the fail-safe were ever to be breached. And look! There it is"—she jabbed her complaint into the air with both hands—"playing out right before our eyes!"

He rescued her hands, drawing them up inside his own. "All is not yet lost."

She squeezed her eyes shut, and a stream of tears started down both cheeks. "If Cupid crosses them past their Liminal Point, his heart will be lost to me forever."

"You underestimate your son's love for his mother."

"I wish that were true. Look what happened when he met Mia, and she wasn't even his Right Love . . . let alone a trained mental health professional! You should have seen the notes that woman made in her notebook!"

Ares knew enough to disengage from a battle he couldn't win. He adopted a softer tactic, sweeping two fingers along her cheek and tucking several strands of auburn hair behind her ears. "How brave you were to foster this union with so much at stake."

"Lest you or the Council fear I've made it too easy for him, trust—I have not. Just because they've made contact does not mean he'll win her over." A smile flickered.

Ah! There she was for the briefest instant, his partner in crime! He could hardly wait to learn what obstacles Aphrodite had placed in Cupid's path. A blast of oxygen ignited the embers of Ares's smoldering desire into full flame.

"That was most wise, my love. Regardless of the outcome, the boy will have been given his fair chance."

"I know it was the right thing to do, but failing to cross the Liminal Point with his own Right Love will destroy him."

How Ares wanted to soothe her soul, to convince her the boy could know other great loves even if his Right Love were to elude him. But Ares's truth was no more flattering than Aphrodite's—Ares could never replace her great love, Adonis, and he had no stomach for reminding Aphrodite of his own deficits.

"Then let us wish Cupid success in his difficult quest, and may the boy be joyfully reunited with his mother."

She looked up at him with pleading eyes. Would that Ares could make it so for her and that he might somehow fit into that picture.

"I suppose we will soon find out."

# 8

# RUNNING

Andre bounded ahead of Pan toward the clearing, and Margaux charged forward to keep pace, grazing Pan's leg as she left him in the dust. Pan could hardly begrudge the Beaucerons their enthusiasm to reunite with their master. Pan's eagerness matched the dogs', even if he was slightly better at masking his feelings.

By the time Pan emerged from the woods, Reed had already been lured outside, crouched near the back door in his beige cable-knit sweater with the dogs' wet noses pressed to his hands and a grin drawn on his face. Happy, little sounds bounced between man and dogs, a love language only a man with wild beast in his blood could ever hope to understand.

Pan slowed to a jog and let the scene seep into his bones. Home. Family. Happiness. *So this is how it feels.*

Sensing Pan's approach, Reed stood. The dogs didn't budge, collapsed with their bellies to the ground, tongues unfurled with their hard panting. Reed's smile grew wider still. "I don't know what you did to these two, but I've never seen them so thoroughly worn out."

Pan pulled up short, hands on his hips, keeping a fair distance so as not to offend Reed's refined nose. "I just ran."

It was the truth but not nearly as simple or common as Pan had made it sound. He hadn't run like that since Vermont, where the woods were thick enough to cover his tracks. Pan had settled for human speed for so long, he'd nearly forgotten the glory of letting go, unfettered by observation and unbound by the limitations of his human appearance.

"'Just ran,' eh?" How well Pan recognized Reed's tone, that slide into demigod worship mode that Pan found impossible to resist. "I thought maybe you got lost back there."

"*Me?* Lost in the woods?" Pan laughed out loud. "Never. In a car? Maybe!"

"I'd love to put a tracker on you and see how much ground you cover next time."

"Oh, would you now?" Pan chuckled. "Then that tracker might be all I wear next time I run." As predicted, Reed's cheeks flamed bright pink. "Yeah, I was thinking I'd ditch the shoes next time and go barefoot. Then I thought, hey, why stop there? A satyr can dream, can't he?"

Chuckling now, Reed shook his head. "I just put up some iced tea. Can I pour you a glass?"

"Sure. Let me hop in the shower first. I don't want to stink up your kitchen."

"*Our* kitchen," Reed insisted. "And your stink doesn't offend me one bit."

"Yeah? Let's see how you feel when I get a little closer." Pan stalked toward the door, pleased beyond reason when Reed stood his ground. "You know, Reed, you're starting to get a little freaky on me . . . and I gotta say, I really like it." Who could've predicted Reed's burgeoning appetite for all things Pan: sweaty gym clothes, nudity at the breakfast table, lewd sexual acts?

Reed's blush returned in full force, and Pan couldn't resist planting a wet kiss square on his lips.

"Feel free to join me in the shower," Pan said, pumping his eyebrows for effect.

Before Reed could offer an answer, his phone rang. His shrug was an amusing combination of disappointment and relief.

"Next time, then," said Pan as he slipped past Reed, his feet halting at Reed's cheery, "Q!"

Though Pan wished more than anything to be the one helping Cupid through his heartbreak, right now, the kindest thing Pan could do was leave his best friend in Reed's capable care. It wouldn't be forever. Still, Pan was no masochist. He forced his steps toward the bathroom where he wouldn't be tempted to eavesdrop.

The fancy showerhead worked its magic on Pan's spent muscles, spooling his thoughts through the pleasure of sprinting through the woods with the hounds at his heels, leaves crunching under his feet, cool autumn air slapping his cheeks. What Pan wouldn't give to share the pure joy of running with Reed just once—even at a jog—but that would never happen. Reed had accepted his fate long ago, and Pan had no right to reopen that old wound. What Pan could do was offer Reed the vicarious pleasure of a good, hard run, and the satisfaction that his dogs were well exercised and content. And wasn't Reed returning the favor by standing in as Cupid's friend when Pan had no choice but to step aside?

Pan turned off the spray and stepped out of the shower. Reed was still on the phone with Cupid. Pan couldn't make out the words, only the soft lull of Reed's half of the conversation. He toweled off, scrubbing the water out of his hair as he strode to the bedroom to grab a T-shirt and jeans from the duffel bag on the floor. He'd continued to pick up clean clothes from home, a few days' worth at a time, though Reed had emptied out half of his dresser drawers and invited Pan more than once to use them.

Pan was ready. Hell, he would have moved in a week ago. There was no question where the two would live once they consolidated—Reed had the perfect property for the dogs, and he'd created a true home here in the woods. It wasn't that Pan worried about giving up his generic rental or even his independence, but Cupid needed all of his energy right now.

Reed glanced up and smiled as Pan entered the kitchen. "Here he is now. Hold on . . ." Tilting the phone away from his mouth, Reed whispered, "Q wants to talk to you, okay?"

"'Course." His short, stilted phone conversations with Cupid were better than nothing.

Reed nodded. "Here's Pan. Keep me posted, okay? And great work, Q. I'm really proud of you."

Reed wasn't lying. Anyone could have seen that glow of pride as he passed Pan the phone. It made Pan gooey inside, and it wasn't even for him.

"Hey, bud. How's it goin'?" Pan took the seat next to Reed at the kitchen table.

"It's good, Pan. Posey is really helping me!"

Pan shot Reed a skeptical glare. "Already?"

Cupid's enthusiasm was undimmed. "Yes! It doesn't hurt to talk to you . . . *at all!*"

"I'm so glad to hear that."

"That's why I wanted to talk to you. I needed to see if it was real, and it is, Pan!"

"That's amazing, Q. Truly. You should come over! Reed and I—" Pan's invitation was cut short by Reed waving his hands around like a lunatic. Pan tucked the phone under his chin and mouthed: *What?*

"Too soon," Reed whispered urgently. He was right, and Pan knew it.

"Yeah," Pan said with a heavy sigh, "maybe we shouldn't push it, Q. If this is good, let's just keep talking like this for now, okay? We have so much to catch up on." Cupid's silence made Pan feel extra crappy. Once he got Cupid talking, everything would be okay again. "C'mon. Tell me about this doctor. What'd you say her name was? *Posey?*"

"Nah, I don't want to go through all that again. Tell me about you. I've missed you so much. Reed seems so in love. Are you happy, Pan?"

Pan's gaze hopped to the man next to him, and Reed leaned in as if pulled toward Pan by his mere notice. Poised and ready, Reed watched his partner, eyebrows raised with the unspoken question: *How can I help?* It took all of Pan's restraint not to close the gap between them and kiss the hell out of him.

"I am." Pan was happy, all right. Except for the giant, Cupid-shaped hole in his heart, he'd never been happier.

"Does Right Love feel . . . Do you feel different?"

Pan huffed into the phone. "You could say that." Pan definitely wasn't ready for Reed to hear him describe the experience of loving and being loved back. "Hang on a second?"

"Sure."

Pan held the phone away from his head and leaned in for the offered kiss, cupping Reed's chin as he pulled away. "I'm going to take this call outside."

"Take your time," Reed answered, his loving gaze warming Pan even after the door closed between them.

9

# RATIONAL DECISION

Posey nosed her front wheel onto the Tahoe Rim Trail with the other early morning riders. Only the punishing mountain ride could unwind her dilemma.

By all rights, she shouldn't have needed twenty-four hours to ponder the decision; she shouldn't have needed twenty-four minutes. This "Q" required in-depth psychoanalysis, the kind a responsible professional would only deliver in person—exactly the kind of therapy Posey had stopped practicing seven years ago, nearly to the day.

So, what's chasing you up the mountain this fine, autumn morning, Dr. Rey?

Q wouldn't be the first applicant she rejected. Thanks to a fat bank account, Posey had the great luxury of being choosy when taking on new patients. If instinct told her she wasn't a good match for a potential patient, she would say as much and even recommend a colleague. No guilt, no lost sleep. Better for both patient and doctor not to start a therapeutic relationship she didn't expect to be fruitful.

If only that were the case with Q, perhaps Posey wouldn't feel as if two chainsaws had wrestled in her belly all night. The thing was, she was sure she could help this one, and that wasn't ego talking. Posey understood his tragic preoccupation with romance and messy attachment issues, and she knew the path to healing because she'd walked those steps herself. But there was more to her confidence than that. Not one given to hippie-dippie notions about what the Universe did or didn't bring into a person's life, Posey nevertheless sensed a deep gut connection even from her brief interaction with Q that tempted her to break all her own rules. Hence, the bike ride, the great diviner of clarity.

The late October chill filled Posey's lungs with a special kind of urgency. Her mountain trails would be impassable soon, blanketed in the season's first snow any day now. She pumped her pedals harder against all the forces beyond her control. *Ticktock*, fading autumn. *Ticktock,* other people's choices. *Ticktock,* biological clock. The last one made her angry with herself, and she pushed harder through the Painted Rock loop.

Q seemed like a decent person. Despite being jilted again and again, he'd spoken no harsh words about Mia, genuinely seemed to want Ruthie to reunite with her husband, and stepped out of the way so his best friend-slash-lover could be with someone else. Honestly, the man seemed too good to be true. Either he was completely full of crap, or he was the least self-preserving human being she'd ever met.

No surprise, then, that he'd gotten himself good and stuck. Thanks to a pathological attraction to unattainable love partners and an inability to tolerate not being in a relationship, he jumped with both feet from one ending directly into the next beginning. The late bloomer piece fit with the rest of the puzzle, but how did a man with such a voracious appetite for romance not experience his first relationship until his thirties?

Past the lava cliffs she rode hard, barely slowing at the peak to take in the view before the trail rolled down toward Watson Lake. *If* Posey were to take this case—which she couldn't, shouldn't, and wouldn't—she would explore his family situation for many of the answers. A child of a broken home, absent father, a mother who withheld her love as soon as Q expressed feelings for another woman? Classic attachment. The deck was stacked against him from the start.

Fascinating how nearly the same pattern of adult behavior could result from Posey's entirely different upbringing—until she'd actively chosen to change the trajectory of her life. Q would have to do the same or be doomed to a lifetime of highs and lows at the mercy of other people's hearts.

The same dense forests that provided relief from the summer sun now trapped the chill in the air at the Brockway Summit, bringing a cool objectiveness to Posey's thoughts. She'd burned off the self-destructive impulses, leaving the only rational choice—but a compromise had been struck between her warring halves.

Q deserved better than an email rejection. She'd work out the language on the way down the mountain.

10

# TOO COMPLICATED

Cupid was pondering the gourd display at the grocery store when his phone caught him completely off guard. He plucked the phone from his rear pocket and stared at the screen, unsure what to make of the name that stared back at him—Wings.

After his chat with Posey yesterday afternoon, he'd waited impatiently for an email invitation for another online session. It never occurred to him that she might call instead. A phone conversation was dangerous—not enough time to think and arrange his words.

His finger hovered over the screen while he pondered ignoring the call. After the third ring, curiosity bested him. "Hello?"

"Hello, Q. This is Dr. Rey. *Posey*. From Wings?" Her voice matched the gentle smile of her screen avatar, but her words tumbled out too fast, trying a little too hard to sound like they weren't trying too hard.

"Yes, hello."

"I hope it's okay to call you. I felt a conversation was more appropriate than sending a message." That sounded ominous.

Cupid pushed his cart out of the main aisle and stared at the array of mushroom varieties without registering anything. "Sure, it's fine."

"I've given your situation a lot of thought, and I'd really love to help you, but . . ." *Blindsided.* That was the word for it, right? When you thought everything was going along just fine, and all of a sudden, you were sideswiped by a truck barreling through a red light. "I'd be happy to recommend another practitioner to work with you."

Another practitioner? But Posey was the doctor Reed had chosen for him, the only doctor Pan had approved.

She'd paused. Cupid was meant to respond, but he'd missed most of what she'd said due to the herd of wild boars jumping on his chest. "I don't understand. Did I say something wrong?"

"Absolutely not. No, Q. Please don't think that." Her rapid-fire assurances were anything but convincing.

"Then why don't you want to help me?"

"I do. Very much. But your situation is beyond the scope of the services I offer through Wings."

"I'm *that hopeless?*"

"Oh dear," said Posey. "I'm making a royal mess of this."

Fear. That was what Cupid had picked up on, Posey's fear.

For the most part, the gods lacked this emotion. Aside from a healthy terror of Zeus's power and Hera's vindictive streak, which Cupid would have done better to respect, the gods had done their worst to one another through the millennia and pretty much exhausted all the outcomes. Eternity tended to breed a kind of trust, albeit a twisted and unstable version.

The mortals were a different story. Fear dressed itself in a wide variety of costumes—fear of being hurt, fear of being alone, fear of failure, fear of loss, fear of looking foolish—and manifested as often as not as the complete opposite of fear. As

Cupid was learning, fear in all its forms made an impressive barrier to Love.

*What are you afraid of, Posey?* He waited for her to continue. "Please know that if I had any concerns as to your personal safety, I would have recommended you seek immediate help."

"Okay." Reed had said as much.

"Okay." Posey released a shaky breath; Cupid drew one in and held it. "Clinical evaluation is not simply a matter of degree," she explained. "There are deeply complicated forces at work in making each of us who we are. Oversimplifying your situation for the sake of trying to fit into the online model would be a disservice to you. Does that make sense?"

"I'm too complicated for you?" That was a first.

"Not for *me*," she was quick to reply, "but for Wings. Certain types of therapies are best suited to in-person psychoanalysis."

"Then help me in person!" The words left his mouth before he could stop them. Pan would never approve such an arrangement. Bad enough they were speaking on the phone.

"I'm sorry, Q, but I can't. I don't do that kind of therapy anymore." The quaver was back.

"But I'm comfortable with you. I already feel so much better. I talked to Pan on the phone yesterday, and it didn't hurt. I'm even buying vegetables again!"

"That's wonderful to hear. You've made a bold start."

"Yes, with your help."

"I haven't done anything."

"You did something. I don't know what, but I felt lighter after our chat yesterday. If we could just do that—"

"It wouldn't be ethical."

"I don't understand. Isn't the whole point to help me?"

She let out a long sigh, the kind Cupid had heard many times before. "That's really not the kind of help you need."

"*What* isn't?"

"I'm sorry. I shouldn't . . ." The yearning in her voice spoke directly to Cupid's heart. She wanted to help him.

"Posey, *please*. Please don't abandon me without at least explaining why."

When she didn't immediately refuse, Cupid knew he had her.

"Okay. Here it is," she said, and Cupid held his breath so as not to make any kind of sound that might cause her to reconsider. "When Mia broke your heart, you substituted Ruthie for Mia. When Ruthie broke your heart, you fell in love with Pan. Each time, you felt better for a while—until you didn't. That's your coping mechanism, starting the next relationship." No, that was his mother's mechanism for punishing him, but obviously, Cupid could not enlighten Posey on that point. "I give you a ton of credit for putting your heart out there again and again, but that comes at a tremendous cost. That's the heartbreak you're feeling."

"But I'm not feeling it anymore." He focused on his heart to be sure. Nope, no more of that dreadful, hollowed-out despair in his chest—but also, no new target revving up. *Strange.*

"I believe that's because you've substituted me to fill the void left by Pan when he turned to someone else."

"You think I'm *in love with you?*"

Cupid's incredulous reply came out perhaps a decibel too loud. A woman reaching for a package of mushrooms drew her hand back and scuttled away.

"No, of course not. But your default solution of replacing one person with another isn't healing. It's avoidance of the core problem."

He bent over the shopping cart and resolved to keep his voice down. "What am I avoiding?"

"This is exactly what you need to explore in therapy."

"I'm *trying!*"

"I'm so sorry I can't pursue this with you."

"Why not?" Cupid asked. "Even though you're making me a little crazy right now, I think you know exactly what I need."

"I have already said too much." And yet, there seemed to be so much more she was holding back.

"As my not-therapist."

"Yes," she said with another heavy sigh.

"How about as my new friend Posey?"

"What?"

"What if you're not my online therapist? What if you're just some person I met on, say, a dating app?"

"Dating," she repeated. "You've done it again. You see that, right?"

"Fine. Not a dating app. What if we'd met at the gym? Just two people whose yoga mats happened to be next to each other?"

Miraculously, he heard her chuckle. "Then you would know what a klutz I am."

"I would still happily go for coffee with you after class."

"And I would very much enjoy randomly meeting you under these completely hypothetical circumstances," she said, then turned serious again. "Unfortunately, that's not how we came to know each other. The only responsible way to handle this situation is for me to recommend a good therapist so you can get the help you deserve. Would you feel comfortable sharing your location with me so I can send you some references in your area?"

He'd never follow up, but if Posey needed to do this to assuage her conscience, he'd play along. "That's very kind of you. I'm in Tarra, Indiana."

"Okay, let me do a little research, and I'll shoot you an email in the next day or two with a few names. Meanwhile, please don't regard anything about our conversation as actual therapy."

"Nope. Just two random people randomly having a random conversation."

"Yes," she said. "I really am very sorry I couldn't do more for you. It's truly been a pleasure speaking, randomly, with you."

"You too, Posey."

The idea of Posey handing him off to someone else made him unbearably sad, but she'd made up her mind, and a woman with her mind made up was a force beyond Cupid's control.

# 11

# DRAWN TO PAN

"I know you're not reading that paper," Pan said without turning from the sink.

Reed smacked the newspaper against the kitchen table with a huff. "I was not aware you had eyes in the back of your head."

"Don't need 'em to know you're gawking." Scrubbing away the last of the scrambled egg crumbles, Pan glanced over his shoulder. Yup, Reed was looking. Pan shot him a wink.

"Hey, I've got a Greek god standing in my kitchen, doing the breakfast dishes buck naked. Damn right I'm gonna gawk."

Pan's booming laughter set off Moses and Bo Peep. The pups barked louder and louder at Reed's feet until he bent to run a calming hand along their backs. Pan knew the feel of those hands; he wasn't above barking for a belly rub himself.

"Now look what you've done," complained Reed. "Not happy until every man and beast in this house is agitated, are you?"

Happy was exactly what Pan was—deliriously so. He dried his hands on the dish towel and sidled up behind Reed's chair. Draping his arms around Reed's shoulders, he dropped a playful kiss in the crook of his neck. "I happen to have the perfect cure for agitation," he murmured with a nip at Reed's earlobe.

"*Again?*" Reed managed a horrified expression.

"Again . . ." Pan swept his tongue around the shell of Reed's ear. "And again . . ." Pan slid his hand down Reed's chest and wriggled it inside his pajama pants. "And again." Reed jerked back against Pan's chest with a muttered curse.

Pan's phone jumped to life with the "Stupid Cupid" ring-tone, first time in over a week.

"Saved by the bell," deadpanned Reed.

Pan retracted his hand. "One of these days, Professor, you're going to stop pretending you don't love that," Pan said, reaching for his phone with a huge smile at Reed's grimace. "Yo," he said into the phone.

"Hi, Pan."

*Shit.* Something was off.

Pan unwound himself from Reed and paced to the other side of the kitchen. "What's wrong, Q? Where are you?"

"I'm in my car."

The car? Was Cupid being led toward his ascension right now for some reason? "Where are you going?" Pan asked through clenched teeth.

"I think I'm heading toward Reed's."

"*Reed's?* Why?"

"My heart is doing its thing again," said Cupid, sounding no cheerier than Pan about this turn of events.

*Crap.* Why was his navigational system pulling him to Reed's house, where two Right Loves were already ecstatically—and, one hoped, irrevocably—mated? How could this be good?

"Listen to me very carefully. Do not drive to Reed's. Meet me at my house. I'll be there in twenty minutes. Go inside and wait for me. Got it?"

"What if my heart won't let me change direction?"

"Just go with it. Hopefully, once I leave Reed's, your GPS will recalibrate."

"Unless it's not taking me to you."

If Aphrodite had figured out that Pan wasn't good enough for Reed and sent Cupid back for a redo, he'd . . . well, Pan had no fucking idea what he'd do.

"I'm not even going to think about that," lied Pan.

"Okay. And Pan . . . I'm sorry."

Pan wanted to be the bigger man, to reassure his friend whatever this was, it was not his fault. But then he glanced over at Reed, now crouched on the floor between the Pyrenees pups, tickling their bellies and babbling utter nonsense into their cute gray faces, and he couldn't find the generosity to let Cupid off the hook if he were to ruin this.

"Let's not get ahead of ourselves. We'll figure it out, Q. We always do. See you soon."

Without waiting for a response, Pan hung up and strode back to the table. "Reed, I'm sorry, but I have to—"

"Go. I know." Reed lifted his gaze to Pan and gave him an encouraging smile. "Do what you have to do, but remember one thing before you leave."

Pan smirked. He was starting to get used to Reed's mushy declarations of love and, if he were being honest, quite enjoyed them. "And what's that?"

"You're not wearing pants."

A loud bleat of laughter rolled out of Pan. *This fucking guy* and his sweet way of letting Pan know he trusted him. "Thanks for the tip. I'll call you when I'm heading home."

"We'll be here," Reed said with his usual flair for the undramatic.

Pan would've bent to kiss him, but he didn't know how to

do that without spilling all the worst-case scenarios swimming in his head. Reed demanded no answers, and Pan had none to give. The best Pan could do for all involved was to get his ass dressed and hit the road.

As Pan's truck bounced over the back roads of Tarra, so did his thoughts. Had he crossed a line helping Cupid connect with a therapist? Were the gods displeased at Pan and maybe even Reed for alleviating Cupid's emotional pain? Had they launched Cupid toward Reed's house to blow all three hearts to bits? What if they were sending Mercury down with another of their special dispensations—a *threesome* this time? How would any of them survive? Could Aphrodite really hurt a Worthy as worthy as Reed?

Pan dialed Cupid, interrupting before Cupid could get out a hello. "Is it still trying to take you to Reed's?"

"No. It changed course when you started driving."

"So it's me you're chasing," said Pan, enormously relieved.

"I guess."

"Be there in a few."

Pan was about to disconnect when Cupid's pleading voice froze him in place. "Pan, I can't do this again. Not with you."

"I know, buddy. I'm not thrilled about this either. You want me to stay on the line?"

"Would you?"

"Sure. How far away are you?"

"I'm in your driveway."

"Sit tight. I'm turning onto my street now."

That was the end of their conversation until Pan pulled into the driveway next to Cupid's Prius. Their gazes met and held as Pan's truck rolled toward the open garage. Pan took a deep breath, hopped out of the truck, and slogged over to Cupid's car. *Please don't let his heart be stuck on me.*

Cupid rolled down his window. A good five feet away, Pan stopped. No need to torture the guy. Pan braced himself. "Well?"

Cupid pushed his face out the window. "Come closer."

"Really?" Was it possible his range had shrunk? Pan inched toward the car. "Anything?"

Cupid shook his head. Confusion creased his forehead. "I don't get it."

"No heart motor? No pain?"

"Nope." A tentative grin lifted one corner of Cupid's mouth.

"Well, get your ass out of that damn car, and give your old pal a fucking hug already!"

Pan barely had time to step out of the way of the swinging door before Cupid jumped into his open arms. "It doesn't hurt to be with you!" cried Cupid, and Pan squeezed him tighter.

The two old friends stood hugging in the driveway. Muffled sobs against Pan's neck brought him back to Cupid's plight. It had been three weeks since Pan had last been able to hold Cupid like this without inflicting pain, three long weeks since the two of them had walked into the Tarra Arms together, knowing that one brief, glorious night was all they'd ever have. How different their fates during those three long, eventful weeks. Pan had found his Right Love in Reed, while Cupid had lost everything.

A tear or two might have stung the back of Pan's eyes too. He covered his emotions with a brotherly slap on Cupid's back. "Hey, hey. What's this, now?"

"Sorry." Cupid pulled away with a sniffle as he swiped at his wet cheeks. "I'm just so relieved not to be in love with you."

Pan pulled a face. "You sure know how to hurt a guy."

"You know what I mean. That doctor cured me even though she says she didn't do anything." Or the gods had released him for their own dark purposes—a theory Pan kept to himself.

"Well, we're here together now. What do you say we go inside and figure out why?"

The house greeted Pan with a cold shoulder, and the feeling was mutual. Since the crossing, Pan had barely set foot in the place. The peace and quiet Pan used to crave now served as a stark reminder of the loveless life he'd led before Reed. Where were the dogs glued to Pan's heels? Where was Reed's warm gaze trained on Pan everywhere he wandered? Where were the sound of laughter and the crackle of a fire burning in the hearth?

"You want a beer?" asked Pan.

"Sure. Whatever." Cupid settled onto his old stool at the counter. For a second, the last month evaporated, and they were best friends hanging out, shooting the breeze.

Pan opened two bottles and slid one to Cupid. They clinked out of habit and downed matching swallows. "Talk to me, Q. What is happening with that ticker of yours?"

Cupid set his bottle onto the counter and linked his fingers around it. "I was definitely pulled to you just now."

"And you're absolutely sure there's no . . ." Pan wiggled a finger back and forth between Cupid's heart and his own.

"Nope. No beats coming from either direction."

*Thank the gods. Every single blasted one of 'em.* "Okay, good. What's it feel like now?"

"It's more of a jumpy feeling. You know how your truck kind of hums and rolls when you're sitting at a red light?"

"When the engine is idling?"

"Right." Cupid nodded. "I think I'm meant to be doing something that includes you."

"And not Reed?"

Cupid took a thoughtful sip of beer. "I don't think the signal would have let go of me if this involved Reed too."

"Agreed."

The worst of his fears had been allayed: Cupid was not in love with Pan or Reed. Tipping back his beer, Pan rearranged the puzzle pieces. "Hey! Remember that first night with Mia? After you screwed her and told her you loved her and tossed your cookies when she didn't say it back?"

"Yes, thanks for reminding me," said Cupid with a scowl.

"The gods guided you back here, to me, to help you figure out the mission. Maybe that's why we're here now."

"Okay, so what's my mission?"

"Let's think about this. Have you met anyone in the past week who sparked your interest?"

"Not that I can remember."

"No? No supercharged Cupid heartbeats?"

"Definitely not."

"Not even a flutter? Maybe it's weaker this time, and you just weren't paying attention?"

"But it's gotten stronger each time. With you, I could barely hear myself think." Cupid's phone chimed. "Sorry, one second . . ." Pulling his phone from his back pocket, Cupid looked at the screen and rolled his eyes.

"Need to take that?"

"No," Cupid answered, setting the phone down next to his beer. "You were saying?"

*Oh, Q.* Pan shook his head, chuckling. "Didn't I warn you about giving out your phone number to every rando you bone? Who's that, one of your dance partners from the other night?"

Cupid let out a huff. "Not even close." He raised his beer and guzzled half the bottle while his other hand scrubbed at his chest. *Whoa.* Pan knew that move.

"You, uh, feeling something there, bud?"

"A little. I didn't eat much for breakfast."

"I wasn't referring to the beer." Pan jabbed his finger at Cupid's heart.

Cupid glanced down and watched his own hand move back and forth as if it belonged to someone else. Indeed, right now, it did. His wide-eyed gaze lifted to meet Pan's.

*Yeah, buddy. I know.*

Pan jutted his chin toward the phone. "You want to tell me who that was just now?"

Cupid drained the rest of his beer. "That was Posey."

"That doc from the app?"

"Yes. She said she was going to send me an email with names of local doctors she thought could help me."

"There are names in that email?"

"I guess. I didn't open it."

"Open it."

"No, thanks. I don't need another doctor. Posey already cured me."

"Dude, you're about to rub a hole through that shirt. Whatever's going on with your heart-motor has to do with that message. Now unlock your damn phone, or I'll do it for you."

"I changed my password," Cupid said with a defiant smirk.

"Did you now?" Pan grinned, despite himself. "Well, well, well. Looks like my little boy's all grown up. So how about acting like an adult for once."

Cupid's self-satisfied expression evaporated. "Fine."

With a weary sigh, Cupid set down his beer, unlocked his phone, and read the doctor's message aloud: "Dear Q, I hope you are continuing to feel hopeful. While I do not wish to minimize your optimism, I do feel it is my professional responsibility to caution you that the reprieve you described from your depressive feelings is not uncommon at the start of therapy. In my experience, however, the relief you are enjoying will likely fade unless you put in the deep work to understand your choices. I urge you to seek the help of one of these providers in your area before you feel desperate again."

Guilt punched Pan in the belly. Sure, he'd seen Cupid at his worst, but to hear a mental health professional label his best friend as "desperate" was sobering.

"I have vetted both therapists and feel comfortable recommending them to you. While much depends on personal chemistry, I believe either one would make for an appropriate match. I wish you all the best in your journey. Most sincerely, Posey."

"Can I see the names?" Pan held out his hand for the phone, and Cupid passed it to him. A man and a woman, neither of whom Pan recognized from his twelve years in this Tarra.

Tapping on the first link, Pan opened the bio of Dr. Wesley Chan. The photo looked like an official hospital headshot meant to instill confidence, white lab coat over a white dress shirt and blue tie. Dr. Chan was not a bad-looking guy, with wisdom in his eyes and a full crop of straight, black hair just beginning to gray around the ears. Pan put him at late forties. He turned the phone to show Cupid the photo.

"How does this guy strike ya?"

Cupid glanced at the screen, frowned, and glared back at Pan. "It doesn't work that way."

"Easy, bud. Just asking a question." *Because however you think this works can change on a dime.* "No pitter-patters?"

"No, Pan."

"Okay, lemme read his bio." *Fancy résumé, prestigious position at the local university hospital, specializing in adult mental health concerns, yada, yada.* "Nothing's jumping out at me. Let's check the other one."

Pan clicked on the link to Dr. April Fairlawn, and a woman who looked to be in her thirties with a kind smile and big glasses popped up on the screen. "How about this one? Anything stirring?" Pan asked.

"This is a waste of time. Pictures don't do anything for me."

"You're right. We need to get you close enough to let your heart tell us what's what."

"What do you mean, 'get me close enough'?"

"I mean, let's get you appointments with Doctors Chen and Fairlawn."

"What? I thought the whole point of the app was so I wouldn't have to talk to a doctor in person."

"Who says you have to talk? Just get into the room, listen to your heart, and leave."

"You have no idea what's involved. You don't just stroll into the room. Ask Reed!"

"Reed's not here," said Pan calmly, though the reminder only made him less patient.

"Then let me tell you how it works. I'd have to first answer all these personal questions about my problems and my feelings and you and my mother and father. And I'm not even depressed anymore, so they'd never agree to see me. I'm not doing it, Pan."

"Yeah, you are," said Pan, grinning at his friend's scowl.

"What are you smiling about?" Cupid snapped.

"I just figured out why I'm here."

12

# SOWING BLESSINGS

For all his ability to sneak up on the enemy, the God of War could make a dramatic entrance when he wanted to—and he wanted to tonight. What better audience than all of Olympus, gathered at Zeus's palace to celebrate the autumn sowing?

By all rights, Aphrodite should have declined Ares's offer to transport her. Did the Goddess of Love truly require a "proper escort"? And by whose imagination would her illicit lover possibly qualify as a proper anything? But oh, how she quivered at the magnificent sight of Ares at her palace gate, garbed in his formal red robes and the gold arm cuff hugging his bicep! How her heart raced at his awed, "My goddess," and the way his eyes widened as he took in his prize.

Her own chariot would have served her just fine—nay, better; her doves would have cut through the sky without making a mess of her hair or requiring her tender feet to endure standing up for the frantic ride. Four sets of immortal hooves thundered over the mountainous roads, kicking up dust and trailing flames. Granted, Ares's fire-breathing steeds were as swift as they were furious, and their journey would be brief. Too bad, really. Aphrodite quite liked being tucked into the meager space with Ares in his carriage designed for one, the way his commands rattled his chest as he urged the horses on into the night. By the feel of him behind her, Ares quite enjoyed the tight squeeze, too.

Maybe she'd accepted out of spite. Hephaestus had left early for Zeus's palace to stoke the ceremonial fire, and he hadn't even bothered to invite Aphrodite to go with him. In fact, Hephaestus hadn't spoken two words to her in a fortnight. If she didn't know better, she might have worried Heph didn't care what was going on between his wife and his brother.

As Zeus's palace came into view, the folly of her decision sharpened to a fine point. It was nothing short of treachery turning up here in Ares's chariot as if the two were on a date.

Ares gathered the reins into one hand and slipped the other around Aphrodite's midsection. With the slightest pressure on their golden bridles, the horses slowed to a trot, then a walk. Liverymen scurried to clear the forecourt of carriages and draught beasts while Zeus's head coachman rushed to greet Ares. If he was surprised to see Aphrodite, he schooled his features well.

The coachman bowed impressively and held the position for the requisite length. "A festive good evening to you both." A hand was extended. "May I?"

Ares surrendered the reins but not the goddess. They stepped out of the carriage as one, as if the velocity of the ride had melded their bodies together.

Aphrodite remembered herself as the music from inside reached her ears. Clearing her throat, she shrugged out of Ares's grip.

"Apologies," he said with a tender laugh as if unaware he was holding her bottom to his hip. "After you, Goddess."

Aphrodite stepped into the front vestibule of the magnificent palace. Black marble flooring veined with rich streaks of gold gleamed beneath her sandals; gold columns glowed to their hand-polished perfection. As befit the King of Gods, the palace inspired awe and envy, but certainly, none would have described the space as warm. It wasn't the massive scale of the architecture or the exotic materials from the finest quarries or even the intimidating immaculateness that caused visitors to shudder; it was Zeus himself. A summons to this residence rarely ended well, and bad news spread quickly on a mountaintop with a small and unchanging population.

Tonight was a rare exception. Puanepsia was an occasion for all to come together and beseech Apollo and Dionysus for their blessings on the autumn seeds. Silk streamers of fiery reds and golds cascaded from the ceiling. Servants rushed about the Festival Hall, arms filled with giant baskets overflowing with the freshest fruits of the season. The hard stone surfaces that normally served as Zeus's echo chamber now pulsed with music and merriment—and true joy, now that Euphrosyne was back. And there she was, in the center of the room, dancing in a circle with her sister Graces, Thalia and Aglaia.

The brilliant snap of a high-licking flame drew Aphrodite's eye to the far window-wall. Tonight's fire was purely ceremonial, the indoor hearth crafted not of centuries of animal remains but of the same decorative marble that adorned her own parlor. Still, the altar sent an ancient shudder through her bones. Aphrodite could never stomach the idea of animal sacrifice.

As expected, the goddess Hestia was busy tending the hearth. Hephaestus would not be far, ever vigilant of the active flame, especially inside the packed hall. *There!* Standing off to one side, chatting with Zeus, was her husband, a blaze of red. Aphrodite's breath caught in her throat.

"Magnificent fire, isn't it?" Ares snagged a fig cake from a passing servant's tray. "Father looks pleased."

Aphrodite followed his gaze to the two gods who looked to be very much enjoying each other's company. "He always did favor Heph."

"Indeed. And proved it by gifting him the most precious jewel in all of Olympus for his wife." Oh, the flattery that rolled off Ares's tongue!

"He hoped Hephaestus would settle me."

Ares huffed. "If only Zeus knew your truest desires," said Ares, depositing the fig cake on his tongue with a naughty grin.

"Yes, well . . ." A blush heated her cheeks. "Speaking of Zeus, I'd best greet him before the crowd thickens."

"Yes, let's." He gave her a chivalrous sweep of his arm. "After you, Goddess."

"Perhaps a separate greeting is wisest," Aphrodite said delicately.

"As you wish," replied Ares, undaunted. "Go and do your duty. I won't have any trouble finding you again. The room turns on your beauty."

This time, Aphrodite rolled her eyes. "Oh no. Have you been reading Sappho again?" His rich laughter trailed him as he turned and disappeared into the crush.

With a determined step, Aphrodite headed toward the fire, steeled for her husband's anger. At least he could not ignore her here. As she drew near, Hephaestus turned from his boisterous conversation with Zeus and met her gaze.

"Aph." His smile faded.

"A very joyous Puanepsia," she said in return, because she couldn't say any of the things that needed saying.

Zeus spun around, his cheer nearly making up for Hephaestus's gloom. "Goddess." He opened his arms wide and pulled her into his firm embrace. "Are you enjoying yourself?"

"I've only just arrived." She stole a glance at Hephaestus, who'd been splitting wood and toiling at the hearth while she and her lover were primping and preening and planning their pre-Puanepsia chariot ride. If Hephaestus knew, he did not let on.

"You must try a pastry!" Zeus plucked a lyre-shaped pastry off the banquet table. Jars of olive oil and honey were laid out atop the sun-colored cloth along with the laurel-wrapped wands to be carried in the traditional *Eiresiônê* procession. "Taste! They're even flakier than last year."

*Flakier?* This was the ferocious, fearsome King of Gods? His childlike zeal brought a smile, but Aphrodite politely refused. "Maybe after the bean stew."

With a shrug, Zeus stuffed the entire thing into his mouth and swallowed it whole. "Truly exceptional! Is it me, or is everything better and brighter this year?"

"It's Euphrosyne's return," Hephaestus said pointedly. Aphrodite followed his gaze to the Graces performing their merry dance. "A happy reunion."

"Indeed," said Zeus, missing Hephaestus's little jab at his wife's handling of Cupid's punishment, "but your fire, too, burns brighter than ever before with the most vivid reds and oranges! Have you seen it, Aphrodite?" Zeus gave Hephaestus's shoulder a hearty clap. "Your husband has outdone himself this year."

Yes, he had. She couldn't take her eyes off his beard—long, carrot-colored coils that resembled tightly spun glass. It must have cost him a solid hour in the barber's chair. The last time he'd submitted to such "frivolous fluffery" was their wedding day.

"Eh, that's just salt coloring the flames," said Hephaestus with a humble chuckle. "The *real* splendor is this vision in purple." Husband and wife locked eyes for the briefest moment before both looked away. Was it the fire or his compliment that flushed her husband's cheeks?

And what about hers?

Aphrodite cleared her throat. "Is that a new chiton you're wearing?" Hephaestus rarely bared a shoulder outside of their bedroom, and the pleated skirt was a definite fashion stretch for him.

Hephaestus harrumphed. "Rhapso had her way with me."

"Did she now?" Aphrodite grinned inwardly, imagining the tiny seamstress running roughshod over her massive husband. "Well, the style suits you. The color, too."

"To be honest, I find the gold trim a bit much, and I *certainly* did not agree to this length," he said, kicking out his leg to glare with great disdain at all the dimpled skin.

Aphrodite had to bite her lip to keep from giggling out loud. "Well, it is quite hot over here."

"Did someone say *hot?*" Ares barged into the tight circle and handed Aphrodite one of the two wine goblets he'd carried over.

Aphrodite grasped the stem, shooting Ares a secret glare. *You promised.*

"Hello, Father. Heph."

Hephaestus responded with a stone-faced nod. Zeus clasped Ares's hand. "How goes the battle, son?"

"Ah, I don't think I'll ever tire of that one," said Ares with a charming smile, then raised his goblet. "*Yamas!*" With clenched teeth, Aphrodite repeated his toast and clinked.

Hephaestus cut in before the wine reached Aphrodite's lips. "If you'll excuse me, I've been meaning to check in with Euphrosyne."

"Pity," mumbled Ares.

"What about the fire?" asked Zeus.

"Hestia has everything well in hand." Hephaestus regarded the hearth one last time before hobbling off, pleats flapping against the backs of his colossal thighs.

Zeus eyed Ares suspiciously. "Are you and your brother at odds?"

Ares attempted innocence. "What quarrel would I have with Hephaestus?" Aphrodite stiffened, her goblet pressed to her lips. "Are you not enjoying the wine, Goddess? Perhaps you'd rather that vintage we enjoyed with our supper last night?"

*Oh, the treachery!* A bead of sweat tugged free from her scalp and slid down her cheek.

Zeus groaned, turning from one guilty face to the other. "Don't tell me you two are—"

"—on the Ad Hoc Subcommittee for Disciplinary Action together." Emboldened by the grain of truth, Aphrodite grasped Ares's elbow. "In fact," she said, eyes flashing with warning, "don't you need to go and gather that evidence *right now?*"

"You see what a tyrant she can be?" said Ares, laughing. "May I at least enjoy my wine, Goddess?"

"As if I could tell *you* what to do." This time, he took her warning seriously.

Lifting his goblet, Ares said, "May the autumn seeds be fruitful." Aphrodite let out a shaky sigh of relief when he left.

Zeus didn't miss a beat: "So what is this ad hoc whatever-it-is project you two are working on?"

"It's Cupid's punishment."

"Cupid is still gone?"

"Have you not noticed your grandson's absence?"

"Huh. Now that you mention it, Hera has been a bit calmer." Aphrodite followed his gaze across the room to where the Queen Bitch of Mount Olympus was loudly berating one of the servants.

"Truly? How can you tell?"

"Careful, Goddess." Zeus shook his finger at Aphrodite. "Don't disrespect your mother-in-law."

Maybe Aphrodite was pressing her luck, but Zeus seemed

in a particularly festive mood tonight. "I just don't understand. You can have anyone in your whole realm—god, mortal, and everything in between—"

"And I have," he said with a pop of his eyebrows.

"Yes, exactly. So why . . .?" She dared not voice the rest, nor did she need to.

Zeus's expression softened. "Come. Let's walk."

Wrapping his arm around her shoulders, he drew Aphrodite away from the fire and gossipy gods and led her out the back door. The few guests who'd made their way outside, paired-off lovers seeking inspiration from the first quarter of the moon, largely ignored Zeus and Aphrodite as they strolled across the lawn.

His arm slipped away as they walked side by side. "Do you know what it is to be the king of all gods?"

"Well, let's see," said Aphrodite. "Omnipotent ruler of sky and thunder, revered and obeyed without question, and able to seduce any lover you want. I suppose it's fairly wonderful."

He chuckled. "Yes, mostly. But at times, it's also exhausting and desperately lonely."

Aphrodite stopped short, turned to face him, and took his hands in hers. "If it's love you desire, you must know I can find you the perfect Worthy any time you say."

"Of course I know that. I already have the mate I desire."

"You love Hera, then?"

His answer didn't come right away. He looked up, and his gaze caught on the stars. "She is the wife I need."

Seeking to understand, Aphrodite craned her neck to the sky. The constellations spread above them like pages of family history—Zeus's indiscretions, Hera's many revenges. "I'm sorry, I don't understand your meaning."

Their gazes returned to each other. "The sky and heavens

are mine to command. Out of all the gods and all of human-kind, there is but one who does not submit without question." A laugh boomed out of him. "Who am I kidding? She does not submit at all!"

"That doesn't bother you?"

"Whether we want it or not, each of us needs a mirror unafraid to show us our true colors. If we're lucky, that mirror is a mate who will at least try to see us in the most flattering light."

*Hephaestus.* She swallowed over the lump in her throat.

"Hera sees me for who I am. There is no hiding from that goddess." He shook his head, chuckling at what might have been any one of a thousand memories. "There truly is no pleasing that woman, but I do believe she brings out the best in me as no other could . . . most of the time." Zeus shot Aphrodite a wink.

She shared a smile with Zeus, but her insides twisted with shame.

Her husband's tenderness in the presence of Ares was no manipulation; it was how he genuinely saw her. If only Hephaes-tus had staged a Hera-style jealous outrage—a dramatic ultima-tum, a righteous dressing-down, a temper tantrum involving flying objects—Aphrodite might have been able to shield her heart from the awful truth: she was horrible, truly horrible.

"Aphrodite," Zeus said gently, "your mate is the right one for you."

"Says the one who chose him for me," she replied, and Zeus matched her grin.

"You would not have been objective."

A huff left her. "Take it from the Goddess of Love, coupling is not meant to be a logical process."

"Please," said Zeus, his mouth twisted with distaste, "let us delve no deeper into the topic of physical attraction."

"Yes, let us not."

Zeus squeezed her hand with his own, a comforting gesture that nearly brought her to tears. "I understand that fidelity is tedious and unnatural when you've already lived forever, and another eternity stretches out ahead of you." *So he wasn't buying her cover story.* "Do what you must, Goddess, but do not try your husband's patience for too long. Every man and god has his breaking point. Even yours."

She slid her hand from his. "Thank you for the advice."

Turning them both toward the great Festival Hall, Zeus offered his elbow. "Come now. The procession is about to begin."

13

# SHRINK

"You're sure this is the doctor's office?"

The multistory brick building in downtown Tarra was not what Cupid expected. The cold, nondescript structure seemed better suited to professions involving numbers and paperwork than humans "spilling their guts" to each other.

Throwing his truck into park, Pan shot his passenger a grin. "If you're looking for Asclepius's altar, it was replaced with a revolving glass door circa 1902."

"Funny." Cupid huffed.

"And you won't find snakes at your feet," said Pan as he hopped out of the truck, "or offering tables or—"

"I get it!" Cupid scurried out of the truck and caught up to Pan. "I can't believe you're making me go through with this as if it's an actual appointment. You know we could have just found out where the doctor lived and pretended to deliver a package or something."

"Oh yeah? Then why didn't they just fire up your heart and send you to his house or his gym or the place he gets his coffee on the way to work?" Pan had a definite point.

"Fine"—Cupid scowled—"but if I don't hear the beat, we're out of here."

"Like hell we are," said Pan, forging toward the door at a furious pace. "We have no idea what part of this trip is meant to provide valuable information. Your next Worthy could be another patient sitting in the waiting area right now or some guy you meet in the john." Pan's hands flailed about as he pulled guesses from the air. "Or maybe your punishment requires actual delving into the type of therapy your app doc believes you need."

Cupid froze in his tracks. "Do you really think I might have to let this doctor dig around in my heart?" That sounded too terrible for words.

"I have no fucking clue! Which is why"—Pan jabbed his finger at Cupid's chest—"we are going to the fifth floor to meet this Dr. Chan, and you are not leaving his office until your time's up. Got it?" There was no arguing with Pan when he was insistent and probably right.

"Fine," replied Cupid, "but you're not listening in on my session."

"Trust me, I have no stomach for hearing your anguish in vivid detail. Besides, I already have my marching orders from Reed."

"Do tell."

Pan's features slipped into an expression Cupid recognized as his "Reed face"—a dreamy reverence tempered by a boyish crush and a hint of amusement. "Well, after *much* convincing, Reed did grant me permission to accompany you inside the building, *but*"—and there Pan switched to his best impersonation of Reed—"under no circumstances am I to breach the sanctity of the therapist's office, nor am I permitted to ask any 'probing questions'"—this Pan marked with air quotes—"after your session."

"I'll be sure to hold you to that."

"After you." Pan followed Cupid inside the revolving door, and soon enough, they were standing inside the lobby.

Cupid pushed the elevator call button and lifted his head to watch the lighted numbers tick down. Their last elevator ride together was inside the Tarra Arms under much different circumstances. The memory only intensified the awful feeling churning in his gut.

"I'll meet you," Cupid said suddenly, cutting away to the stairwell before Pan could answer. He clambered up the five flights and located the door with Dr. Chan's name listed along with five others. Before turning the knob, Cupid paused to read his heart. His pulse beat quicker from climbing the stairs, but that was all.

Pan glanced up at him from his chair, settled into his *People* magazine with his legs splayed out in front of him as if he'd been sitting there an hour. "What took you so long?"

Cupid glared. If not for the other patients, Cupid would have told Pan where to stick his magazine.

Smirking, Pan pointed his thumb toward a woman sitting behind a counter. "Go check in. If she asks for your insurance, give her that blue card in your wallet."

Cupid trudged to the counter on lead feet. On his left, he passed a series of closed office doors labeled with name placards. On his right stood a line of matched chairs, mostly filled. Every head turned as Cupid walked by, but there was no Love motor to be found.

He announced himself to the cheerful receptionist and filled out another five pages of questions. Cupid had already spent over an hour on their patient portal four days ago, answering all the same questions he'd answered for Wings. He was actually a bit surprised when he'd received the callback from Dr. Chan's office to schedule the appointment, considering how much less dire his responses were now than his first time through.

He strode back to Pan, sat down, stood up again, and paced some more.

"Hey!" Pan whisper-shouted, peering over his magazine. "You're making everyone anxious. Go find something to read." He jerked his chin toward a stack of magazines on the side table.

Cupid recognized most of the titles from the ever-present pile by his mother's garden chaise. He thumbed through *Vanity Fair* and *Entertainment Tonight* and settled on *Psychology Today* before returning to his seat. Flipping to the article that had caught his attention, "Psychology Apps—The Virtual Doctor Is In," Cupid glanced up when Pan peered over to see what he was reading.

"The virtual doc is *out*, buddy. Let it go."

"I'm curious what they have to say about it," Cupid said with a shrug. It still bothered him that Posey had refused to treat him, and he wanted to understand why.

"As long as you're not perseverating," Pan said.

"Okay, new rule—no more using big, obnoxious words when it's just the two of us."

"Sorry. Reed finds it sexy," Pan said with a not-sorry grin. Cupid rolled his eyes. "It means you're stuck on something you can't do anything about—like that doctor, for example. She's got her reasons, and you're not gonna change her mind, so let it go." Pan huddled closer and lowered his voice. "Besides, you don't even need a therapist anymore, so what's the big deal?"

"I don't know, Pan. I kind of liked her. I felt comfortable talking with her. I told her a lot of personal things, and then she decided she didn't want to help me anymore. I just feel . . ."

"Like a kid thrown off a mountain by his mom?"

A door opened. A woman blotting her eyes with a tissue exited the office and headed toward the outer door. A man resembling the photo Pan had shown him yesterday stepped into the doorway and scanned the row of faces. "Mr. Arrows?"

Cupid stood slowly and slipped the magazine onto his seat. "Yes, that's me."

"Good luck, buddy." Cupid felt Pan's gaze on his back all the way to the doctor's door.

Cupid clasped Dr. Chan's offered hand. "Please, call me Q."

"Nice to meet you, Q. I'm Doctor Chan. Come on in."

Heart check: nothing.

Pan craned his neck, seeking clues Cupid refused to offer, until the closed door separated them. If Cupid had to suffer through the next hour, so would Pan.

It turned out to be fifty minutes, and Pan was already on his feet when Cupid emerged from Dr. Chan's office. A dozen questions danced in Pan's eyes, but Cupid's attention was drawn to the magazine grasped between his fingers: *Psychology Today*. Cupid's mouth opened into a broad grin.

"Learn anything?"

"What?" Following Cupid's gaze, Pan seemed to notice the magazine for the first time. "Oh. I was just reading about the importance of boundaries. *Well?* How'd it go in there?"

"That sounded like a probing question," said Cupid, striding toward the outer door.

Behind him came Pan's rushed steps. "Oh, come on!"

Pan zigzagged after Cupid down the five flights of stairs, their footfalls echoing off the hard surfaces. They crossed the lobby like two horses straining for the finish line. Cupid darted into the revolving door, and Pan crowded into his bay. Cupid pushed on the glass, but the door wouldn't budge.

Cupid spun around to find Pan with a boot wedged against the glass and a cross look on his face. "You're not getting out of this contraption until you tell me what happened in there. I'm not asking for the gory details. Just give me the executive summary."

"Fine." Cupid's hands found his hips even in the tight space.

"No beat. Not going back. And I don't think Reed would appreciate your tactics."

Pan relented. Cupid stole the opportunity to give the door a shove and escape into the parking lot.

"Hey, wait up!" Pan yelled, but Cupid charged toward the truck without slowing.

Cupid mounted the passenger seat, slammed the seat belt into its buckle, and fixed his stare out the side window. Pan started the engine, and the Titan popped and rumbled around them like a crowd of spectators at a boxing match. They drove away, lost in their separate thoughts until Pan blurted out an apology.

"I'm sorry, okay?"

Cupid swiveled toward Pan. "Tell me, what did you learn about boundaries?"

"Not enough, apparently," Pan answered with a snort. Cupid couldn't help but smile. "C'mon, buddy. You know I only have your best interests at heart."

"I'm pretty sure that's what my mother said the last time we spoke."

"Ouch."

"Sorry. I'm a bit raw right now."

"Understood." As Pan steered them out of downtown Tarra with his left hand on the wheel, he scrubbed his right hand across his mouth. Back and forth, back and forth. A quick glance at Cupid, back and forth again.

Cupid sighed. "Just ask."

Pan dropped his hand as he turned. "Really?"

"It's more annoying watching you try *not* to ask."

Pan huffed, the beginnings of a smile on his lips. "Okay, but I wouldn't want to be reported to the professor. He might turn me over his knee." He added a naughty pop of his eyebrows in case Cupid had missed his meaning. He hadn't.

"Boundaries, Pan. Boundaries!"

They chuckled together.

Air cleared, Pan ventured a question. "Was it awful?"

"Yes and no. He dredged up a lot of painful memories from my childhood. How I never fit in with my peers, Mother's infantilizing"—another unpleasant addition to Cupid's vocabulary—"behavior, Ares always poking his nose in and trying to toughen me up, people I love abandoning me—"

Pan's shoulders sagged as he let out a soft curse.

"Fun stuff, right?"

"Fuck, man. I'm sorry . . . for all of it. Then and now."

"I know, Pan. And don't beat yourself up. Dr. Chan said I'm remarkably well-adjusted despite the truly impressive emotional scars I'm carrying around. *That's* why I'm not going back."

"Huh. Well, good for you."

Cupid leaned back against the headrest and released a cleansing breath. "I'm just glad I'm done with that."

"Yep. On to Dr. Fairlawn."

Cupid turned a murderous glare on Pan. "Now I know how Mia felt."

"Hey, it all worked out well for her in the end. Let's stay focused on that."

14

# HOME OFFICE

Dr. Fairlawn's approval process involved exactly two emails: Cupid's request and the doctor's response. No questionnaires, no chat rooms, no admin assistants, and no excruciating paperwork. "Also no insurance," Pan pointed out with a half-snort.

She worked out of her home in the same wealthy neighborhood where Ruthie used to live. Thanks to Dr. Fairlawn's patient load consisting of predominantly at-home mothers of schoolchildren, her afternoon schedule had an opening two days later, giving Cupid just enough time to recharge his emotional batteries.

Pan had insisted on driving him again. Memories assaulted Cupid as Pan took the off-ramp to Tarra Heights: sneaking up Ruthie's driveway that morning after meeting her at Versailles; seeing her for the first time without the big hair and face paint to mask her natural beauty; finally earning an invitation to help her create her writing sanctuary; showing up with all his earthly belongings in a garbage bag when Pan kicked him out of the house . . .

He was beginning to feel more at home here than on the Mount—not that it mattered one bit what Cupid felt or wanted. The truck got quiet and stayed that way until Pan pulled up in front of the doctor's house.

"I'll be right here waiting." The gods had involved Pan for some reason, and he was determined to see this through.

"Thanks." Cupid hopped out and took his first heavy steps up the brick path.

"Hey!"

Cupid whirled around to find Pan wedged between his truck and the open door, his head and shoulders the only body parts visible above the roof. "*What?*"

"Don't come out of that house until you get what you need. This doc is the end of the line."

"Gee, thanks for the reminder." With a heavy exhale, Cupid plodded toward his next gut-spilling.

Dr. Fairlawn had instructed him to ring the bell at the side door. She buzzed him inside, where there was a small waiting area with two chairs—both empty. He crossed the room and stood with his nose pressed to the closed inner door. *Nothing,* not a love-beat from his own heart, let alone the other side of the door.

He leaped back when he heard footsteps approaching from inside the office, giving him just enough time to appear to have been sitting innocently in one of the side chairs. He listened again as the previous patient walked past him. No beat.

"Mr. Arrows?" The doctor's benevolent smile matched the photos he'd found online last night, hoping for any clue, however minor, to help him understand why he was here. She was dressed in gray trousers and a shirt that might have come from Dr. Chan's button-down collection.

"Please, call me Q."

"Dr. Fairlawn. Pleased to meet you." She gestured him inside and closed the door behind them. "Please have a seat anywhere."

He was greeted by a confusing choice of furniture: a small couch, a low chair upholstered in a nubby beige fabric, two simple wooden chairs resembling those in his current kitchenette, and a brown leather armchair the doctor was backing into while he deliberated. He settled on the beige chair opposite Dr. Fairlawn and released a breath as he sat.

"So, Q, how can I help?"

Slogging through every detail from the beginning was becoming tedious. He tried for an abbreviated version: "I'd been going through a rough time and decided to get some professional help, so about a week ago, I signed on to use an online app. The therapist decided I needed to be treated in person and referred me to you."

"Mind sharing which app you were using?"

"It's called Wings."

"Ah," she said. "That would be Mariposa Rey?"

"Yes! Do you know Posey?"

The use of the nickname lifted Dr. Fairlawn's eyebrows. "Yes. We worked together in the same practice when we were first starting out."

"So you're friends!" Cupid's spine tingled where his wings used to hinge.

"We lost touch years ago, sadly. She must have found me in the APA directory. But I'd like to redirect this conversation back to you, Q. What brings you here today?"

But wasn't that precisely what Cupid had come to find out? "I'm here because Posey recommended you," he said truthfully.

"Maybe we should start with your encounter, then . . . with Dr. Rey."

He recited the facts for the doctor as he had for Dr. Chan.

"I filled out all the forms online, and she emailed me back to set up a chat conversation."

"Just to clarify, this was to be a written conversation?"

"Yes. In a private chat room."

"All right. And how did that conversation go?"

"I thought it was going fine. I was even feeling better."

"What was the nature of your initial complaint?"

*Here we go,* thought Cupid as he rattled off the words that no longer weighed him down. "I had just broken up with someone I loved very much, and I was in a lot of pain."

"I'm very sorry to hear that."

"It's fine now."

The slightest tilt of her head gave away her skepticism. "Did Dr. Rey offer you a perspective you found particularly helpful?"

"No, not really. She was just asking questions."

"But you did experience some relief from your emotional distress after the initial chat?"

"Yes."

"That's helpful. What happened after that chat conversation took place?"

"I was waiting for Posey to email me with some possible times for our next chat, but she called me instead to tell me she couldn't help me."

"Did she offer a reason?"

"Not exactly. She said I was using relationships as my coping mechanism and that I had substituted her to fill the void in my heart."

"'Her,' meaning Dr. Rey?"

"Yes."

"I see." Oh, Cupid had seen that "I see" many times before. *Mother.*

*Your geometry teacher sent another note home about applying yourself to your studies.*

*Artemis said you were in the woods again, distracting her maidens with your arrows.*

*Mercury said you and Pan were chasing nymphs again.*

That familiar ache of having screwed up was upon him, but this time, he genuinely didn't know why.

"I don't understand what I've done wrong."

"Nothing. Nothing at all," Dr. Fairlawn replied immediately and unequivocally. Seeing that Cupid was unconvinced, she added, "Dr. Rey was alluding to a situation called 'transference,' where the patient subconsciously projects feelings about some-one else onto his or her therapist."

"No offense, Doctor, but I'm pretty sure that didn't happen in the chat room. I can't be in love with someone I've never even met."

Dr. Fairlawn's lips disappeared between her teeth for a thoughtful moment. "Of course, I cannot presume to know what took place between you and Dr. Rey. I can only tell you that transference is an extremely complex phenomenon requir-ing skilled navigation by the therapist. This is a perfect illus-tration of where the online therapy model falls short, in my opinion—though I have no doubt Dr. Rey provides the gold stan-dard of care in the field."

Cupid might have agreed after their first chat, but now, he wasn't so sure.

The doctor offered a warm smile. "Personally, I believe in the old-fashioned model—two people in a room together, putting in the time and emotional elbow grease. Having practiced psy-choanalysis for many years herself, Dr. Rey surely understands the limitations of her online medium, hence, the rigorous cull-ing process. If she made the determination that the traditional model will better serve your needs, I respect that decision."

"As do I. I asked Posey to see me in person, and she said she doesn't practice that kind of therapy anymore."

"Right. The last time she saw a patient was seven years ago." Dr. Fairlawn immediately seemed to regret giving away the information.

"Was she not good at it?"

The leather at the edge of Dr. Fairlawn's armrests crinkled under the curl of her fingers. "She was wonderful, and she helped a great deal of people. But we should get back—"

"Then why did she stop?"

Her smile thinned. "I'm sorry, but I really have to cut you off right there, Mr. Arrows—"

"Q."

*Heavy sigh.* "Q. Let's focus on *you.*" Dr. Fairlawn folded her hands in her lap. "The good news is, you're here. And I am ready, willing, and able to help if you're open to doing some hard work on yourself. I must warn you, psychoanalysis is a very intense, very rigorous course of treatment. We'll be delving into your childhood memories, and this often brings out emotions that are unpleasant or even disturbing in the short term. I will be here to guide you every step of the way, of course. The plan is to work through these difficult and sometimes painful memories, so you will emerge healthier and stronger on the other side."

"Like the butterfly. Posey's app."

"Yes," said Dr. Fairlawn, her expression softening. "That's exactly right."

Clearly, Dr. Fairlawn held a great deal of respect for Posey, though she seemed reluctant to elaborate, and Posey must have held Dr. Fairlawn in high regard. Why else would she have referred Cupid to her? Were they once close friends? Lovers? Why would these two women have lost touch if they had the means to find each other?

Was this Cupid's mission, then—to reunite the two? It was only a stab, a wild arrow let fly without a target in sight, but for the first time, Cupid felt a flicker of light inside the dark box holding the answer.

But why, if Dr. Fairlawn was his next Worthy, had Cupid not succumbed to love's sweet stupor once again? The only direction from his heart-motor was the drive toward Pan almost a week ago. And why, come to think of it, did Dr. Fairlawn seem oblivious to Cupid's charms? Nothing added up, but the urgency was gathering like storm clouds.

With more questions than ever, Cupid scanned the office for clues. *Who are you, Dr. Fairlawn?* Compared to Dr. Chan's generic office, Dr. Fairlawn's read more like an extension of her home. Warm tones, a giant standing clock with a soothing *tick-tick-tick*, colorful paintings on the walls, wood cases crowded with books. That said, she hadn't left many personal items lying around to be discovered.

Cupid was about to give up on his treasure hunt when he saw it on the shelf behind her. Tucked away between stacks of hardcover books was a small silver frame with a photo of Dr. Fairlawn with a man and a young boy.

"Is that your family?" he asked, pointing just above her head.

She appeared puzzled by his question, but he'd knocked her off-balance so many times already, she recovered quickly and glanced over her shoulder. "Oh. Yes."

"Is that a recent photo?"

She studied Cupid as if performing some kind of high-level analysis on the therapeutic merits of answering, then stood to reach the photo off the shelf. Regarding it fondly, she handed it to Cupid. "That was Myles's sixth birthday. He's ten now."

Present tense. There was no note of melancholy marring her joy, no broken heart searching for its mate. This doctor did not need Cupid's help. So much for his aimless arrow.

Fingering the frame in his lap, Cupid dropped his chin to his chest. *Now what?*

"Do you have family nearby?" she asked gently. She'd returned to her armchair and now sat forward, elbows on her knees, hands carefully folded between them.

Cupid shook his head.

"Have you seen them recently?"

He lifted his face toward Mount Olympus and added up the days since his fall. "It's been months now."

"That can be rough."

He nodded. Elaborating would have required a side trip Cupid did not have time for.

After several beats of the giant clock, Dr. Fairlawn broke the silence. "I know this is a scary path to embark on, but you came to me today for a reason, Q." Her voice held great compassion. *She must be a wonderful mother to Myles.*

Tears pooled in Cupid's eyes. "I know."

"So, what do you say, Q? Shall we begin this journey together?"

A tense breath fluttered out of him. "I don't think I can."

"That's okay, too," she said. "If you change your mind, my door is open."

They stood, shook hands again, and Cupid attempted one last time to discern some kind of message from their hearts, but there was no connection at all. His mind raced as he jogged down the path toward Pan, yanked open the truck door, and climbed inside.

"I have to find Posey."

"Posey? Dammit, Q, we've been over this. She's not going to be able to help you."

"I know. I think I need to help *her.*"

15

# APRIL CALLING

The downside of the quiet house at the lake was that the closest decent grocery was a twenty-minute drive on a light day. While the ride through the mountain pass might have charmed Posey that first summer on the lake, seven years of trekking up and down Route 28 had taught her to plan her meals carefully. Twice a week was enough, thank you very much, even with the lull in tourists between summer's water sportsters and winter's ski bums.

Breezing through Wednesday's pre-rush hour traffic, her eco-friendly bags filled with provisions to last her through the week-end, Posey cast her gaze to the rich yellow and deep red hues all around her. Autumn had its ways of cushioning the blow, one bright explosion of color before gray took over the landscape, but it was almost time to hang up her bike for the winter.

Home again, she unloaded the groceries, poured herself a glass of wine, and set the oven to preheat before checking her Wings emails. Addie had left her a request to chat in the morning; Posey's bike ride would wait.

Posey was just about to confirm with Addie when the last message caught her eye, a generic subject line indicating a message received through the Wings contact portal. Curious, she opened the message.

**Need to talk about your recent referral.**
**Please be in touch soon.**
**—April**

Posey collapsed into her desk chair, swiping the wine off the shelf on her way down. *He'd contacted her.* A wall of heat smacked into her face. *What the hell were you thinking, bringing April into this?*

But of course Posey would refer Q to April. How could she *not* when she discovered her old colleague was practicing in the very town where he lived—and how crazy was that? It was the professional and ethical way to handle the situation.

The oven chimed. Posey chugged half the glass of wine on her way back to the kitchen. What, exactly, did April need to talk about? Posey muttered to herself as she unwrapped the salmon and set it on the broiling pan. Had Q been to see her? *What was he like?*

"Christ," she said out loud, slamming the pan into the oven. *Jesus Christ, Posey. Really?*

Posey took another sip of wine, then loaded her arms with salad ingredients pulled from the refrigerator. *"Please* be in touch soon," she said, then repeated it, emphasizing "soon" this time. What was she expected to do now, just pick up the phone and call her as if Posey hadn't carefully avoided contact for the last seven years?

The knife flew over the cucumber. *Watch your fingers. You're agitated.*

What if Q was in danger? Once awakened, the fantasy would not be silenced, not by peeling carrots or slicing onions or downing another glass of wine.

"Goddammit!" Posey screamed to her empty house.

She scooped the chopped veggies off her counter into a big plastic bag and shoved it into the refrigerator. After refilling her glass once more, *definitely my last,* she plucked her phone from her bag and plodded to her office as if marching to her death. She owed it to April and Q—and honestly, to herself—to make the call. Taking wine and phone to her comfortable chair, she pulled up April's mobile number, hit send, and held her breath until she heard the familiar voice on the other end.

"Posey," said April. "I'm so glad you called."

The pain that lived inside of her all day, every day rose up like a sea dragon punching its ugly head through the surface of the water. *Breathe.*

"Hello, April."

"Are you okay?"

A strange laughter rolled out of Posey. "In general, or right this moment?"

"Both. Either." Posey could still picture the kind smile she'd last seen at the hearing.

"I'm doing okay," Posey answered. "How are you?"

"I'm good. Listen, I didn't call to torture you with personal questions. I'm concerned about the patient you referred to me."

"How concerned? He's not going to hurt himself—?"

"No, no. Nothing like that."

Posey released the breath she'd been holding, sipped her wine, and folded her legs underneath her. "Okay."

"He came to see me, and we had a session together."

"Good."

"I believe he would benefit greatly from therapy, and I know I can help him, but he seems to think you've already healed him somehow."

"We had two encounters," Posey was quick to reply, "but he was never under my care."

"Yes, he was quite clear on that. In fact, he spent most of our time together trying to understand why you won't treat him."

The fingers of guilt wrapped their icy grip around Posey's neck once again. "I'm sure you explained why that was impossible?"

"To the extent I was able."

"Thanks, April. I'm sorry if I put you in an awkward position."

"Not a problem. This isn't about me. I contacted you because he's unreceptive to the idea of beginning treatment with me. I thought you might want to revisit your decision."

"Oh. Had he contacted the other doctor yet?"

"I wasn't aware you gave him another recommendation."

"I had no idea if you'd have room for him in your schedule or if he'd be more comfortable with a man . . . I just wanted to give him a couple of options."

"Sure. No, he didn't mention talking to anyone else. Who was the other doc?"

"Wes Chan. Know him?"

"I do. He's a good guy. But honestly, whether Q has seen Wes or not, I think whatever connection you and Q have is both his best chance and, at the moment, his biggest obstacle." *Way to rub salt in the wound.* "From what I can glean, which, to be honest, is based on very little data, you were spot-on with the transference call. I'm afraid he sees your refusal to treat him as one more abandonment in a long line. You may be the only one who can help him right now."

"But I really can't. Psychoanalysis is well beyond my scope now. You know this." *And you know why.* "Not to mention the physical distance."

"There are technologies available. I've used both FaceTime and Skype quite effectively in my practice . . ."

Was she honestly suggesting it was as simple as that? "You know I can't, April."

April didn't answer right away. "Actually, Posey, I have no idea where your head's at. You sent this man to me, so I'm trying to follow up responsibly. What you do with the information is up to you."

"I appreciate that."

Were they finished, then? Neither seemed eager to end the call.

April took the first leap into the deep void between them. "I miss you, my friend."

"I miss you too." Tears sprang to Posey's eyes. "How's Myles?"

"Myles is . . . ten!"

"Ten! Dear God, how did that happen?" *I've missed his whole life.*

"I know," April said, chuckling.

"I suppose Jarrod's older too?"

"Mm-hmm, but somehow I haven't aged."

"I believe you." Would those laugh lines framing her mouth be deeper now?

"What about you, Posey?"

"What? Have I aged?" A hollow laugh escaped her.

"Have you . . . met anyone?" *Since Evan,* she meant.

"No," she replied. "Nobody special." The only thing she'd had between her legs in months was her bike seat.

"How's your practice?" April asked.

She'd clearly found Posey through Wings, so there was no need to fill her in on that part. "It's good. I average between four and seven patients at a time. It's . . . enough."

"Sounds like you're getting on," April said,

"Most days." Today might not be one of them.

April sighed into the phone. "I'm sorry, Posey. I didn't call to upset you. I just wanted to update you on the referral. The guy's tied up in knots, and you can help even if all you do is encourage him to talk to me. You don't need this on your conscience."

No, she really didn't.

"Look, give him a call. He's not your patient yet. Say what you need to say."

"I'll think about it."

"And know you can call me anytime, Po. *Anytime.*"

*What is that smell?* "Oh shit! I forgot I have fish in the oven!"

"Go!" She could hear April laughing as she tossed the phone away and bolted for the kitchen.

16

# CARPOOL

"Remember, Reed, no sloppy goodbye kisses in front of Q."

Without taking his focus from the road ahead, Reed rolled his eyes, but his blush was everything. "I'll try to restrain myself."

The truth was, they'd been sloppy-goodbyeing each other since Reed had woken him by nuzzling the ticklish spot below Pan's armpit. Soundlessly, so as to draw out the sweet, predawn, dog-free bubble that belonged to just the two of them, Pan had burrowed beneath the covers and given his lover a very sexy memory to tide him over for as long as this mission might take. Their tender pawing had continued all through the day's first cups of coffee, and still, they couldn't quite keep their hands to themselves.

Chuckling, Pan drew Reed's hand from the steering wheel and laced their fingers together. He couldn't believe he was about to get mushy. "I hate that I have to leave you."

"The dogs are not going to be happy with me when I come back without you."

"The dogs, huh?"

The red light gave Reed a chance to cock his head at Pan one last time before taking the turn into the South Side Apartment complex. "I can't even remember what my life was like before you."

"Well, for one thing, you didn't have to wake up at the ass-crack of dawn to drive two gods to the airport."

"I didn't wake up to drive you. I woke up to give you a proper send-off." *Sweet, sweet Reed.*

"You know I love it when you talk dirty, Professor. Man, I'm gonna sext the shit outta you while we're apart."

Reed's blush returned, and so did the shy smile Pan had fallen in love with. "Oh boy. I'll do my best."

"I can't wait," said Pan, chuckling to cover his anxiety about how long that wait might be. If not for those dogs, there was no way Pan would have let Reed stay behind while he and Cupid scoured Lake Tahoe looking for this Posey Rey for reasons they had yet to understand. "Seriously, though, you know I'll be back as soon as I can."

"I know." Reed drew their joined hands into his lap. "Don't worry about me. Just do what you need to do. We'll be here when you get home."

*Home.* There it was. Of all the places Pan had left, this was the first time he'd ever felt as though he were leaving home. The light turned green, pulling Reed's focus back to the road

Their headlights washed the circular driveway with an arc of light as Reed pulled around to the front door. "There he is," said Reed.

Pan retreated to the passenger side, releasing Reed's hand in the process. Cupid had yet to be in the presence of Reed and Pan together since they'd crossed two weeks ago, and though he claimed to be over Pan, there was no need to rub Cupid's nose in their bliss.

Cupid followed his suitcase into the back seat. They'd agreed on seven days' worth of clean clothes. Neither had a clue what might happen or how long they might need to stay. "G'morning."

"Morning," Reed called cheerfully, then guided his SUV onto the main road.

"Did you remember your driver's license?" asked Pan, peering over his shoulder.

"Yes, Mother. You've reminded me four times since yesterday!"

"Hey," said Pan, "you won't believe what earthlings have to go through in order to fly. If you're not careful, you'll earn yourself a cavity search." Reed shot Pan a stern warning.

"Did you bring my arrow?"

Pan wheeled around. "We discussed this. The arrow is a no-go."

"But that arrow might be my only chance."

"Your only chance for *what?*" asked Reed, shooting Pan a grim look.

"To fix love," said Cupid.

"Sorry, pal. You're gonna have to find another way. Sharp, pointy weapons tend to make people nervous in airports these days."

"Pan's right," said Reed. "I daresay even your charms won't sway the TSA agents from enforcing the rules."

"We don't want to give them any reason to detain us," said Pan. "If you find yourself on the no-fly list, it'll be a long damn drive to Nevada."

Cupid harrumphed against the back seat like a scolded teenager.

"Hey," Pan said, "you're sure this is what you have to do, right?" After spending all day yesterday tracking down the good doctor and booking flights and accommodations in the Lake Tahoe area, Pan had not stopped to seriously consider the wisdom of this half-assed plan.

The last time Pan had stepped outside the Tarra network of divine penal colonies spanning the globe was in the early 1900s. Triton had tricked Pan into leaving Oklahoma for what he claimed was a burning compulsion to be near the water. After convincing Pan to deliver him to the Texas coast, Triton promptly shifted into merman form and dove into the Gulf of Mexico. Mercury discovered the sea god in Nigeria a week later. Pan and Triton had spent the next twenty years wandering the Sahara together. Not an experience Pan was eager to repeat.

"It's the only thing that makes any sense," Cupid replied. "Everything keeps bringing me back to Posey."

"May I slip in a question at this juncture?" asked Reed.

Smirking, Pan replied, "Go for it."

"If the gods wanted you to end up at Posey's door, why do you think that heart-motor of yours hasn't simply dragged you there already?"

Pan jumped in. "She's way out of his range. My fallens usually interact exclusively with the inhabitants of whatever Tarra they land in. Q's first three Worthies and their Right Loves were all here. If Posey's office were here in town—and a bigger if, assuming she is his next Worthy—Q would've probably been pulled directly there."

"Maybe," said Cupid, "but that would have been a far different kind of initial meeting. You were dead set against letting me talk to a therapist in person at that point."

"No, you're right," said Pan. Truthfully, he hadn't fully gotten past that uneasiness, but there didn't seem to be another way. "Which is why I thought one of those two references Posey gave you would turn out to be your next Worthy, but that would bring us right back to Reed's question. Why not just compel you to Dr. Chan or Dr. Fairlawn directly?"

Reed chimed in with the answer to his own question. "I suppose you needed to first connect with Dr. Rey through Wings, specifically around your heartache and depression. Sorry, Q," he added, hastily checking Cupid's expression in the rearview mirror.

"It's fine," said Cupid with a nonchalant wave. "Go on?"

Reed nodded at Cupid's reflection. "While you felt better after the initial contact, clearly your conversation triggered something that caused Posey to bow out of treating you and set off this chain of events that has you convinced you need to find her." *Damn*, that brain of Reed's was one sexy organ.

"Yes," agreed Cupid.

Holding Cupid's gaze in the mirror, Reed ventured deeper. "I'm curious to hear your take on your appointment with Dr. Chan."

Cupid's lips twisted into a grimace. "He asked me all these personal questions about my childhood and my love life and dredged up how I keep losing the people I love most. I'd rather have taken my chances with Scylla."

"The six-headed sea monster? Yikes!" said Reed, eyes wide. "Was there no therapeutic effect at all, then?"

"Hey, don't forget he said you weren't fucked up anymore. That's something." Pan's comment earned a groan from Reed.

"I guess. If I'd gone to Dr. Fairlawn first, I'd probably still be in her office, slogging through my feelings about Mother, instead of focusing on how I'm supposed to help Posey."

"To fulfill your assignment from the gods?" Reed had a way of making the Divine Council's punishment sound like a page of math homework.

Cupid shrugged. "I assume so. I'm still here, which means I have more work to do."

"Does that mean you expect to fall in love with Posey as you did with the others?"

"If the pattern holds, it should be a lot worse."

Reed flinched, his gaze shifting across the front seat.

"Good times," Pan mumbled under his breath.

Reed caught Cupid's eyes in the mirror again. "Are you sure you can handle that?"

"Does it matter?" Cupid replied.

"Sorry," said Reed, "I just meant . . ."

"It's okay, Reed. At least I have a therapist lined up for when Posey doesn't beat back."

The car went silent after that, the three of them staring out the nearest window into the predawn sky. When Reed pulled up to the drop-off area, they all huddled together on the curb.

Reed was a ball of nerves, poor guy, stuffing his hands into his pockets and trying not to make an awkward display, per Pan's request.

"Fuck it. C'mere," Pan muttered, then pulled Reed into a hard kiss.

Reed pressed his hand to Pan's chest, but he didn't offer any real resistance. They broke apart after a couple of minutes, blushing and grinning at each other as if it were their first kiss.

Cupid cleared his throat.

"Sorry, man," Pan said.

"We didn't mean to—"

"No, it's fine." Cupid's eyes were glued to the sidewalk. "I was just thinking I should probably say goodbye to you, Reed." *Right.*

Pan had grown somewhat numb after so many goodbyes that turned out not to be, but Reed was positively stricken. His head whipped toward Pan as if he could provide answers or prevent the inevitable; all he could do was shrug. *I should have warned him about this.*

"All right," Reed said as he ambled forward toward Cupid and opened his arms.

Cupid stepped into the hug. "Thank you, Reed. For everything."

"It's been an absolute pleasure knowing you, Q." Reed's voice caught halfway through the nickname, making it come out more *kuh* than *kyew*. "You will be missed."

"I know it's asking a lot," said Cupid, squeezing Reed around the shoulders, "but please take good care of my friend."

Reed's gaze met Pan's over Cupid's shoulder. "I promise." He pinched his eyes shut, sending two tears rolling down his cheeks.

*Crap.* Pan was tearing up, too. Goodbyes sucked.

Their arms slid to their own sides as both men staggered away from their broken bond. Cupid turned and strode between the glass doors that slid open for him, dragging his suitcase behind.

"You better go before he does something he shouldn't," said Reed, forcing a smile.

Pan nodded. He'd swallowed so many doubts, he could feel the pile sitting in his belly. "Tell the dogs I'm sorry I had to leave?"

Reed clapped him on the shoulder. "They'll understand."

17

# MIDDAY SURPRISE

The *clip-clop, clip-clop* of his wife's sandals skipping down the stairwell to his workshop was the very last thing Hephaestus expected, let alone her carting around the lap-tray delivered by the kitchen servants when the gods wished to be served in bed. Aphrodite's face dipped below the ceiling line as she peeked to see if he was there before descending the last flight.

Hephaestus lifted his chisel with the utmost care from the gold medallion clamped to his anvil, but it was too late—his engraving was ruined. He'd need to start over with a new piece of gold once Aphrodite had gone.

He braced himself for the highly unusual visit. *What is it you've come to extract, Goddess?* If not for the disappointment that surged within his old, knowing bones, Hephaestus might have felt remorse for his suspicion.

"There you are!" Aphrodite sounded relieved and more than a little surprised herself, though Hephaestus could not imagine why. He'd scarcely left his workshop since the Festival. Had she been searching for him an entire week?

"My goddess, what brings you to the bowels of my workshop? And what mouthwatering treats have you brought with you?" He set down his mallet and chisel and leaned in to inspect the delicacies giving off their tantalizing scents: spinach and cheese pie, pork belly over mashed potatoes, and four triangles of baklava gleaming with butter. A full carafe of wine stood in the center of the tray. His suspicions doubled, but his belly growled without conscience.

"It's been weeks since we've shared a meal. I had the cooks prepare your favorite dishes. I, um, hoped we might catch up over our midday meal?"

He covered his astonishment with genuine delight. "Sounds perfect." Surveying his blacksmith shop for a nonexistent clean surface, he relayed the sad truth. "I'm afraid my accommodations are sorely lacking for such an occasion."

She followed his gaze around the room, her eyes landing on the blankets piled in one corner. "Is this where you've been sleeping? On the cellar floor?"

Surely, the adulteress could not be indignant! He nearly laughed out loud at her audacity.

"Would you have me sleep at the foot of our bed while you and Ares toss about in the sheets?"

At least her cheeks had the decency to redden. "Ares has not slept in my bed but that once."

He bent at the waist in a dramatic and extremely sarcastic bow. "Gratitude, Goddess. Still, I'll take the stone floor and the warmth of my hearth any day over a bed sullied by my brother's cock."

She absorbed his cruel blow without missing a beat. "There *are* other bedrooms in the palace, you know."

"Ah, I see now. I should keep Cupid's bed warm while you and your lover dream up your evil plans to keep him away."

Her neck lengthened almost imperceptibly. He'd wounded her. "You've misread my intentions."

How on earth had Hephaestus been made the aggressor here? A terrible image of Ares rejoicing at their bickering popped into his head, and just that flash of Ares's smug smirk made Hephaestus want to put a fist through his brother's teeth. For all he knew, Ares's own hand had roused this battle lust between husband and wife. He regretted every harsh word.

Hephaestus softened. "Forgive me, darling. Shall we have ourselves a picnic among my bedding?" He hoped she might read his tone as romantic whimsy.

All but a fraction of her outrage subsided. "Sure. Why not?"

They set to spreading the quilt and laying out the banquet, working more *around* than *with* each other, averting their glances when fingers accidentally brushed. She sank gracefully onto her bottom, legs folded demurely beneath her, while Hephaestus grunted and tugged his legs into a pretzel.

Aphrodite arranged a dainty place setting in front of him—iron-creased linen napkin, gleaming silverware, a porcelain dinner plate—then passed him food platters one at a time until his plate was full. Without asking, she poured him a goblet of burgundy nectar, apparently intent on serving her husband one of everything before partaking of even a morsel for herself. His unease increased with each of her attentive gestures, but whatever her game, the food and drink were pure bliss to his system. He'd been living on dried meats and hummus for weeks now, not counting the Festival.

"Mmm. The spanakopita is still warm from the oven!" he said, eyes rolling back into his head as a clump of feta melted on his tongue.

"Here, have another."

He waved her off as she reached to refill his plate. "I'm saving room for that baklava."

She answered with a nod and a sip of her wine. He didn't love this small-talk game, but he could outlast his wife's patience six days out of seven.

Another sip of wine for Aphrodite; a large gulp for Hephaestus. A delicate forkful of shredded pork placed on the edge of her tongue; a mound of mashed potatoes shoveled into his mouth. A tap of her napkin at the sides of her mouth; all ten of his fingers individually inserted between his lips and loudly sucked clean. A soft sigh escaped her. Oh, how hard she was working not to criticize his manners.

He leaned back onto his palms and tested her with a large belch. Her eyes went wide, but she buried her distaste behind her goblet. Whatever this was, Hephaestus seemed to have the upper hand.

She really was an extraordinary beauty, no less stirring for all her tension: copper hair rolling like gentle waves over her milky shoulders, pale green chiton belted tightly around her trim waist, fingernails painted a deep garnet that might have been inspired by the wine. Eyeing her perched among his bed-sheets and treating him with such deference, Hephaestus could not ignore the fantasy that perhaps his wife had stopped in for a conjugal visit—or at least, that such activity would not be out of the question in order to achieve her as yet unstated goal.

She nibbled at the corner of her spanakopita, her eyes flitting like a nervous bird to and from her husband's watchful gaze. "Were you engraving something when I came in?" More small talk? Or was there something more behind her question?

"Mm-hmm. A gold medallion."

Her interest was definitely piqued. "You're making jewelry? It's been a while, hasn't it?"

Hephaestus laughed. It was true; he mostly churned out horseshoes and tools. "It's a gift." It seemed the wrong time to enlighten Aphrodite about his recent visits with Euphrosyne, their long chats about Cupid and Pan and life on Earth. In fact, it was Euphrosyne who had entreated Hephaestus to craft matching gold necklaces for her two sister Graces after receiving the welcome-home gift at the Festival, a twenty-four-karat gold chain and medallion engraved with a beautiful script E.

"I see." Aphrodite's eyes flashed with an emotion Hephaestus might have read as jealousy if it weren't so outlandish. "You don't, by chance, have any more of Cupid's arrowheads prepared?"

*Well now.* This was an intriguing line of questioning, especially since Aphrodite had expressed distinct displeasure over the last arrowhead he'd forged. "I do not. Why do you ask?" Aphrodite would have to dangle far more enticing bait on her line if she wished to catch a fish today, even a minnow.

"Oh, it's just that we're—I mean *I'm*—expecting him home relatively soon and just want to make sure everything will be ready."

"Soon? Huh. What did I miss?"

Aphrodite studied him with disbelief. "You really haven't been watching Earth, have you?"

A tired sigh rolled out of him. "I don't see the point in it, to be honest." Hephaestus had already tried everything from guiding vehicles to trying to persuade Aphrodite to do the right thing to dropping Cupid's bow and arrow right into his hands. Clearly, his efforts were unwanted and ineffective.

"I would have thought you cared about your family's welfare."

*His* family? Exactly when had she begun referring to Cupid as Hephaestus's son again?

His jaw dropped open, and he covered by quickly filling his gaping mouth with one of the buttery baklava triangles while the questions tickled his brain. He chewed thoughtfully, dizzied by his wife's bizarre behavior. Could she honestly have believed for one moment that Hephaestus didn't care about Cupid? About *her*?

He clapped the crumbs off his fingers, then, moved by sudden tenderness toward his estranged wife, unfolded his napkin and used it to wipe his face and hands. The situation required finesse, and he certainly wasn't going to manage any while sitting on his ass. He rocked onto his feet and offered Aphrodite a hand up. It struck him, as it often did, how very small her hand was inside his. Emboldened when she didn't pull away, he cupped her chin and tilted her face toward his.

"Of course I care," he answered her finally, "but tell me the truth, Aph. Surely, you didn't suffer through a meal with me in this dark cellar just to ask me for a batch of arrows. Why have you come?"

Her cheeks pinked, and she would have looked away, but he held her firmly to his gaze, and they both knew he could outwait her. Trapped, she pinched her eyes shut, forcing out tears as she gave in to the confession tumbling from her lips.

"Apparently, I'm a monster." An awful sob caught in her throat.

Hephaestus brushed his thumb along her jaw. "Come now, Goddess. Who told you that?"

"Nobody told *me*," she said, her lower lip quivering. "It's Cupid who's going to learn all about it."

"What do you mean? From whom?"

Her labored swallows rolled like boulders along her throat. "Psyche."

"Ah." *Wow.* A lot had happened since Hephaestus had last watched.

She released a ragged sigh. "It was time." Her sad eyes beseeched him for solace, and he understood at once why she had come. He hadn't seen her this fragile since Adonis was gored to death.

Hephaestus pulled her into his burly arms and pressed a soft kiss to his wife's head. Neither spoke for a long time—she, because she was weeping; he, because he had yet to find the right words.

His wife was proud, a goddess second in rank only to the Queen of Gods. Admissions of wrong were few and far between. If he pressed her now in her weakened state, he might extract an apology for her latest indiscretions along with earnest promises of renewed loyalty—promises she would break the next time it suited her. No, he would not put them both through the humiliation, nor would he whisper empty words into her ears. They all deserved better than that.

"Goddess." He drew his fingers through her hair, rocking her gently until she calmed. "What's done is done and cannot be changed." He was grateful for the lack of eye contact afforded by their hug. If her affair with Ares was not done, Hephaestus really did not want to know. "Whatever mistakes you may have made in raising Cupid cannot be erased, but through the wondrous gift of eternity, we all have a chance to atone and try to do better. The length of our days is greater in front of us than behind. Hold on to that."

She pressed on his shoulders, leaning out of the hug. Her tear-streaked cheeks caught the reflection of the fiery forge as she blinked up at him. "How will I ever be able to face Cupid after hearing his sordid accounts of his childhood rehashed over and over?"

He shrugged. "I recommend not listening."

"I can't help it. I can't tear myself away from the gaia glass."

Taking her hands in his, he fixed his expression to radiate kindness as best he could. "Trust me, Aph. It's better not to hear than to try to unremember after the fact. Leave the boy to his conversations, and let us attend to our own concerns, hmm?"

Her voice was a mere whisper, but of course, he heard every word. "I don't know what to say to you right now."

"When you figure it out, I'll be right here, ready to listen."

She bowed her head with shame. "I've treated you so poorly."

He agreed with a gruff chuckle. A strange giddiness had made him bold. "Feel free to practice atoning on me until Cupid comes home."

His wife smiled up at him. "I could use the practice."

"I'm easy."

Snaking her arms around his neck, she surprised him with an affectionate kiss. "How was that?" she asked with a sly grin.

"*That,*" he replied, firing back a grin of his own, "was a very good start."

Her gaze shifted to the blankets under their feet before meeting his again. She raised her eyebrows—a gauntlet thrown. They both sank to their knees on Hephaestus's makeshift bed, piled the dishes onto the tray as quickly as divinely possible, and moved the tray well out of their way. As Aphrodite climbed astride his hips, Hephaestus tried to stay present, but it was hard to keep from wondering if his wife would have Ares between her legs again before his own bliss had faded.

18

# BOW RETRIEVAL

A mere three weeks ago, Reed would have thought the muscle-bound redhead and his dark-haired friend were just two ordinary guys walking into an airport together. Before the serendipity that still made Reed pinch himself several times a day, he wouldn't even have noticed that the two were ridiculously hot. Now, by the grace of the gods who used to be his life's work—and whom he now understood to be alive and well and living on Mount Olympus—Reed knew better.

*TSA hath no idea what cometh their way.* Reed chuckled to himself. The visual of a winged Cupid flying through the metal detector, brandishing bow and arrow, lifted Reed's spirits as he pulled away from the drop-off curb—as long as it took him to picture the rest of the scene: armed agents swarming poor Cupid and dragging him into an interrogation room until the guys with the straitjackets arrived. *Youch.*

But of course, Pan had quickly shut down Cupid's fantasy of bringing his bow and arrow on the plane. If they'd been traveling by car, now that would have been a different story. . .

*Boom!* That's when the bright idea hit Reed right between the eyes.

By the time he arrived home, Reed had a full-blown plan. The two-thousand-mile shot across I-80 wouldn't be the most interesting drive, but if he could manage three consecutive ten-hour days behind the wheel and find a couple of dog-friendly motels close to the highway, he could be in Reno by . . . *hmm*, the sun was barely up. Could he leave yet *today?* The daydream of an early reunion with Pan kicked Reed's dreaded, lonely, lazy day right into high gear.

Job number one—go and get that arrow. Off he sped to Pan's, ticking through a mental checklist of practicalities of driving four dogs across the country and more than one demoralizing objection along the way. *This is nuts. Pan will be furious I made this long, hard drive alone! And how will he feel about my first deception?*

Each doubt was in turn countered by the image of Pan's face, lit with joy and surprise and awe. *"Reed! How did you . . .? You* drove *across the country with all four dogs?"* But even clouded by love, Pan might not let him off the hook so easily. He could draw together those furious eyebrows of his and open with, *"You really shouldn't have . . ."* In which case, Reed would flash the bow and arrow, and Pan would burst with pride at his lover's initiative and all would surely be forgiven. If not, Reed would dig into his ever-expanding repertoire and find another way to smooth things over with Pan. Those plans brought a different kind of smile to Reed's face, which he set aside as Pan's garage door rolled up its tracks.

The last place Reed had seen Cupid's equipment was the front hall closet. Heart hammering in his chest, Reed made a beeline for the door, wrapped a sweaty palm around the knob, and pulled.

A *whoosh* of cool air hit the top of Reed's head. Reed jumped back, stunned and dismayed that opening the closet had somehow burst a pipe in Pan's ceiling. A column of vapor descended, but there was no rush of water. Instead, as Reed stood squinting, the translucent field solidified into a nearly opaque male form with a petasus on his head, winged sandals on his feet, and a loincloth around his middle.

Just as Reed's brain had begun to process the confounding data delivered by his eyeballs, the being spoke: "Greetings from the gods."

Clutching his heart, Reed staggered away. "Holy shit! You're . . ."

"Your boyfriend's father?" he offered with a grin. "Indeed."

"Oh! Right! Yes! That too!" Reed's overtaxed brain hadn't even made that connection yet. "Hermes?"

The god nodded. "I prefer Mercury." Right, the Great Syncretism.

"Mercury. That's it, then. Wow. *Wow.*" Reed was babbling and he knew it, but watching another of his favorite fictional characters come to life had knocked him quite off-balance.

"It's a pleasure to meet you, Reed, and I apologize for startling you. I'm afraid I don't have a lot of options for earth landings. I hope you won't hold it against me."

"No, it's . . . I'm . . ." Reed closed his lips on the stream of nonsense pouring out of him without his consent. Studying the vibrating form of the gods' messenger, Reed ventured, "Can I shake your hand, or . . .?"

"We can try," said Mercury, still smiling as he offered his shimmering hand. "It won't hurt. You might just go right through me."

Heart in his throat, Reed reached for the offered hand. Wonderment and awe flooded him as their palms clasped, sort of. It felt like clapping hands underwater. *I'm shaking hands with Mercury!*

"You know," said Mercury, a merry twinkle gleaming in his eyes, "we did meet once before, very briefly, in your kitchen."

"That was you! You were the column of light that took Euphrosyne!"

Mercury nodded, then cocked his head. "You look like you have questions for me."

Reed cackled, then belly-laughed, then made a valiant attempt to regain his sanity but dissolved again into gales of thigh-slapping, tears-rolling-down-his-cheeks laughter. Holding his sore stomach and wheezing, Reed held up a "give me a moment" finger to Hermes-Mercury-Pan's dad, who now surely thought him crazy.

"Please excuse my outburst," said Reed, wiping the tears from his cheeks. He met Mercury's gaze, finding nothing but benevolence. "I have an entire lifetime of questions for you, not that I'd presume a god of your import would have time to stand here and satisfy an old man's curiosity."

Mercury chuckled. "I can stay until I am pulled away by a god of *true* import," he said humbly. "In the meantime, I'll happily answer whatever I can for you."

"I guess, for starters, why are you here?"

"Ah." Mercury swooped away and returned with Cupid's bow slung over his back and the arrow in his hand before Reed could close his gaping mouth. "Same reason you are."

*Well, shoot.* Reed shuffled from one leg to the other, wishing he hadn't left his cane in the car. He could have used a little grounding right about now. "I, uh, I'm very sorry, but I can't let you take those."

It was Mercury's turn to be surprised—and amused. He threw his head back, and a musical chuckle issued from his mouth. "I do admire your pluck, sir."

Humiliation washed over Reed, but even worse, a sense of

deep disappointment and failure. He'd so badly wanted to be Pan's knight in shining armor.

Reading Reed's dejection, Mercury's grin fell away. "The arrow is not the solution, friend." Mercury placed his not-quite-human hand on Reed's shoulder, sending an electric buzz through his body. "Nor is it your best opportunity to help Cupid."

"No?"

"You already know how this story is supposed to end," he said with a bright smile. "I suspect that will come in handy."

"It *is* Cupid and Psyche!"

With a wink, Mercury jabbed the arrow toward Reed. "A-plus, Professor Scully."

"I don't understand. If the outcome is predetermined—"

"Ah. No," said Mercury, shaking his head, "that's not how it works. Say, would you care to sit down?"

"Of course. Where are my manners?" As Mercury glided to the couch with all the grace of an Olympic skater, it struck Reed that his suggestion to sit was entirely for Reed's benefit. "May I offer you something to drink? There's probably some lemonade in the fridge. Might be some chips in the cupboard, but Pan hasn't . . . oh! Are you even able to . . . uh, process . . .?"

"Doubtful, but thanks anyway." Mercury settled onto the chaise-end of the sectional, where the bow hung off the edge.

Situating himself catty-cornered, Reed steered them back to their conversation. "You were saying, about predetermination?"

"Only that it's not a thing. The gods tend to find it all quite boring if they already know how everything is going to turn out."

Reed was trying very hard to read between the lines, but Mercury was being frustratingly vague. *They're always watching,* Pan had cautioned Reed more than once.

"So, I gather, then," Reed began equally cautiously, "that Cupid is about to meet his true soul mate?"

"It would be difficult for him to avoid it at this point."

"That's wonderful!" Reed's heart surged with joy for Cupid.

"It may well be, yes," said Mercury, lacking most of Reed's enthusiasm.

"It *may?*"

Mercury sighed. "The love story you are familiar with was written two thousand years ago, just after Pan's descent, about two souls that were supposedly mated one thousand years earlier. As we all know, that is not how events proceeded at the time, which explains why Cupid and Pan laughed when you brought it up."

"And chalked up the story to myth."

Nodding, Mercury went on. "Cupid's soul, of course, has only lived inside its one divine body. The Psyche soul, on the other hand, has been recycled a hundred times over and knocked about in innumerable encounters through the centuries—not all bad by any stretch, but not once in relation to its own Right Love. You might not be aware of the rarity of the situation, but trust me, you're looking directly at Aphrodite's fingerprint."

This news dropped like a boulder to the bottom of Reed's stomach, and part of him worried for Mercury's safety at having shared what felt like a rather huge secret. "Wouldn't all of that make Posey's soul even more ecstatic to meet its perfect mate?"

"One would hope," said Mercury inscrutably. "By the way, nice job on puzzling out the Mariposa connection." The compliment sent a rush of warmth but also a reminder that they were all being watched by the ultimate Big Brother. "Now, if Cupid can win his way to Psyche's soul through the layers of . . . *hmm*, remind me of the current lingo for weighty emotional burdens?"

"Baggage?"

"Yes, that's it. The mortal presently housing the eternal soul has some"—Mercury huffed—"impressive baggage."

*Ugh. Poor Cupid.* "The woman's heart was hardened before Cupid even had his chance?"

Mercury set a gentle hand on Reed's damaged leg, a reminder, perhaps, of the healing power of positivity. "As long as the heart still beats, it can open to love. But it's up to Cupid to earn her trust and cross them over. There are no shortcuts. That is why I was sent for the arrow." *To protect them all–Cupid, Posey, Pan, and now Reed as well.*

Reed swallowed hard over the lump in his throat. "Thank you," he said simply.

"You're a good man, Reed. You've been a tremendous influence on Pan since you came into his life. Keep up the good work, Professor." Mercury shot him a wink.

Reed felt the blush heat his cheeks. "I believe we bring out the best in each other."

Mercury chuckled as he released Reed's leg with a friendly pat on the thigh. Reed was starting to appreciate where Pan's demonstrative nature came from. "Would you be open to a bit of fatherly advice? Not to brag, but I do have thirty-four centuries of experience."

"Please," replied Reed, "and thanks for making me feel young."

"It's all relative," Mercury said with a knowing grin. "My hard-won wisdom is thus: Be patient with him. Pan can be a hothead at times. Perhaps you have discovered this already?" He paused for confirmation and Reed gave him a shy smile. "It's not his fault, really. It's probably the red hair. Either way, I blame his mother."

Which reminded Reed of another slew of questions about Pan's parentage, around which there were so many conflicting accounts. Those questions would have to wait.

"That said," Mercury continued, "don't be afraid to challenge him. True growth is hard to come by when you've lived as long as we have. He may squawk and fuss, but he loves it, and he's better for it. I suspect you know this, too."

Reed lowered his head in reply. "What else can you share?"

Mercury stood. "You already know the rest. Be well, Reed. I must leave you now."

And Reed was alone.

Alone with the dazzling memory he wanted to hold and share word-for-word with Pan. Alone with his relief at being spared the chance to screw up Cupid's mission, along with a new appreciation for Pan's job. And most importantly, alone with Mercury's implied missive to use his knowledge to help guide Cupid to success.

But how? This was the dilemma Reed turned over and over in his mind all the drive home.

19

# FLYING LIKE MORTALS

"Here's your boarding pass. Stick to my back like glue, and do exactly what I do. Do not speak to anyone unless someone wearing a uniform asks you a direct question."

So many details and documents and hallways and lines. As guilty as Cupid felt over separating the lovebirds, he couldn't have managed this without Pan.

"No wisecracks, no questions, no flirting. Got it?"

Cupid replied with a solemn nod. He couldn't remember seeing Pan this serious over anything.

They plodded forward in the long queue as if performing a line dance at the Versailles—minus the music and merriment. They peeled off jackets and shoes and phones and wallets. When Pan unbuckled his belt, Cupid glanced around anxiously to see how much more he would be required to strip off, relieved to discover the other passengers still wearing pants. When it was Cupid's turn to lift his arms inside the giant tube, he held his breath well after the required interval, only releasing it once he and Pan had dumped their armloads of discarded clothing on a bench some distance from the security area.

They arrived at their so-called "gate," though Cupid saw nothing of the sort. In fact, the lines of chairs reminded Cupid of Dr. Chan's waiting area. The two slipped into empty seats across from each other. Pan stared blankly ahead. He seemed lost in thought, and by the lines creasing his forehead, those thoughts didn't look to be happy ones. The faster Cupid accomplished his purpose, the sooner Pan could get back to Reed, and Cupid would get . . . whatever was inflicted next.

An announcement about boarding roused the sleepy lounge into a sudden burst of activity. Their papers were scanned, and Cupid followed Pan down the ramp leading to the plane. Cupid's eyes went wide as he stepped inside the enormous machine, so much bigger than it seemed from his vantage point on Olympus. He was greeted by a cheery, uniformed woman whose face lit up at the sight of Cupid.

They shuffled down the center aisle to row six. Pan lifted his suitcase and then Cupid's into the overhead compartment. "You take the window seat," said Pan. Cupid climbed in, and Pan plopped into the middle seat and lowered the armrest between them. "Seat belt time—your favorite," Pan said with a smirk as he clicked his own into place. "And you need to turn your phone off until we land." They both tucked away their phones, then Pan slouched in his seat, folded his arms over his chest, and closed his eyes.

Cupid sighed heavily, causing Pan to squint one eye open to check on him. "You okay?"

"Are *you*?"

Now both eyes popped open. "Huh?"

"You seem sad."

"I'm fine," Pan replied, but he wasn't.

"Are you angry with me?"

"Not yet, but you're starting to get on my nerves. Close your eyes and get some rest."

There was no way Cupid was going to sleep through one second of his first—and possibly only—airplane ride. He shifted to look out the window at the bustle of people and vehicles coming and going, about as different as Cupid could have possibly imagined from his own solitary, silent flight.

"How many of the other gods have flown on an airplane?" Cupid asked, pulling Pan once again from his rest.

"A few," he answered without opening his eyes. "Why?"

"Nobody ever talked about it when they ascended, at least not to me."

Pan's eyes blinked open, and his Adam's apple bounced hard when he swallowed. "I guess they had to be careful."

"That won't be an issue now that I know about you."

Pan straightened in his seat. "You aren't planning to make a nuisance of yourself about a Permanent Descent, right?"

Cupid was aware of the answer he was supposed to give, but he was not prepared to make any promises. "Do you think they'll at least let me see you through my gaia-sight now and then?"

"Who can predict what the Council will decide?" Pan shifted toward Cupid as much as his seat belt allowed. "And who says you'll even want to see me?"

"What? Why wouldn't I?"

"I . . . *pshhh*. Reed? It wouldn't be too hard for you?"

"To see you happy? Never, Pan."

Pan shook his head. "Fucking hell, Q. I hate this so much. The longer you're here, the harder it gets to imagine you gone."

"Reed will get you through it," said Cupid, knowing full well he would have no such friend or lover to lean on back home.

"Reed," Pan said, his Right Love's name bringing an incredulous smile to his lips. "He'll probably try to distract me with some demanding reading assignment that will occupy all my brain cells."

"That can't be too hard to find," Cupid said, grinning now.

"Hey!" Pan snapped his arm, whacking Cupid on the chest. "You could do with reading a book or two yourself, mister. It's not as if you don't have time."

"Um, no thanks. Just because you're in love with a smarty-pants professor doesn't mean I have to suffer, too."

Pan chuckled. "I'm suffering, huh? I'll have to tell Professor Scully you said that."

"Scully? That's Reed's last name?" It had never occurred to him to ask. In Cupid's world, there were only first names.

"Yeah, it's nice, huh? I was thinking I might use it, too, instead of Gauthier."

"Wow! Does that mean you and Reed are talking about marriage?"

Pan's bushy eyebrows popped up to his hairline. "Me? Married?" He shook his head, chuckling. "Can you even imagine it?"

Cupid shrugged. Three months ago, could he have imagined sitting next to his dead best friend inside a mortal flying machine?

"Is it really that crazy? You and Reed are obviously perfect for each other."

"But that's just it," said Pan. "When you've been mated by the Goddess of Love, the construct of marriage seems pretty trivial."

"I don't think Ruthie and Zach would agree. If they hadn't made a commitment to each other before they started drifting apart, would they have stuck around long enough to try to put their love back together?" Cupid shuddered. A Right Love squandered was a tragic waste.

"It is possible for two people to commit without a piece of paper saying they're married. Reed and I have had that discussion, and we're both all in."

"That much is obvious." Painfully so, at times. "Still, there must be some benefit to the institution of marriage. Otherwise, why would mortals still bother with it after all this time?"

Pan blinked back at him, forehead creased from Cupid's question. "You're not wrong," Pan finally replied. "Marriage does have important legal ramifications, especially for same-sex couples. If Reed were ever, say, in an accident or required some kind of medical intervention"—a scowl flashed across Pan's face—"I might not be able to advocate for him unless his sisters deferred, which, who the hell knows . . ." Pan threw his head back, eyes pinched shut.

Gently squeezing Pan's arm, Cupid waited for Pan's pensive green eyes to open again. "Something to think about, then? For Reed."

"*More* thinking." Pan sighed, the hint of a grin creeping in. "Guy's gonna make my head explode with all the thinking I've been doing since I met him."

"Yes, I've noticed. Your vocabulary is quite annoying."

Pan guffawed in a very goat-like way just as his aisle-side neighbor was strapping himself into the seat. Pan glanced over his shoulder and gave the man a friendly tip of his chin. "Hey, man."

The man answered with a nervous nod. "Hey." Reaching into his satchel, he pulled a fat headset over his ears.

Pan turned back to Cupid with an amused huff. "Guess we won't have to worry about our friend here eavesdropping."

"Good. I was hoping you would help me figure out what to say to Posey."

"Obviously, you know her better than I do—"

"Not much," Cupid admitted. "I know she is going to be furious that I tracked her down."

"I would imagine so," said Pan in his extremely unnerving

way of bluntly speaking the truth. "What if you don't tell her you're the one from the app?"

"Are you suggesting I pretend to be meeting her out of the blue?"

The yoga mat next to hers . . . Hadn't Posey said she would have happily met him for coffee afterward? The idea was tempting.

"She doesn't know what you look like, right?"

"Not exactly. But I had to make an avatar for our chat."

"Like a 'pick a head shape' kind of avatar?"

"Yes."

"I think you're good. There's just no way any cartoon prefab could possibly capture your . . ." Pan lifted his arm like a singer about to hit a high note. Cupid rolled his eyes, and Pan brushed it off, as usual.

"We did speak on the phone. She might know my voice."

Pan's eyes narrowed to a squint. "You really think she'd put that together? I know your charms are unforgettable and all, but I can't see her associating some stranger standing in front of her with the voice of a guy who told her he lives in Indiana."

"Let's say she doesn't realize right away that I'm the Q from Wings. What am I supposed to tell her about myself? I'm a terrible liar." Cupid's stomach lurched at the prospect of an extended charade.

"Yes, I am aware," Pan said.

Cupid gripped his armrests and searched his friend for answers. "I can't do this, Pan."

"Sir? Are you all right?" The woman who'd greeted him at the front of the plane leaned in with a kind smile, and Pan's neighbor craned his neck to watch. "Would you like some water?"

"He's fine, thanks," Pan answered. "First time on a plane."

"Ah. I have just the thing." She pulled a small object from her pocket and reached over to hand it to Cupid. "You're never too old for your first set of wings," she said with a wink. As he took the toy airplane pin, a blush rose to Cupid's cheeks, not helped any by Pan's gruff laughter.

"Gotta admit, she nailed it!"

Cupid watched the safety briefing with great fascination, especially the simulation of the oxygen masks dropping from the ceiling. With a myriad of opportunities for mechanical failure, let alone intentionally malicious attacks, it was a wonder anyone chose to fly.

The sudden burst of acceleration pinned Cupid to his seat back. The plane's nose lifted, and he felt a jolt of exhilaration as the back wheels left the ground. Airborne! The airplane's wings didn't flap but held their majestic pose as the plane cut higher and higher with a loud whine. Cupid watched wide-eyed as houses and roads shrank into tiny specs farther and farther beneath him. A white haze blanketed the windows, causing Cupid to turn anxiously toward Pan.

"It's just a pocket of clouds. Don't get nervous if we bounce around a little." That seemed like an excellent reason to get nervous.

Cupid remembered the horrible, out-of-control tumble he'd taken through the sky after his wings had disintegrated, but this wasn't the Great Cloud at the base of Mount O, and he wasn't falling again. This was just an ordinary cloud in Earth's sky. His best friend was sitting beside him, perfectly calm, and the pilot knew what to do.

Some eight hours later, their second flight touched down at the Reno-Tahoe Airport—though with the time zone adjustment Cupid had yet to wrap his head around, it was not yet noon. Cupid stared out the window while they coasted toward the building, more anxious than ever now that he was actually within striking distance of Posey. This whole thing might just blow up in his face, and then what would he do?

Pan's phone chimed about ten times, drawing Cupid's attention to a huge smile pushing Pan's beard out to both sides. *Reed.* Pan's thumbs flew over his phone with his replies.

Cupid fished his phone out and turned it on. He, too, was greeted with notifications of the day's emails and texts downloading all at once. How someone who only knew fewer than twenty mortals by name could manage to attract so many emails was beyond Cupid's comprehension. He didn't even bother deleting them anymore, just swiped his screen up, up, and up . . .

Cupid's thumb froze in midair, mirroring the breath stilled in his lungs. He sensed people around him getting out of their seats, pulling on coats, gathering their belongings, but all he could do was stare at the screen, a swarm of butterflies beating their mariposa wings inside his belly.

"Time to go, pal," said Pan, pulling both of their cases from the bin above. "C'mon! This is your favorite part, the unbuckling of the belt—hey, what's wrong?"

Stricken, Cupid met Pan's gaze. "There's an email from Dr. Mariposa Rey."

20

# HITTING THE TRAIL

Two days of perseveration did not make for a relaxed Posey by Friday morning. She knew what needed to be done, and she knew her conscience was not going to release her to the mountain trails for the weekend until she had addressed the non-patient who shouldn't have been taking up so much real estate in her brain, and still, she procrastinated until every other item on her to-do list was finished.

It was almost eleven by the time she sent the email to Q though it required no wordsmithing: **May I call you?**

She half hoped he would answer right away so she could get this over with, but as five minutes became thirty and Q still hadn't replied, she acknowledged a definite sense of relief. Even her mother's phone call provided a respite though their annual conversation about the family's Thanksgiving celebration was so predictable, Posey could have recited both sides by herself.

"Your father and I would really love you to come home this year."

"Thanks, Mom, but I'm going to have to decline." *Again.* "You and Dad are more than welcome to come to Tahoe anytime."

"Oh, Posey. You know it's not the same."

"No, it's not. Sofia wouldn't be there to shoot daggers every time my eyeballs happened to venture within a mile of her perfect"—*slimeball*—"husband."

A tenacious social climber, Sebastian Adams had been the house chair of the Ivy Club, arguably the most exclusive undergraduate eating club at Princeton, when sophomore Sofia Rey bickered for entry. Sebastian charmed the pants right off her, literally, the suave senior with his sights set on Goldman Sachs and the single-mindedness to make it happen. Miracle of miracles, Sofia was accepted into the Ivy Club. After that, every other word out of her mouth, when she deigned to talk to her little sister at all, was Sebastian-this or Sebastian-that.

Posey's first impression of the guy was the flash of dollar signs in his eyes when Sofia brought him home to meet the family that spring break. He didn't even bother trying to mask his glee at hitting the mother lode, his neck craning to take in every detail of their opulent home—including Sofia's well-endowed fifteen-year-old sister.

If using Sofia to scratch his way up the social ladder were the worst of Sebastian's faults, Posey could have written him off as yet another opportunist and called it a day, but he made Posey uneasy from the get-go with his lingering gazes and lecherous smiles. Sebastian was a boy used to getting his way, and it seemed the only thing he wanted more than Sophia's trust fund was Posey. Bright Princeton boy he was, he'd done the math, which worked out the same no matter which of the three Rey heiresses he seduced.

Sebastian's unwelcome intimacy made Posey's skin crawl. He loved to make Posey blush, and she hated that she kept obliging. He made a habit of standing too close and pushing his verbal teasing too far. What she despised even more was his way of appearing angelic whenever anyone else was around. *Aww, look how sweet he is to Sofia's baby sister.* Nobody seemed to notice he wasn't so solicitous to Alicia, the middle sister.

Posey started avoiding him at all costs, which only made him seek her out more doggedly. This cat-and-mouse chase went on for two full years. Posey cut her hair short, wore baggy clothes whenever Sebastian visited, spent the weekend holed up in her room. Her driver's license became her saving grace. She counted the days till Sofia's graduation, after which they would be moving to Sebastian's apartment in SoHo, and their visits home would be few and far between. She nearly made it, too.

Sofia's graduation party was to be a lavish affair held in the backyard of their stately home. The afternoon of the party, Sofia and Alicia had left with their mother for the hair salon—an invitation Posey had passed on—and her father was out playing golf, leaving Posey home alone when Sebastian arrived for the festivities. With no time for a graceful exit, she found herself stuck in the kitchen with him, enduring his uncomfortable compliments and wandering eyeballs. When she got up to rinse their plates, Sebastian came up behind her and trapped her against the sink. She tried to squirm out of his grasp, claiming she needed to supervise the vendors outside, and Sebastian spun her around and planted a kiss on her lips.

Sofia burst into the kitchen right then, bright-eyed and immaculately coiffed and so excited to be reunited with her boyfriend. Her perfectly made-up face twisted in horror as the scene registered in her brain. Sofia burst into tears and darted off, followed closely by Sebastian, leaving Posey to explain herself to her mother and sister. More than two decades of family occasions had passed—both her sisters' weddings, the births of Sofia's two kids and Alicia's triplets, Christmas dinners and anniversary parties and her father's retirement—and still, the memory and shame were as fresh in Posey's mind as the day Sebastian drove a wedge between Posey and the rest of her family.

The long-suffering sigh from her mother said it all. While Posey strongly suspected her parents believed her side of the story, she also understood they were truly stuck in the middle. Sebastian was their daughter's husband, the father of their grandchildren. Hence, the decision Posey had made many years ago not to put them all through unnecessary full-family gatherings. With her move to Tahoe seven years ago, avoidance was that much easier.

"And how about Alicia's snide remarks every time I pass up dessert?"

"Alicia lost eight pounds since she started that Keto diet in August!"

"So she won't be insufferable at all," Posey said, unable to stifle her sarcasm.

"But the kids . . ." *are brats*, Posey would have interjected if she were a less evolved human being. ". . . will miss their auntie Posey."

"I doubt it, Mom. Cort was two the last time I came for Thanksgiving, and the triplets weren't even conceived . . . so, yeah, I think they'll survive. Honestly, it's just easier for everyone if I don't come."

"Family's not always about what's easy, Posey."

"That's beautiful, Mom. Maybe you can start your own line of reality greeting cards."

*Another sigh.* "How are you, Posey?"

"All good," she said brightly.

"Well, if you change your mind, even at the very last second, you know there's a place at the table for you."

"Mom, please don't hold your breath."

Her mother filled the phone line with a soft chuckle. "I'm not going to asphyxiate myself, but I shall remain ever hopeful."

"That's sweet. Please give Dad my love."

"You could give it to him in *person*," she singsonged, fully aware she was stating the impossible—or at least the highly improbable.

"Have a wonderful day, Mom."

With familial and professional duty out of the way, Posey geared up for the ride ahead—her favorite loop, with the views of Squaw Valley that had clinched her decision to settle at Carnelian Bay. The ride down Highway 28 was a necessary evil, but Posey relaxed when she left the heavy traffic behind at the Dollar Point turnoff. She barely slowed at the busy Cross-Country Center trailhead, pushing on past the old logging road at Burton Creek State Park. There, the mountain biking began in earnest, with the 1.5-mile climb to the Tahoe Rim Trail. The chilly autumn air stung her lungs, but there was no stopping Posey before she reached the ledge known as Painted Rock.

No matter how driven by personal demons, Posey could never resist stopping here and taking in the view. This was her long-standing promise to herself, and she had yet to break it. She was used to sharing her not-so-secret happy place with fellow bikers, but with the colder weather, the number of visitors had dwindled. Today, she was alone.

Clicking out of her pedals, she dismounted and leaned her bike against a tree. She soaked the scene into her bones; it might have to tide her over till spring. Shaking out her legs, she pulled a deep breath in through her nose. It didn't take a PhD to intuit why she'd chosen this ride today. The mountain's demands left no room for Posey's guilt. The old baggage was manageable— her inability to resolve the family feud, her mismanagement of

Evan's case and the resulting fallout—but learning she'd failed the prospective new patient brought a fresh guilt that wasn't going away so easily. Sometimes clarity sucked.

She closed her eyes to concentrate on the next deep breath, and that's when she heard the soft crunch of approaching tires.

# 21

# MEETING AT
# PAINTED ROCK

Cupid emailed Posey back—**Yes**—first typing the message in all caps before changing it to appear less desperate. There were so many questions he'd wanted to add: What had made her reach out when she'd seemed so against it earlier? What did she want to say to him now? Had she changed her mind about helping him?

"Can I at least add an exclamation point?" Cupid had asked Pan, earning an amused headshake but a firm no. He questioned the wisdom of Pan's advice when Posey did not reply. Not everyone enjoyed the hard-to-get game, Cupid reminded him, scowling as the minutes stretched on.

Pan ignored him, wheeling his suitcase through the airport to the rental car counter, where he took forever making arrangements for their car. At least, it felt like forever because while Pan was filling out paperwork, Cupid's heart motor revved up worse than every other time.

Clutching his heart, Cupid squeezed in next to Pan at the front of the line. "Almost done?" he asked as politely as possible while his insides tried their best to jump out of his skin.

"This takes a few—*holy shit!* What's the matter with you?" Stricken, Pan eyed the hand Cupid was furiously rubbing across his chest. Suddenly clear, Pan turned back to the woman behind the counter. "Yes to the tank of gas, no to the insurance. Can we speed this up?"

"I'm doing my best, sir."

Pan drummed his fingers on the counter, shooting anxious glances over at Cupid every few minutes. "Can you tell if it's Posey?"

"No idea." The pull had no face, no gender, no voice, no soul.

"At least we know we're on the right track now, eh?" Pan seemed far cheerier than Cupid felt. Any delusions of keeping his heart at a safe distance were now fully shattered.

"Seems so."

The agent finally passed Pan the keys, and he set off at a jog, practically lifting the suitcase off the ground, while Cupid ran beside him. They located their white car among a sea of white cars and threw their suitcases indelicately into the trunk. Pan climbed into the driver's seat. "I'll follow my GPS to the address I have for Posey. We're at least an hour away by highway, and zigzagging through old mountain paths to try to follow your signal is going to take us forever. Just tell me if you feel like we're heading way off track."

Cupid nodded. The winding route to the airport exit was the worst, but he knew Pan had no choice. Once they reached the highway, Cupid's heart eased to a sufferable squeeze. For the next hour, Highway 28 took them in the same general direction of his heart's demands, leaving Cupid plenty of time with his thoughts. Was it Posey his heart was dragging them toward? Would she hate him for tracking her down? Would he be up to the task ahead, knowing success would almost certainly bring him the most excruciating pain yet when she beat for someone else?

At Carnelian Bay, Pan's phone instructed them to exit, but Cupid's heart said otherwise. Slowing to the speed limit, Pan turned an anxious eye on Cupid. "Nothing?"

"Nope. Keep going."

"Okay. It's on you now to tell me where to turn. By the way," Pan said, thumbing toward his window, "you might want to take a gander at Lake Tahoe while we're here."

Cupid sat up straighter so he could peer out Pan's side of the car. Despite his physical discomfort and emotional turmoil, the view stole Cupid's breath. Maybe his vision had been dulled from his time on Earth, but it seemed the planet's full color palette was on display, lit by the afternoon sun to its most advantageous effect: tall trees sporting vivid yellow and bright orange foliage guarding the banks of the stunning lake, itself alive and rippling with dazzling blues and greens.

"Wow."

Pan turned toward him, eyes glimmering with yearning. "Right?"

"How do you not live here?" Cupid asked.

Pan sighed, smile fading with the intrusion of reality. "There's no Tarra here."

"But you're here now."

"You need me here, so I'm here." The reminder that even Pan was bound by the will of the gods sobered Cupid. "Hey. Don't waste your time feeling sorry for me, Q. I have a good life here, no complaints . . . and thanks to you, I have Reed now."

"Back in Indiana," Cupid said sheepishly.

"How 'bout you do your job, and let me do mine, huh?"

A sigh escaped Cupid along with his tight nod. They drove on well past Carnelian Bay before Cupid's heart pulled them off the highway at a place called Dollar Point. Three turns later, they reached a dead end, and Pan was forced to stop in the parking lot of a place called the Tahoe XC Center. Cupid's heart lurched like a slingshot pulled back before releasing the stone.

"This is as far as I can drive you." Pan swore under his breath as he jumped out of the car to investigate.

"What? Wait!" Cupid threw open his door and scurried to Pan's side. "We're not there yet! What am I supposed to do, run the rest of the way?"

"Which direction is it pulling you now?"

Cupid pointed, and Pan followed the direction of his finger toward the impassable forest. "Gimme a sec," Pan said, then jogged over to a big sign at the entrance of the woods, which he studied for an agonizing few minutes before returning. "There are miles of trails in there. You can't possibly do this on foot. The only way that makes any sense is a mountain bike. I don't suppose you've ever ridden a bike."

"I've seen them at the gym," Cupid said.

Pan huffed. "Not exactly the same, but I'm sure you'll pick it up quickly. C'mon."

The line to rent bikes was several people deep, and the wait felt like a thunderstorm inside Cupid's chest, but Pan made good use of the time. He fit them both with special shoes and helmets and taught Cupid how to switch gears and use the brakes without causing a flip over the handlebars.

"So basically, I'm driving with my hands."

"Yup. Powered by your legs."

The man who finally brought around their bikes seemed to have even more to say than the car rental lady. He eHewarned them about the downhill slopes they were likely to encounter and made them sign a paper saying they understood the risks. Geared up and thoroughly cautioned, Pan pedaled to the middle of the parking lot and made Cupid ride a practice lap around him. It reminded Cupid of the day Pan taught him to drive, that day his heart fired up for the very first time with love for Mia. Forever ago.

"Okay, you're good to go," Pan said after just one lap. "You lead. I've got your back. Stay on the marked paths. If you need to stop, signal me like so, and keep to the right, just like driving a car. And please remember what the guy said about riding downhill. A broken neck is really gonna slow us down."

As Cupid's fat front tire met the beginning of the trail, the full weight of the moment caught up to him. This person they were pursuing had not set out into the deep woods to be followed. One mistake in their first interaction might cost him everything.

He stopped short and turned around. "Pan, what if it *is* Posey in there? What am I supposed to say to her?"

"My advice? As little as possible."

Cupid gave him an exasperated scowl.

"Look, man, even if she doesn't recognize your voice right off the bat, the two of you are due for a phone conversation in the very near future, right?"

"Right."

"So don't give her another chance to figure this out before you're ready to reveal yourself."

Slightly relieved, Cupid nodded.

Walking his bike right up next to Cupid's, Pan set his hand on Cupid's shoulder and squeezed. "Hey. You're fucking *Cupid*. You'll know what to do."

"Thanks for the vote of confidence, but the fact that I'm still here means I've pretty much screwed things up three times now, so . . ."

"Whatever, man. There are three deliriously happy couples right now because of your screw-ups. You must be doing something right."

"This isn't helping." With one final cleansing breath, Cupid set off. Almost immediately, the trail pulled uphill. A relentless incline stretched out ahead of them as far as the eye could see. Of all the forms of physical exertion he'd subjected himself to on Earth, pedaling uphill was his least favorite. Between the cramp in his side and the burn in his thighs, Cupid was a collection of spent body parts by the time they reached the Tahoe Rim Trail, but his heart motor overpowered the rest, and he had no choice but to obey.

He was close now; the signal was stronger than the pull to Mia's yoga studio or Ruthie at Versailles or the rush of love for Pan, who'd been standing right next to him at the time. Another turn and another rise and Cupid could barely feel his legs moving the pedals.

He crested at a place called Painted Rock and caught sight of her for the first time. She stood alone at the edge of the grassy knoll overlooking the lake, her back to the trail, arms raised, palms together above her head. A gentle breeze lifted her wavy, brown hair from her shoulders. Cupid's heart flipped over and ended its demanding pull. He'd reached his destination.

He pedaled to a stop where her bike leaned against a tree, helmet dangling from the handlebars, and clicked out of his pedals. Pan sailed past him with a thumbs-up, leaving Cupid to his labors.

The woman turned at the sound of crunching tires, and he instantly regretted disturbing her—and yet, the first glimpse of her face was worth everything. Even at a distance, her features matched the cartoon likeness he'd somehow felt drawn to for reasons he only now fully understood. He pushed her name to the bottom of his throat so as not to speak it aloud.

Posey turned abruptly back to the lake, her shoulders carrying a tension that wasn't there before. Cupid stood locked in place with his feet planted on either side of the bike while Love, shiny and new, bloomed in his chest. The pounding of his heart could only mean one thing—Posey was his next Worthy.

Before he could draw another breath, there was one more thing he had to know. He removed his helmet and clipped it over the bar between his legs. Bracing himself, Cupid listened across the still, cool air only he and Posey shared. Not even the most expert handbrake technique could have saved Cupid's heart from its end-over-end tumble when Posey's perfect echo beat reached his ears.

# HEART READING

Bent over her gaiascope with the weight of a mother's love bearing down on her, Aphrodite wept. The die was cast. The signal she'd initiated had brought Cupid and Psyche together, two souls united at long last, two hearts beating each other's perfect echo so loudly, Aphrodite's ears rang with the truth a world away: her son was lost to her.

She listened intently through her own muffled sobs for Cupid's grand proclamation, but he said nothing. Aphrodite squeezed the tears from her eyes to get a closer watch on his movements. Surely he'd rush to the woman's side! *Nothing.*

Heavy footsteps approached Aphrodite's bedchamber, the uneven *step-clomp, step-clomp* of her husband's gait. Clutching the gaiascope between her hands, she turned toward the door. After their earlier reconciliation of sorts, she thought Hephaestus might cross the room and wrap a comforting arm around her stooped shoulders as was his manner. Instead, he stopped short of the entrance.

"Goddess," he said quietly. "I couldn't help but hear your weeping." He'd dragged himself up from the depths of the palace to check on her. That was something, even if he had taken a stand, as it were, outside the bedroom door.

"Cupid knows."

Hephaestus nodded. "It is for the best, my love."

She answered with a sniffle.

"Have they spoken?" he asked.

"Not a word. Cupid is hesitant to reveal himself and fears she will recognize his voice."

"That seems wise at this point."

"Perhaps. But how does the mortal resist his pull?"

"Is she immune to his charms?"

"Oh no. She is fully receptive to the attraction. She just isn't acting on it."

"Huh." With just that one, innocent syllable, Hephaestus had made his point. Aphrodite deserved his sarcasm and a whole lot more, but right now, she was grateful for his company.

"She didn't even acknowledge his presence."

"Is there someone else in her life right now? A love interest she owes a debt of loyalty?" A *husband, maybe?* He didn't say it, but she heard it just the same.

"No, nothing like that. She hasn't been with anyone in a long time." Aphrodite had made sure of that, but revealing her role in Posey's loveless life wouldn't score her any points with Hephaestus.

He leaned against the doorjamb. "She's afraid."

"Of Cupid?"

"Of herself. Fear of reliving past mistakes? Guilt and regret over hurting people who cared about her? Of course, I'm just guessing."

Of course, he was not guessing at all. He was reading his wife's heart like a storybook. Who would have anticipated her sweet Hephaestus would make her work so hard to win back his fealty?

"I suppose her reluctance is justified . . ." She left her comment open for Hephaestus to contradict, to absolve his wife's guilt by proxy, but he did no such thing.

"As is his." Hephaestus gave her a tight smile as he shifted away from the wall. "The boy is wise to stay silent until he is sure he can trust her." With a curt nod, he turned and ambled away. *Step-clomp, step-clomp.*

Inside the Earth-glass, Cupid mounted his bike and rode off.

# HOME WITHOUT PAN

Reed needed to be with them. Wasn't that what Mercury was trying to say?

Or was Reed's reasoning simply the foolhardy conjuring of a lonely, recently oversexed, middle-aged man? The thought made him ill.

He was drained by the time he returned to his Pan-less home. The click-clack of sixteen paws and slobbery kisses from four eager faces didn't quite fill Reed's heart all the way to the top as they had before Pan had burst into their lives, and Reed wasn't the only one feeling the loss. The dogs were agitated the rest of the morning, sniffing around for Pan and moping when they couldn't find him. Reed did his best to distract them, even tried out some Pan-style rough-and-tumble play, but Reed was no Pan.

*Pull up your big-boy briefs.* Yes, he missed Pan's constant, playful touches, his relentless cuddles, his physical way of expressing himself without a shred of embarrassment, but honestly, could Reed not go one stinkin' week without the guy by his side?

Around three p.m., right on schedule, the phone Reed had been carrying around all day chimed with a text notification: **The gods have landed.**

Reed's reply: **Would Godspeed be the appropriate wish?** was answered with: **Depends which god. Things might get crazy now. Will contact you ASAP.**

During the next two hours of helpless waiting, Reed made up his mind to go. Without Cupid's bow and arrow to transport, there was no reason to waste three days by driving. The dogs were staying home.

Amid Reed's calls to dog-sitters and airlines, Pan's next message arrived: **Wish you were here**, followed by a spectacular picture of Lake Tahoe.

**So do I**, Reed replied, skirting the line between truth and deceit. **What's happening there?**

**Q found Posey. He's with her now. We're on bikes. Will call when I can.**

**Enjoy the mountains.**

**As much as I can without you. Later, Prof.** Pan's mushy message brought a smile.

Reed booked his flight for the following morning to arrive in Reno midafternoon. He went to his bedroom, pulled out his suitcase, and piled seven of everything onto his bed while the dogs paced in anxious circles around him.

"I know, I know," Reed soothed as he shuffled around the reckless paws. He'd make it up to them tonight, break with the new routine and let them sleep in the bedroom—but not in his bed. Pan would give him hell if he caved on that one, and with that nose of his, he'd know.

After dinner, Reed settled into his armchair to read. A fire blazed in the nearby hearth, but Reed couldn't seem to get warm. On the side table, Reed's phone lit up with Pan's smirking face as "Wild Thing" started playing. Reed shook his head, grinning. *When had Pan done that?*

Reed accepted the call, acutely aware of pulling off his very first—and likely, his only—deception of his otherworldly partner.

# 24

# THE JUGGLED PATIENT

"Fuck you, Sebastian! Fuck you, fuck you, fuck you, Sebastian."
All down the mountain, with gritted teeth, Posey repeated the
phrase until the words lost their meaning.

She pulled in a deep, cleansing breath as her tires met the
parking lot at the trailhead, then pushed the air out of her lungs
along with all the toxic anger. *Better.* "I am way too fucking
evolved for this shit!" Hearing the words spoken out loud gave
her the perspective to pull back from the weird moment in the
woods and analyze what was going on inside her to produce
such an outsized response to a total stranger.

The call from her mother had frazzled her, awakened
ancient guilt and shame from their fitful slumber. *And when
Sebastian was conjured, Evan was never far behind.* All the dried-up
scabs covering everything Posey had done and not done—the
careful boundaries she'd so rigorously constructed, for all any of
that was worth—were ripped open again for a fresh examination.
Raw and exposed, she'd let down her guard at Painted Rock,

her happy place, and just at her most vulnerable moment, he'd happened upon her.

That had to be why Posey's cold, black heart had jumped into her throat when their eyes met. Not because of the way he looked at her as if he'd finally found what he'd been searching for his whole life. And certainly not because he was easily the most attractive man she'd ever seen. Posey would never be that giddy girl.

Pounding the pedals, she resolved to get her mind on something more productive and to do herself the favor of lightening the load she'd been carrying lately on her conscience, the juggled patient. She didn't need to add Q to her list of mishandled situations.

She rolled her bike inside the garage and hung her helmet on its hook. Bending to unlace her cleats, Posey pressed her palms to the floor and gave her tired muscles a long stretch. The quickly approaching winter had seeped into her bones, and all she wanted was to warm up her insides and clear her head.

She moved with purpose to her bedroom, stripped off her sweaty layers, and stepped into the hot shower. By the time she emerged, her skin pink from all that blood rushing to the surface, she knew what she needed to say to Q. She toweled off her hair and pulled on a pair of cozy sweatpants and an old, faded T-shirt.

It would be around seven in the evening where Q lived. She hoped he wasn't out with friends, and then she hoped he was. She hoped he had at least one really good friend to lean on because he was trying to manage an awful lot on his own. She sat down at the kitchen table with a cup of hot tea and placed the call.

Distracted by her thoughts, Posey was startled by his warm, "Hello, Posey."

"Hello. And thank you for allowing me to contact you again."

"Of course." Agreeable as ever. "How are you?" he asked, throwing her off-balance once again. It was the wrong question. By all rights, he should have demanded, *What do you want from me now?* Lucky for Posey, he didn't seem to know that.

"I'm fine. Thanks for asking." She didn't return his question; it was both too pointed and too vague for this conversation. "Dr. Fairlawn contacted me, and I wanted to loop back with you."

"Am I in trouble?" If there was teasing in his tone, she couldn't hear it.

*If anyone's in trouble, it's me.* "No, nothing like that. We both wanted to make sure you were properly covered, that's all."

"I appreciate your concern, but I'm good."

"Oh. You found someone else, then?"

"No. I mean I'm fine now."

"I see." Denial was strong in this one. "Look, Q, I realize it took a lot of courage for you to reach out, and you used my online portal for a reason. I get that. And I'm sorry it didn't work out for us to work together through the app—"

"Me too. I was really enjoying speaking with you."

"Yeah, so here's the thing. I can't, in good conscience, just pretend I don't know you're out there alone with all that pain you brought to me last week when we spoke."

"But I'm not. I promise."

"I understand that you feel better right now, and I'm glad for your relief. The thing is, we humans can be mighty crafty at burying uncomfortable feelings. This defense mechanism can protect the mind so successfully that it actually feels as if those unpleasant emotions have gone away, but our issues don't just evaporate like that. In fact, the better we are at burying them in the present, the more powerfully they surge up later to do their damage." *Like when you're out taking a relaxing bike ride one afternoon.*

He listened politely to her whole speech and followed up with, "Or maybe you're better than you think."

A hollow laugh left her. "I truly wish I were. I don't think anyone's that good. And right now, I feel as though I've done you a tremendous disservice. You came to me for help, and now, because of me, you're not getting that help." *And I really need to sleep at night.*

"According to Dr. Chan, I'm fine."

"Those were his exact words?" There's no way those were his exact words, not if he were half the doctor April seemed to think he was.

"He said I'm remarkably well-adjusted, considering all the crap I've been through." Not exactly a spotless bill of mental health, but she could see how a patient could interpret the comment the way he had. "And believe me, Posey, I told him all the gory details, so he knows what he's talking about."

"Well, that is certainly encouraging," she said. Maybe Posey would have taken some comfort in Dr. Chan's lack of urgency and left it there if not for April's call. "May I ask, if you were satisfied with Dr. Chan's analysis, why did you go see Dr. Fairlawn?"

A long pause followed before he finally came back with, "That's a good question."

*Which you deflected.*

"May I respectfully suggest you were seeking something further because deep down, part of you feels unsettled?"

His second pause gave her hope. If she had him thinking, maybe his mind could open to the idea that he still needed therapy.

"Maybe I was . . . *then*," he said, "but I'm good now."

"Are you saying something in your life has meaningfully changed in the two days since you went to see Dr. Fairlawn?"

"Yes. In fact, just a little while ago."

"Would you mind sharing this life-altering event with me?"

"You're not going to like it," Q said, and she was pretty sure he was right.

"Try me."

"I'm in love."

"I see." *Check that disappointment, Doc.* It was neither fair nor useful. After all, romance was his go-to coping mechanism, and she'd done nothing to help him change that.

He went on, no doubt starry-eyed. "What's that saying? 'Love heals all wounds'?"

"*Time.* The saying is 'time heals all wounds.'" Though Posey was no believer of that old saw either.

Regardless, Q was not deterred. "Well, I'm in love *and* I'm healed. My heartbreak over Pan is gone. Completely. So good job and case closed and thanks for your concern, but I don't need any more therapy."

It really sucked that he kept making her convince him he was still a mess, but she would do what she had to do. "Don't you see? You're doing it again. Romance is not the solution. Love is"—a farce, a lie, a distraction, a curse—"an illusion."

Q answered her in a hollow, resigned tone that told her she hadn't convinced him of anything except that he was growing tired of arguing with her. "What is it that you want me to do, Posey?"

"I'd like you to go back to Dr. Fairlawn and let her help you work through your issues."

"I'm sorry, but I'm not going to do that."

"In that case, I feel a responsibility to take you on as a patient." What the hell was she saying? She hadn't practiced that kind of analysis in seven years. She didn't even know if she'd be any good at it now, let alone, the risks . . .

"No, thank you," he said politely as if refusing a second helping of broccoli. "You're worried about me, and that is very sweet.

But I don't want to be analyzed, Posey. Not by Dr. Fairlawn, not by you, not by anyone."

*Time to let go.* She'd referred him out to two excellent practitioners. She'd followed up. She didn't believe him to be a danger to himself or anyone else. Due diligence done. "I hear you—"

"*But*—"

"Yes?" Posey pressed the phone to her ear, holding her breath.

"If you wanted to just talk," he said, "I'd be good with that."

"You mean, like this?" she asked.

"Sure. Why not?"

*Why not, indeed?* She'd be able to keep tabs on him, to know he was really okay.

"I have to tell you, this is a gray area for me. Not exactly your therapist, not exactly *not* your therapist . . ." Oh boy, was she skating on thin ice here! There wasn't even any language for what he was proposing.

"*Oh.* I get it," he said. "I can go through the Wings app and pay you for your time."

"No! It's not about the money. I don't want your money."

"Why not? Isn't this exactly what you do?"

"I don't treat people who don't want help. I didn't call to force myself on you."

"But it wouldn't be fair of me to take your valuable time away from your other patients."

"It's okay," she said, talking herself into this insane arrangement while justifying it to him. "I have plenty of patients and plenty of time to talk to you outside of my work hours. That's not a problem."

"I have to be honest with you, Posey. If we're just going to talk about me, that feels an awful lot like therapy. If we're going to do this, we have to talk about you too. That's the deal."

"Is it now?" His consideration of Posey's needs brought a smile to her face. In the transactional relationship between patient and doctor, she'd found it rare for the patient to express concern for the doctor. "And what am I going to talk to you about?"

"We can start with why you're so down on love."

A brief burst of maniacal laughter escaped her before she could rein it in. "A light topic, then?"

"You talk to me. I talk to you," he said, and she could visualize his shrug. "Nobody's anyone's patient. Just two friends who meet in a yoga class and go out for coffee afterward." His vision of their hypothetical first meeting made her smile again as it had when he'd mentioned it last time. If only it could be that uncomplicated between them.

"So how does this work, hmm? Seeing as you and I live at opposite ends of the country?"

"Seems to be working fine just like this," he said. "At least, it will once you let go of the idea that you need to fix me." Well, *there* was a page right out of the couples therapy playbook. It made her smile. Who was shrinking whom?

She didn't quite understand why she was letting this guy make up the rules as he went along, and that scared her more than a little bit, but her gut was telling her to keep him close. He needed her somehow; she was sure of it. And Posey wasn't about to fuck this up.

"You've got yourself a deal, Q."

25

# EARLY HIKE

Pan's snoring was obnoxious, but that was not what woke Cupid at 3:35 a.m. Those secrets he was keeping were weighing heavy on his heart. Pure necessity might mold him into a more skillful liar the longer his stay on Earth, but he'd always have this awful tangled-up feeling in his belly.

Cupid snuck quietly out of bed, threw on some clothes, grabbed his phone and room key, and headed to the bay in the predawn stillness. He stood for a while, watching the water lap at the pebbled shore. Lifting his gaze to the stars, Cupid easily picked out the nymph Callisto and her illegitimate son by Zeus, placed forever in the sky as Ursa Major and Minor to spare them Hera's revenge. There were Zeus's lover and son, his to view in the night sky whenever it suited his whim, but what kind of existence was that for Arcas and Callisto, frozen in the black void of a distant world and so very, very alone? It sent a shiver down Cupid's spine. Whatever could be said of his own torturous punishment, he was less alone now than he'd ever been—which would only make leaving that much more painful.

The night had not brought him any answers, but knowing Posey was his Right Love did make one thing as clear as the mountain sky: Posey would be his final trial. Success or failure, whatever those looked like, would determine not just his own future but Posey's too. He had to do this right—for her sake.

Because she was a Worthy. *His* Worthy.

*And I am hers!* He had been so distracted by coming face-to-face with his Right Love, he hadn't made that leap yesterday, but now, the realization knocked the breath from his lungs.

A tap on Cupid's shoulder made him spin around, clutching his chest. "Pan! What are you doing out here?"

Pan gave him an odd look. "You okay, man?"

"I was until you snuck up on me!"

"I *snuck* . . .?" Pan threw his hands up in surrender. "Sorry. Your heart going again?"

"No." Following Pan's gaze to his chest, Cupid dropped his hand away. "I couldn't sleep."

"Yeah. Jet lag sucks. Wanna take a walk? Nothing's gonna be open around here for a couple more hours."

"Sure."

Pan jerked his head and started down the small stretch of beach. "C'mon." The two walked side by side until the trees took over the shoreline. Without hesitating, Pan slipped inside the dense woods with Cupid right behind. They tromped through the wilderness in silence, Cupid's mind cycling through hope and confusion, fear and determination, until they emerged from the woods onto the main road.

"Jog back?" Pan asked.

"Can we talk instead?"

"'Course."

"So, I've been thinking . . ."

"Yes, I gathered," said Pan with a chuckle.

"Why would Mother choose me to be Posey's Worthy if she was still trying to punish me?"

"A very good question."

"I keep running this over and over in my mind, and all I can think of are all the ways they could turn this sour."

An anxious look came over Pan. "If you're about to list a bunch of sordid scenarios *out loud*, please, just . . . *don't*."

"Look, I know how you feel about that, but honestly, Pan, if the God of War and the Goddess of Love are planning to use Posey to punish me further, do you really think any of my ideas haven't already occurred to them?"

Pan drew his hands to his hips and scowled with all his might. "I have no idea what to think, and neither do you."

"Agreed. But if we can talk about this, maybe you can help me figure out some kind of strategy, or at least help me not lose my mind. Isn't that why you're here?"

Pan rolled his eyes to the sky and blew out a long, loud breath. "Maybe it's good we're out here in the open. No roof to give you a false sense of privacy. You hear what I'm saying?"

Swallowing the lump in his throat, Cupid nodded. Pan nodded. They began walking again, and Cupid spun out his fears between them.

"My first thought was Tantalus." Trapped between a spring of water at his feet and low-hanging branches of a fruit tree just overhead, both of which receded each time he attempted to partake, Tantalus was eternally deprived of the nourishment just beyond his grasp. "What if Posey is my forever temptation, and every time I reach for her, she is pulled away?"

"You mean, what if you can't have sex, like, *ever*?" Pan asked.

"I'm not talking about sex, Pan. Think bigger."

"Um . . ."

"What if Posey's heart is good and truly sealed? What if I can't make her love me? I'd be doomed to an eternity of unrequited love."

"Okay, *that*," said Pan, jabbing his finger at Cupid, "is impossible. Posey's not going to live forever. Your punishment would end with her mortal life."

"Your heart's going to forget Reed after he's gone?"

"Of course not!"

"Exactly," said Cupid, feeling no better at all but determined to voice the rest of his fears. "But maybe that's not it at all. What if I'm not really a Worthy? What if I made up the echo beat in my head because I was so desperate to be Posey's Right Love?"

Pan's head turned sharply. "Did you?"

"I don't think so."

"Neither do I," said Pan. "You were sure of what you heard. I could see it written all over your face. You can't start doubting yourself. You know hearts." Pan's logic was leaky, but Cupid wasn't strong enough to dispute it right now. "Next?"

Time to share the one that had kept him up all night. "Posey and I are meant to be, but she finds out I've been keeping secrets from her, *massive secrets,* and she won't speak to me again. I never get a chance to prove she's wrong about Love. I will have squandered the greatest of all possible gifts, and Posey will go on to live a lonely, loveless life."

When Pan didn't offer a quick comeback, Cupid knew he was truly in trouble. A few minutes down the road, Pan finally responded. "Okay, yes, I can see that being an issue—"

A soft moan left Cupid.

"*But* once she knows the truth about who you are and why you're here, she will also understand why you had to keep things from her along the way."

"And which of my many identities do you think I could be

truthful about without shutting down the conversation so I could tell her the other?"

"Another very good question. Not everyone is as open-minded as Reed," said Pan, pausing a moment to marvel at his good fortune. "Look, you've already identified both Worthies, and one of you is already all in! I have confidence you'll figure this out, *but*—"

Pan's feet froze in place. He peeked up at the sky without moving his head, met Cupid's gaze with an intensity that captured his full attention, and stirred the air with a hurry-up motion. "Feel me?"

Cupid nodded. Time was not on his side. At any moment—even right now—the gods could force him into Posey's presence again, and whatever careful progress he'd made could be undone with a single glance.

Pan set off again, always more comfortable in motion. "I have faith in you, buddy," he said, knocking his elbow with Cupid's as the two continued down the deserted road.

"Let's say you're right, Pan. Let's say I do somehow manage to get us to our Liminal Point. Maybe we even have one bright spark of joy. Then what?" Cupid held up two fists, then spread his fingers wide. "*Boom!* I ascend. She's down here. I'm up there. Right Love-mated until she dies, and we're apart the whole time!"

"*Orrrr,*" Pan said, winding up like a singer practicing his scales, "the two of you will have a wonderful love story with a happily ever after—whatever the hell that means."

Whatever *did* that mean? Cupid pondered the question until his head started to hurt, and the only answer he could come up with was that every couple's happy ending was different. For Mia and Patrick, that could be PB&Js in the park with three little boys tumbling in the grass, maybe even creating new life together. For Ruthie and Zach, maybe it was working side by side to make the world a gentler place. For Pan and Reed, who'd both found their fireworks in a most unexpected partner, happily ever after seemed to be a passionate trail of physical and intellectual adventures.

What could happily ever after look like for Cupid and Posey? There was only one way to find out, and that was by living their Right Love together. Cupid could not remember ever wanting anything more powerfully in his whole, eternal life.

"Do you really think I have a chance, Pan?"

"You're the freakin' God of Love! Who has a better chance than you?" Pan didn't wait for an answer. "Let's go find a damn cup of coffee."

26

# COFFEE TALK

Q's text—**Good time to talk?**—was waiting for Posey when she woke up from her first easy sleep in a while.

She felt the smile form on her lips as she lazily messaged him back: **Coffee first! Some of us are just waking up ;)** She hit send before it struck her she'd tacked on a wink. Too late now.

**Understood. I have a 2-cup lead :)**

Of course he did. He had a three-hour lead on life. She was grateful for the emoji he'd returned. It made her feel less silly about hers.

She rolled out from under the covers and strode to the window to peer through the curtains. Another clear day. Unfortunately, it was also the weekend, and she'd have to share her beloved trails with other humans. *Wouldn't mind too terribly if I saw that guy again.*

She laughed and shook her silly head. "Yeah, I definitely need that coffee!"

Posey made quick work of her morning routine, grabbed her phone, and shuffled to the kitchen in the boxers and T-shirt she'd slept in. As she absently watched the coffee drip, a sense of peace washed over her. The annual Thanksgiving conversation was behind her, and she was pleased, too, with how she'd dealt with the Q situation. She'd met yesterday's issues head on—*yay, me!*—and today's ride, a less punishing route, would be her reward. She'd earned it.

*Hmm,* but who was Posey to squander this gift from the cycling gods, a bonus ride to her favorite spot while the colors were their most spectacular? Yes, she really should make the effort one last time, and if Mr. Handsome happened to swing by Painted Rock again, maybe she wouldn't scare him away so quickly this time.

Not that Posey was planning her day around the hypothetical schedule of a total stranger, but why not take her time this morning? It was the weekend, after all, and not for nothing, she was oddly excited about speaking with her new . . . whatever Q was.

Definitely not a patient. He'd slammed on the brakes to any kind of therapeutic relationship, and yet, he'd been the one to initiate this highly unusual back channel. They weren't exactly friends, though she did like him. She found his positivity almost naïve, albeit utterly authentic. His obsession with love intrigued her, and he seemed equally fascinated by her total disavowal. Were they sparring partners, then?

*Sheesh!* Did she have to analyze every damn thing down to its atomic level? Could she not just admit to herself that she liked being phone pals and leave it at that?

Mug in hand, she curled up on the window seat banking the kitchen table. Staring out over the bay, Posey was filled with gratitude. She really loved this simple life she'd carved out for herself. She'd planned to relax with her first cup before calling, but eagerness won out.

Q answered with a chuckle in his voice. "That was fast."

"I didn't want to give you a chance to change your mind."

"Posey, you're the one who changed her mind about talking, remember?" His gentle teasing brought a smile to her face, and she imagined his avatar-face smiling back.

"Hmm. I think I'm gonna need more coffee for this conversation."

"Do what you gotta do." His tone was airy and light. If he was faking happiness, he was doing a fine job of it.

"So, how's your day going so far? Still in love?"

"Most definitely," he answered.

A twinge of longing tugged at Posey. Oh, to have that much faith in an emotion that was about as tangible as God. She wasn't wired that way, but once in a great while, she could see the appeal.

"Would you like to tell me about this new love of yours?" It struck her she had no idea if his latest love interest would be male or female or something that might not be so conveniently labeled.

"That depends," he said. "Are you planning to try to talk me out of it?" Man, did he have her number.

"I don't know yet," she said with a playful lilt. "Are you worried I'll ruin it for you? Because if it's that easy to talk you out of it, maybe it wasn't what you thought it was."

"You don't scare me. I know what I found."

She sighed; she couldn't help it. "Really? Number four's the charm?"

"Posey," he said, taking her right into his confidence with a tone as sweet and sticky as honey, "this one is different."

She hated feeling so damn cynical when he was so damn optimistic, but if Posey had a nickel for every brokenhearted soul who'd ever told her this time was different . . .

"Oh, Q."

"No, really." This one was hard to discourage. "I knew right from the start the others weren't going to work out."

"And yet you plunged, heart-first, into each of those."

"I had no choice." At last, common ground!

"No," she agreed, "we can't exactly control who we fall in love with, can we?"

"So you *have* been in love."

A sweat broke out on her forehead. *This is what happens when you let down your guard.* She set the mug on the table and fanned her face.

Q's voice came through, gentle but worried. "Have I already pushed too hard?"

*Yes.* "No, it's fine. But before we get to that, can we go back to your love life for one more second, please?"

Easy laughter tumbled through the phone. "Sure."

"The suspense is killing me. I need to know if it's a man or a woman this time."

"It's a woman," he said.

Why did his answer make Posey happy? Why did that make Posey anything at all?

"Name?"

"Yes, she has a name," he said pointedly, "but your one second is up."

*Well, hello again, feisty sparring partner.* There was the guy who'd flat-out refused to go back to April and warned Posey against trying to "fix" him.

She pictured a blue-eyed, dark-haired man wearing red satin trunks and puffy, red boxing gloves, springing gracefully on his toes in a wide swath around the edge of a boxing ring with Posey at its center, throwing punch after punch at his chest. Each of her rapid-fire jabs was effortlessly repelled—until that last punch, which he'd definitely dodged. Highly trained analytical thinker she was, Posey observed he could've batted the conversation back to her a whole lot quicker with a simple answer.

Still, he had redirected the flow, and in all fairness, it was her turn to pony up some personal information. She gathered her knees to her chest even while rolling her inner-shrink eyeballs at herself for the transparent fetal position.

"Yes, Q. I was once in love." The rare admission tasted bitter on her tongue.

"Once," he repeated. She caught a shift in his tone, a gravitas.

"Yes," she answered simply, allowing him to properly infer every nuance of the word. Past tense. One and done. Never again.

"Was it very long ago?"

"Feels like another lifetime," she said.

"I know what you mean." If Q's breezy attitude had made Posey temporarily forget the despair that originally brought him to Wings, his sympathy for her lost love reminded her now. "Were you together very long?"

"We weren't together at all."

"Oh no! He didn't love you back?"

"He did." Beautiful, broken Evan. "Very much. But we couldn't be together."

"Why not?"

Posey forced out the shameful confession. "He was my patient."

"I'm sorry, I don't understand." No, she wouldn't expect him to.

"It would have been a serious breach of my professional ethics."

"*To fall in love?*" The horror in his tone almost made her smile.

"I know this is going to sound like a cliché, but it's very complicated. There's a process called transference by which the patient identifies with the doctor as some important figure in their life. It can also work as countertransference where the doctor returns those feelings. Transference is not inherently bad—in fact, it can be a vital element of the therapeutic process—but can often lead to romantic feelings, which, again, are not necessarily harmful *if* properly managed. That's the therapist's job. That was *my* job . . . and I failed. I failed Evan."

She was tempted to tack on that she was cleared by a panel of her peers, that in a profession fraught with gray areas and intimate entanglements of the mind, Posey had technically done nothing wrong. She would have loved for this new person in her life not to regard her as a monster. But the truth was, it didn't matter that she'd never acted on her feelings. Evan's downward spiral was Posey's fault, and no piece of paper could ever relieve her of her guilt. The best she could do was avoid repeating her mistakes on anyone else.

"What happened to him?" *Fair question.*

"He ended up in a bad place for a while. I'd rather not get into specifics with you."

"No, of course. I understand."

"I'm told he's doing better now."

"You haven't talked to him?"

"I'm not allowed to have any contact with him or his family."

"That sounds incredibly painful, Posey. I'm so sorry."

"Thanks. Me too."

They were both quiet for a bit. She liked that he didn't fill her ears with platitudes.

"You sure you're not a therapist?" she asked, breaking their long silence.

His soft chuckle felt like a warm hug. "I don't know anything about any of that stuff."

"Maybe not, but you just extracted something from me I haven't spoken about in seven years." There lay Posey, flat on her back in the ring, Q standing over her.

"I wasn't trying to make you say something you didn't want to say. I'm sorry if I hurt you."

"You didn't hurt me." But no, he wasn't standing at all. He was kneeling beside her on the mat, cradling her, his gloves tossed away. "And maybe I *did* want to say it." *Maybe I was just waiting for the right person to listen.*

"You're the expert, I guess."

"Oh yeah, some expert I am." Unwinding her limbs, she reached for her coffee. "Now do you see why I promised myself never to get into that situation again?"

"Being in love?"

"No, treating patients in person. It's hard to fall in love with words on a screen and disembodied voices."

"Is it?" Q asked, stunning her into silence.

*Huh. Was it?*

She thought of her excitement with each new application that crossed her desk, that picture she painted in her mind, the story she pieced together, how it all came to life each time she'd meet a prospective patient in the chat room and they'd start to interact. And what about the voice in her ear right now? Did she not hop out of bed with a little more bounce in her step this morning in anticipation of this talk? Could she honestly say she wasn't getting attached to the person behind the voice? *Now who was being naïve?*

"It's worked for me so far," she replied, hoping she sounded more convinced than she felt.

"Well, I guess there's that." He sure had a polite way of telling her she was full of shit.

"So what do you think, Q? Are you still into this phone-a-friend deal now that you know my ugly truth?"

"No, not really," he said, causing Posey's jaw to drop one last time. "To be honest"—she braced herself because yeah, she cared what he had to say—"I'd much rather be doing this in person. You sound like you could use a hug."

She blinked away tears. "Yeah, that'd be nice."

"Hey, are you gonna be okay?"

"Yep. I'm going to get on my bike right after this and ride to my happy place."

"Oh yeah? Where's that?"

"It's called Painted Rock. The views are spectacular this time of year."

"Sounds amazing. I wish I could join you."

"That'd be nice, too," she said, smiling to herself as she pictured Q waiting for her at Painted Rock, boxing gloves hanging from a cord tied over his shoulders.

"Can we talk again soon, Posey?"

"I'd like that."

They parted gently with reluctant goodbyes and well-wishes for each other's day.

As the piping hot stream of fresh coffee warmed her tepid drink, anticipation churned Posey's insides like the steam swirling in her mug. It was then she remembered she'd already slotted in Mr. Handsome for a Painted Rock appearance this morning. My, my, what a crowd was forming in Posey's happy place today.

27

# THE TROUBLE
# WITH MORTALS

"No more coffee for this one." Pan flipped Cupid's cup upside down on the saucer just in time. "Bring him a Blue Moon, extra oranges. I'll take one too. Thanks, man."

"I don't want a beer, Pan." Sad Cupid was a depressing sight.

"You need to relax, and we're not doing tequila shots before two o'clock."

"How am I supposed to relax while Posey is riding around those trails with her heart cracked wide open? What if she catches her tire on a tree root because she's not paying attention and does one of those endos! She could be lying there right now, broken and bleeding and alone." He picked up his phone again, checked his calls and texts, and set it back down with an agonized groan.

"She's not alone. C'mon. She told you exactly where she was going." Which was why Pan had led Cupid in the opposite direction. "She's riding one of the most popular stretches of trail."

"Yes, to see the view from a very high cliff. What if she walks too close to the edge and falls to her death? She might already have fallen!"

"Wow, I've never seen you this worked up before."

"She's my Right Love! And I've put her in a really fragile state. And she's mortal! How could I possibly *not* be worked up?"

Pan's phone picked that moment to ring. *"Don't stand so close to me . . ."*

Trying hard to stifle his grin, Pan jerked his chin at Cupid's plate. "Eat your sandwich. It's not good to drink on an empty stomach, especially after a hard ride." He swiveled in his seat and brought the phone to his ear. "Good morning, Professor."

"Hello, wild thing."

"Oh, damn. I think I really dig it when you call me that."

Reed's laughter filled his ears. So did a loud *honk!* followed by a stream of curses—not Reed's.

"Are you in your car?"

"No."

"Why did I just hear a car horn?"

"I'm in an Uber."

"Why?" Pan leaped out of his chair. If not for the bike shoes, he would have already been pacing. "Did your car break down? Don't tell me you were in an accident!" *I leave the guy for one day . . .*

Glancing up from his meal, Cupid asked, "What's wrong?"

Shrugging, Pan pointed to his phone.

"I'm fine, Pan. My car is fine. It's at home."

Screw the clips. Pan was pacing. "And where are *you*?"

"Um . . . almost there?"

"Almost where? Reed, you are making no sense!"

Cupid jumped to his feet and joined Pan at the edge of the restaurant floor, pushing his ear next to Pan's so he could hear Reed too.

"Almost to Carnelian Bay, near Incline Village."

Cupid asked, "He's in California?"

"Not yet," Reed answered. "Hi, Q."

"Hi, Ree—"

"Wait, *what?*" Pan was beginning to think he'd made the wrong call on the tequila shots.

"I'm still in Nevada." And there was Reed, explaining everything, calm as ever. "We haven't crossed the border yet."

Pan jerked the phone away from his ear, sending Cupid stumbling backward. "Do you have a fucking clue what Reed's talking about? Because I sure don't."

"It sounds like he's flown out here, and now he's in some guy's car, heading toward Carnelian Bay to try to meet up with us."

"We're not even in Carnelian Bay."

Cupid pointed at the phone dangling from Pan's fingertips somewhere around his left knee. "Might want to tell that to your mortal." Cupid shot him a wink and snuck away before Pan could slap him.

"Sorry for the interruption, Reed. Q was having an issue." Cupid and Pan exchanged obscene gestures. "Am I to understand that you've flown out to Tahoe, and you are currently driving around in an Uber heading toward the address I found for Posey?"

"Yes, that would be correct."

"Oh-kayyyyy." Pan stood there, nodding to himself like a lunatic. A million questions raced through his head, most of them starting with *why*.

"So, can you please tell me where to direct this nice young man?"

"Yes. Have him take you to a very elegant establishment called the Carnelian Lookout Lodge. When you get there, speak with the manager and get us a room with a king bed, then text me the room number. Q and I are twenty miles away from there on the other side of the lake, but I'll meet you back at the room as fast as these bikes can carry us, and I will deal with *you* when I get there."

"Should I be scared?"

"*Very.* And I hope you brought a change of clothes because I plan to destroy whatever you're wearing."

Reed's laughter poured into Pan's ear. "For a minute there, I thought you were really angry with me."

"How could I be angry? But why didn't you tell me you were coming when we spoke last night?"

"I thought you might try to talk me out of it."

"For a smart guy, Reed Scully, you sure can be a numskull."

"Thank you," Reed answered. "See you soon."

Clomping back to the table where Cupid was polishing off his lunch, Pan tipped his face to the ceiling and blew off the head of steam he'd gathered. He flung his phone onto the table and sat down heavily in his chair.

Cupid lifted his untouched beer and waited for Pan to do the same. "To mortals!"

# LEAVING SANITY

There was nothing elegant about the way their bodies crashed together when Reed opened the door of room eight or the way they clawed each other's clothes off in the bathroom. Pan needed a shower, but he needed Reed more. He economized and took them both at once. Spent and sore—Reed more so than Pan, obviously—they emerged from the shower stall wrinkled like two plump raisins.

It wasn't until afterward that Pan, wrapping one of the threadbare towels around his waist, spoke for the first time. "I just realized I have no clean clothes. Meet me in room three when you're dressed?" Cupid was a loose cannon, and Pan had already left him for too long.

"Pan, wait!" Reed called as Pan turned for the door. "There's something I need to tell you—while we're alone."

The ancient hackles at the back of Pan's neck sprang to attention. "Okay?"

"I, uh . . ." Reed pushed his fingers through his wet hair. *Fuck.*

Pan headed for Reed, crossing the room in four swift strides.

He cupped Reed's chin and looked straight into his lover's brown eyes. Reed hadn't put on his glasses yet after their shower, so there was nothing to obscure Pan's view. Still, he didn't see anything that gave him cause for alarm, so what was this?

"Speak. Quickly."

"I met your father."

Pan's hand fell away from Reed's chin. "Huh. I was not expecting that."

Reed let out an amused huff. "Yeah, it was a bit of a shock to me too."

Pan sat down at the edge of the bed, and Reed joined him. "How did this come about?"

"I think I brought it on myself."

Pan side-eyed him. "What have you been up to, Professor?"

"After I dropped you and Q at the airport yesterday, I got to thinking—maybe it wouldn't be so terrible to have a backup plan in case things didn't go so well with Posey." That was Reed, always three moves ahead.

"I see."

"Long story short, I went to your house to get Q's bow and arrow."

"What the hell, Reed? You know you could never bring that on a plane."

"Which is why I was going to drive it to you, which meant I could bring the dogs too."

"Oh! *Now* it all makes sense. You've completely lost your mind." *In a heroic, sexy kinda way.*

Reed looked over at him, nodding his head like a dashboard hula doll. "Well, let's see. I'm sitting in a towel in a questionable motel room in Lake Tahoe, next to a demigod who has just, *ahem*, had his way with me, discussing how his father, Hermes—excuse me, *Mercury*—came down from Mount Olympus in a pillar of clouds to take Cupid's bow and arrow so he couldn't use it to an unfair advantage to win the heart of his eternal love, Psyche, who is actually a real-life psychotherapist living in a secluded cabin less than a mile from here. Does any of that sound sane to you?"

"Uh oh," said Pan, grinning ear to ear. "I think I broke you."

"*Meanwhile*, I had a lovely chat with your father."

"Did you now? He didn't just pop in, do his thing, and *shweep*?" Pan swept his finger in a swift line toward the sky.

"Nope." Reed sat there smiling with secrets Pan would work out of him later. "But he did take the arrow with him when he left."

"And . . . here you are?"

Reed threw up his hands. "I know! How nuts is that? I made arrangements for the dogs and booked the first flight out here."

"Please don't take this the wrong way, but why did you decide to come out here now when you were pretty dead set against leaving the dogs two days ago when I booked my flight?"

"Well, while I was talking to your dad, which still sounds way too banal considering, yeah"—he waved his hands maniacally—"he mentioned that I might have some value to add to this whole process, being somewhat of an expert in mythology—which, as I now know, isn't actually a *thing*—but as it turns out, there are some clues in the ancient Cupid and Psyche story that might inform Cupid's quest, and if I can help in any way, this is where I should be."

"So, this isn't a booty call?"

It took Reed a couple of beats to realize Pan was pulling his leg, which Pan chalked up to the insanity.

"Get dressed, Professor. Cupid needs you."

29

# THE GOLDEN ASS

Cupid stared at the sent message on his phone, unease nagging at his gut. *Please call me when you're back from your ride.*

Fighting off images of twisted limbs and a bloodied, scraped-up face, he pictured Posey returning home from her ride, unzipping her jacket, and pulling her phone from the pocket. In his mind's eye, Posey's pretty lips formed a grimace as she read his message. Had he already violated their newborn intimacy? Would she roll her eyes and regret telling him everything?

This messaging game was tricky. He'd have to be more mindful of his word choices.

*Just making sure you're ok*, he typed, read, reread, and sent.

Feeling slightly relieved, Cupid peeled off his sweaty clothes and tried not to think too hard about what Pan and Reed were doing a few doors down. It felt right to have Reed here, whatever the circumstances. At least Pan would be more relaxed.

Cupid was sitting on his bed, tossing his phone from one hand to the other, when Pan barged in wearing only a towel and a smirk. "'Sup?"

Cupid took one look at him and snorted. "Nice reunion?" he asked, hoping Pan wouldn't expound on the details.

"Yeah, ya know, Reed's a freak, so . . ." Pan whipped off the towel without ceremony, rooted through his duffel, and reappeared fully dressed at the foot of Cupid's bed. "What's happening here?" Pan asked, mirroring the path of Cupid's flying phone with his finger.

"Waiting for Posey to call me."

"Know what you're gonna say?"

"So far, what's come out in the moment has been working pretty well."

Pan drew his hands to his hips. "Reed has some ideas for you. He'll be over in a minute."

"I don't see how Reed can know Posey better than I do."

"As it turns out, he has some inside information. Anyway, he's here, so you might as well hear him out." A soft knock came at the door. "Cool?"

"Sure."

"Great. Okay." Pan clapped his hands together and jogged over to open the door. "*Hola!*"

Reed peered around Pan with a shy grin. "Hope I'm not intruding?"

"Of course not!" Pan assured him as Cupid approached Reed and offered a warm hug.

"Always good to be with you, Reed. Do you want to sit down?"

Following Cupid's gaze toward his cane, Reed nodded. "Airports." Then, jerking his chin at Pan, he added, "And this one!"

Pan guffawed loudly. "You're welcome."

Reed settled against the headboard of the bed Pan would no longer be using, legs extended, and Pan squeezed into the space beside him. "I imagine you're wondering what I'm doing here."

"You've come a long way," said Cupid. "If I know you, there's a good reason."

"I went back and forth about coming, believe me," said Reed. "I had a very interesting conversation with Mercury yesterday."

Cupid's gaze shifted to a surprisingly unsurprised Pan, who must have already learned this much from Reed. "Mercury came to you?"

"We were both going for your bow and arrow."

"You were?" Had Reed somehow—

"Don't get your hopes up. He took it with him when he left."

"Oh."

"*But* he did hint rather forcefully that my knowledge of *Metamorphoses* might be instructive. Remember that one from your studies?"

"Wasn't there something about a donkey?"

"Very good, Q!" said Reed. "The novel is referred to as *The Golden Ass.* If you'll recall, the protagonist Lucius has an insatiable curiosity, especially for all things magic. One day, while attempting a spell to transform himself into a bird, he accidentally turns himself into an ass."

"Aside from the obvious," said Pan, "what does a story about an ass have to do with Q?"

Dismissing Pan's mischief with an indulgent grin, Reed went on to explain. "Embedded within the novel is a series of stories, one of which happens to be called 'The Tale of Cupid and Psyche.' Sound relevant yet?"

Cupid and Pan exchanged confused glances, and Reed continued.

"When I first brought up the Cupid and Psyche story, you both shrugged it off as myth, but now that we know Posey is your intended, it makes sense—and I use that term with a great deal of poetic license—that the Apuleius telling of the ancient love story could serve as a roadmap for your own courtship."

Cupid angled forward and asked the question on his heart. "Does the story have a happy ending for Cupid and Psyche?"

"Ultimately, yes," answered Reed, giving Cupid his first glimmer of hope yet. "But there were many serious pitfalls along the way, mistakes made, impossible tests thrown at the lovers by—" Reed stopped himself midsentence and cleared his throat.

An icy chill shot through Cupid. "*Mother?*" How was he still astonished at the idea of his own mother conspiring against him even after all he'd been through? And clearly, the worst was yet to come.

Pan snorted. "Surprise, surprise."

"I'm sorry," said Reed, struggling to meet Cupid's eye. "But that's why I'm here, to help you navigate the turbulence."

Cupid's thoughts shifted to the oxygen masks dropping from the airplane ceiling.

"Y'okay, Q?" Pan asked.

"Fine," Cupid whispered.

"Okay, then." Reed clasped his hands together and continued brightly. "The first order of business, as I see it, is the three of us studying the text together."

"Let's do it!" said Pan, shocking Cupid with his eagerness. To *study?*

Encouraged, Reed pressed on. "Any translation is, inherently, an inferior rendering, but I thought we'd study the Stuttaford translation in English—unless you'd rather wrestle with the Latin?"

"English is fine," Cupid answered swiftly, half expecting Pan to disagree.

"Good. I have copies for you both in my suitcase. In the meantime, why don't you catch me up on what's happening here so I might save your heart some wear and tear?"

30

# NOT SO HAPPY PLACE

Cupid brought Reed up to date while Pan paced the tiny room, chiming in whenever an important detail had been omitted. Reed listened intently, occasionally tapping his fingers on the handle of his cane lying on the bed beside him.

"And right now, I'm waiting for Posey to read my message and hopefully call me."

"That would explain your highly agitated state." That and Cupid's worry that his probing might have caused Posey to act carelessly. "When she does call—"

Just then, Cupid's phone rang in his hand. He was about to answer when Reed reached his cane over the gap between the beds and jabbed the end at Cupid's leg.

"Ouch!"

"Sorry."

"*What?*" Cupid asked, staring anxiously at *Posey calling* . . . with his finger hovering over the screen as the seconds ticked away.

"Before you say another word to Posey, know that secrets are what drive Cupid and Psyche apart in the story." Reed's words sank like a rock to the bottom of Cupid's heart. Was it already too late?

With a tight nod acknowledging Reed's advice, he accepted the call. "Hi, Posey. Thank you for getting back to me."

"It was very sweet of you to check on me."

"You'd do the same for me. In fact, you already have."

"True."

Reed had left the bed and was busy coaxing a reluctant Pan toward the door, the two of them bickering the whole way: "Give them some privacy . . ."

". . . just gonna have to repeat everything afterward."

". . . nosy Nelly."

". . . big bully."

Cupid covered the phone with his hand until he heard the door click shut behind them. Only then did he resume his conversation with Posey. "How was your happy place today?"

"It was fine," she answered flatly.

"Just fine?"

"It was good," she said—but it wasn't really. He could hear it in her voice.

"Did something happen? Please tell me you're not hurt—"

"No, nothing happened. Nothing *at all* happened." Posey sighed into his ear. "It's just me being silly."

She was keeping something from him. Reed had warned Cupid about secrets, but he hadn't specified whose. Wouldn't Posey's secrets destroy them just as handily? He'd have to venture gently into the new territory of Posey's mind. She'd had a lot more practice at hiding than Cupid.

"You know you can talk to me, Posey. Remember, that's our deal. You're here for me, and I'm here for you."

The silence between them stretched for so long, Cupid worried he'd scared her back into her shell . . . but then came the confession. "I think I asked a little too much of my mountains today. A spectacular view and a good, hard ride used to be enough."

"I'm sorry, Posey. I feel responsible for ruining your happy place."

"You know, come to think of it, it *is* your fault! All this talk about love. You've got me seeing things that aren't really there."

*Love?* Could it be that Posey recognized love at Painted Rock yesterday?

Attempting to contain the jubilation threatening to burst out of him, Cupid took care to keep his tone steady. "What kind of things?"

"Oh, don't worry," she said, a scary, hollow laughter trailing her words. "I'm not hallucinating or anything. I would know if I were psychotic, right? I'm an expert."

"Not about love, you're not."

"Oh, excuse me, and you are?"

*No more secrets.* "If there is such a thing, yes. The way you know souls, I know love."

"That's quite a claim from someone broken by love three times over," she reminded him almost cruelly, "and possibly a fourth any day now."

"Just because I recognize love doesn't mean I can control my heart any more than you can."

"I was doing just fine controlling my heart until you came along, thank you very much!"

"But were you, Posey? What was it you told me about sup-pressing our emotions?"

Posey's grim laughter worried him. "Wow. If I didn't know better, I'd think April put you up to this."

"Put me up to what?"

"Oh, challenging my belief system? Excavating my heart from the ancient ruins?" Once initiated, Posey's fiction gathered momentum at an alarming rate. "I'm impressed, truly. April must have gone to a lot of trouble to concoct such an elaborate scheme. Did she fill out the DASS for you too? Brilliant profile, by the way. April would have known I wouldn't let this go."

As she ranted on, Cupid half wondered if the Maniae had sunk their hooks into poor Posey.

"Where did she find you, Q? You can't possibly be an actual mental health professional, or you'd know this is cut-and-dried malpractice, career suicide. I'm thinking you must be an actor . . . improv, yes? Who else could play the part so perfectly? Boy, I hope she's paying you well. But what I really don't get is, after all this time, why would April want to torture me now?" Cyclone Posey died down, or at least stopped for a breath, and Cupid seized his chance.

"Posey, I'd never heard of Dr. Fairlawn before you emailed me her name. I'm not an actor, and nobody is trying to torture you. I promise." He stopped short of saying he wasn't part of an elaborate scheme to excavate her heart because she'd actually hit on a much larger truth than she could know. "Those were my genuine answers on all the forms. I was a complete mess when I filled them out. My pain was real, and I didn't know where else to turn."

"Oh god. Forgive me, Q. I don't know what's come over me. That was inexcusable." She groaned. "I seem to have moved from psychosis straight into paranoia."

"Posey, please don't beat yourself up. I understand. I hit a nerve."

"But it's not just you. There was this guy in the woods yesterday. I barely got a glimpse of him, but—here's the part where I sound crazy again—I swear, something passed between us."

So she *had* felt it. "That's who you were hoping to see today at Painted Rock," he said.

"If I'm honest, yes. I went and got my hopes up. Happiness is all about expectations, you know. There's a little piece of therapy you can tuck in your pocket, free of charge, not that you're probably too interested in taking advice from the loony girl over here." She laughed unkindly at herself. It made him sad.

"Well, I'm sorry you were disappointed," he said though he couldn't deny he was also thrilled.

"Eh, it's probably for the best. I didn't even tell you the part that gets really *woo-woo*."

"Oh?"

"Mm. The whole ride home yesterday, I couldn't stop thinking about that weird connection. The answer was knocking at my brain, floating just out of reach. And then when I went to call you, and your avatar popped up on my screen, I knew at once why he'd felt so familiar. The resemblance was uncanny."

If Cupid's tongue weren't tied in knots, he might've made a joke about the mysterious stranger's obvious good looks. He'd have to untie that tongue of his and quick. The moment of truth was upon him.

His heart began to thunder the same way it used to when he and Pan played hide-and-seek as kids, a ridiculous game to play with a creature whose nose was as sensitive as Pan's. Cupid well remembered that thrill of approaching hooves, that breathless anticipation of Pan throwing open the cupboard door and discovering him inside. This time, there was so much more on the line. Posey was seconds from discovering Q's hiding place, and when she did, she might never speak to him again.

"I know it's more silliness on my part, or maybe some kind of wishful thinking, especially since you're in Indiana . . ."

Cupid threw open the cupboard door. "I *was*."

"You *were*? And now . . .?"

"I'm much closer."

"Uh-*huh*. Just curious—if I were to ask you the time right now, what would you say?"

He pinched his eyes shut. "Two fifteen."

"I see." An unnatural tightness entered her voice. "And what time was it yesterday when you and I stood on Painted Rock together?"

No turning back now. "Around the same time."

When Posey spoke again, she seemed just shy of hysteria. "Well, Q—whatever that stands for—I don't know why you tracked me down or how on earth you found me in the middle of the woods, but I have to tell you I'm feeling all kinds of creeped out right now."

"I'm sorry, Posey. I hope you'll let me explain . . ."

"I don't feel safe right now. I need some time to process." As horrible as it was to hear how his deception had harmed her, she hadn't shut him out for good—at least, not yet.

"Whatever you need, Posey."

"What I need is for you to promise you won't show up on Painted Rock or attempt to contact me again. If and when I'm ready, I'll be in touch."

"Yes, of course. I really am sorry."

"So am I." She hung up without a goodbye, a mercy to them both.

Lost and forlorn, Cupid shuffled through the room, opened the door, and nearly stumbled into the two friends waiting for him just outside.

Pan took one look at Cupid and pulled him into a firm hug. "We're here, buddy. We're going to get you through this."

"I don't know if she's going to give me another chance," Cupid said, choking back a sob.

"We have to believe she will." Pan gave him a hearty slap on the back as he pulled away, and Reed stepped in, taking Cupid by the elbow.

"Come. You'll tell us what happened, and we'll study the story and come up with a plan together."

They crowded in close on both sides and moved him forward when he couldn't feel his own two feet. Across the street, Cupid was lowered to the grassy shore, where he stared out at Carnelian Bay and did his best to relay the conversation.

"So we wait," Pan said.

"And in the meantime, we learn," said Reed, producing a copy of Cupid's so-called love story for each of them. "Pan, why don't you read aloud from the beginning?"

"Sure thing, Professor Scully." Pan batted his eyelashes like a lovesick schoolgirl. "'The Story of Cupid and Psyche,' translated from the Latin blah-blah-blah. Once upon a time, there lived in a certain land a king and queen who had three daughters of rare loveliness."

A powerful burning in Cupid's chest propelled him to his feet. "Oh no!"

"What'd I say?" asked a startled Pan.

"It's not you, and it's not the story." Out of habit, Cupid fisted the shirt over his heart, but this was a new kind of fire raging deep in his belly.

"So much for waiting." Pan rose, then pulled Reed up beside him. "Well, Professor, looks like class is dismissed."

# OFF THE LEDGE

"Well, Po, you sure can pick 'em!" Propelled by a stream of disparaging self-talk, Posey stormed into her bathroom and whipped off her sweaty clothes. If only it were that simple to peel off the self-loathing that slumbered just beneath the surface until awakened by the slightest provocation.

Even the sanctuary of her river-stone shower walls couldn't shield Posey from her scorn. *I should've known better. Why am I so weak? This is why we don't do people.* She stood under the stream until the water turned into punishing, icy pinpricks, and her outside was as numb as her insides.

Toweling off, Posey was able to observe her situation with practiced objectivity as if the glass shower door had acted as a dividing wall between reactive patient and composed therapist. Physical attraction caused blindness, which was exactly why Posey had spent all these years building up her immunity. Yes, she'd unquestionably been drawn to the man in the woods, and she was self-aware enough to admit it, but that didn't account for the allure of the prospective patient's story on her screen or the sympathetic friend's voice in her ear. What was it about *that* Q that had made her let him in?

Cocooned in her favorite sweatpants and hoodie, Posey passed through the kitchen to put on a kettle for tea. No more caffeine today. Chamomile, that's what she needed. She readied her mug with a tea bag and attempted a quick meditation while the water boiled. The whistle rescued her from her wandering thoughts.

Dabbing her tea bag in the hot water, Posey walked to the sink, stared out the window, and sighed. *You can run, but you can't hide.*

A terrible thought popped into her head. What if he was watching her house right now? She darted away from the window, narrowly avoiding scalding herself on the wave of hot tea that sloshed to the edge of the mug.

"And now you're being dramatic." Posey didn't suffer drama, and she particularly disliked being at its center. It was true what she'd told Q, that she didn't feel safe, but she never believed he'd cause her physical harm. *If I had a nickel . . .* said Dr. Rey, while giving her a you-know-better-than-this eye roll. If Q knew what was good for him, he would honor her request to leave her the hell alone.

Posey took her tea and her warring halves into her office, where she plucked the composition notebook from the top of the stack. The Q on the cover mocked her now as it hadn't before, the first half of "Q & A," wasn't it? And where were the answers, huh? Had she missed some obvious warning sign that Q was a crazy stalker?

Flipping to the lines she'd jotted down on page one only reminded Posey how little she'd needed to hear before making the decision to refer him out. "At least I did one thing right," she said aloud, laughing mirthlessly.

Reviewing her early notes brought Q's issues into clear focus. Possible situational depression brought on by repeated loss of intimacy, attachment issues with one or both parents, abandonment themes, jealous mother. There at the very bottom in all caps was Posey's characterization—SERIAL ROMANTIC. Oh yes. "Love heals all wounds." *Please.* And that wasn't even counting his latest love, the nameless woman he'd met just yesterday. Wait, *yesterday?*

*Holy shit, Po! You're it! The woman with no name is you!* Well, no fucking wonder he'd dodged the question!

And didn't that prove her point? She'd been there too. Not a word was spoken, and he just up and decided he was in love, and he was over the last guy just like that?

Okay, yes, Posey had felt . . . *something.* It still made her head spin to try to conflate the two separate experiences of Q into the one man . . . and yet, his admission—that Mr. Handsome was the living, breathing avatar of Q—hadn't really come as a surprise at all. She'd known on some cellular level in that first blink of an eye.

Clearly, he'd already known exactly who *she* was. This was so fucked up.

She wished she'd been recording their conversations all along so she could go back now and analyze every word. All she had left were gut feelings and scattered recollections, both of which were becoming less reliable by the minute. Taking her pen in hand, she began scribbling feverishly in the notebook, writing down every snippet of conversation and impression she could remember.

As the words filled the page, certain patterns emerged. His conviction in love and her corresponding doubt were no great revelation to Posey, nor was his equally confident claim that his depression had disappeared. But what the discovery of his

THE QUEST FOR PSYCHE

tracking her and flying out West to find her had overshadowed was her overarching sense of Q's kindness and empathy—outstanding traits to find in one with so turbulent a childhood.

Truly, Q's happiness for each of the three love recipients who'd preceded Posey was extraordinary. This man's broken relationships sounded healthier than most of the ongoing ones she knew of. And what about Q's concern for the state of Posey's heart? It certainly felt genuine even now, knowing he had a vested interest.

Without understanding why, she'd felt drawn in by his online application, and she'd genuinely liked him right from their first eye-popping chat. He seemed like a solid guy, except for the whole creepy stalker thing. *Crap*, she had to cut him off, didn't she?

*Ugh.* Her brain was about to explode. She let the pen slip from her fingers. Scrubbing her hands over her face, she released a weary sigh. So much for objectivity. *Might need to call in the cavalry on this one.*

One name came swift and certain—*April.*

Hadn't she said to call anytime? The offer was as sincere as they come; Posey knew because she felt exactly the same.

Posey picked up her phone and walked to the French doors. She was aware of glancing at the lock before finding April's number in her recent calls. It might be dinnertime in Indiana, but she wouldn't be waking anyone from a dead sleep.

April picked up right away. "Posey? Are you okay?"

"Yes. Mostly. I'm sorry to interrupt, but—"

"Don't be silly. Hold on. Let me just get to where I can hear you." Then, muffled, "Be right back, Myles. One sec . . ." A door closed. "Hey. What's up?"

"I need you to talk me off the ledge."

"Just to be clear, the ledge is metaphorical, right?"

"Absolutely."

"Okay. I'm listening." God bless April.

"It's Q. He's here."

"Here *where?*"

"He's in Lake Tahoe."

"What? Are you sure? He was just *here!*"

"Yep. I actually saw him yesterday on a bike trail, but I didn't realize it until he admitted it on the phone just now."

"Jesus, Posey. This is not okay."

"Yeah, that's what I was thinking too." It felt good to know she wasn't crazy for being freaked out.

"Are you in a safe place right now?"

"Yes," she answered easily despite her earlier doubt. "But it's weird and eerie, right? For him to go to the trouble of tracking me down and the expense of flying out here?"

"What did he say?"

"I didn't give him a chance to say much of anything. I told him to give me some time to wrap my head around this. I've been sitting here for the last hour trying to figure out what to do."

"You don't think he'd come to your house, or . . . God, Posey, you don't think he'd hurt you?"

"You met him, April. Do you think he's dangerous?

"Look, anyone is capable of anything, but I sure didn't get that vibe. Come to think of it, he seemed way more focused on your issues than working on himself."

"How so?"

"He asked me a bunch of questions about your former practice. Were you good, why you quit, that sort of thing. Do you think he might have some connection with Evan?"

"That doesn't fit. I told him about Evan, and he seemed genuinely surprised. Besides, what would anyone gain from dredging that up?"

"I don't know. Maybe someone's sick idea of punishing you?"

"I guess it's possible, but if anything, he was the opposite. Super empathic. I even thought . . . eh, it sounds so foolish now. I wondered if you'd sent him here to try to help me."

"Oh, Posey."

"I'm sorry. All kinds of wild theories were flying through my head. This guy is pushing my buttons like he's holding the instruction manual, you know?"

"Yeah," April said with a soft sigh. "I suppose there's really only one way to find out what's motivating him."

"I'm pretty sure he thinks he's in love with me."

"Well that escalated quickly," April teased.

Posey retorted, "Right?" and the two shared a cautious chuckle. Posey teetered on the edge of truthfulness before taking the plunge. Really, how was April supposed to help if Posey wasn't being honest with her? "So, before this thing kind of blew up, I was starting to wonder if I might, I dunno, have some kind of feelings for him."

"He's not your patient, right?"

"Definitely not."

"Thank God!" April giggled a bit more freely this time. "Not for nothing, Po, did you get a good look at him? I mean, the guy *is* drop-dead gorgeous."

"Yeah, I noticed." Posey turned away from the door, her feet carrying her to the couch, where she collapsed with a dreamy sigh. "Shit, April, I like him. I *really, really* like him. I liked him before I ever saw him and put two and two together. He's sweet and easy to talk to and he believes in things I wouldn't mind believing in again. But . . . y'know."

"Evan."

"Evan. Sebastian. Ted Bundy."

April burst out laughing. "That's quite a collection."

"You know what I mean."

"Yes, of course, and you're not foolish to worry. You could check him out, you know."

"I could . . . if I knew his name."

"He wouldn't tell you his name?"

"I never ask for names. I've just been calling him by the screen name he chose, 'Q.' Wait! Do *you* know it?"

"Yes. Quentin Arrows. Not one you easily forget."

"Arrows, as in, 'the slings and arrows of outrageous fortune'?"

April chuckled. "Sorta, yeah."

"*Huh.*" Posey turned the name over on her tongue.

"If I were you, Po, I'd run all the usual checks, and don't feel bad about it for one second. Trust me, he didn't find you in the white pages."

"Very true." James Bond's Q had nothing on this guy's intel.

"Let's get real for a minute, Po. This guy already knows where you live. Ignoring him isn't going to make you any safer. If he checks out, meet him in person somewhere very public. Let him know you've got friends watching out for you. Then look him right in the eye, and ask him all your questions. You'll know if he's bullshitting you."

"You think I should hear him out." As the words left her, Posey realized that was exactly what she'd hoped April would say.

"My friend, you moved clear across the country, and you're still running. Aren't you exhausted? I know I would be."

Tears rolled down Posey's cheeks. "Yep," she choked out.

"The choice is yours this time. You can stand and face Q, or you can keep on running."

32

# TICKING TIME BOMB

Ares himself answered Aphrodite's frantic knock at his palace entrance. He'd been expecting her, and she had not dithered. He'd only just revved the boy's heart minutes before. Trap set, he'd dashed from the War Room to the entry hall and shooed the guards away. He wanted that first, undiluted blow of Aphrodite's battle lust all to himself.

Casually munching on an apple as if he'd just meandered into the kitchen for a snack, Ares swung open the foreboding iron door. There stood his lover, absent of late, fully present now. Oh, the passion of her boiling blood! The wild chop of stormy seas churning in her eyes!

"*Why?*" she demanded.

*For exactly this.*

"For the good of the boy," Ares answered with ease. "Why else?" A slight tip of the head, a dare. Go *ahead, Goddess. Challenge me.*

"You take me for a fool." Her luscious curves, crafted for the purpose of love, tensed for battle. Cords of muscle throbbed against the creamy skin of her neck, stirring Ares to his own state of throbbing readiness.

"Never, my love. Would you like to come inside and discuss this?"

"What's to discuss? Make it stop." Spittle pooled at the corners of her furious lips. He wanted to lick them clean.

He sank his teeth through the apple's brightly polished skin and pulled a juicy wedge of flesh onto his tongue. She narrowed her eyes. He leaned against the doorjamb, chewing. She would blink first, of this he had no doubt.

With an irritated growl, she tugged open the strings of her gaiascope pouch and consulted the glass. The temptation to peek was great. Ares hadn't checked on Cupid since stoking the boy's battle lust. If the prize weren't so dear, curiosity might have won out.

Aphrodite's expression screwed up with anguish. "You're hurting him!"

Ares shrugged. "There is no pain if he doesn't resist the pull."

"But he is." She held the glass to Ares's view, and he peered inside. There stood Cupid on the bank of the great lake, clutching his chest but not moving his feet. *Huh.*

Ares harrumphed, leaving the boy to his mother's watch. "Then he is a fool."

"Only a fool for love. He's respecting the girl's wishes, even at the cost of his own pain."

"Bah! He should go and take what is his."

"*Nothing* is his unless he can cross the Liminal Point with Psyche."

"Which is exactly why he needs to go to her. *Great Father!* I could smell the pheromones from here!"

"Yes, their attraction is powerful—"

"And Cupid needs to cash in on that. Clearly, *I'm* the only one with the *orchis* to put them in the room together." By all rights, Aphrodite should be kissing his feet right now, not standing here arguing with him. "This might be Cupid's last chance."

"I disagree . . . and so does Hephaestus."

Ares spat out the half-chewed apple in his mouth and tossed the core to the hedge. "Do tell, Goddess. What does my brother have to say about my son's punishment?"

"We *both* believe that Cupid's only chance is gaining the girl's trust. That is never a simple process."

"As we are all painfully aware." Did she honestly believe Ares didn't know she'd betrayed him?

Lowering her gaze, Aphrodite continued. "The girl's faith has been shaken. She needs some space to think things through, and she's asked him to leave her alone in the meantime."

If things had not deteriorated between them, Ares would have cupped her chin just then and drawn her gaze to his. Instead, he tucked his arms over his chest, a reminder to keep his hands to himself. "And what if that 'meantime' turns into forever, *hmm*?"

"I believe in their Love. She'll give him the chance he deserves, and he will win her without trickery or deceit. That's why Heph sent Mercury to retrieve the bow and arrow."

A guffaw escaped him. "Oh, the hypocrisy! Who crafted that arrow and decided to send it down there in the first place? And *who*"—Ares glared into Aphrodite's soul so there could be no misunderstanding—"now has the gall to decry deceit?"

"Oh . . . whatever! This isn't about us anymore." She raised her Earth-glass to her eyes once again. "Great! Now he's picked up Pan's horrible habit of pacing."

Ares pushed off the wall. "Cupid's still holding out?"

Aphrodite shoved the gaiascope toward Ares, and he peered inside. It was true. Flanked by Pan and Reed, Cupid paced the grass, his fist rubbing at his abdomen and his expression twisted in agony. *Huh.* The boy had manned up after all. Ares didn't suppose this would be a good time for I-told-you-so's.

"Happy now?" Aphrodite's raised eyebrows were waiting for Ares on the opposite side of the glass.

No, Ares wasn't happy. His plan had backfired, and he'd come off looking like a brute. Surrendering was his smartest option, but why give up the last of your pride when you'd already lost the war?

"We'll all be happy when Cupid wises up."

Aphrodite lowered the glass and met Ares's gaze without a shred of fear. "Make it stop right now, or I will. I'll not have you use my son's body as a battleground."

"*Our* son. He's mine too. Or have you forgotten?"

"You are no father to Cupid."

"And you, fair goddess, are no paragon of motherhood." *Well, he'd said it out loud.*

She drew up like a cobra about to strike, and he braced himself for the final blow.

"I'm warning you, Ares. Stay out of it. I'll handle this with Cupid's real father, the one who cares about his well-being." She hadn't tried to defend herself, he noticed.

"Need I remind you that neither you nor the husband you cuckolded *yet again* holds a seat on the Council? Your only authority in this situation is by the goodness of my heart, and I'm not feeling so generous anymore."

"I'll take my chances with Athena," she said, stuffing her gaia-scope away into its leather pouch and turning for her chariot. "I expect Cupid to be free of your curse by the time I get home."

33

# STORY TIME

"It stopped."

Reed and Pan blinked at him, their expressions widened by the same disbelief Cupid was feeling. "Just like that?" asked Pan.

"As suddenly as it started."

"So, no pull, no pain?"

Cautiously, Cupid lowered his hand. *Nothing.* He shrugged.

"Okay, that's weird," said Pan.

Reed glanced back and forth between Pan and Cupid. "Maybe because you resisted?"

"Maybe. I don't know," said Cupid. "It felt different this time."

"How so?" asked Pan.

"Like it wasn't my heart pulling me, but anger."

"Anger? At Posey?" Reed asked, sounding somewhat alarmed.

"I guess," Cupid replied. "You know that feeling when you're itching for a fight?"

"Battle lust," said Pan, sharing a knowing glance with Cupid. *Ares.*

"Was it some kind of a test?" asked Reed. "Does the fact it stopped mean you passed or . . .?" Reed swallowed the alternative, along with its possible consequences, leaving them all to the worst of their imaginations.

Pan took up the pacing for all three of them, scrubbing his hand across his beard as he grappled with the puzzling new event. "Could be. No way to know. Maybe someone changed their mind."

"Maybe someone changed someone *else's* mind," Cupid speculated.

"This is good!" said Reed. "Now we have time to get back to the story and develop a strategy." Reed waved the papers in front of Pan, who was still a moving target, and Cupid, who had used up the last of his energy.

"I'm sorry, Reed. I don't think my brain can absorb anything else right now."

Pan clapped a hand on Reed's shoulder. "How about you give us the Twitter version?" When Reed cocked his head, Pan added, "The answer key. We need the answer key."

"I'll do my best. Say, can we get something to eat?"

"I'm sorry, Reed," said Cupid. "I've been completely preoccupied. You probably haven't eaten all day, with the crazy flights."

"You"—Pan wagged his finger at Reed—"start talking while we walk back to the car. We'll grab a bite in town."

"Just make sure we don't accidentally bump into Posey," Cupid warned.

"Right," said Pan. "We'll head in the opposite direction of wherever your gut was trying to take you."

They crossed the road and piled into the rental car—Pan at the wheel, Reed in the passenger seat, and Cupid in the back. Cupid pointed, and they set off.

"Okay, Professor. Enlighten us."

Reed slipped easily into his role. "As we were about to learn, Psyche's beauty is so rare, men all over the world start to worship her instead of the goddess Venus."

Pan piped in, "Areful-cay, Eed-ray."

Reed nodded before continuing. "Venus sends her son Cupid to avenge her by choosing a, quote, 'lowly mate' for Psyche. Meanwhile, Psyche's father becomes concerned and consults an oracle who advises him to take Psyche to a mountain crag where she is to wed a winged serpent. Not wanting to prolong the agony, Psyche hastens to the cliff and prepares to throw herself over. Peering over the edge with her back to Cupid's approach—"

"Just like at Painted Rock!" Cupid said.

"Yes," Reed replied, "but when Cupid comes upon Psyche there, he is so taken by her beauty that he accidentally nicks himself with his own arrow and falls madly in love with her."

"Ah," Cupid said, reliving that rush of emotion he felt when he first set eyes on Posey.

"Psyche is lifted by the Zephyr wind. She awakens on a grassy bank at the entrance of a palace clearly built by gods: ivory ceilings and gold pillars and silver moldings and marble tiles laid out in intricate patterns on the floors."

"Sounds like Ruthie's house!"

Pan sniggered. "It actually does."

"She ventures inside, where a staff of servants assure Psyche everything belongs to her—delicious foods and the finest wines, music produced by unseen instruments, room after room of furnishings fit for a goddess. Sated and exhausted, she retires to her couch and is greeted by a, quote, 'gentle noise,' which turns out to be her unseen bridegroom taking her virginity."

Pan slapped the steering wheel. "Hold the damn phone! Posey's a virgin?"

"Why does that matter?" Cupid asked.

"Dude, we are going to have a whole different kind of talk after story time."

"May I?" said Reed, continuing only after Pan mumbled an apology. "This lover visits her nightly, but she is never permitted to see him or know his true identity. Still, they live happily this way for quite some time, her loneliness relieved by the comfort of his voice and the, quote, 'pressure of his limbs.'"

"*Phew!*" Pan fanned his face comically. "Is it hot in here, or is it just Reed?"

Reed gave his arm a playful slap. "Are you watching the road for a lunch place?"

"Yes, Professor Hangry. I got this. Now tell us more about the pressure of Cupid's loins."

"Limbs! I said limbs!" Shaking his head, Reed swiveled around to face Cupid, now perched at the edge of the seat. "What I wanted to highlight was the love that built between Psyche and Cupid before she knew who he was."

The question Cupid feared most shook out. "And then?"

"And then," Reed said, holding Cupid in his gentle gaze, "as these tales are wont to do, this one grows dark. All this time, Psyche's family has presumed her dead by the winged serpent of the oracle's prophecy. When the sisters go searching for her remains, Psyche wants to reassure them she's alive and well, but her still-unseen husband warns that doing so will eventually bring about the destruction of their marriage."

"Lemme guess," said Pan, shaking his head.

"Mm," Reed answered absently, flipping through his papers. "There's a lovely passage here where Psyche persuades her husband to let her meet with her sisters. May I read it to you?"

"Go for it, Professor. And FYI, we're here." Pan pulled into a parking space at a sandwich shop and turned off the car. Nobody moved to get out.

Reed found his place and began: "Pressing luxurious kisses on him, whispering soft words and intertwining her limbs, she wooed him with passionate caresses. He fell, conquered by the power of love, and promised all."

Touched by the poetry, Cupid sighed. "That's beautiful."

Pan spun in his seat. "You do realize that was the kiss of death for Cupid, right?"

"Come," said Reed. "Food first, and then we'll deal with the rest."

During their meal, Cupid learned that the envious sisters convinced Psyche she had indeed married the hideous serpent and that her only course of action was to cut off his head while he slept. Armed with a sharp knife and an oil lamp, Psyche looked upon her husband for the first time and discovered the beautiful, winged Cupid.

"And then?" asked Pan.

"There's a scuffle, a drop of hot oil spills on Cupid's shoulder, and he flees. Psyche tries to follow him and falls from a window."

"She *dies?*" Cupid wailed.

"No!" Reed quickly assured him. "But she's bereft, and she attempts to drown herself . . . until none other than Pan convinces her to fight for her love."

Pan straightened his shoulders. "I'm not even a little surprised I turn out to be the hero of this story."

"And so humble too!" Cupid laughed.

"Hang on," said Reed, wiping the crumbs off his fingers before flipping through the booklet. "You guys are going to love this passage."

Pan shot Cupid a wink while Reed found his place.

"Okay. Here's Pan convincing Psyche not to kill herself: 'Do not try to throw yourself from a precipice, nor by any other means to seek a violent death. Dry your tears and pursue Cupid, the greatest of the gods'"—Reed grinned but did not look up from his papers—"'for he is young and voluptuous and may be persuaded by your charms,' which, I think we can all agree, you definitely are."

"Naturally, Psyche takes my fabulous advice and runs back to grovel at Cupid's feet and they live happily ever after."

"Almost," said Reed. "By now, Cupid is home nursing his wounds, and it's Venus who requires the groveling—and a whole list of tasks she's sure Psyche can't possibly complete."

"But she does?" Cupid asked hopefully.

"Long story short—"

Pan huffed. "That ship sailed two hours ago!"

Reed gazed across the table into Cupid's worried eyes and nodded. "She does."

"And?" Pan raised his wide-open arms.

"And Psyche is eventually welcomed and made Cupid's immortal wife."

Cupid released a tense breath. "Thank the gods!"

"Yes," said Reed, with far less enthusiasm.

Pan snuck an anxious glance at Cupid before pushing Reed for more. "But?"

"It's a bit premature for celebrations," Reed said with a sigh. "Your Posey seems destined for the same treacherous path until you are willing to reveal your most treasured secret—that you are Cupid, God of Love."

Cupid turned sharply to Pan. "Are you okay with this?"

"I don't disagree with Reed's logic. You're going to need to go all in—but *carefully*." Frowning, Pan added, "The last thing we want is for Posey to have you committed to a mental hospital, and she totally could."

Cupid did not like the sound of that.

"True," said Reed, "but then, what better leap of Love to show your gods above?"

Reed was right. Pan was right too. Cupid turned the old tale and his friends' advice and the decision he needed to make over and over until he couldn't make sense of it anymore.

"Every choice feels wrong."

Pushing aside the plastic tray holding his sandwich wrapper and empty drink, Reed clasped his hands in front of him. "Meet Posey in person. Remind her why she couldn't stop thinking about that man in the woods."

Pan shifted into the corner of the booth, angling his body to better take in Reed, seated next to him. "You're saying Q should seduce her?"

"Yes, *but*"—Reed broke off with a stern look at Pan—"still as 'Q,' the man who opened her heart to love."

"Even if Posey gives me that chance, and it works, I'll still be stuck on the Cupid piece."

"But she will be stuck *with* you, don't you see?" Reed asked, gazing back and forth between Cupid and Pan, who were exchanging blank stares.

"We'd like to buy a vowel, please."

Cupid didn't get the joke, but Reed chuckled. "Right. Okay. It's one thing for Posey to understand intellectually that her man in the woods was actually Q, but being in your presence *while* relating to you as Q will help her internalize that connection, and she'll be emotionally invested in making it work. That's when you tell her everything—gently."

Pan snorted. "Yes, do be gentle while dropping a house on your mortal's head."

Reed elbowed Pan's side. "Some of us do survive it."

"Only one of you, so far," Pan said, "but of course, we're all hoping for Posey to be number two."

Cupid's phone bleeped with a text notification, and he whipped it out of his pocket. "I just got a text from Posey."

"Good," Pan said. "At least she didn't ghost you."

Ever the calm counterbalance, Reed asked, "What does it say?"

"It says: 'If you want to talk, I'll meet you for coffee tomorrow morning. But first, text me your real name before 7 tonight.'"

"Oh dear," said Reed.

"In other words," Pan said, "*fuck.*"

34

# FOLLOWING HER GUT

"Flip a coin," Posey would tell her patients when they couldn't decide between two choices. While the coin hovers in the air, we realize what we really want.

And so it was that evening between 5:24 (when she'd sent Q the text demanding his name) and 5:29 (when he'd answered) that Posey Rey found out exactly how badly she wanted Mr. Handsome and Q to get their collective act together and convince her they were worth all the trouble—starting with coming clean on the name.

*Quentin Arrows, my ass.* It had taken a mere two-minute background search to learn there was no such person.

Posey would never have pushed a patient to reveal his identity. Anonymity was the foundation of her work, but that was where Posey and Dr. Rey diverged. Posey had a right to know what she was dealing with before she put herself in a room with the guy.

When his text came in, Posey was mindful of her heart's heavy thud against her chest. Q's response did not line up with her wishes.

*I understand your request. I would very much prefer to tell you my name in person tomorrow.*

"What the actual fuck!" she yelled at unhearing words on her screen. Posey tossed her phone onto the couch and went to the kitchen to pour herself a big glass of wine. As she returned the recorked bottle to the fridge, she made no promises she wouldn't be back for refills.

"What the hell are you hiding, Q?"

She set down her glass on the stone mantel and scraped one of the long fireplace matches along the box's sandpaper edge. Lighting the Rey family fire had always been her father's job. Therefore, it brought Posey a unique sense of self-sufficiency to manage the wood-carrying and log-poking and fire-wrangling without a man's help. The flame at the tip of her match met yesterday's junk mail, carefully tucked between the logs. The fire flared instantly but thinned as it widened, as if the fire were as uninspired by the bills and solicitations as Posey had been. She grabbed the bellows and pumped some air from below to throw the flame onto the dry twigs she'd gathered for tinder. The flames flickered and jumped and eventually found purchase in the medium-sized logs. Confident the fire could now sustain itself, Posey traded in her bellows and poker for the wine she'd neglected.

Sitting her bum down on the bearskin rug, she shimmied backward until her spine met the ottoman. She sipped her wine, then gazed through the Chardonnay at the flames, turning everything a murky yellow-orange. Clarity was nowhere to be found this evening, it seemed.

*What to do, what to do . . .* He'd failed to honor her request. She'd be well within her rights to end it right here. She owed him nothing, not even the chance he'd squandered.

*Jesus,* why wouldn't he give her his damn name?

Sex offender sprang to mind first, and a chill shuddered down her back despite the heat from her now-roaring fire. Though she hated herself for it, her mind followed that stark path through half the glass of wine. Did the pathology of a typical sex offender line up with what she knew of Q? He hadn't struck her as narcissistic—quite the opposite, actually. His empathy felt real. Oddly, considering his recent trio of rejections, his self-esteem appeared to be remarkably robust. But then, she couldn't ignore the history of troubled relationships, attachment issues with both parents, the fact that he was a late bloomer . . . *sigh*. Could there be some sexual dysfunction he hadn't confessed? She couldn't rule it out.

What about some other searchable criminal record? Couldn't have been too serious if he was out on the street now, in his early thirties. An incarceration could explain the lack of opportunity that resulted in his romantic innocence. Ah, but how could she forget? Q was the self-proclaimed expert on love! *Christ!* She threw back the rest of the wine and headed to the kitchen for more.

The puzzle tugged at her as she wriggled the cork free, and she knew she'd never be able to let this one go without solving the riddle of Q. Decision made, her father's oft-repeated warning rang in her ears: "*You know what curiosity did to the cat, Posey girl.*"

"Okay, Q. If you won't tell me your name, I'm gonna make you work for this."

She settled into a cozy corner of the couch and took a healthy swig before trading in her wineglass for her phone. She tapped out her first text, an opening volley. **Why?**

His answer was swift but not exactly instructive. ***I'd rather you meet me as a man without everything that goes with the name.***

She read it over and over again. "Meet me as a man." *How*

*else?* "Everything that goes with the name." *The* name, not *my* name? Some family name she was supposed to recognize?

Could it be about money? Posey huffed. "Dude, if you're filthy rich, just wait till you find out how little I care."

What was he trying to say? What was he trying *not* to say? She was going mad!

A new explanation struck Posey, so foreign to her, it made her laugh out loud. Maybe he was a celebrity—*a movie star?* Oh, he had the pretty face, without a doubt, and the body to match, and the whole incognito lifestyle fit the profile, but wouldn't she or April have recognized him if he was so famous?

**You're famous**, she typed. Holding her breath, she sent the message.

He responded right away. **Posey, I promise to tell you my name when we meet tomorrow morning. Please give me that chance.**

Whatever he was or wasn't, Q deflected like a pro. He wasn't budging on this. Fuck. Now, she was stuck. "Fine," she said aloud, "give him a chance. But don't be stupid about it." If he cared about her the way he said he did, he wouldn't want her to put herself in peril.

She put the question to him. **How do I know it's safe to meet you?**

The answer he gave wasn't half bad. **You set the terms. I will meet you wherever you say. Bring a friend if you need to.**

He'd already ruined Painted Rock for her and invaded the sanctity of her shower. She wasn't about to give up the Daily Grind too. She'd choose a place she could willingly never frequent again. As for the friend part, Posey didn't have a friend like that, not here anyway. She'd arrive early and get a table in plain view of the counter. If their meeting didn't go well, they would part ways.

But he knew where she lived. Life in the deep woods had its disadvantages for a single woman. How did she know he wouldn't continue to stalk her?

Posey hated revealing her fear, but she needed to know his response to the real question, the one he'd understand because she'd told him all about Evan. So she typed it—*What if we meet and I decide I don't want you in my life?*—and sent it before she chickened out.

This response was his swiftest yet. *Then I will leave Lake Tahoe and you will never see or hear from me again.*

Welp. That was the right answer, the only answer, but it wrapped around her heart and squeezed. *And how do I know I can believe you?* She was grasping at straws, and she knew it. Would she ask a serial killer how to avoid his clutches?

*You asked me not to contact you earlier and I didn't. Not a word. Not a glimpse.*

"Seriously?" She barked out a laugh at his effort. "Four whole hours? Should we give you a damn trophy?"

Having spent her sarcasm on the outburst, Posey was able to deliver a gentler response. *One afternoon is not a terribly long time.*

He sent back an emoji, one of those anguished faces that moved from yellow to blue to green, followed by a message that sounded very much like the Q she'd come to know. *I disagree. It was for me. Longest of my life.*

"Yeah, it was right up there for me too, pal." There was nothing further to be gained from making them both twist in their nooses.

She sent her final message. *See you tomorrow at 9 at Café Carnelian. Bring your ID.*

She waited, finger on the lock button, for his response. *Thank you, Posey.* Just as she was about to push the button, another message came through—a heart emoji.

# Q IS FOR CUPID

The parking lot of Café Carnelian was crowded. Finding the closest open spot around the side of the building, Cupid pulled the rental car neatly between the lines.

"She's already here," said Cupid, tensed over the steering wheel.

Beside him, Reed glanced at the windowless brick wall. "You're sure?"

"I heard her from the main road. Her echo beat is louder than ten Stentors."

"That's loud," Reed said, a warm smile in his voice. Reaching across the front seat, Reed gently placed his hand on Cupid's arm. "Turn off the engine, Q. Breathe."

Cupid released a juddering breath. "Right."

"I'm ready when you are, but take your time. You have six minutes."

"I can't wait another second." He'd waited an eternity already. Cupid reached for the handle.

"Q." Cupid halted at Reed's urgent tone and turned back to meet his waiting gaze. "I know you're eager to get through this, but please try to keep in mind how anxious Posey must be right now. It's . . . different for a woman, no matter what. That's not fair, but that's how it is. Do you understand what I'm saying?"

Cupid's gaze slipped to Reed's ruined leg and the fingers clutching his cane. "Reed, I am nothing like that terrible man. You know I'd never in a trillion years hurt Posey, right?"

Reed was quick to reassure him. "Of course I know that, but Posey doesn't."

Yes, she'd told him as much yesterday. *How do I know it's safe to meet you?* His heart had nearly torn in two.

"Thank you, Reed. I appreciate the reminder," Cupid said with a solemn nod. "And thank you for coming with me today. I hope Pan isn't upset he had to stay back."

"No. After some guided self-reflection, he realized that his passion might not have been entirely productive in this morning's enterprise."

"Agreed."

Reed's plodding shuffle tested Cupid's patience though it served as a reminder, too, of his own warning to Pan about Reed's fragility. Cupid grabbed the massive wood door handle and waited for Reed to catch up before chasing the cold November air into the café.

Posey raised her head toward the open door and locked eyes with Cupid. Her anxiety was palpable from across the busy room, but so too was her desire for him. Through the pleasant bouquet of coffee and fresh-baked pastry came the far more enticing aroma of Posey's attraction. Cupid pulled it into his lungs as he strode toward her table.

*Gods,* but she was a vision—a living, breathing work of art! Even more beautiful than she'd appeared on Painted Rock, or maybe it was just that she didn't turn away this time. Her wavy brown hair spilled from a woolen cap with a big, fluffy ball on top, and she had yet to remove her puffy blue coat though she was already seated with a cup of coffee. Posey was prepared to make a hasty exit.

The longer he was allowed to gaze at her, the more deeply her beauty touched him. No painter could have created more perfect tones than the honey-kissed warmth of her cheeks or the deep caramel of her eyes. No sculptor could have chiseled a more perfect composition of forehead and eyes and nose and lips and chin than the delicate artistry of her face.

A sharp rap at the back of Cupid's leg made him twist around to find Reed mouthing the words *Slow down.*

Right.

Cupid slowed to a stroll but still outpaced Reed to Posey's table. Their heartbeats aligned in perfect precision, one's *tha-thump* starting exactly where the other's left off, pitch and volume attuned so as to make one beat indistinguishable from the next. For all his musical gifts, Apollo himself had never inspired a more harmonious duet.

Cupid ached to tell her she was the most beautiful woman he'd ever met, but he was sure she would discount his compliment along with everything else he needed her to believe. *Another time.* "Hello, Posey."

Posey rose, woodenly, arms folded over her chest. "Hello, Q." Her voice shook. She seemed to be struggling as much as Cupid to hold back a flood of emotions.

Despite his burning need to wrap her in his arms and rejoice, Cupid pushed his hands into the pockets of the fleece jacket he was wearing to fit in with the mortals. "Thank you for meeting me."

Her gaze shifted as Reed reached Cupid's side. "And you are . . . ?"

"Reed Scully," he said, switching his cane to his left hand to offer his right. Cupid watched with envy as she placed her hand in Reed's and allowed him the first touch.

"You're Pan's partner."

A lover's smile bloomed on Reed's face. "That's right."

"Is Pan here too?" She craned her neck to peer around the two of them.

"No," said Reed. "He's back at the motel. And don't worry about me. I won't get in your way."

"Well, it was very nice of you to come to support your friend."

Reed leaned in. "Please allow me to double as a character reference for this fine young man, if one is needed."

"I'll keep that in mind." Posey released him with a charming smile.

Reed nodded. "May I get either of you a coffee?"

"Thanks, I'm all set," said Posey.

"I better not," said Cupid.

"All right, then." Reed squeezed Cupid's arm as he walked behind him toward the counter.

Wasting no time, Posey placed one hand on her hip and extended the other, palm up. "I'll take that ID, please." Whatever warmth Reed had won from Posey left with him.

Cupid sighed. "It's not my real name, Posey."

"Humor me."

"Of course." He pulled his wallet out of his back pocket, worked the driver's license from its sleeve, and handed it to her.

A puzzled look came over her face. "Huh." She glanced up at Cupid's face, then back down at the photo. She held it up to the light and tilted it this way and that. She might have been examining a newborn for all its fingers and toes. "Why does the Indiana Bureau of Motor Vehicles believe your name is Quentin Arrows?"

"Because Pan is very good at his job."

"Your best friend is a forger? What's Reed? A fence?"

The idea of Reed dancing around waving a sword almost made Cupid giggle. "No, Reed's a professor, and someone else makes all the cards for Pan."

"All the cards? *Jesus.* What are you, a drug lord with a drawerful of fake IDs and passports from twenty different countries?"

"No, Posey. All I have is this driver's license, one credit card, a health insurance card, and two gym memberships."

"Right." Her gaze rolled down his chest before snapping to his eyes again. "But Quentin Arrows doesn't exist."

"No, not really."

"Never mind." Shaking her head, she thrust his license toward his open wallet. As Cupid slipped it inside, Posey grabbed her phone from the table and snapped a picture of him, then proceeded to tap and swipe her phone.

"Now what are you doing?" Cupid asked, peering at her screen.

"Searching Google Images for your face."

"You're not gonna find—"

"Oh! Look at that! Quentin Arrows, hero of Tarra, Indiana." She flashed the screen toward Cupid. "Huh. At least you were telling me the truth about saving those three little boys."

"Yes, that's all true. But Posey, my name isn't Quentin Arrows."

"All right." She swiped the news story from her phone and tapped her finger into the search bar to clear it. "You have exactly ten seconds to give me a name that checks out, or I'm outta here, and we are through." Finger poised, Posey was acting tough, but he could tell the effort was taking its toll.

"Posey, could we possibly sit down?"

"Nope. Nine . . ."

Cupid gestured to her phone. "You're not going to need that."

"No? Why not? Eight . . ."

"Because you're going to recognize my name."

"Kinda cocky aren't ya? Seven . . ."

"No, I don't think so."

"Six seconds, pal. Five, four, three. . ."

*Tha-thump, Tha-thump.* This could be it. He might vanish or . . .

"Two, one . . ."

He pinched his eyes together. "I'm Cupid."

Cautiously, he opened one eye. He was still in the café, and Posey was still standing in front of him, and she looked even more exasperated than before.

"Excuse me?"

He leaned in, repeating himself quietly but firmly. "I said I'm Cupid."

"*The* Cupid?"

"Yes."

"That's your final answer?" Oh, they had definitely not crossed. "It's the truth."

Her mouth twisted with anger. He'd realized the god revelation would be a challenge for her, possibly insurmountable, but it was necessary. "Did you honestly show up here just to feed me this bullshit line?"

"No, Posey, I was hoping to—"

"What kind of a sick joke is this? I'm done!"

Quaking with fury, she pushed past him. Cupid's reflexes were faster. He stepped diagonally backward and placed his body in her path.

"Posey, please don't leave like this!" He reached for her hands, and she snapped back as if scorched by fire.

"Don't touch me!" Her eyes were wide with fear and rage.

"I'm sorry. Sorry, sorry, sorry." This was all going so wrong, and he didn't know how to stop it. If Posey walked out, he wouldn't get another chance. He'd promised her that much.

"Whoa! Hey! You okay, miss?"

They both turned toward the voice behind the counter to find a very big man who looked ready—and honestly, quite eager—to jump the counter and pound Cupid into the floor. Reed had stood too, cane in hand, prepared to defend Cupid with all the big words in his arsenal. Cupid's stomach lurched. If anything happened to Reed, he'd never forgive himself.

Holding up her hand to the big man, she nodded. He nodded back and returned to his customers.

"I'm so sorry, Posey. I promise I won't touch you again."

"Damn right you won't."

Cupid shoved his hands into his coat pockets again. "Okay?" She nodded.

"Look," Cupid said with the calmest voice he could muster, considering his entire life and Posey's hung in the balance, "you said you would give me a chance to explain if I told you my name, and I did that. So may I have my chance? Please?"

As she studied him and considered his plea, the anger seemed to seep out of her. "As long as *you*"—she jabbed a finger toward his chest—"remember the rest of the deal. I say 'go,' and you are outta here on the next flight."

"Yes. Absolutely." More likely, he'd be straight up to Mount O on Mercury's back, but either way, he'd be gone. "Can we please sit down?"

"Fine." She returned to the seat where her abandoned coffee was sitting.

He wanted to offer her a new drink, but he didn't want to interrupt the footing he'd finally gained, weak though it was. He pulled out the chair across from her and sat down.

"So? *Talk.*" This was definitely not his gentle, diplomatic Posey, but she was in there under the fear and hurt and anger.

"I'm trying to figure out where to begin," he said.

"How about answering a question for me, then, while you figure that out?"

"Of course. Ask me anything."

"Have you ever been admitted to a mental hospital?" she asked.

"No. I told you that on my Wings application."

"I figured it was worth revisiting some of the facts, seeing as you did leave out a rather massive detail about your identity." Her tone was not encouraging, but as long as they were both still here, there was hope.

"No, to the mental hospital question."

"But you say you're Cupid."

"I am."

"Well, I guess I can see why you wouldn't want to write that down on your intake survey. Aren't you supposed to have wings?" He detected a hint of amusement.

"I do—*did*. They disintegrated while I was falling."

"Falling from . . .?"

"Mount Olympus."

"Of course. So, you're a . . . *what*? A fallen angel?"

"Not an angel, a god."

"Right, right. Sorry. And do gods often go slipping off Mount Olympus?" At least she found him entertaining.

"Never. I was pushed."

"Who would push the god of love off Mount Olympus?"

"My mother."

"Aah! Your mother . . . Now, that would be Venus, right?

"She goes by Aphrodite since the Great Syncretism." When Posey returned a confused expression, he added, "Yes. Venus, Aphrodite, one and the same."

"Wow, okay. And here, I thought we were just dealing with a garden variety borderline personality disorder." Cupid didn't understand the term, but he was pretty sure his mother wouldn't like it.

He leaned forward, hands locked in his pockets. "Please be careful how you talk about my mother." He found himself speaking softly even though it made no difference whether he whispered or shouted.

"Why?"

"Because it's dangerous. She can hear you."

Her eyes popped wide. "Right now?"

"Yes, if she's watching us."

Posey's eyes darted around the room. "Is she?"

"I don't know. I can't see her."

"Is she . . . *invisible?*"

Cupid reminded himself to be patient. This was all a lot to take in, and Posey had been taught the gods weren't real. She didn't know any better.

"Mother is not invisible. She's just not here. She's on Mount Olympus. She has a special glass she can look through to see Earth."

"A glass that sees through plaster ceilings and whatever this roof is made of?"

"It goes through everything. Hephaestus made it for her."

Posey pushed her coffee mug to the side. "Okay, I'm officially off caffeine. Let's go back to why your mother pushed you off Mount Olympus."

He figured they'd get to this eventually, but he'd rather hoped Posey would have come to know and love the man Cupid had become before learning about the obnoxious flying pain in everyone's backside he'd been before. "Because I had aggravated Hera and Hades, and the Divine Council was called in to decide my sentence. And then Ares came up with the idea—"

"Ares, the God of War?"

"Yes. Also my father."

"Wow. I really need to study up on my mythology."

"Reed can teach you anything you want to know."

"Because he's a professor," she said, nodding.

"A professor of the classics. Well, a former professor. He hasn't worked since his accident."

"Does he know? That you're"—she leaned in and whispered—"Cupid?"

Cupid followed Posey's gaze to where Reed was sitting, watching, fully aware they were both staring at him. "Yes. Should I ask him to join us?"

"Maybe later. Let's talk more about why you're here."

"I was sent to Earth to fix Love. First, I had to help Mia, then Ruthie, then Pan, and now you."

"Wow." She gathered her thoughts, and folding her hands on the table, Posey formed a tight smile with her perfect lips. "I don't mean to sound ungrateful, *Cupid*, but I don't need you or your mom trying to fix my love life, okay? Actually, I don't need a love life at all. So, thank you, but no thank you."

A grin tugged at Cupid's lips, and before he knew it, he was shaking his head and smiling ear to ear.

"Why in the world are you smiling right now?"

"I think I might have said the exact same thing to you when you insisted on trying to help me."

Her mouth dropped open. She said nothing for several long moments as the two sat blinking into each other's eyes. For the first time since Cupid had entered the café, he felt she was truly able to hear him.

"I'm curious, Posey. Do you feel you made the right decision when you reached out to me after I visited Dr. Fairlawn?"

"Yes. A hundred percent. I needed to know you were okay."

"Even when it meant breaking your own rules? Reopening old wounds and sharing painful memories from your own past?"

"Yes. I really believed you needed my help. I couldn't turn my back on you."

"And that is exactly why I'm here now, 'spilling my last gut,' as Pan would say, trusting you with all my secrets, secrets that could get me in all kinds of trouble if you choose to use them against me."

Their gazes locked, his challenge lodged but unanswered. He freed his hands from his pockets. How he would have loved to stretch across the table and take her hands in his, but he settled for clasping them in his own lap.

"So here we both are," Cupid said. "Two people who—"

"One person and one god," she said, her mouth lifting into a smirk. "Just staying with the theme here." She was poking fun at him, but Cupid didn't mind, because Posey didn't look scared or angry anymore.

"Okay," he answered, allowing himself a matching smirk. "One person and one god who desperately wanted to help each other, and if you're honest with yourself, Posey, I think you'll admit we were doing just that. You helped me over my heartache, and I opened your heart to love again. It was just a start, but it was something."

Her expression turned serious. "Yes. You were a kind, sympathetic voice on the phone. A total stranger I'd never meet. Someone I could talk to without being judged. It was nice. You were lovely."

*Gods*, how he ached to hold her. "That voice on the phone is still me, you know."

"I'm still trying to reconcile all the different . . . Q's."

"Look, Posey, I know you think all this talk of gods is crazy, and that's okay for now. I just really needed you to know the truth."

She studied him for several terrifying thumps of their hearts before saying anything else. "I'm going to be honest with you, Q. I don't believe in *a* god, let alone many gods, and frankly, the jury's still way out on love, but I do believe *you* believe all of it. After hearing everything you've said, I'm pretty comfortable you're not a danger to yourself or anyone else. And if I'm being *totally* honest, I like you. Probably a little too much."

Cupid's heart soared. "Does that mean I don't have to leave?"

"Not yet. I have a lot more questions for you." With that, she pulled off her hat, set it down on the table, and ran her fingers through her brown waves. Standing, she took off her coat and arranged it over the back of her chair. "But I do think we should both stick to decaf."

36

# THE MAN WHO BELIEVED
# HE WAS CUPID

Posey's alluring but delusionary companion stood swiftly and draped his coat over the chair across from hers. Underneath it, he wore the most ordinary, plain blue T-shirt over the most ordinary pair of jeans. He might have blended in with any crowd of hikers or ski rats or cyclists throwing back a beer at the end of the day but for the otherworldly beauty that set him apart like an actor in the only spotlight on a pitch-black stage. It wasn't so easy to breathe, strolling up to the counter next to this guy who claimed to be an actual Greek god (or was it Roman?) even though he was keeping a careful distance as per Posey's demand, his hands shoved into the front pockets of his nicely fitting jeans.

*I am mindful of a powerful biological response to the drop-dead gorgeous man walking next to me: a flutter in my belly, sweaty palms, a pleasant buzz in my head, a weakening of the knees, a tug of want in my nether regions. (Deep breath in, deep breath out.)*

Mr. Handsome believed he was a god.

*I do not have to act on these feelings. I can observe and watch them flow through me without judgment.* (Deep breath in, deep breath out.)

And the man's eyes? Iridescent, layered, the shimmery surface of a deep, deep ocean. *I am aware of feeling captivated by those eyes.*

As they approached the counter, Reed-the-former-classics-professor swiveled on his stool. Posey read anxiety behind the wire-rimmed frames as Reed's gaze bounced back and forth between Posey and the man who believed he was Cupid.

"Anything I can do?" Reed asked. *You might try not enabling him,* Posey could have answered had the two been alone.

Q smiled as he clapped a hand on Reed's shoulder. "We're getting some coffee."

"Oh!" Reed brightened considerably. "Excellent. I'll update Pan."

Pan. She'd thought the name a bit unusual, but up to this moment, she hadn't even considered connecting it with the satyr from Greek myth. She gawped at Reed, Pan's lover, while profane, horror-movie-worthy images ran through her head. Surely this man's partner wasn't half goat?

"Can I get you something to eat with your decaf?" Q asked as they stepped into line.

"Hmm? No, I'm good. And you don't have to buy my coffee." This wasn't a date, and even if it were, Posey was never much for the traditional, male-provider role.

"I'd like to, if that's okay?" He pulled out his wallet again.

There was a generosity about the gesture that touched Posey well beyond his offer to pay, something so open and innocent about the way he moved through the world. She'd put him through the wringer, and he hadn't balked once. She was certain he would have handed over his cell phone password without a second thought.

Posey's heart went out to him. No wonder he'd been wounded so deeply. The world could be awfully cruel to such a vulnerable soul. Here was a man who required Posey's compassion, not her fear.

"Sure. Thank you," she said, then registering his delight, she allowed a playful moment, inclining her head toward his so as not to be overheard. "Hey, that's not counterfeit money you're passing around, is it?"

"Knowing Pan, it could be." His rich laughter bounced off Posey and gave her goose bumps. Their first private joke.

*I am aware of a giddy, swoony crush.*

And Posey wasn't alone in that, judging by the froth her companion had kicked up all around them. Q turned heads, which was understandable—the man truly was unfairly gorgeous—but the response seemed, well, exceptional, especially for a sleepy Sunday morning. It wasn't Posey's imagination. Many other customers—girls, mostly—laughed a little too loud, stood a little too close, stared a little too long.

Settling in together at their table with their steaming mugs of coffee had the feel of returning home after a shared adventure. Après-ski, minus the skiing. *I am mindful of insanely romantic scenarios crowding my thoughts.*

"I'm ready for your questions," Q said. There he went again, inviting her into his secrets.

Questions, questions . . . she had so many for him, it was impossible to know where to start. "Okay, so you explained about the wings"—*do not roll your eyes*—"but why doesn't the rest of you look like the Cupid I know?"

Amusement crinkled the corners of his eyes. "What Cupid do you know?"

"A chubby little cherub, flying around in a diaper, firing off arrows every which way?"

"Ouch!" He chuckled, slapping a hand against his chest.

"You asked," Posey said with a shrug. It would have been a whole hell of a lot easier to stay objective if he'd looked like that, not like this being who might have been handcrafted to Posey's "ideal man" specifications.

"Even before my fall, I didn't look like that hideous, winged toddler I keep seeing around. I don't know who down here decided to portray me so unflatteringly, but I reached my fourteenth year before my body stopped aging on Mount Olympus."

"You seem to have, uh . . . matured . . . well past fourteen now." *Jesus Christ, Posey. You're acting like a silly teenager yourself.*

He smiled at her awkward blush. "That happened when I fell." He leaned forward as if to share a secret, and she found herself meeting him halfway. "I was pretty excited about it, to tell you the truth. Being freed from that useless body definitely has its advantages." Eyes dancing with glee, he drew his coffee to his lips and left Posey to read between the lines: *all the sex.*

She remembered wondering why he'd only recently lost his virginity at thirty-three. This explanation certainly fit. His story was cohesive, if nothing else.

"Well, you must be having yourself a grand old time."

"You won't hear me complaining . . ." He chuckled to himself as he set down his mug. "But it's not like I have so much free time to do whatever I want. They're keeping me pretty busy with my punishment."

"I'm your punishment?"

"No!" Both of his hands flew up like a man about to be hit by an oncoming truck. "You're not like the others. I thought you would be, but when I found you in the woods, I knew—"

"Yes, can we talk about that? How did you find me? How long have you been stalking me? Did you register on Wings as a ploy to draw me out? Was this whole thing one big, fat lie from the start?" She caught up on her breathing at the end of her rant.

*Tell me, Q, how big of a fool am I anyway?*

"No, Posey," he answered softly, looking very much like the truck had hit him after all. "I told you, I was wrecked over Pan." Q glanced over at Reed, then let out a small huff. Clearly, the two held nothing but fondness for each other. *An odd response toward the man who stole his lover away.* "Reed thought it would help me to talk to someone, but Pan wouldn't allow it."

It took all of Posey's restraint not to launch into a lecture on macho men and therapy shaming. "Sorry, but why is Pan in charge of your mental health?"

Q's gaze dropped to his mug, both hands wrapped around it again. "Pan's in charge of everything while I'm here."

*Wow. Svengali much?*

"Well, that's troubling, especially considering your history."

Q's head whipped up. "Pan's my best friend. He was only looking out for me. And when Reed found Wings, Pan did agree to let me talk to you online."

"Big of him."

"I wasn't stalking you or anything, Posey. I was just so sad, and it seemed like you were the only one who could help me. And then you did, even if you don't believe that."

"Ah yes, Posey Rey's magical miracle cure." *Nobody's that good.*

A soft huff escaped Q. "We didn't understand it either at the time."

Ignoring his disconcerting use of "we," Posey asked, "And now?"

Q met her gaze full on. "And now, I realize I was already in love with you. I just didn't know it yet."

Posey's hackles stood on end. "You loved me? Before we'd even spoken on the phone?"

"I knew you wouldn't believe me," he said. His defeat rang in her ears. It was painful to pull the scales from someone's eyes, the hardest part of her job but maybe the kindest.

"So you decided to fly out here and prove it to me?"

He seemed surprised by her conclusion. "That's not what happened." Taking a deep breath, he folded his hands on the table. "When you called me and said you couldn't talk to me anymore, I was very disappointed, but I accepted your decision. Then, I got your email about the other doctors, and . . . this thing happened to me." A pained expression crossed his face.

"This thing? Can you say more?"

"Yes. I came here today to tell you the truth, and that's what I'm going to do." Posey followed Q's right hand to his chest again. He fisted his shirt between tensed fingers. "My punishment from the gods starts up like an engine inside my heart and pulls me in a very definite direction. If I don't follow the signal, it gets very unpleasant."

*Points for the creative twist on hearing voices but dangerous just the same.*

"My email started your heart engine?"

"Yes."

"Because you thought you loved me?"

Something flashed behind his eyes—hurt that she didn't believe his story? Pity that she couldn't share his happy fantasy? "No," he said evenly. "I didn't know that yet."

"I'm sorry, I don't follow how that email landed you here. Are you saying your heart engine brought you all the way out to Lake Tahoe?"

"No, we were too far apart. I first had to follow the signal through Dr. Chan and Dr. Fairlawn." *So that was the justification his subconscious had provided him for going to see Wes and April—the gods were punishing him, and he had no choice.* "After speaking with

Dr. Fairlawn, I felt sure I was meant to find you. Pan helped me find your address."

"But you didn't find me at my address. You found me miles away, deep in the woods."

"I'm so sorry if that scared you, Posey. Once we landed in Reno, my heart pulled me directly to Painted Rock." *Which would explain how he found her in the middle of nowhere—if it weren't so completely outlandish.* "Pan and I drove as far as we could, but then we had to rent bikes, and Pan had to teach me how to use the gears and the brakes."

"Wait, that was your first time on a mountain bike, and you just hopped onto one of the most challenging routes on the trail?"

"I'm a quick learner." *And maybe those two gym memberships came in handy.* "Anyway, I didn't even know for sure it was you I was riding toward until you turned around and looked at me. Your face matched the picture from our chat."

"Yeah, so does yours." And here she'd thought that perfect face too good to be true.

"Did you notice we both picked the same lips?" he asked.

"Cupid's bow," she said, nodding. "Quite the irony."

While they studied each other's mouths, both unfurled into full, matching smiles. She couldn't help imagining how perfectly they would line up when pressed together. The thought made her woozy. *Get a grip, Po.*

"Look, I have to be honest with you, too. I'm having trouble buying this heart signal story." Spell broken. Nothing killed the mood quicker than a cold, clinical dissection of the psyche, and the man in front of her had basically offered up his mind to science.

He slouched against the back of his chair, smile mostly wiped away. "Okay. Why don't you tell me how I found you at the top of a secluded mountain trail in the middle of nowhere?"

She huffed. "Hey, you're the one with nefarious connections. I have no idea what this friend of yours is capable of. Maybe you figured out how to track my cell phone . . . or my Fitbit. Or maybe your family members in outer space have their sights set on me, and they're feeding you information via satellite from Mars."

"That last one actually makes sense," Cupid said, cracking a grin. "My explanation sounds almost boring now."

The suggestion earned him a genuine smile from Posey. "Boring is not a word I would associate with you. I have many other words you probably don't care to hear, but that's not one of them."

"Oh, I don't know. I think I might like to hear some of them." *Ugh, is that a damn dimple in his cheek?* "You know what I'd really like to hear about, Posey? That man you saw on the mountain."

"You mean, you?"

"Before you knew he was me. When you were telling me about your encounter, you said something passed between you."

Feeling the heat spread to her cheeks, she glanced away. "I can't talk to you about that. It's too weird."

"Okay. Can you tell me about *now*?"

She swiveled back to meet his gaze. "What about now?"

"Do you feel that 'something' between us right now?"

She attempted to laugh off his question, but her blush had already given her away. "Sure. Me and half the customers in this place."

"Excuse me?"

"You haven't noticed everyone has been jockeying for your attention since you walked in?"

"Have they?"

She laughed, shaking her head. "Seriously? You haven't noticed?"

"Honestly, Posey, it's taking all of my concentration to keep up with this conversation."

"Eh, whatever. I'm sure I'm not the first to inform you that you're an attractive man."

A guffaw fell out of Cupid, and Reed's alarmed face wheeled their direction. "I'll admit, there's something about earth-me that seems to have that effect on people, but I'm not the least bit interested in seducing you with my godly charms."

"You know, of all the claims you've made today, that might be the most unbelievable of all."

Cupid shrugged. "I would much rather you love me as an equal than adore me as a god."

Posey blinked back at him, as mesmerized as she'd claimed. "That's one hell of a pickup line, Mr. Cupid."

"Does that mean it's working?"

"You're the expert," she said. "Why don't you tell me what I feel?"

"Really?" he asked, as if he'd been waiting for the invitation for days now.

"Please."

"Will you try to keep an open mind?"

She shifted in her chair. "I'll do my level best."

Cupid released a heavy breath. "Okay, here goes. Each time I've fallen in love in the past—Mia, Ruthie, Pan—I've been able to tell that the other person was not going to return that love. That's the punishment the gods chose for me. I fall deeply in love, more so each time, but the other person isn't my match. I have to find their Right Love and bring the two together. Once that happens, my heart breaks into a million pieces, and I stay that way until the next punishment kicks in."

"That's a misery, to state the obvious."

"Yes. That's what brought me to Wings. The last one was

more than I could handle on my own. Without understanding why, almost as soon as you and I started chatting online, I was released from my heartbreak over Pan."

"So you're saying I am your punishment?"

"I'm saying you're most definitely my heart's target. When I stood near you at Painted Rock, I knew right away that you were my next Worthy."

"Worthy?"

"Yes, a person marked worthy of Aphrodite's greatest gift, a perfect love match."

"So that means . . . what? You're supposed to be finding me my heart's true love or some such nonsense?"

"That's exactly right. It also means, whether you believe it or not, I am in love with you . . . but it's different this time." She recalled he'd told her that when they'd talked on the phone, and she'd called him out for his latest avoidance tactic.

"How so?"

He leaned in urgently. "Posey, if I disappear, it's not your fault, and I'm sorry."

Mr. Handsome had the crazies again.

"I have no idea what you're talking about."

"I know, but I needed to say that before I could go on. You heard me, right?"

"Yes. Not my fault. You're sorry." *But please don't disappear.*

"Okay. I also knew, in that same moment, that you were—you *are*—my Right Love match." He blinked hard, then squinted at her.

"Are you telling me I'm in love with you?"

"Yes." He kept flinching as if expecting to be struck by lightning at any moment. Honestly, it wouldn't have surprised Posey if he were. This was officially the weirdest conversation of her life, and she'd treated more than one schizophrenic in her career.

"Okay." She pressed her fingers to her temples and rubbed deep circles into her skull. "Aphrodite, your mother, the same woman who pushed you off a mountain, has now decided to grant you the perfect love?"

"She's complicated."

Posey brought her hand over her mouth, but her giggles escaped her fingers. "I'm so sorry I'm laughing. I feel like I might be having a psychotic break."

Cupid slumped back in his chair. "Would it help if I brought Reed over to talk to you? He's very good at explaining things."

"No. Uh-uh. We got this." *Deep breath in, deep breath out.*

Q eyed her anxiously. "Are you okay?"

"Mostly," she said. "How did you learn all this? Does your mother communicate with you somehow while you're down here, and she's . . .?" Posey pointed toward the ceiling.

"I can hear when two hearts are meant for each other. They echo each other's beat. It's like music, two instruments playing the same melody in perfect sync." He tapped his chest—"tha-thump"—then pointed to Posey's—"tha-thump"—then his—"tha-thump"—then Posey's again—"tha-thump."

"Our hearts are doing this right now? And you can hear it?"

"Yes. We have the most perfect echo beat I have ever heard. Posey, I've been alive over three thousand years. I've heard a lot of heartbeats."

"You know I can't hear it, right?"

"Yes, I know." He dropped his hands to the table. "I'm the only one who can hear it."

"Oh shit." *And we were just starting to have kind of a normal time.*

"Can you not find a place in your heart for the possibility that what I'm telling you is true?"

"As much as I might want to, Q, it makes no sense. None of this makes any sense."

"Love isn't supposed to make sense, Posey."

"I guess the god of love would know," she replied with a dark chuckle.

"I do. Our hearts have finally found each other. I just want a chance to make you believe." He slid his tightly clasped hands to the middle of the table. "Do you think you could try?"

Damn, whether he meant to or not, he was pumping some kind of supernatural hotness out of every pore. And she really did like her phone-friend Q even before she met Mr. Handsome in person. Setting aside the god stuff and the love talk, she actually might've felt a certain ease in his presence if she weren't fighting it with such aggressive mindfulness.

*Do you want to keep running, Posey?*

"I suppose I could try if it'll save you from eternal damnation or whatever happens to fallen gods."

His dazzling eyes teared up, and the bow of his luscious lips stretched open in wonder. "You will?"

"Sure. Why not?"

37

# FALLING

Cupid dropped the car keys into Reed's palm with a triumphant smile. "We're going for a hike. I trust you can get back to the lodge okay?"

"That's wonderful, Q. Just wonderful. You told her the truth?"

"I told her everything." Cupid glanced over at Posey, half expecting her to have run when he'd given her the chance. But no, there she was, standing near their table, pulling on her coat and hat and checking her phone.

"I'm so happy for you. You did it!"

Cupid wasn't sure exactly what he'd done, beyond earn himself some more time to convince her they were in love, but that was better than any of the alternatives. "Thank you for being here, Reed. I really appreciate it. And if it's okay, I think Posey will have some questions for you later on."

"Of course. You know I'll do anything I can to help." Reed stood and gave Cupid a solid hug. Pulling back, he asked, "You haven't crossed yet, have you?"

"Not yet. And if I should happen to vanish into thin air, you'll explain for me? I tried to warn her, but I don't think I really got through."

"Sure, sure. I'll take care of it," Reed said dismissively. "But keep a good thought, okay? Maybe you won't be separated at all. You might be on your way to your great immortal love story." Reed's starry-eyed optimism was almost too much to bear.

"Talk to you later, Reed."

"Yes, please keep us posted. You know Pan will be digging a trench with his pacing until we hear from you."

Cupid gave him a wink. "Distract him."

"I'll do my best." They shared a knowing grin, followed by the sad acknowledgment that would haunt all of their partings from now on, it seemed. *If I don't come back . . .*

Cupid's melancholy faded away as he turned toward the love of his eternal life, who stood waiting for him with an expectant smile on her face, and he swiftly closed the distance between them.

"Ready?" Posey asked.

He almost laughed. He'd waited nearly thirty-four hundred years for her. "Lead on."

He opened the door, and they stepped outside together into the crisp California air, pregnant with possibility. It was strange being alone with Posey after the clamor of the café, and Cupid quite liked it.

"Gimme one minute?" Posey said, jogging over to her car. "I just wanna grab my pack. I've got a couple of water bottles and emergency supplies."

As he had been doing obsessively since walking into the coffee shop, Cupid once again read her echo, read her pulse, read her desire for him. All systems go. And she'd been the one to suggest a hike.

"Hey, Posey, I was wondering . . ." He made sure his hands were tucked deep into his pockets before she spun around from her open car door.

"Hmm?"

"Is there anything I can do to make you feel safer with me?"

Her lips tugged up at the corners. "Sweet of you to ask. I already sent your picture to three of my friends, told them exactly where we'd be hiking, and made them promise to call the police if they don't hear from me by noon."

Her answer caught him off guard, and all he could do was laugh. "That's good, I guess?"

Strapping her pack across her back, she grinned. "You're fine. Just be yourself—unless you're a serial killer."

"Who else can I be?"

"Honestly, I can't imagine dreaming up anyone more out-there than Cupid." She closed her car door and walked over to Cupid, glancing briefly at his waist. "And you can take your hands out of prison now." With a playful pop of her eyebrows, she took off at a fast clip. "Coming?" she called over her shoulder without slowing down.

Cupid had to jog to catch up. He took her up on the invitation to free his hands, but that only made it harder to resist reaching for Posey's hand as they strode side by side down the road.

"The trail starts just past that curve ahead. You good for a four-mile loop with a fair bit of grade? It should take us about an hour."

*An hour alone with Posey.* "Sure, whatever you like."

"I suppose that was a silly question," she said with a chuckle. "How does this god thing work anyway? Do you have unlimited stamina? Do you have to sleep? Do you need food?"

He'd decided at the coffee shop to ignore her teasing tone. At some point, she would either tire of placating him, or she would start to believe him. In the meantime, each question she fired at him would earn an honest answer and none of Cupid's defenses.

"My Earth body requires food and sleep, much like yours, but even with the worst abuse, everything pretty much resets within a couple of days to the body they gave me when I fell."

"What kind of abuse are we talking?" That was concern, not mockery.

"Oh, the usual brokenhearted behavior, I guess. Days of nothing but ramen and beer and frozen pizza, lack of sunlight and fresh air, too much sleep, no sleep at all." He kept the poor personal hygiene to himself. No need for Posey to picture him at his worst.

"What if you get hurt? *Can* you get hurt? Physically, I mean."

"Yes, though I haven't suffered more than sore muscles from working out too hard in the weight room. I believe I can bounce back from anything short of death, and maybe death, too, but I haven't been too keen to test that theory."

"That sounds wise," she said.

Cupid caught her gaze, and they shared a smile. They'd arrived at the trail's entrance. Posey's next question came as they turned into the woods together.

"Does that mean you're eager to get back home, where you're safer?"

Cupid lifted his eyes to the treetops. Surely, Mother was watching and listening. Too much honesty made him vulnerable with the gods; not enough made him useless with Posey. His decision wasn't difficult.

"No, Posey. Not if it means leaving you behind." *Go ahead, Mother. Use that against me.* It was worth it for the stutter in Posey's pace, for the hitch in her next breath, for the way she planted her next step close enough to brush the sleeve of his coat with hers.

"You mean that," she said.

"Of course I do."

Her knuckles tapped the back of Cupid's hand. Without a word or glance his way, Posey slipped her hand inside his and curled her fingers into all his waiting spaces. Cupid's heart hammered faster; Posey's echoed his love song.

He'd never been happier in his life . . . but that all could change at any moment.

They had to be sitting on the razor's edge of their Liminal Point, a whisper from crossing. Sadly, if he were ripped from Posey's grasp right now, she would know everything he'd told her was the truth, but understanding wouldn't do either of them a lick of good. He wanted to prepare her, but how could he when he had absolutely no idea what to expect?

Her pace slowed to a more leisurely stroll, linked hands swinging like a rope between them. That suited Cupid just fine. The longer he could keep her to himself, the better, especially now that they were holding hands.

"Tell me about Pan." Not where he expected her to start.

"What would you like to know?"

"He seems to play a very big role in your life."

"Pan was my best friend—my only friend, really—growing up." It shamed Cupid to admit that to Posey. He hoped she wouldn't dwell too much on his life before the fall. There wasn't much he was proud of.

"They say you only need one good friend to get you through, and I believe that."

"Yeah, maybe. I guess that's why I was so lost after they told me he'd died."

"What? Was he not immortal? How could he die?" Posey looked stricken, but a part of him wanted to rejoice. She'd started to believe him.

"Turns out he didn't," Cupid replied.

"Then why would anyone tell you he had?"

Cupid had that uneasy sensation of being cracked open and examined through a magnifying glass again. It hadn't been pleasant when Dr. Chan had done all his probing, but this was even scarier. How would Posey see him as a man worthy of her love if he only showed her the wounded child?

"Pan was never really happy on Olympus. I guess you could say he was restless, always longing for nymphs he couldn't have and causing trouble for everyone. When Pan requested a Permanent Descent, the Divine Council realized it would be beneficial for all involved to grant it. They didn't want me to find out because they thought I would want to stay down here with him, I guess. So it was easier to just tell me he'd died."

"I take it your mother was aware of all this?"

"She's very protective." Cupid squeezed her hand and glanced upward to remind Posey not to say anything to bring on Aphrodite's wrath. Posey gave him a serious nod.

"How long ago did that happen?"

"Your year fifteen."

"One-five?"

"Yes."

"Wow. When did you learn the truth, that Pan was alive?"

"The day I fell. Three months ago."

Posey's mouth dropped open. "Well, that must have been one amazing reunion! After two thousand years apart?"

Cupid chuckled, remembering his joy and confusion. "Indeed. Pan is in charge of all the fallen gods. That's the trade they made him for letting him stay on Earth. He manages everyone's needs while they're down here. Documents, living arrangements, clothing, what-have-you, and he helps us figure out what we need to do to earn our ascent back home."

Posey angled her head abruptly toward him. Had she forgotten Cupid was only a visitor here?

"And if one of us messes up down here, they hold Pan responsible. It's a big job."

"I guess that explains why he was in charge of your therapy decisions."

"Right. We're supposed to stay out of the spotlight. Pan wasn't too happy with me after that car accident that landed me on the news."

"Sounded like a traumatic night for everyone."

Cupid shuddered at the memory of screeching metal and the smell of smoke and gas at the scene, the look on Mia's face as Cupid had stood in the headlights of Patrick's cruiser. "It was a terrible night."

Posey's thumb stroked the back of his hand. "You've been through a lot in a short time."

Cupid huffed. "And almost nothing for three thousand years before that."

Posey stayed silent. Any talk of his life on Mount O seemed to shut her down. *Patience.*

"And after all that drama, they made Pan one of your punishments as well?"

"Correct."

"Well," she said, "I'd love to hear more about *that*. But maybe another time." Cupid couldn't imagine a good time to tell Posey about his brief but exuberant affair with Pan, but if she asked, he would answer. "He and Reed are extremely happy together."

"So, I know this is a crazy question, but I'm gonna ask anyway. Isn't Pan a . . . *satyr?*"

"He was, before his descent. Now, he's as human as I am," Cupid said, "at least on the outside. There are, however, a few notable differences in our abilities."

Posey's giggle turned Cupid's head. He squeezed her hand, drawing her gaze to his. She was blushing again, and from the sweet tang swirling in the air around her, Cupid had a pretty good idea why. "What's that for?" he asked.

"Would it be rude of me to ask the god of love about his 'abilities'?"

"Extremely!" Cupid joined in her laughter. "But I would be delighted to provide a demonstration at your request."

"Oh, I'll bet you would," she said, suddenly serious.

She stopped in her tracks, and he, in perfect step beside her, stopped too.

*Wait . . .*

She angled her body toward his, met his steady gaze with her deep, soulful eyes. Her heart raced, taking Cupid's on a wild chase.

*Wait, wait . . .*

Rising onto her toes, she placed her free hand over his heart.

*Wait, wait, wait . . .*

Her lips parted. "Maybe just a sample?" Her gaze darted to his mouth, then back to his eyes, searching for his answer.

His joy broke free. "Anything, Posey."

Closing her eyes, she cocked her head just before pressing her perfect Cupid's bow to his. The first taste made him weak in the knees. His head fizzed and popped as if a shaken can of ginger ale had opened inside his brain. He couldn't breathe, and he didn't want to ever again if it meant breaking their perfect kiss.

He unlaced his fingers from hers and brought his hands to Posey's cheeks, cupping them ever so tenderly, cradling this moment as much as the precious kiss that had been waiting his whole lifetime to find them together, right here, right now. A dizzying pleasure passed back and forth between them, give-and-take merging into one brilliant blast of bliss.

He pulled back slightly, tracing his thumb across her shining lips. It wasn't that he was sated, but he'd already taken in more than he could absorb. Settling flat on her feet again, Posey blinked up through glassy eyes, neither speaking as their mouths formed mirror-image smiles.

She tipped her forehead to his chest. "You sure can pick 'em, Posey," she mumbled into his jacket.

Cupid's laughter floated past the fluffy ball at the top of her hat, and he wrapped his arms around her. "If it makes you feel any better, you didn't pick me."

She shook her head against his chest, an odd but arousing tickle at his breastbone, then let out a deep sigh. "Nope. I don't think that helps." Lifting her head, she chuckled. "We haven't gotten too far on our hike."

"Oh, I wouldn't say that at all," he replied.

# 38

# TO LOVE A GOD

What was sure to be the strangest night of Posey Rey's life so far began with a knock at her front door. Q stood at the front of the motley group on her stoop, a meadow's worth of lilacs spilling over his arm. She could not ignore, nor did she want to, how utterly delicious he looked in his blue-and-white-plaid button-down.

"I've been told light violet lilacs signify the first pangs of love," he said, transferring the cellophane-wrapped spray into her arms.

"Thank you. They're beautiful, and so is the sentiment." *And so are you.*

He melted her with his smile, then stepped forward to place a sweet kiss on her lips. *Damn, he smelled good.* She had an almost irresistible urge to run her fingers through his wavy hair. Why, again, had she invited the others when she could have had Q all to herself in front of a roaring fire?

*Oh, Posey Pie. Where are your manners?*

"Come in, come in. You must be cold," she said, noting that only Reed wore a coat, and he was carrying a box with a decadent-looking cake inside. "Would that be a Black Forest cake?"

A proud grin spread across Reed's face. "Q mentioned it was your favorite. Pan and I drove to Kings Beach this afternoon to pick it up."

She had to admit, they were all pretty adorable—and impressive. She'd barely mentioned the cake to Q in passing last night—"I wouldn't even be able to make room for one bite of Black Forest cake right now"—over burgers and beers at Whitney's, their first official date. It was no small thing that Q had picked up on it and had sent his friends out to find one today while she and Q had spent the day getting to know each other better.

"Well, thank you all. I'm glad you're here to help me eat this," she said, relieving Reed of the box and leaning in to kiss him on the cheek.

"We'll help you drink this, too," said the brawny redhead holding a bottle of wine in each hand.

"Ah. The famous Pan." Despite the image of the mythological creature locked in Posey's mind, the ginger in her foyer was indeed all man—and one who fit in perfectly with the flannel-wearing, bearded, lumbersexual contingent populating the Tahoe area—though the pairing of this strapping young he-man with the slight, erudite professor certainly fascinated her.

He extended the bottle in his right hand to Posey, then offered his freed hand to shake hers. "It's nice to *finally* be allowed to meet you." His grin indicated there were no hard feelings.

"Likewise," she answered.

"I hope you like the 2013 Silver Oak Cab. Personally, I've been leaning toward the Cab Francs from the Loire Valley, but when in California . . ."

"He's a bit of a wine snob," Reed said in a mock-whisper.

"Moi? Look who's talking! You only let me into your house because I was holding a bottle of Duckhorn."

"That's actually true," Reed said, earning a giggle from Posey.

"Please don't mind Pan," said Reed, breaking into her thoughts. "We haven't fed him since 5:30. He's *hangry*."

"It's only six now," she said, playing along.

"Uh-huh." Reed and Pan exchanged hungry glances having nothing to do with food. *Projecting much, Posey?*

While the two lovers bantered on, Posey's attention drifted to Q, who stood gazing at her as if he, too, was remembering the sweet day they'd shared, hiking up to the more intimate picnic area at Skylandia Park, which turned into a massive make-out session. The man certainly kissed like a Greek god anyway.

Mindful of a powerful desire to kiss him again, Posey waved them all into the kitchen. "Let's get some cheese and crackers into Pan."

They marched behind her in a line to the island where she'd set out the appetizers. "If *you*," she said, handing the corkscrew to Pan, "could open that very nice bottle of wine, and *you*," she said, digging out a vase for Q, "could put these beautiful lilacs in some water, and *you*," she said, sliding the salad bowl and dressing toward Reed, "would toss the salad, I will throw our steaks on the grill, and we'll all be eating dinner in fifteen minutes. Think you can make it, Pan?"

"No problem, Doc." Pan shot her a wink.

"Good." Posey clapped her hands together as they all took up their duties. "I will be out back." She picked up the tray of strip steaks and slipped out onto the deck. The cold air was bracing, and her breath puffed into a cloud in front of her, but it felt good to clear her head of all the testosterone swirling around inside her house.

She lifted the round lid of the preheated grill and transferred the four slabs of meat onto the grate. Rich laughter floated to her ears, and she peered through the French doors into her kitchen to the lively scene of the three friends enjoying the simple pleasure of one another's company. Not in a long while had such a sense of happiness and belonging filled her heart.

She cast her eyes to the darkened sky. The night's first stars had poked through the black velvet curtain, faraway lights from another world. *What if . . .?* For a fleeting moment, she was able to suspend her disbelief and imagine Atlas holding the heavens on his broad shoulders.

*Yeah, right,* she huffed to herself. *Let's just throw out the last two thousand years of science and go back to the ancients and their gods. May my sacrifice of sirloins be worthy, oh ye lords on high.*

The door clicked shut, and Q appeared, holding two glasses of wine. "I thought the chef might like a drink."

"Thank you. That was very sweet." *So, so sweet.*

She took the goblet he extended and clinked with his. "*Yamas!*" he said.

"Cheers!" she said.

Smiling at their separate toasts, they sipped.

"Wow, this is really nice wine," Posey said. "Your friend Pan doesn't mess around."

"Nope." Cupid grinned, but his smile faded when he saw her shivering. "You're cold." Stepping in close, he drew her into a two-armed hug, flooding Posey with a rush of unfamiliar emotions.

She closed her eyes and nestled her face into the collar of his shirt. His sexy scruff tickled her nose as she inhaled his alluring musk. Whatever soap he was using was working for her.

"How are you so warm?" Her lips formed the words against his neck, feathery almost-kisses.

"I don't really get cold."

*Did he have to go and ruin the moment with that again?*

A soft chuckle vibrated in his throat. "It's okay, Posey. I know you don't believe me yet. That's why I brought Reed and Pan, so you can ask all your questions."

Posey wasn't so sure Q's friends were any more credible, but by the time they all sat down around the table, her curiosity was off the charts.

"I'd like to make a toast, if I may?" All eyes turned toward Reed, who was holding his glass aloft.

"Please," Posey said.

The others raised their goblets, the deep red wine reflecting the flickering votives at the center of the small round table.

"To open minds and open hearts," Reed said.

Beside her, Q caught Posey's eye, then added, "And the first pangs of new love."

Four glasses clinked in the center; four voices toasted in unity: "*Yamas!*" Q's eyes popped wide with pure delight.

*Could it be just this easy to slide into their world?*

"The steak is delicious," Pan said, setting off a string of compliments from Reed and Q.

"Glad you're enjoying everything," Posey said. "It was fun to cook a hearty meal for a change."

Pan sliced off a generous bite of steak and raised it toward his mouth. "I'm available if you want to have more fun tomorrow night." With a wink, he opened his mouth and delivered the meat to his waiting tongue.

"Good to know," said Posey, grinning across the table at Pan. "Maybe let's see how tonight goes?"

"Fair enough," Pan replied around his mouthful. "How would you say it's going so far? *Ow!*" Pan bent to rub his leg. "What the hell, Q!"

Q froze, fork poised over his baked potato. "What'd *I* do?"

Reed cleared his throat. "That was me."

Pan turned his glare toward Reed, and the irritation dissipated as quickly as it had sprung up. "Oh, come on. Like you aren't curious?"

Reed's forehead angled toward Pan and delivered a stern but loving rebuke. "Curiosity is not a license to pry."

Chastened, Pan turned to Posey, hand over his heart. "Apologies. I withdraw my prying." Pan returned to his steak as if nothing had happened, as did Reed, having educated his student.

"He means well," said Q.

"It's all good," said Posey, "and for the record, I think tonight is going extremely well. I can't say I had a clue what to expect when I invited two gods over for a home-cooked meal, but so far, I'm having a pretty great time."

"One and a half, actually," Reed said, just loud enough to be heard.

Pan shook his head with a good-natured smile. "You're killing me, Reed."

Posey was lost. "Sorry?"

Q leaned in. "Pan's a demi. His mother was mortal."

"Reed's a bit of a stickler for details," said Pan.

"Occupational hazard, I'm afraid," Reed said. "But if any of my knowledge on the subject of classical mythology might be helpful to you, Posey, I am entirely at your service."

"I'll keep that in mind, thanks."

"Though I have to say," Reed continued, "the basic premise of everything I thought I knew went right out the proverbial window when I met these two." He laughed to himself, stabbed a tomato wedge, and resumed eating.

Yes, the retired professor had done an admirable job right there reminding Posey of his real value. Even more than his encyclopedic grasp of the subject matter, what Reed brought to the table, literally, was corroboration of a wildly fantastical story by an intelligent, presumably stable, fellow human, setting up Posey for the most important psych evaluation of her life. And off she went into the depths of Reed's mind.

"The basic premise being . . .?"

"That mythology is a body of stories that aren't demonstrably true. Once you know the gods actually existed, *and still do*"—he paused to gesture at Pan and Q—"any so-called mythology becomes, at a minimum, historical fiction."

"Okay, since you offered . . . I'm curious how you explain away the obvious conflict with scientifically proven facts." Three pairs of eyes blinked at Posey, and she understood how Galileo must have felt facing the Inquisition. "Can we agree that our sun is not pulled across the sky by a god-driven chariot?"

Reed reached for his wine, chuckling. "Either of you boys care to field that one?"

Pan continued shoveling food into his mouth at a steady clip. Q set down his fork and stared sadly at his plate. Posey's heart sank. Had this house of cards come crashing down so quickly?

"Nobody has *anything* to offer?"

Reed smiled. "You wish to be convinced."

She felt Q's head turn her way, and she met his tense gaze. *The coin flip . . . heads or tails?* "I think I do." Nobody was more surprised than she. Q's face lit up with pure delight.

"May I try?" Reed glanced at the two so-called gods, whose relieved "Yes" and "Please" fell on top of each other. "I'm not naïve, Posey. I know there are questions I can't answer, too many details that just don't fit when I line up the ancients' explanations versus what I know as an enlightened inhabitant of the twenty-first century."

"Then how do you . . .?" She could only finish the question with a shrug.

Reed shot her one of his gentle smiles. "I don't see this as an all-or-nothing proposition. I can't—nor do I want to—throw out my certainty that these magnificent creatures in our presence are indeed gods simply because I can't prove out the rest of the workings of the universe."

"Nor do I," said Posey, "but sadly, I've seen where delusionary thinking can lead. It's not a place I want to see any of us end up."

"That makes four of us," Pan interjected with a pointed glare at Reed.

Unruffled, Reed replied, "I appreciate your reservations, Posey." She let the gross understatement pass. "At the end of the day, I'm a man of letters. I believe in stories with multiple, often diverse, points of view, which is how I've always regarded the works of the ancient poets. Good luck to anyone claiming there's a cohesive, definitive canon. The more you study, the more you'll dig up wildly contradictory stories of the universe's origin or the parentage of certain divine beings, to take two easy examples."

"I'm not quite catching how you made the leap from literature to reality."

Seemingly possessed with endless patience, Reed took in her question with a fixed smile. "It was less leap than it was a series of small steps that burrowed into my consciousness. Look at our two friends here. Their human bodies are invulnerable to aging or climate or wounds. The first time Pan visited my home, he exhibited a connection with my dogs that could best be described as primal." Pan huffed, and the two shared a glance laced with lovers' secrets. "If you have the great privilege of watching Pan move through the outdoors, you'll see a grace one simply doesn't find in humans, no matter how athletic." Clearly humbled by Reed's words, Pan took a break from his snappy retorts. "His senses are extraordinary, his reflexes finely honed, and he possesses a stamina that cannot be explained away by youth and fitness."

At that, Pan burst out laughing. "Reed, come on, man! We're in the presence of a lady."

"I was referring to your epic runs." Ignoring Pan's smirk, Reed pressed on. "As for the god seated to your left, within an hour of putting his head underwater for the very first time, he had completely mastered both breast and crawl strokes, and I'm told he learned to drive a car with similar dispatch. I'm fully convinced his ability to read hearts is not some con artist's trickery, but you'll have to judge that for yourself. I'm sure you've noticed the superhuman sex appeal?" Posey's cheeks heated, and she pulled her goblet to her lips. "Forgive me for putting you on the spot, Posey. You don't need to answer that, of course."

"I believe Q is well aware I find him attractive," Posey said, though if he had a clue of her most intimate thoughts on the topic, Posey would be even more mortified than she already was. "But Reed—"

He held up his hand to stop her. "Yes, I know. They could have all these amazing abilities and still be fully human. Which is why I wasn't one hundred percent sure, myself, until I had a conversation with Mercury three days ago."

*Oh no.* "There's a third god wandering the streets of Indiana, calling himself Mercury?"

"Not at all. He appeared in a column of vapor, his body not fully solidified due to the speed at which he comes and goes between Mount Olympus and Earth. We talked for several minutes, he answered some questions, we shook hands, sort of."

Posey was out of practice and slightly drunk and way too unguarded to disguise her disbelief. Her jaw dropped. She swallowed hard. *Well, there goes the whole shootin' match.* So much for her reliable witness.

Pan angled his body close to Reed's. "Um, I don't think she believes you."

"I can see that," Reed replied, his smile undimmed. "Say, Pan, if you and Q have finished your meal, why don't you two go for a little stroll?"

"Yep. Got it." Pan stood and poured out the last of the second bottle into Q's glass. "C'mon, buddy. Let's leave the mortals alone so they can talk about us."

Q swiveled toward Posey. "You want me to go?" She could feel the tension pouring off him.

"Maybe for a little while?"

He sighed deeply. "Fine," he said, then leaned in and kissed her square on the lips. "Try not to forget me."

"Shall we sit by the fire?" Posey asked.

"That would be lovely," said Reed. "The gas log at home has its advantages, but I do miss the smell of burning firewood."

"Nothing like it." They settled in with their wine. "I really appreciate your candor, Reed. I don't mean to poison you with my doubts. I hope you know that."

"Don't worry about me, Posey. I have what I need. You'll have to find your own way, if you can—if you want to."

"I do want to. I know that now. I'm just not there yet."

Reed nodded. "I can imagine what you must think of me, the eccentric classics professor who's willed his books to life like some fairy tale."

"Actually, I was thinking what a great couple you and Pan make. You're obviously smitten with each other. I wish it could be that easy for me."

"Easy?" Reed's eyes crinkled with his laughter. "Which part was easy for me, loving a man or loving a god?"

"Oh! Are you saying you didn't . . . you were . . . you never . . .?" Posey shook her head. "Sorry. I had no idea Pan was your first man."

"Yeah, that whole concept took a bit of time to penetrate my skull."

"I can understand that. As you said, they're unfairly alluring."

Reed's eyebrows popped. "I don't believe I used the word 'unfairly.'"

"I may have projected." They exchanged grins.

"You know," Reed said, "Pan wasn't the first man who turned my head."

"No?"

"Q didn't tell you how we all met?"

"He told me he met you at the pool while he was trying to get over Pan, and you were kind enough to teach him how to swim."

"Ah, yes. And the silly old man proceeded to develop a confusing crush on the handsome young man in a pair of wet trunks."

"At least it wasn't a Speedo!" Posey said with a giggle.

"No, that would be Pan," Reed said, shaking his head and blushing a bit at the memory, "but I didn't meet Pan until after Q and I had become close. It all happened so quickly. When Q offered me something more than friendship, I just wasn't ready. And by the time I wised up, he'd already decided I was meant to be with Pan." Reed shook his head, chuckling. "Yes, I hear how this all sounds."

"So, you and Q were never together?"

"Only as friends. You don't have to excise any images of the two of us together," he said with a wink. "But he had me thinking about it, believe me."

"Oh, I do," Posey said.

"Sorry, is this weird?"

"No weirder than anything else we've talked about tonight."

"Good point. You know, Posey, it's a relief to be able to talk to you. I have had to keep all this to myself. Don't get me wrong— it's a trade-off I'd take any day, but I've been going crazy a little bit, you know?"

"I can see where not sharing would be the smart route." She had a pretty good idea what April would have thought about Reed's vision of Mercury. "Honestly, Reed, I'm just fine with the world not knowing anything about my love life. I've stayed in the shadows for seven years. I've made my peace with it."

Reed sipped thoughtfully. "Tell me to go suck an egg if you don't want to answer, but what about your family? Don't they miss you?"

"No egg sucking required," she replied with a smile. Reed's old-world charm had quickly swept away Posey's defenses. "I keep in touch with my parents. I know it's hard for them that I don't do the big family events anymore, but I have a strained relationship with my two sisters, and it's just better for all involved this way."

"By chance, do you come from royalty?"

"*Royalty?* Why do you ask?"

"Just a guess based on the etymology of the name Rey. I thought perhaps there was a king somewhere in your lineage."

"As far as I know, we're just a plain old dysfunctional family."

Smiling, Reed waved his hand in the air as if to sweep the conversation away. "Please, don't mind me and my curiosity. Pan loves to tease that I can't help myself." The man was positively beaming. Reed wore his partner's affection like a badge of honor.

"So, give me the scoop, Reed. What *is* it really like? Loving a god, I mean."

"Ah." He set his wine down and shifted to face her, a warm glow spreading across his face. "Amazing on every level. For starters, they're going to stay perfect—and alive—for as long as we know them." The "we" startled Posey. She wasn't quite ready to put herself in Reed's category. "Our lifetimes are not even a blink of an eye for those two. Have you ever tried to contemplate what it means to live forever?"

"Not really. I can't even imagine wanting to."

"Even in a body that never ages? Just think, Posey! They'll never get love handles or wrinkles or gray hairs or—"

"Stop!" Posey was quickly approaching forty, and though she had always felt attractive "for her age," envisioning life with a partner who wouldn't age with her was daunting. "Jeez, do you think they'll still want *us* when we're all those things?"

"Look at me, Posey," Reed said with a melancholy note in his voice. "Don't you think Pan knows he can do better?"

"I'm guessing he doesn't like it when you talk that way."

"No. And I almost believe him when he says it doesn't matter."

Posey covered Reed's hand with her own, overcome with affection for the gentle professor. "I believe it. Pan's had enough experience to know what really matters."

Reed huffed. "He knows he can have all the sexy young partners he wants after I'm gone. It's so hard to wrap my head around it still. They've seen worlds rise and fall, the best and worst of humankind, and weathered it all with grace and humor. And yet, in many ways, they're still boys. I happen to think they're both pretty remarkable."

"Do you ever worry someone up there might just arbitrarily decide to break you up the same way you were thrown together?"

"No. Aphrodite seems to have a soft spot for these Right Love matches. To be perfectly candid, Posey, as invulnerable and omnipotent as Pan and Cupid appear to be, you know who poses the biggest threats to their well-being right now? Two little mortals. You and I." He took no pleasure in the observation.

Reed's phone buzzed, and begging Posey's pardon, he checked the text message. "Cupid wants to know if he can come back now."

"Tell him yes."

A soft knock came at her door, and Posey rushed to answer.

39

# NO MORE RESISTANCE

"Stay the night." Posey's offer floated across the table she and Cupid were clearing. Time stood still for Cupid; the clatter Pan and Reed were making in the kitchen faded into the distance. Posey met his gaze between the soft candle glow and the low-hanging chandelier. "Will you?"

"You really need to ask?" The mouths that had spent the afternoon kissing now formed two shy smiles.

With their hands full of plates and glasses and serving bowls, they sealed their secret deal by sweeping into the kitchen together with a common goal—getting rid of their company as quickly as possible.

"We'll finish up here," Cupid called to Pan and Reed, working a wash-and-dry routine at the sink like an old married couple.

"It's really no bother," Reed said. "You know how much Pan loves to do the dishes."

Pan roared with laughter. "I think you meant to say, 'You know how much I love to *watch* Pan do the dishes.'"

"No, *really*," said Cupid. "I'm going to *stay* and help Posey with the dishes."

Two heads turned together, understanding dawning on Pan and Reed as Cupid set down everything he was carrying and wrapped his arm around Posey's shoulder.

"And *we* are going to *go*. C'mon, Professor." Pan pulled the dish towel from his shoulder and snapped it playfully at Reed's bottom before tossing it onto the counter. "Posey, thank you for the delicious meal. Q, see you tomorrow, or . . . whatever." Unable to put words to their possibly permanent goodbye yet again, Pan pulled Posey and Cupid into a group hug. "Love you guys."

As Reed occupied Posey with his thank-yous and goodbyes, Pan took the opportunity to jam a handful of condoms into Cupid's front pocket. "Remember, Psyche was a virgin. Be careful."

Not five minutes later, Cupid had shooed his friends out the door.

"I thought they'd never leave," Cupid said. "Do you have any idea how badly I've been wanting to do this?" He pulled Posey in close and pressed his lips to hers.

Posey smiled against his mouth. "Yes, I think I do."

Well practiced by now, the two fell quickly into a deep, sexy kiss. Posey's thin, gray sweater had been taunting him all night, or rather, what was underneath. And now, feeling her curves pressed to his chest, Cupid was dizzy with want. Her need swirled around him too, pulling them together like a belt around their hips.

Posey inched her hands upward and looped them behind his neck, baring a tantalizing sliver of her belly where her sweater tugged free of her jeans. He swept the pads of his thumbs across her soft, warm skin. Posey wriggled into his body. Her jeans brushed against his, but he hardly needed the encouragement.

Was their Liminal Point waiting for them inside this joining? Mia and Patrick had only needed that initial flicker of recognition. For Ruthie and Zach, a single moment of mutually dropped defenses opened two hearts that had nearly given up on each other. For Pan and Reed, the crossing came when both men experienced fireworks. What was Aphrodite waiting for this time? And even more troubling, what would happen to Cupid and Posey if they did cross?

The only happy outcome Cupid could imagine—being allowed to stay here with Posey, Pan, and Reed—seemed impossible. Mother hadn't spent three thousand years keeping Pan's descent a secret only to let Cupid slip out of her iron grasp now. Didn't he owe Posey at least some hint of what they might bring about?

He broke off the kiss with a gentle slide of his tongue that left them both wanting. "Posey, we need to talk."

Shaking her head, Posey pressed her hand to Cupid's mouth. "I'm all talked out. I need to feel."

Yes, it had been two solid days of nonstop questions and answers. If worse came to worst, Pan and Reed would explain Cupid's sudden disappearance.

Cupid hoisted Posey to his hips, drawing a surprised squeak. "Done. Where am I taking you?"

"The bedroom." Posey wrapped her legs tight around Cupid's waist as he pivoted toward the hallway to his left. "No, wait," she said, "the fireplace."

Cupid chuckled as he spun her in a full circle. "You sure?"

"I've always wanted to do it on the bearskin rug."

"I would be honored to make that happen."

She kissed him all the way to the mantel, where he sank to his knees and lowered her back gently onto the rug. Straddling her, Cupid dropped onto his palms on either side of her head.

His shirt fell open, enveloping Posey in a canopy of blue plaid. When had she unbuttoned his shirt? He gaped down at Posey to find her grinning up at him.

"You're a tricky one," he said, flexing his arms so he could dip to reach her with his mouth. He trailed a line of kisses up her jawline and finished with his lips next to her ear. "Go on, then. Finish the job." Her mouth formed a smile against his cheek.

She pressed her warm hands to his belly, and a soft grunt left him. He nibbled his way into the crook of her delicious neck as she slid her palms up his abdomen, fingers splayed as they crawled up his chest. He drew in a sharp breath, tickling the shell of her ear and making her squirm beneath him. If this were to be Cupid's last night making use of his human body, all he wished for was the chance to bring Posey bliss before being ripped away.

Her hands crested his shoulders, easing the shirt up and over his back until it would go no farther. "A little help?" she said, pushing playfully at the fabric.

Cupid lifted his head and mirrored her smile. Pressing up onto his knees, he took in the beautiful offering gazing up at him with hunger in her eyes. He unbuttoned his cuffs, tugged the sleeves off, and tossed his shirt away.

Her lips fell open as she took in the sight of him, releasing a puff of her irresistible musk. The firelight danced in her eyes, bright sparks of gold and amber playing in tranquil brown pools. *I love you, Posey.* Her heart answered in perfect agreement.

He slipped his fingers under the edge of her sweater and pushed the material out of the way as he bent to touch his lips to her belly. Posey arched into his kiss, filling Cupid's ears with a moan that strained his groin.

Delirious with desire, he slid the sweater higher, trailing feathery, wet kisses through the hollow of her firm belly until he reached the edge of her bra. He wanted all of her, desperately needed to know every inch of her body, but only if Posey wanted that too. It wasn't enough that she was as aroused as he or even that their hearts had found their truest mate. Cupid raised his head and searched Posey for permission.

Meeting his gaze, she stretched her arms over her head. "Don't stop," she whispered.

Pushing her sweater over the mounds of her cream-colored bra, he inched forward on his knees until the fabric was bunched at her chin. "Close your eyes," he said, then started the sweater over her head. Her perfect lips disappeared behind the swath of gray, and he couldn't resist kissing them when they reappeared. Together, they wriggled the sweater up and over Posey's arms.

The moment she was freed, Posey looped her arms behind Cupid's neck and tipped him over sideways like a hot dog spilled out of its bun. She climbed astride him, looking very proud of herself.

"I guess I best stay alert," Cupid said, grinning up at her.

"That would be wise." Without a thought to modesty, Posey reached behind her back with both hands, unhooked her bra, and tossed it away. "Maybe these can hold your attention?"

Without breathing, Cupid reached to cup his lover's breasts. They filled his palms as if his hands were the molds into which her flesh was poured. "My *gods*, you are so perfect."

"Funny, I was kind of thinking the same about you," said Posey just before she covered his mouth with hers. There followed four frantic hands at buttons and zippers and a whole lot of wriggling and kicking jeans down legs until finally, mercifully, they were both naked.

So fixated was Cupid on Posey's taut, athletic body and the muscular thighs that had so deftly flipped him, he failed to notice her gawking until she reached out and slid her hand down his erection. Her touch nearly ended his self-control.

*Enjoy this. It may be the last time.*

"Okay, wow. Maybe all that Greek god stuff is true." Posey grinned at him, not a hint of a blush on her cheeks. She seemed utterly unembarrassed.

"So, this isn't your first, um . . .?"

"Penis sighting? No, but thanks for asking." She leaned in and gave him a peck on the lips. "I'm a thirty-eight-year-old woman. I've been around the block. If you have some old-fashioned notion in your head of deflowering my maidenhead, I'm afraid I'm not your girl."

"I don't have any notions in my head, and you are definitely my girl," he replied, feeling majorly relieved.

"Good!" Posey jumped to her feet. "I'll be right back."

Cupid grasped her fingers before she bolted away. "Where are you going?"

"I may not be a virgin, but that doesn't mean I keep condoms stashed in my living room sofa," she said.

"I have . . . one," he said sheepishly, reaching for his jeans. "Pan shoved it in my pocket just before he left."

"Of course he did." Posey watched with great amusement while Cupid reached for his jeans and not one but three packages fell out.

"Your friend has a lot of faith in you," she said with a smirk.

He didn't want to think about how Pan knew Cupid could burn through three condoms in an evening. "So, shall I . . .?"

"I can do it for you, if you want."

He'd planned on building up to their big moment, but Posey was all business. Her emotions were locked away from Cupid—and from what he could see, perhaps herself as well.

Cupid handed her the packet and leaned back onto his elbows to watch. Posey casually plopped down cross-legged between Cupid's legs. She shot him a flirty smile as she rolled the hateful sleeve down around him. This wasn't the romantic lovemaking Cupid had hoped for, but if this was the only door Posey could hold open, Cupid would make the most of it.

She stood abruptly, straddling his thighs, and Cupid feared she was about to sink down and end things all too quickly. Acting with haste, he wrapped his arms around Posey's hips and pulled her to his mouth. The first stroke of his tongue surprised her, and the second drew a moan. He slowed the pace even as Posey fisted his hair to spur him on, and he wrested away her tightly held control one lick at a time. Her orgasm tore a shudder from the depths of her throat, and Cupid held her tight through the last of her quivers.

With a bliss-filled sigh, she slid down his body. Cupid guided her on top of him, fitting their bodies together as if nocking one of his arrows onto its bowstring. They rocked together slowly at first, kissing and touching everything they could reach, then sped up as the tension grew unbearable. The dread thought occurred to Cupid that he might disappear the moment he peaked, but once that tingle started in his groin, he couldn't have stopped it if he'd tried. He closed his eyes and prayed for the first time in his life. *Please don't take me now . . .*

Whether or not the gods were moved by his plea, Cupid was still there when Posey's second orgasm triggered his own. Afterward, when they floated back to Earth like two leaves tossed by a tornado, Cupid was still there to wrap Posey in his arms. Forehead to forehead, they sat catching each other's quick breaths.

Through his postcoital brain fog, Cupid made out the sound of Pan's ringtone coming from his phone. "I'm so sorry, Posey, but I need to answer that."

"Wow. Three condoms *and* a phone call. That is definitely protective."

"Agreed, and yet, I *do* need to answer that." He lifted her out of his lap as tactfully as he could.

"I'll go get us a towel . . . unless you have one in your pants?"

"Funny girl." He stretched for the phone and accepted the call. "Present."

Cupid's reminder of Pan's very first cell phone lesson made Pan laugh out loud as it had that day. It felt as if forever had passed since then. "Okay. Just checking."

"That's it?"

"Yeah, pretty much . . ." Pan trailed off with a chuckle. "Sorry, man. Carry on."

"Night, Pan."

"Yep. See you tomorrow?" The silence between them was heavy. "I think so."

The towel landed in Cupid's lap, and he turned to catch Posey grinning at him. She'd pulled on a T-shirt and a pair of baggy boxers, and she looked completely adorable. "Did you give your buddy the blow-by-blow account?"

"No! I would never. He called because he thought—we both thought—I might have ascended."

"Speaking of ascending . . . *wow*. Thank you twice over. You sure you were a virgin until very recently?"

"Yes, quite sure." He was trying to manage the condom removal gracefully, but Posey had sat down beside him, and she seemed overly intrigued by what was happening between his legs.

"Well, Reed was right. You are a quick learner."

"That's not exactly something I had to learn, not like driving or swimming. I know you're not sure you believe me, but I *am* the God of Erotic Love. Even though I couldn't do anything about it before my fall, I guess all of that's been inside me, waiting to get out."

"So you're telling me that fucking is your superpower?" She waited, eyebrow cocked and daring him to correct her.

"I guess."

"Well, how lucky am I?" She gave him an openmouthed kiss that threatened his efforts to complete the job, but he finally got the damn thing tied off and the whole mess wrapped up in the towel. "One down, two to go," she said with a wink.

Cupid grunted. "I'm gonna need two minutes and a big glass of water."

Posey's phone rang. "Saved by the bell, big guy," she said, pushing against his shoulder to rise to her feet. "I'll bring that water when I come back."

"Thank you."

Cupid listened with half a divine ear, quickly becoming concerned at Posey's tone. "Mom? Why are you calling so late? . . . Oh my god! Is he okay?"

Cupid sprang to his feet and rushed to her side.

"Yes, of course I'll be there as soon as I can. I'll text you after I've worked out the flights. All right . . . Oh, that's good, I guess. Okay, Mom. Try to get some sleep. Love you."

Posey hung up, stunned.

"What is it, Posey? What happened?"

She answered without seeming to see the man standing right in front of her. "It's my father. He's had a heart attack. I have to fly home."

40

# GOODBYE FOR REAL

"Why do I have the feeling this is goodbye for real?" For once, Pan's expression did not include a trace of sarcasm. Beside him, Reed slipped two fingers under his glasses to wipe away tears, but the poor guy was losing the battle.

"Because you're smarter than you look?" Cupid's attempt to lighten the moment just made all three of them sadder.

Posey would be there any second now to pick him up from the lodge. They barely had time to make the midnight flight from Reno.

Pan yanked Cupid into a hug. "I know some of this sucked, but these past few months, having you down here with me, have been the happiest of my life."

"Me too, Pan," Cupid replied, trying hard not to shed the tears pooled in his eyes.

Pan gave him a hard whack on the back, then released him from the hug. "Look at it this way—your next visit to Earth is only one wrong arrow away."

"Cheery thought," said Cupid with a forced smile.

Reed, as usual, was the serious one. "Are you sure we can't come with you to Connecticut?"

Cupid shook his head. "I'm lucky she's letting *me* go with her." That had taken some convincing. Posey was not one to lean on others.

"In that case . . ." Reed pulled some rolled up papers out of his coat pocket and pressed them into Cupid's hands. "Take this with you." The edges opened to reveal the title of the ancient love story.

"Reed, I appreciate—"

"I beg you, Q, read this on the plane." Reed closed his hands around Cupid's, sealing the papers inside. "Her sisters are going to try to sow doubt. You need to be prepared."

"Honestly, after all Posey's told me about her sisters, I don't want to make it any harder for her to be around them, especially now."

"That's admirable," Reed said carefully, "but your good intentions might be misplaced. If their venom persuades Posey to reject your truth, you will not be the only one hurt. You're not doing Posey any favors letting her sisters discredit you."

Cupid replied with a tight nod. "I hear you."

"That's not all." Reed paused, and Cupid steeled himself for more bad news. "There's a large chunk of this story where Aphrodite puts Psyche through some terrible trials, and Cupid sits by and lets it happen."

"That's horrible!"

"Truly," said Reed, leaning in closer, "and you are so much better than that."

Cupid swallowed the lump in his throat. *Am I?*

Answering the unspoken question, Reed nodded.

"Thank you, Reed. I'll do my best."

"We know you will," he replied, glancing at Pan.

"If I mess this up, would you please make sure Posey knows I will never stop loving her and that she has to find a way to love again?"

"We won't need to," Reed said, squeezing Cupid's hands one final time before letting his grip slip away.

"Here she comes," Pan said.

As Cupid turned toward the approaching car, he realized he'd half expected her to leave without him.

"Good luck, buddy," Pan said. "I hope everything works out for you guys."

Cupid drew in a deep breath, then pushed it out of his chest.

Posey pulled to a stop in front of them. The trunk popped open, and Cupid placed his suitcase beside hers. With one final glance at his two best friends in the cosmos, Cupid climbed into the passenger seat, fastened his seat belt, and turned toward his destiny.

# 41

# RED-EYE

"Are you sure you're okay to drive?" Q asked soon after they'd hit the main road.

"I'm fine," she replied.

*Nothing's fine.* Her dad was in ICU, her mom was a wreck, and her sisters would already be camped out at the hospital when Posey and Q arrived. But then, Posey was a ninja-level compartmentalizer. Defense Mechanisms 101: Shut the valve and choke off those painful emotions.

"Okay," he said gently, "but I'm happy to take the wheel if you're not up to it." And he could, too. Whether or not the man beside her turned out to be the God of Love, he was most definitely "Racer Q."

She turned and met his gaze. Looking into his eyes was like looking into the sun—brilliant, dazzling, and probably bad for her health. She was lucky for the excuse of driving to turn away. "Thanks. I got this."

Q offered his hand on the armrest between them, and Posey took it gratefully, threading her fingers between his. She had the urge to crawl into his lap and pull his arms around her. It had been a long while since she'd felt that way about anyone. The last guy who'd made her feel that safe was currently lying in a hospital room, fighting for his life.

"I'm guessing this isn't exactly what you expected when I asked you to stay the night."

"Every second with you is a gift, Posey." Anyone else would have earned an eye roll for that cheesy line, but damn, if he wasn't sincere.

They remained interlocked in comforting silence until Posey turned into the airport parking lot. He offered to roll her suitcase to the gate, but she chose to hold his hand instead.

While Posey was too exhausted to do more than fall into her middle seat on the plane, Q sweet-talked the passenger sitting in the window seat beside Posey's to trade him for his middle seat three rows back. Next thing Posey knew, Q was standing in front of her, urging her toward the window. He sat down in the dreaded middle seat and lifted the armrest separating them. She leaned over and kissed him.

His lips curled into a surprised smile. "What's that for?"

"I appreciate you. You were really brave to make this trip with me. Let's face it, this is gonna suck, and we barely know each other."

He reached up and cupped her cheek. "How can you say that to the man who made love to you on your bearskin rug?" He looked at her as he had last night while their bodies were gliding together, somehow leaving her feeling giddy despite the anxiety brewing inside her.

"Yes, I suppose there's that."

"You should sleep." He shifted to offer his whole body as her own personal pillow.

She collapsed into his arms and fell into a fitful sleep, laden with visions of her father lying unconscious on the floor. The last dream was so vivid, it drew a strangled wail from Posey's throat and startled her fully awake.

Q tightened his arm around her and pressed his lips to her temple. "I'm here, Posey. I've got you." By god, he did.

"Sorry," she mumbled as she straightened into her own seat. Stale airplane air gummed up her tongue. She took a long drink from her water bottle, rubbed her dry eyes, and squinted at Q, who was reading a pile of papers by the light of his phone's flashlight. "Aren't you going to try to get some sleep?" she whispered.

"I need to finish this."

"What is it?"

He scrunched up his face. "You sure you want to know?"

"Now I do." She peered into his lap. "You're acting kinda sketchy."

Q heaved out a sigh. Flipping to the front page, he handed her the packet of papers and lit up the title, "The Tale of Cupid and Psyche."

"Oh." *That again.* "Why are you studying this like you're about to have a test on it?"

"Because I am, in a way." If this was a part of some self-improvement project by Reed to teach mythology to "the boys," as he called them, he was totally stressing Q out.

"Oh, Q—"

"We both are," he said.

"Huh?"

"This is us, Posey. Our story. Or some version of it anyway."

"This old myth? How is this us?" She held the stapled papers, at once incredulous at his absurd claim and somehow cognizant of the kernel of truth working its way into her brain, as Reed had described, in tiny increments.

"For starters, Cupid is Cupid, and Psyche is the most beautiful mortal in the world."

"So, it's obviously us."

He didn't even crack a smile at her sarcasm. "I tried to head off the worst parts by telling you the truth about who I am, but I'm not sure you entirely believe me, and your sisters might use your doubt to try to drive a wedge between us like they do in this story."

"Enough." She reached around Q's fingers and switched off the light. "I can promise you I am not about to be swayed by my sisters' advice, *especially* where men are concerned. You don't have to worry about that. Okay?"

He gave her a tight nod. Maybe he'd been hoping to hear that she did entirely believe him, but Posey didn't have the strength to lie.

"And *you* don't have to worry about the whole last part of the story, where my mother puts you through the wringer to prove your love. I already know you're my Right Love. I'm not going to let anything bad happen to you, Posey."

"Good to know," she said, offering him whatever hint of a smile her mouth was able to form, which couldn't have been much, considering. "I don't suppose your superpowers extend to my dad's health?"

His shoulders slumped, and a deep scowl darkened his expression. "I'm so sorry, Posey. I wish I could help. The length of each person's life is set by the Fates at the time of birth. Once the thread is measured and cut, there is only one way to extend a mortal's life, and that's by granting immortality. I do not have that power."

*Well, shit.* She'd seriously made the guy feel guilty about not being able to turn her father into a goddamn immortal? "Oh, Q. Please don't burden yourself like that. I didn't bring you with me to perform some hocus-pocus on my dad."

"I almost wish you had. That would mean you believe me."

He tried to smile but only managed a flat line. "Still, I wish I could do something to ease your worries."

"You are doing it." She slipped her hand just inside the sleeve of his T-shirt and squeezed the very firm bicep that had cradled her sleep. "You're here."

He smoothed the hair off her face and feathered a kiss to her forehead. "Of course." He tucked her head beneath his chin, fingers playing at her nape.

She let her eyes drift closed. This man beside her was certainly real enough—the warm skin and taut cords of muscle beneath her fingers, his affectionate caresses at the back of her neck. It felt wrong now to recall how beautifully their bodies had moved together just hours ago—the passion and power and pleasure—but the memories were part of them both now, written in permanent ink on two souls. No one and no fairy tale could take that away from her.

And yet, the papers in her lap held a definite weight. If Reed could pick and choose from the ancient legends, why couldn't Posey?

Easing out of Q's embrace, she flipped to the last page. "You know, I seem to remember this story having a happy ending." She wriggled the phone from Q's hand and made to turn on the light, but the phone had locked.

"Oh. Whoops." Posey passed the phone back his way, but Q didn't take it.

"It's 5555." And there it was, the secret no man gave away— and she hadn't even asked.

In the eerie light of the darkened plane, she found his trusting gaze. *Who are you?* she wondered, followed quickly by *How did I get so lucky?*

Shaking her thoughts back to the story, she scanned backward from the end to find her answer. What she discovered there was not the sweet vignette from her high school memories—the dizzying union of heart (Cupid) and soul (Psyche)—but something much more three-dimensional and not entirely flattering to any of the characters involved.

Snuggling close so she could place her mouth next to Q's ear, she read aloud. "*HH*'He,' meaning *you*, 'has chosen a maid,' meaning *me*, 'and has robbed her of her virginity.' Is that why you asked me if it was my first time?"

Q nodded. "I would have proceeded differently."

She tucked a kiss behind his ear. "You are completely adorable. And now I'm kind of curious what I missed."

Turning his head to close their tight circuit, Q whispered his reply into the shell of her ear. "There's always next time."

Grinning now, Posey returned to their story. "So Jupiter says to Venus, 'Do not grieve, nor fear, by reason of a marriage with a mortal, that the honor of your great house and name will be dimmed. This marriage shall neither be disproportionate nor irregular.'" Setting down the pages, Posey asked, "What the hell does that mean? What could possibly be *regular* about their marriage?"

Q chuckled. "I have no idea. I don't know of one marriage among gods that is anything close to regular."

"Oh, here comes the good part." Posey continued from where she'd left off: "He then ordered Mercury to find Psyche and carry her up to the heavens. When this had been done, he took a cup of ambrosia and said, 'Drink, Psyche, and be immortal. Never more shall Cupid leave your side, for your marriage shall last throughout eternity.'"

Their gazes locked as their happily ever after spooled out toward the unseeable horizon. The vision was both glorious and terrifying, like peering over the edge of the Grand Canyon.

Inside the white noise of the airplane, Posey became

hyperaware of the heartbeat pounding in her ears. If Q was right, his heart would be thrashing just as wildly. Posey leaned her head against his shoulder.

*Coin flip time.* Inching downward, she held her breath. *Yes, please.*

She pressed her ear to his chest, took Q's hand in her own, and pulled their joined hands to her heart. His heartbeat galloped against her cheek, and hers responded in the gaps between. She couldn't hear it the way he claimed to, but she felt it vibrating in her bones, the way the two hearts filled each other's spaces as completely as their bodies had done last night. Her tears spilled all over his shirt, but Posey refused to tear herself away.

He curled his arm around her side and drew her closer yet. She felt his spoken words rumble out of his heart. "I love you, Posey."

Her answer was barely a whisper mouthed against his chest, and yet she had no doubt he heard her perfectly. "I love you too, my sweet Cupid."

42

# MEET THE REYS

Posey's sister was waiting for them in the hospital lobby. With her puffy face and wide-set frame, Cupid could barely make out the family resemblance.

"Oh, Po! You came!" Arms thrown wide, the woman lunged at poor, sleep-deprived Posey, who held tight to Cupid's hand before, during, and after the collision.

Posey wriggled free. "What's the latest on Dad?"

"He's stable." She shot a pained glance at Cupid. "You brought a date to Dad's heart attack?"

Cupid offered his free hand. "Hello. I'm Quentin."

Posey's sister clasped his hand, and before she could speak, Posey rattled off an abrupt introduction. "Quentin, Alicia. Alicia, Quentin. How's Mom doing?"

"She's shaky, as you would expect. Dad had a quiet night, but we can't breathe easy until he passes the twenty-four-hour mark."

"Can you take us to see him, please?"

"I can take *you*," Alicia said, "but it's just family, and they're only allowing two of us in at a time."

"Of course," Cupid said before Posey could even think about feeling bad. "I wouldn't dream of getting in the way."

Posey shot him a look of gratitude, and the three of them stepped into the elevator. On the second floor, Alicia led Posey and Cupid to the Coronary Care Unit visitors' desk, where they presented their licenses and aimed unsmiling faces toward a merciless camera. Two plastic badges were produced and set on the counter.

"Mr. Arrows, you'll have to wait in the lounge area. Ms. Rey, cell phones silenced past this point, and when you get inside, please ask one of the others to step out."

"Okay," Posey answered wearily, switching off her phone. The giant double doors swung open, and a sob caught in Posey's throat.

Cupid grabbed her hand. "Need a minute?"

"No, I can do this," she answered while staring into the stark, white space on the other side of the doors. "I think it all just became real."

He pressed his lips to her head. "I'm sorry I can't go in there with you."

"Yeah, me too." She gave his hand a squeeze, then let go and walked forward in measured steps. Cupid stood watching until the doors swooshed closed behind her.

"So where'd you come from, Quentin Arrows?" Alicia's voice shook Cupid from his second entreaty to the gods in twelve hours: *Please let Posey's dad be okay.*

"Hmm? Sorry, what do you mean?" He sat down in one of the stiff chairs across from Alicia in the small waiting area.

"Did Mother know about you?" Alicia's hostility toward Cupid took him by surprise despite his thorough digestion of the cautionary tale of Psyche's sisters *and* Reed's directed warnings *and* Posey's anecdotes. He hadn't encountered another earthling who'd disliked him so much since his initial confrontation with Ruthie's husband.

"Did she know what?" Cupid asked.

"That Posey was bringing someone with her?"

"Honestly, I'm not sure what Posey told your mother about us." Cupid shrugged off his coat and leaned back into his chair. He noticed a TV sitting on a bracket over Alicia's head. Some news show was playing, thankfully with the sound off.

"So, there's an 'us'?"

Warning bells clanged in Cupid's head. "I think you should probably ask Posey your questions."

"What should she ask Posey?" The second sister had emerged through the double doors into the waiting room—the oldest, angriest arrangement of the Rey genes. Tall and brittle, this sister reminded Cupid of one of the dried twigs in Posey's fireplace, ready to burst into flame at the slightest spark.

Cupid jumped out of his chair and offered his hand. "Hello. I'm Quentin."

"Sofia," she said, her lips pursed in what seemed to be a permanent expression of disdain. "What should Alicia ask Posey?"

"Whatever she wants, I guess," Cupid said with a shrug. "How's your father?"

Sofia sank down heavily next to her sister, leaned back against the arm of the couch, and tucked her legs beside her. "No change."

"That's good, right?" asked Cupid.

"I guess." Sofia sighed and closed her eyes. "He's just had a metal balloon inflated inside his heart, so all things considered, stable is good."

Cupid nodded. "It's been a long night for everyone. If you two would like to go back to the house and get some sleep, I can take care of things here."

Sofia squinted her eyes open just enough to shoot Alicia a look that sent a chill down Cupid's spine. "Thanks, but we're not leaving our mother with a total stranger."

"Posey can vouch for me."

A hollow laugh left Alicia. "Another stranger."

Overpowered by their resentment, Cupid raised his hands in surrender and sat down. "I didn't come here to make this difficult situation harder for any of you. I'll just wait here for Posey."

He pulled his phone out and began composing a text to Pan. *At hospital now. Posey is in with her fa—*

"How old are you, Quentin?" Sofia had pulled herself upright, her back propped up with a folded coat.

Cupid lowered his phone and met her narrowed eyes. "Thirty-three."

Both sisters huffed. Sofia folded her hands in her lap and attempted a pleasant tone. "And what do you do for work?"

Cosmic matchmaker seemed the wrong answer for the moment. "I'm a builder," he replied.

"You're a general contractor?"

He recognized the term from his work at Ruthie's, but with the ground shifting beneath his feet, Cupid picked a simpler truth. "I'm more of a hands-on guy. Carpentry, painting, that sort of thing."

"*Hands-on*," Alicia repeated, nodding slyly to Sofia.

"Is that how you and Posey met?"

"No, actually."

"If you weren't doing a build-out for our sister," Sofia pressed on, "what was it, then? A dating app?"

Posey would be furious if she knew they were interrogating him this way and even angrier if he revealed how they'd really met. With all the fallout after her entanglement with that other patient, her sisters would never understand. He and Posey hadn't gotten around to discussing how to present their relationship to her family, and he knew better than to dig a hole she'd have to climb out of. The truest answer he could have given was, "None of your business," but he'd come to help them heal, not deepen the wounds.

"I met Posey on a bike trail. We'd both stopped to admire the same scenery." There was no way he would divulge the name of Posey's happy place to these two.

"Wow," Alicia said, "you work quick."

Picking up her sister's thread, Sofia asked, "Is that your move? Waiting at a scenic overlook for an unsuspecting woman and then sweet-talking her into giving you her number?"

So preposterous was her version of events, it made Cupid laugh out loud. "I seem to spend much of my time defending myself for other men's poor behavior." To be fair, after meeting Mia's Tinder dates, Cupid could certainly understand the reputation of the average male mortal.

"Oh puh-*leez*," Sofia said, fainting dramatically against the couch. "Don't tell me we're on to Sebastian *again?*" Whoever this Sebastian was, he caused Alicia to fold her arms over her chest in supportive defiance.

"I'm afraid I don't know who you're talking about," Cupid said.

"Oh? Little Posey never mentioned how she made a move on my husband?"

"Sebastian is your husband?" Cupid was trying very hard to absorb the information being thrown about.

"For the time being," Sofia answered ominously. "Well, I'm not surprised she didn't tell you about that. Not her finest moment." And likely the source of all the bad blood between them.

"Was this recent?" Cupid asked, feeling a little disloyal to Posey even for the question.

"She was seventeen at the time, so I should say not," Sofia answered.

Alicia chimed in with a snide, "You do know she's nearing forty . . . or has she failed to mention that, too?"

Anger was not an emotion that overtook Cupid frequently, but these two were trying their hardest. He could easily visualize the Rey sisters' faces superimposed on Psyche's meddling sisters, hear the damning accusations issuing forth in their voices, convincing Psyche that her husband was a poisonous serpent she must slay for her own safety.

Well, their evil efforts would have no effect on Cupid's love for Posey. Nor would he allow them to steal his even temper.

"Oh, no," Cupid assured them, "Posey did mention her age. I was so shocked, we nearly had a disagreement over it." For once, Cupid lied well, made them believe he was recalling a vivid memory. "I made her show me her driver's license." That part was half true, anyway.

"How long ago was that bike ride when you met Posey?" asked Sofia.

"Five days."

"Well! A whole five days!" Sofia hmphed. "It's a wonder you don't know everything about us by now."

"I'll bet he knows the balance in Posey's trust fund."

"Hush, Alicia!" The two sisters glared at each other, seeming to forget their common enemy in the heat of the moment.

"Oh, get real, Sof. Why else would Thor and his magic hammer fly across the country with our sister after knowing her for less than a week?"

*Money.* Was that the source of their animosity? It certainly didn't seem to be making any of them happy people.

Two heads swiveled toward Cupid, and Sofia shot the question like an arrow right between his eyes. "Well, Mr. Hands-on? What do you have to say for yourself?"

Cupid stood and shook the life back into his legs. "I could

use a cup of coffee, and I'll bet you ladies haven't had anything to eat yet today. I saw a diner down the street. What can I pick up for you?"

Alicia scoffed. "I'm on Keto."

"I don't eat before noon," said Sofia.

"Okay, then." He pulled his coat on mostly because he didn't want to leave anything of himself behind with the two of them. "If Posey comes out, please tell her I'll be back soon with breakfast."

43

# WHIPPED

Posey and her mother entered the waiting area, arms linked. "I'm so excited for you and Dad to meet—" Q's absence hit Posey with a force she could not have anticipated. "Where's Q?"

Alicia rolled her eyes so hard, Posey was almost impressed by her stamina. "Isn't five days a little soon for nicknames?"

So they'd been grilling him. Well, no wonder he'd left.

Posey pulled out her phone and smiled when she saw his text, starting with a string of coffee-cup emojis. **I hit the wall. Back soon with food and coffee**. His message ended with the heart emoji with an arrow through it.

"Wow, that boy's got you whipped," said Alicia, sneering at Posey's smile.

Nodding, Sofia added, "Who would've guessed the iron maiden would fall for a gold digger in a pair of tight bike shorts?"

"Don't forget the tool belt," Alicia said.

"Wait, what?" Posey asked. "What tool belt?"

Sofia smirked. "You and your boy toy never discussed what he does for work besides shakin' the sheets with you?"

"Come on, Sof," said Alicia. "You saw the guy. You don't really think she's keeping him around for the scintillating conversation."

"*Girls*," started their mother wearily, rubbing her temples in a gesture familiar to Posey.

"No, they're right, *mostly*," Posey said. "He does look fantastic in his bike shorts. And yes, he's got the body of an Olympic athlete and the face of a supermodel and *damn*, can he shake those sheets—not that we've made it to an actual bed yet—sorry, Mom. So yes, I am thoroughly, blissfully whipped even though we only met a few days ago."

She paused for a wistful, melodic sigh as her sisters sat blinking at her, mouths agape. Posey could have left it right there at the "Suck that, bitches!" moment, but she was so very tired of being underestimated and condescended to. Posey was better than that, and maybe—just, maybe—her sisters were, too.

"If you'd bothered to look past the pretty packaging, you would have learned that he also happens to be a wonderful listener. We've talked for hours and hours, and yes, it's been more scintillating than I can convey, and yet I still have volumes to learn about him . . . and I plan to spend the rest of my life doing exactly that."

Her mother reached a shaky hand onto Posey's cheek. "Posey? What are you saying?"

"I'm saying he's the one, folks. My soul mate, delivered on a silver platter, and I plan to savor every bite. It would be nice if you all could be happy for me, but it's not a prerequisite. By the way, Dad's awake, and he's asking for you both, so you might want to retract your fangs and go give your father a kiss."

"You could've led with that!" Sofia hopped off the couch and pulled Alicia to her feet.

*You didn't ask,* Posey could have answered, but she didn't need to be the keeper of their consciences. "Mom, get your coat.

We're going out for some air, and I'm going to introduce you to my extremely hot boyfriend."

Her mother answered with a smile and a hug. "I'm so happy for you, Posey."

"I can't wait for you to meet him."

They linked arms for the short elevator ride to the street level. The automatic doors opened, and Posey's mother lifted her face to the sun like a prisoner leaving jail.

"I don't think I've properly breathed for twelve hours."

"It does help," Posey said gently. "Take your time."

"No, no, I need to meet this soul mate of yours."

Posey's phone vibrated with an incoming call, and she slowed to dig it out of her purse. *Q calling . . .*

"Go ahead," her mom said. "You can walk and talk at the same time. I'm not about to keep you from your sweetheart."

"You sure you don't mind?" Posey was already accepting the call. "Hi. We're heading down Hubbard now."

"I hear your father is alert and doing well."

"Yes, he's feeling much—*wait*. How did you hear that?" Posey's shoes grew suddenly heavy. "Q?"

"Posey, you did it!" His cheerfulness sounded off. He was a terrible, terrible liar. It was one of his very best qualities.

"Did *what*?"

"You crossed us. All that stuff you said to your sisters about soul mates. You believe in our perfect love."

"Why does this not feel like a good thing?" *And how did he know?* Her feet were no longer moving.

"Posey?" came her mother's worried voice.

"Do you remember how I told you that each Right Love couple has to cross a liminal point? And at that point, my heart is released?"

A cold sweat broke on her forehead. She was about to lose

her shit. "Are you saying you're done loving me now? No more echo beat? You're moving on?"

"No! Our love is eternal. Forever and ever and ever. Longer than your mortal life. That will never, ever change."

"I'm being dumped." And she was about to be sick right there on the street. Posey's mother moved in front of her and grabbed her by the arms. "Po? You okay?"

"Gods, no, Posey. Slow down. Take a breath."

"No! I'm not breathing until you tell me what's happening!"

"Mercury has come for me. I've served my sentence, and it's time for me to go home."

"Oh my god. You're leaving." The sidewalk tilted. "Where are you? Can't we talk about this in person?" She frantically searched past her mother, but Cupid was nowhere to be found.

"I'm so sorry it has to be this way. They allowed me this one phone call, and our time is almost up. Posey, listen very carefully. This is extremely important."

Her heart was beating so hard, she could barely hear him, and she imagined his doing the same. *Calm down so you can take this in.* "Okay, I'm listening."

"Good, good. I can feel you relaxing."

"I'm trying."

"Me too," he said, and this time, she could picture a genuine smile on his beautiful face. "I have to ascend now, alone, but Mercury is going to come back for you."

"*What?*"

"We can still be together on Mount Olympus if you want that. The choice is entirely yours, but you need to understand that your decision is final. If you go with Mercury, you can never return to Earth."

"What are you saying? I'm going to fly up to the heavens and become immortal like it says in the myth?"

Posey's mother shook her. "Posey! What are you saying? You're talking like a crazy person right now!"

Posey tipped the phone away from her mouth. "I'm aware, Mom. Just let me hear this, okay?" Her mother threw up her arms and spun away. Posey would have to fix that later.

"I can't promise you immortality. Only Grandfather can extend that offer. The only promise I can make you about eternity is that I desperately want to spend mine with you." *My heart.* "But if all we are allowed is the length of your mortal life, I would be privileged to share that life with you."

A sob escaped Posey. Tears streamed down her cheeks as she managed a reply. "That sounds like the weirdest proposal ever."

"Don't cry, my sweet Posey. My heart can't bear it."

"I know. I can feel it breaking." *Along with mine.* "Do you have any idea what you're asking of me?"

"Yes," he said simply. "I'm asking you to choose love."

One week ago, the concept of romantic love would not have moved Posey Rey to cross the street, let alone to give up everything she had ever known and cared about. And now, well, she had become that exact fool she'd thought *him* to be.

"How will Mercury know my decision?" *How will I know my decision?*

"You must meet him at the Rosa Hartman Park. It's a short ride from where you are. Start out on Tenney's Trail until you come to a small wooden bridge. He'll find you there. Three p.m. Please don't be late. He won't be able to wait for you."

"Three p.m. *today?* I'm supposed to tie up a whole life in four hours?"

"I know time is short, but it's all they would grant. I've texted you Pan's number. He can take care of your house and car and whatever else you need."

"I don't care about my stuff! What am I supposed to tell my family?" Her mother shot her a look of pure terror. "What about my patients?"

"Please believe me, Posey, it wasn't my choice to spring this all on you or leave without a proper goodbye. I tried to warn you, but we just didn't have enough time."

The echo of her lover's pain reverberated off the walls of Posey's hollowed heart. "There could never be enough time with you, Q."

"I want you to know I will always love you, no matter what you decide. I'm so sorry I have to leave you this—"

*Call dropped.*

44

# ASCENSION

Call dropped.

Cupid's gaze remained so transfixed on the words on the screen, it took a few beats of his anxious heart to register that the hand holding his phone had shrunk. Unable to process what his eyes were reporting to his brain, he slapped his free hand to his chest. Gone was the T-shirt that had absorbed Posey's tears, along with the swollen muscles and firm abdomen that had so nicely filled it out. Even belted, his jeans sagged below his soft belly and pooled on the marble foyer of Aphrodite's palace.

His head jerked up. Aphrodite and Hephaestus stood before him. Mercury had already vanished.

So, that was it! Cupid's gravity-powered fall had produced its requisite torments—loss, shame, anxiety, fear—but this instantaneous ascent was its own punishment. No time to grieve all he'd lost, no time to prepare for reentry into his world, his family, or his sad joke of a body.

Barely holding his dread at bay, Cupid rolled his shoulders. As if their absence had been but a dream, his wings hinged open and readied for flight. That was all the data he needed to know the reversal was complete. He could not have stomached confirmation of his diminished manhood.

Mistaking the spread wings as an invitation, Aphrodite started toward him, arms open.

"Welcome home, son."

He stood woodenly as she hugged him with the same hands that had pushed him off the Mount not so long ago. The once-comforting embrace now only deepened his eerie disconnect of time and place. An outcast on Earth, now an alien on Olympus.

She pulled back, studying the wings as her fingers trailed down the edges. "Hephaestus repaired your wings. I think he did a beautiful job."

*We give you back your wings.* What Posey meant as liberation, his mother used to enslave him.

"I need to warn Posey." Cupid startled at the honk of his old voice. It was impossible to sound tough, but he forced the words out anyway. "She has a right to know she'd be choosing life with a grotesque monster."

"Whatever happened to 'love is blind'? Or 'hello, Mother,' for that matter?" Mother certainly hadn't lost her pluck while he'd been away.

"Hello, Mother. Hello, Hephaestus."

"Welcome home, Cupid," Hephaestus said, stepping forward to kiss Cupid on both cheeks. "We're very proud of you."

"You are?" Cupid searched both faces. "Does that mean I *am* released from my punishment?"

"Of course, dear," said Aphrodite. "You were released when Pan and Reed crossed."

"What? How? After Pan, my heart was in the worst kind of agony."

Hephaestus placed his hand at his wife's back. "Your mother"—

he shot a gooey smile at Aphrodite—"wanted to reward you with the chance to experience your own Right Love."

"And then tear me from her side when she needed me most?" Cupid couldn't recall the term Posey had used to label his mother's behavior, but he was confident this latest revelation would support her diagnosis.

Taken aback, Aphrodite jabbed her finger at Cupid's chest. "The one who tore you from Psyche's side was you! *I* sent Mercury for both of you. You're the one who begged for her to be able to make her own choice."

"You could have left me there with her. What's a few more hours?"

"What kind of choice is it if her decision comes under the influence of your divine gifts?"

Cupid crossed his arms over his chest, wings shadowing the roll of his shoulders. "If you're insinuating that Posey is too weak to know her own mind, you haven't been paying attention."

Hephaestus cut in again, a gentle smile in place. "I believe what your mother is saying is that sometimes, the heat of passion can sway . . . *people* from their best judgment."

"Not if your passion is for the right person," Cupid countered.

"Ah," Hephaestus said, nodding. "You have learned much during your one hundred days of exile."

"Yes. I may look and sound like the boy you forced off the Mount, but I am not that boy anymore."

Aphrodite's brow shot up. "Yes, we are all well aware of your sexual awakening." *Thanks for reminding me you were spying on me every second.*

"I do hope everyone was thoroughly entertained," Cupid shot back. "You'll have to forgive me if I fogged up your gaia glass, Hephaestus. That's what happens when you uncork 3,375 years of sexual repression."

Head hung, Hephaestus said, "Apologies, Cupid. It was wrong to watch."

"Thoroughly," replied Cupid, shooting them both a stern glare. "But I wasn't speaking of sex. I understand about love now, all of it. So, congratulations! Your punishment worked. No more mischievous arrows shall be launched by these fingers."

"I am delighted to hear that," said his mother.

"As am I," said Hephaestus.

"And I also understand that you lied to me about Pan and made all of Olympus keep your secret for two thousand years. How could you, Mother?" The words shattered under the weight of his emotions.

He prepared himself for Aphrodite's usual fare—justifications, excuses, bullying—and just when Cupid had thought he'd heard everything, she surprised him with contrition. Closing the space between them, she unearthed his hands from the fortress of his folded arms.

"I made a terrible mistake. I was afraid of losing you, and I . . . I knew I couldn't bear it if you wanted to leave me. I'm so sorry, my love."

Hephaestus slid to his wife's side, wrapped his arm around her shoulders, and dropped a kiss into her hair. *Well, well, well. Aren't these two cuddly?*

Cupid's reply sounded all the more desperate in a higher register. "If Posey decides not to meet Mercury, my life might as well be over. I'll serve out my days doing your bidding. I really don't care what becomes of me."

Aphrodite squeezed his hands as an anguished look crossed her expression. "Don't say that, son—"

"But if Posey *does*, miraculously, make the choice to give up her life on Earth to be with me," Cupid pressed on forcefully, "things are going to be different around here."

Surprise, then irritation flickered across Aphrodite's forehead. *That's right, Mother. My voice may be squeaky, but at least I've finally found it.*

Her hands slipped from Cupid's, and he did not try to hold on. "Speak your concerns with respect, then, and they shall be heard." That was as open an invitation as he'd ever been granted.

Cupid squared his shoulders and dug deep for his most assertive timbre. "For one thing, I've read that old tale, and I won't allow you to run Posey ragged proving herself to you."

"I see," said Aphrodite, one eyebrow raised but giving away nothing.

"Also, we will require a gaia glass so Posey can keep up with the family she's leaving, and I can follow Pan and Reed's life together."

"Oh dear," said Hephaestus, sharing a knowing glance with his wife.

Aphrodite clasped her hands together and tipped her head in a gesture of empathy Cupid wasn't ready to absorb. "You'd condemn your Psyche to watching her beloved mortals age and die?"

A sharp ache flared in his chest as Cupid recalled receiving the news of Pan's death. He'd felt Ruthie's losses, too, a deep current of grief that ebbed at times but never left her. Still, Cupid was certain Posey would prefer to experience the full range of emotions rather than sever all ties with her family. "It's called being a grown-up, Mother. Losing is part of loving."

Without so much as a glance at his wife, Hephaestus replied. "I would be honored to craft you such a glass." *Huh.* No ingratiating himself with his wife, no appeal for permission. It seemed the last hundred days had brought changes on Olympus as well.

"Have we heard the last of your demands?"

"Almost," he said, drawing up to the full extent allowed by his withered stature. "I want my Earth body back."

Hephaestus trapped his amusement between pressed lips. Aphrodite's response was not so charitable. "*Do* you now?"

"Yes," he said firmly. "I was more fully the God of Erotic Love during my brief life in human form than I have ever been here, trapped in this ridiculous body!" His voice cracked toward the end, but wasn't that just making his point? He couldn't even verbalize his rage, let alone physically express his passion.

"Ridiculous, is it?" Aphrodite huffed. "Not everyone is gifted with a sculpture-worthy physique, you know. Lovers make do." Hephaestus shifted uncomfortably at her side.

Cupid couldn't help but picture his chubby fingers inching toward Posey's pleasure zones, a boy's hands on a woman's body. Even if Posey were to close her eyes and picture him as he once was, her touch would speak the truth. They'd made love exactly once. How long could her imagination bridge the gap?

"I don't wish to discuss the mechanics of carnal activity with you, Mother. Of course I will use whatever gifts I have to please my lover, but I would think your Worthy deserves better than a child for a partner?"

"Well, aren't you the clever one!" She regarded Cupid with what might have been admiration. "Asking not for yourself but for the sake of your Psyche."

"I exist only for Posey now. Without her, I have no need of a body at all."

"I see," she said with a scary grimace that made Cupid picture his own disembodied head with wings for ears and a bow and arrow for arms. Boldness had its risks. "Tell me one thing, son. Would she not still love you even without your fancy body?"

*It's a test,* rang Pan's voice in his head. And wouldn't it be just like Aphrodite to let Posey give up everything only to show up on Olympus and find Cupid in this sorry state? He couldn't let that happen to her.

"Have Posey and I not walked through enough fire already, Mother? Why am I here if we haven't crossed, hmm?" A ghastly thought occurred, so dark that even the possibility made his chest ache. Could he have been wrong about everything? "Are Posey and I truly Right Loves, or have you deceived your own son in the most malicious way imaginable?"

"Enough!" Aphrodite held up her hands to fend off further vitriol, of which Cupid had no shortage right now. "Yes, yes, *of course* you are each other's cosmic Right Love match, and yes, Psyche crossed you when she declared to her sisters you were her soul mate." His mother almost looked proud. "You caused Love to blossom again where it was all but extinguished."

Hephaestus cleared his throat. "In more hearts than you know," he said in an emotion-choked voice that caused Aphrodite to pull her husband's arms tighter around her waist.

Cupid recognized that look in his mother's eyes. He just couldn't remember her ever looking that way over Hephaestus. He could only hope this marital awakening would translate into maternal generosity.

"So? What do you say, Mother? May I have my fancy body back if Posey comes?"

Her expression softened, bringing an almost angelic smile to her lips. "How else would you make me a grandmother?"

# DECISION TIME

What scared Posey most about leaving was how easy it was to tie a neat bow on her "earthly existence"—as she now viewed her life so far. There was barely a doubt in her mind that Cupid was exactly who he claimed to be, hence, she did not agonize over her decision. In fact, there was no decision, only details to attend to.

Beside her walked her mother, thoughtfully chewing her egg sandwich and swallowing her questions with every bite. It would have been nice to leave them all with some reasonable explanation. Problem was, Posey didn't have one.

"Am I permitted to speak now?" asked her mother.

"Yes, and thank you for your patience." Posey unwrapped her sausage burrito, briefly pondering what she would be eating from now on.

"Why can't you tell us where you're going?" *Fair question*, and the quick answer—*you wouldn't believe me*—wasn't going to satisfy.

"His job requires complete secrecy."

Her mother leaned in and whispered, "Is he some kind of spy?"

The idea nearly made her giggle. Cupid would be the worst spy ever. "I really can't say," Posey said, adding a meaningful glance she hoped her mother would interpret as a yes, "but we won't be allowed to contact you by phone."

Her mom took another bite of the sandwich. "How will we know you're safe?"

*Hmm.* Maybe she had stars in her eyes, but the chance to dwell among gods felt more exotic than perilous. Granted, if the myth played out as written, Posey was in for some serious trials even with the answer key tucked in her back pocket. But the psychotherapist in her was far more concerned with the fraught mother-son relationship she would soon be stepping into and how Cupid might behave in his mother's thrall. Would've been nice to meet the folks before committing to spending an eternity with them, but that was a luxury Posey did not have.

"I'll do my best to get messages to you and Dad. I'm sorry, Mom. I just don't want to promise you something and make you worry when I can't deliver."

"I understand." Her mother tossed the crumpled sandwich wrapper into the bag.

They walked hand in hand to the hospital entrance. "I need to make a couple of phone calls," said Posey. "I'll be up in a bit."

Her mother squeezed her hand. "Promise?"

"Promise. I don't have to leave until 2:30."

"Okay. I'll prepare your father privately so you don't—" She cut herself off.

Posey frowned. "Give him another heart attack?"

Her mother tipped her face to the midday sky and let out a weary sigh. "Yesterday, I was sitting at the kitchen table, making my grocery list for Thanksgiving dinner. Today, I don't know which way is up."

Posey joined her mother's skyward glance. Posey's new home was somewhere up there, far beyond any boundary she could fathom. "It's gonna be okay, Mom. Dad's getting better, and I'm great. Please don't worry about me."

Her mom forced a smile. "At least we all got to see you. Silver lining."

Posey nodded. She wasn't looking forward to the goodbyes, especially with her parents, but it helped that this wasn't her first time cutting the cord. They'd all rehearsed for this.

Posey checked the time. It would be nearing ten in Indiana. Hopefully, April would have an opening in her schedule this morning to call her back. Posey was preparing to leave a message when April picked up.

"Please don't tell me he turned out to be a serial killer."

"If he is, he's got me snowed. Do you have a minute?"

"I have eight. What's happening?" *God*, how easy it was to fall back into this friendship, to pick up the phone and jump into a conversation with no beginning and no end. What a shame Posey had wasted so much time. "First of all, I know this is all going to sound crazy, and I promise I didn't call you to talk me out of it."

"Should I be scared?" Posey heard the shift in April's voice; the doctor was in.

"Nope. It turns out Q and I are quite in love."

"That escalated quickly!"

Posey chuckled. "It probably doesn't feel that way to him. I fought it tooth and nail."

"I'm sure you did," April said, "but I'd be the last person on earth to talk you out of love—assuming you've kept far away from the doctor-patient relationship?"

"Oh yes."

"In that case, I could not be happier for you. That's the very best kind of crazy."

Tears sprang to Posey's eyes. *Dammit.* She swallowed hard before continuing. "The reason I called is that I need to take an indefinite leave from my patients, and I wanted to be able to offer them your contact information. I have five active—"

"Whoa. Hang on, sister. What's this 'indefinite leave'?" April wouldn't be as easy to sneak past as Posey's mom.

"Q and I are going away together. Actually, he's already gone on ahead, and I'm leaving very soon to meet him. The point is, I don't know if I'm coming back, and I can't leave my patients hanging."

"Hmm, isn't the big advantage of what you do that you can do it from anywhere?"

"There won't be an internet connection where I'm headed."

"Wow. Does this guy have a private island or something?"

"Something like that."

"Oh-kay? You do hear yourself, right? You realize this is a little concerning."

"I understand how it might sound that way, yes."

"Well, that's a good sign anyway," April said with a lighter tone. "Has anyone in your life besides me met this guy?"

"Uh, strangely, yes." This next part would most likely shock April more than anything Q-related. "He met my sisters this morning."

"You took him home to meet your family? Wow, wow, *wow.*"

"It wasn't exactly like that. Actually, my father had a heart attack last night—"

"Damn, Po, I'm sorry to hear that."

"Thanks. He's gonna be okay. Anyway, Q insisted on coming to support me."

"Nice. Seems like a stand-up guy."

"He is. He's the real deal, April. I know it in my bones."

"Not that it necessarily matters, but what did your sisters think of him?"

"Oh, they gave Q quite the interrogation while I was in with Dad, but you know my sisters—they always think everyone's after the famous Rey fortune."

"And you're sure he's not?"

"Positive." Cupid needed Posey's money like an eagle needed a diamond tiara.

"All right, then."

"I know it's asking a lot to trust my judgment on this, but really and truly, I called you on behalf of my patients so I can leave with a clear conscience. Can you do that for me, April?"

"Of course. You know I just want you to be safe and happy."

"I am. Promise. And while I'm at it, I—" Posey's voice broke with the tears that finally escaped. "*Shit.* I need to tell you how sorry I am I cut you out of my life for so many years."

"Oh, Posey. We all did what we had to do. Let yourself off the hook already."

Posey moved the phone from her mouth until she had regained control of her voice. "When I grow up, I want to be half as good a person as you are."

"Eh, you totally are." April's teasing lightened the somber mood.

"I hope you know how much I respect and admire you."

"I love you too, Po. Go be deliriously happy with your insanely good-looking and apparently obscenely wealthy young stud, and if you two make any babies, consider naming one after me."

"Will do," Posey said. "Love you," she said because it was easier than saying goodbye.

With April's warmth and forgiveness pumping through her veins, Posey sat on the bench outside the hospital, called each of her patients, and then made the call she'd saved for last—Pan.

"Hey, Doc. I'm gonna put you on speaker so I don't have to repeat everything to Reed."

"Hi, Pan. Hi, Reed."

"Posey," came Reed's gentle voice. "How's your father?"

"He's doing much better, thank you."

"That's great news. How are you holding up?"

"Surprisingly okay," Posey answered, realizing it was true.

"Q's gone, isn't he?" The sadness in Pan's voice tore at her heart. She'd stolen the last few hours he and Cupid would've spent together.

"Yes, he called me about half an hour ago, just before Mercury took him."

"They let him make a phone call? That's a first!"

"He had to tell me how to meet Mercury when he comes back for me."

"You're going up to *Mount Olympus?*" That was an awed Reed.

"I don't understand," Pan was saying, almost to himself. "Why didn't Mercury take you both at once?"

"Maybe because I was with my mother? I have to go to the meeting point alone at three o'clock today."

"*Ah.* He wanted you to make the choice for yourself," Pan said.

"Yes, he said that too. Well, I've decided. I choose Cupid."

"Yeah, all right." Obviously reluctant, Pan continued. "Q, buddy, if you're listening from up there, I'm so fucking sorry, but I know you'd want me to warn her."

"He would," murmured Reed, and Posey could feel the love between the two of them along with her growing dread at whatever Pan was trying so hard not to say.

"Please, just say it, Pan."

"Okay. Here goes. Did you two ever discuss Cupid's physical state on Mount O?"

"Yes, he told me how he used to be." He'd been quick to debunk the myth of the diapered cherub.

"The thing is, when a divine ascends, they revert to their Olympian form."

"*Usually*," Reed added.

"Kinda *always*, Reed," said Pan, regret dripping from his tone.

"I see," said Posey. "To be clear, we're talking about a winged fourteen-year-old boy?"

"Yep. Still the same good-looking guy, just . . ."

"Jailbait with wings," said Posey with a sigh.

"Basically," said Pan, "though the age taboo is a purely mortal construct."

"*Pan*," chastised Reed.

"Think about it, Reed. We've all been alive for thousands of years. It's really not the same."

"*Still—*"

Posey's mind raced while they bounced the argument back and forth. How could she conceive of a relationship with a teenager, regardless of how long she lived or what everyone around her was doing? Where would that leave them? In love but with no sexual intimacy?

"Who says I'll keep *my* body when I ascend?"

Wrenched from his debate with Reed, Pan answered, "What?"

"Why *wouldn't* I have a different body on Olympus? Everyone else does," she said. "Maybe they'll turn me into a winged teenager to meet Cupid where he's stuck."

"And that would be okay with you?" asked Reed.

"Sure. Why not?"

"Why not?" Pan's guffaw nearly drowned out Reed's groan. "Only because fourteen is the worst age in a lifetime to be frozen. Just ask your mate."

"Maybe it's only the worst age if you're stuck there alone," she replied.

"Sorry, Doc, that's just—"

"Possibly the most romantic idea the goddess of love may ever entertain," said Reed, stunning Pan into momentary silence.

"Oh yeah? Tell ya what, Reed," said Pan. "If they turned me back into a satyr and gave you the choice to stay as you are or become a monster, too, what would you choose?"

"Immortal life as your physical equal? Easy," Reed said. "Satyr. In a heartbeat."

Posey teared up again. "Sounds like we're about to have one hell of a party up there."

Pan chuckled. "You know, you two almost have me wishing for it." Beneath the quip, Posey could hear the pain of Pan's separation from his best friend.

"Tell me this, Pan. What happens if I don't go with Mercury?"

"Cupid would have you believe you will love again."

"While he's up there watching it all happen?" She could never.

"He wants you to be happy, Posey. I know that for sure."

"But what happens to *him*? What becomes of Cupid after my life is over?"

"That I don't know," said Pan. "Reed?"

"I can only conjecture based on the literature."

"Come on, Reed," said Posey. "Don't sugarcoat this."

"Psyche is Cupid's great love story," said Reed morosely.

Summoning a bravado she did not know she possessed, Posey declared her final decision. "Then I better get up there and make this one last him an eternity."

"Well, Doc, when you get up there, you tell my bestie that he is one very lucky sonofa—oh, wait, not that! One lucky mother—*oh hell no!* Never mind!"

All three of them laughed till they cried. Tears streamed down Posey's cheeks. Two men in scrubs exited the hospital and offered sympathetic nods.

It was Posey who spoke into the last gasps of their sniffles. "Hey, guys? No more goodbyes, okay?" Before they could agree or disagree, she ended the call.

Time was short. She had a little more than an hour to resolve a lifetime of sibling rivalry. "Good thing you're a mental health professional," she joked to herself as she climbed the stairs to the second floor. Posey emerged to an empty waiting room.

"They're all inside," said the nurse at the desk, adding a wink. "Go ahead in. Dad's doing great."

Posey pressed her hand to her racing heart. "Okay. Thanks." The scene she walked into was straight out of a Norman Rockwell painting: Dad, sitting up in the armchair, her mother and sisters close to his side, smiles all around.

Her dad's face lit up when he saw Posey approaching. "Well, why didn't you tell me my Posey Pie was in love?"

Posey chuckled as her sisters parted to make room for her. "I figured your heart had enough to deal with right now."

His laughter set off a coughing fit. Her mom pressed a big heart-shaped pillow to his chest. "Squeeze and breathe, honey."

"Sorry, Dad." Posey flinched at each of her father's grimaces.

"No, it's good," her mom said. "They want him to clear his pipes."

"So, Mom says your man just up and left," Sofia said.

*I am mindful of a full-body clench. I choose not to engage.*

Her mom countered. "That's not exactly how I said it." *I know, Mom.*

But Sofia hadn't finished gnawing on that bone. "What's wrong? Things get a little too real for him? Just like a man." Drawn to her father's coughing, Sofia added, "Present company excluded, of course."

"Q was called away," Posey said evenly, "and I have to leave soon to meet up with him."

"Wow. That's it?" asked Alicia, rising to her feet in front of Posey. "You're here for five minutes, and you're leaving us again?"

Posey gave her dad's hands a squeeze, then let go and stood toe-to-toe with her sister. "I understand how that must feel to you, but yes, I'm afraid I don't have a choice."

Sofia shot to her feet, her face twisted with fury. "What kind of man would make such a selfish demand, and why the hell would you let some guy you just met tell you what to do? Has your free will left you along with your senses? Is that what you think it means to be in love?"

Their father lapsed into another pained coughing fit, and their mother's sharp voice cut in. "Girls!"

"Sorry," said Sofia in a not-sorry tone, "but I think *someone* needs to point out to our baby sister that she's letting her vagina do the thinking again!"

"Can anyone say 'pattern'?" Alicia added.

"Oh my lord," mumbled their mother.

Dr. Rey exited Posey's body. She floated to the ceiling and hovered over the blurred family portrait. Was this how it felt to live with wings? Not a bad way to gain perspective. *They're hurt,* she told her earthbound self, *and maybe a wee bit jealous. And that old resentment is always right there, just below the surface.* Alicia was no more than a parrot, but what was going on with Sofia's hair-trigger rage? Trauma from nearly losing their dad? Maybe.

*I can choose to forgive them everything.*

Releasing a deep breath, Posey reentered her body. She surprised her sisters into silence by grasping their hands in hers. "Maybe it takes a horrible event like Dad's heart attack to remind us our lives on this planet are a gift that can be retracted without a moment's notice. I know we've had our issues in the past, but it takes way too much energy to stay angry. I'm done with all that. We're always going to be family, and I love you, no matter what."

Drawing Sofia into a hug first, Posey felt her sister's body tremble with stifled tears. "Let it out, Sofia. Just let go."

As Posey held her sister tight, Sofia broke down with a violent quake and soaked Posey's shoulder with her tears. Her crying jag peaked with shuddering sobs and a long, breathy sigh. Posey readied herself for an "I love you" or an "I'm sorry," but she was fully unprepared for her sister's declaration.

"I'm leaving Sebastian."

Posey drew back, holding Sofia at arm's length. "*What?*"

"He's a cheating douchebag."

Their dad could be heard asking, "What did she say?" over Alicia's, "What the fuck!"

Posey pulled Sofia to the bed, and they sat down together. "Oh God. I'm so sorry."

"It's not your fault," said Sofia with a huff. "Turns out, it never was." She swept her sleeves over her wet cheeks. "I'm the one who should be apologizing. I'm sorry, Po. I couldn't see it. I was an idiot."

"He was very slick," Posey said.

"Sleazy, you mean," Sofia said, smiling through the tears.

"That too." Posey tipped her sister's chin so their eyes were level. "I forgive you, sister."

A fresh river of tears ran out of Sofia's eyes. "Thank you, but can you do me the favor of not repeating my mistakes?"

Ah. "Q is not Sebastian."

"Sebas-*tard*," said Alicia, sliding to Sofia's other side and wrapping her arm around her sister's shoulders.

"My fierce protector," Sofia said, sighing into Alicia. "Ugh. Love sucks."

Sebastian sure did. "Look, I know I'm the person least likely to make the case for love, but there are good men out there. Don't close off your heart because of one—"

"—cheating douchebag," Alicia said.

The three sisters drew together and swayed in silent solidarity until it was time for Posey's final goodbye.

# 46

# REUNITED

*Tick, tick, tick* . . . Three more minutes left of not knowing how the rest of his life would go. Would Posey arrive soon in Mercury's wake, to love Cupid to the depths of his soul for all eternity? Or would Cupid remain loveless and alone? Or would Mother invent some twisted in-between to imprison them both?

His mother and father and probably Hephaestus would have their noses pressed to their gaia glass, keeping tabs on Posey's every move and utterance, but Cupid couldn't bear to watch. He skipped the midday meal and retreated to his bed-chambers, where he could pace without being observed. Mercury had promised to return directly to Cupid's quarters either way; Cupid would reunite with Posey in privacy . . . or be left to his solitude to suffer the devastating blow.

*Tha-thump, tha-thump, tha-thump.* His heart was too far away to feel Posey's, and that might have been the worst part of their separation, might be the worst part of eternity. *Tha-thump, tha-thump, tha-thump.* One heart left to beat its unanswered half of the perfect whole that might never be again. One heart that would never stop its relentless, lonely beat, even if it wanted to.

Glancing at his cell phone, no more than a glorified stopwatch now, he caught the shift to double digits—fifty-nine seconds to go. Why had he not taken a single picture of Posey or the two of them together? Why had he not recorded one second of Pan and Reed shooting each other gooey glances or fighting like an old married couple? Or Ruthie petting her beloved Pookie? Or Mia's boys building their blanket forts?

*Tick, tick, tick* . . . Fifteen seconds . . . eleven, ten . . .

He stilled his feet. Pinching his eyes closed, Cupid willed Posey to him with all his might. *THA-THUMP, THA-THUMP, THA-THUMP.*

*Tick, tick, tick* . . . Three, two, one . . .

The air around him hummed like an approaching storm. Alone, Mercury could sneak up on Cupid no problem, but a passenger would slow his flight. Cupid's skin prickled; the tiny hairs on his arms and his neck stood on end. He picked up her scent on the incoming gust. Every inch of him tensed.

*THA-THUMP THA-THUMP! THA-THUMP THA-THUMP! THA-THUMP THA-THUMP!* His thundering heart heard hers a split second before she arrived in Mercury's arms, wide-eyed and off-balance.

"Posey!" Cupid lunged forward and steadied Posey with his hands at her waist.

"Q?"

Mercury vanished.

"Are you okay?" Cupid asked, even as he performed his own inspection. She was dazed but she was breathing. The swift ascent had plastered her hair to the sides of her head like that day in the coffee shop when she'd removed her hat. She was still unsteady on her feet as she blinked back at Cupid, stunned.

"Say something, Posey!"

Swallowing heavily, she raised two quaking hands toward his shoulders and then beyond. "My god! You're . . ." Her hands snapped back just short of meeting the tips of the wings folded behind him.

"Grotesque." His head hung with a heaviness he would have to carry into their forever.

Cupping his chin ever so gently, Posey tipped Cupid's head to meet her gaze. "You're magnificent!"

"What?"

She leaned in as if to kiss him. He braced. Surely, she couldn't—

Her soft lips closed over his. Their mouths danced together as they had for the few glorious, kiss-filled days they'd shared on Earth. Tender and greedy, sated and hungry for more—*more he could no longer provide.*

Moment ruined, Cupid leaned away. "I'm so sorry, Posey," he whispered.

Her eyes fluttered open. "About what?"

"Me. This." He took a step back, though it physically pained him. Keeping his gaze locked on hers, he swept his hands in a downward motion to the left and right of his winged form.

"You're apologizing for being the most dazzling creature I've ever laid eyes on?" Posey's gaze rode down his body, a lusty leer that filled Cupid's nostrils with her desire. A bright blast of *want* hit him right in the groin, and very much to Cupid's astonishment, his body responded like an adult male in the prime of his sexual life.

For the first time since Posey's arrival, he chanced a look down at his own body, starting with the muscular chest straining against the fabric of his chiton. The wool folds that had, just moments earlier, hung loose to his knees now skimmed his thighs and bunched tight in the groin.

She'd done it! Aphrodite had fully restored Cupid's Earth body, complete with the deep voice he might have noticed earlier if not for the severe stress of the situation.

*But the wings!* Had she forgotten to remove the sad little chicken wings? Cupid lifted his shoulders to assess the damage. His wings flapped open with a dramatic *swoosh* that ruffled Cupid's hair and sent a shiver down his spine. A stunning array of brilliant, white feathers fanned out on either side of his head. His jaw dropped in disbelief as he followed his impressive wingspan to where it stopped just shy of the ceiling. Wings fit for a god—a virile, man-sized god.

Posey's gasp drew his attention. "Can you fly?" she asked in an awed whisper.

He shrugged, making his new wings hop. "I have no idea."

"Aren't you kind of dying to find out?"

"Not right now," he replied. Too many questions about their future still weighed on his mind.

With an understanding nod, she stepped closer. "Is it okay if I touch you?"

Cupid laughed, a much-needed release that felt almost as good as having Posey nestled into his side. "Yes, please. Touch everything!"

Her quivering fingers met the feathers near his elbow. "Can you feel this?" she asked, studying his face as she caressed his wing.

"Oh, yes." And things were getting fairly dire as a result. How could he have known the wings were one giant erogenous zone?

Slipping an arm around Posey, he swept her right off her feet. She looped her arms around his neck and gazed up into his eyes, a smile playing at her lips. "Is that a hint?"

"Mm-hmm." He was smiling too—two pairs of Cupid's-bow lips smiling at each other.

He carried her to his bed, custom fit to the perpetual youth, far too small for this new and improved version and definitely too small to accommodate his mate. He bent to set her gently onto her back, then stretched out over her body. "Don't worry. I'll ask Hephaestus to make us a new bed right away."

She giggled. "I wasn't worried," she said, pulling him down to kiss her, "*but . . .*"

He lifted his head with great effort, nuzzling her with his nose and making her giggle some more. "But what?"

"But why don't you build our new bed yourself?"

He popped up onto his palms. "What?"

"Where's this magic tool belt you told my sisters about?" She gave him a sly grin.

"Challenge accepted," he said, earning an excited look that reminded him of Ruthie and her fascination with Henry the handyman. "I'll build us a whole new house if that would make you happy." He bent to kiss her again. "How many bedrooms should we have, hmm? Four? Ten? Twenty?"

Posey's eyes widened. "Oh my! That's a lot of rooms to fill. Maybe we could table this discussion for a few hours?"

He laughed. "Sorry. I might have gotten a little carried away. I'm so happy you're here, Posey!" He rolled off her body and crowded next to her, his head propped up with his hand. "Are *you* happy you're here?"

"Crazy happy. The God of Love is my soul mate! I can't believe this is all real." She pushed her fingers through his hair, sighing. "I really didn't think you could get any sexier, and now I come to find these gorgeous wings on your back! I don't know how I'm supposed to control myself."

"Who says you are?" *Gods*, it felt good to be with her again. Joking one second, intense the next. "How was it for you? Leaving your family?"

Catching his shift in mood, she stilled her hand in his hair. "It would have been harder if my dad hadn't improved. You really didn't have anything to do with that?"

"I wish I had that much influence, believe me. But I'm really glad to know he's well."

"Yes, much more settled than this morning. I even made peace with my sisters," she said.

"More good news!"

"I gave Sofia my house," she said, "the place I bought expressly to hide from her."

"You know Pan would've taken care of all that for you."

"I know, and thank you, but I didn't need to trouble him with all that. My parents have lawyers to handle all the details. My family's kind of filthy rich. Did you know?"

Cupid chuckled, nodding. "Your sister mentioned something about a trust fund."

"Yes," Posey said, rolling her eyes, "the National Park Service has been getting a fat check every year since I turned twenty-five."

"Mm, that sounds like you." He dropped a kiss on her forehead.

"I did call Pan and Reed to let them know you'd left." Cupid's eyes slid shut. He missed them already. "Pan felt the need to warn me that you were going to lose your hot bod."

That opened Cupid's eyes. "He told you that?"

"You're not angry, are you?"

"No, not at all. I'm grateful. I would've told you myself if I'd had more time. I'm just a bit shocked you came anyway."

"Well," she said, snaking her hand behind his neck and playing at his nape, "for one thing, I happen to be in love with your mind and your soul in addition to the very hot wrapper. And two, I figured if you'd been turned back, I would just ask to be changed to match."

"Ugh, no!" Cupid pinched his eyes shut to ward off the image of the two of them flying around Mount Olympus, forever locked in puberty. "Please, don't *ever* put that awful idea into Mother's head!"

He opened his eyes to Posey's giggles. "None of that matters. Clearly, Pan was wrong."

"No, Posey. Pan was right."

Her smile evaporated. "What?"

"When I got here earlier, I *was* the old me again. Mother only changed me just now, when you left with Mercury. If you'd stayed back, I'd still be the old me—at least on the outside." His old self definitely would not have spoken up to his mother as he had this morning.

"Well, I cannot wait to meet her so I can say thank you in person."

Cupid leaned in and whispered into Posey's ear, "Soon enough."

She whispered back, "I memorized the trials that were put to Psyche. I will do what I have to do."

He answered her with a kiss. "My brave girl," said Cupid. "I do not believe that will be necessary. You have already stood up for our love once. Mother was most impressed with the way you handled your sisters." A frown settled on Posey's face. He stroked a finger down her cheek and tucked away a few strands of hair that had fallen over her eyes. "What is it?"

"I'm sorry for the way my sisters treated you. This is not meant to excuse her behavior, but my sister Sofia learned that her husband was cheating on her. That's why I gave her the Tahoe house. I figured she might need a place to go with the kids."

"That was kind of you."

"It's not as if I need it now." Posey smiled at him, reaching for his hip as if to hold him close. She needn't have bothered;

Cupid wasn't going anywhere. "You might be amused to know I implored Sofia to keep her heart open to the idea of love."

Cupid's brows shot up. "Well, look at you! Another goddess of love in the making!"

The door to Cupid's chamber flew open, and in burst Aphrodite. "Did I hear my name?"

"Mother!" Cupid bolted out of bed. Pure instinct fanned his wings to shield Posey.

"Wow! I do believe I've outdone myself!" Aphrodite strode straight over for a closer look. "I expect your mate is pleased with this manifestation?"

"Yes!" came the answer from behind him. "Very much so!"

Aphrodite peered around the wings to find Posey scrambling to her feet. "Aren't you going to introduce us, son?"

Cupid retracted his wings, eliminating the barrier between mother and mate. "Mother, please meet Dr. Mariposa Rey—Posey—the love of my eternal life."

Posey's cheeks pinked as she offered her hand to Aphrodite. "Hello. It's a very great honor to meet you." Cupid became aware he'd been holding his breath, but he wasn't quite ready to let go.

"Welcome to Olympus," said Aphrodite as she took Posey's hand.

"Thank you. If I may ask, how shall I address you?"

Something flashed behind his mother's eyes—surprise? "Aphrodite will be fine for the time being."

Nodding, Posey said, "*Aphrodite*, thank you for choosing me to be your son's Right Love match. And thank you for the opportunity to choose life on Olympus. I am most grateful to you." Posey dipped her eyes to the floor, a touch of humility Aphrodite did not fail to notice.

"I, too, am grateful, Mother." Cupid preferred not to enumerate his mother's recent gifts lest she decide he'd been overly enriched.

Aphrodite tipped her head. "Your gratitude is well noted." Cupid felt his shoulders loosen just a bit.

Posey set her left hand atop their two clasped hands. "I want you to know, Aphrodite, you and I have the same goal— to make your son happy." She held Aphrodite's gaze until the goddess nodded.

"Of course."

"And in the spirit of our shared goal . . ." Noting a sudden, marked increase in the heart rate he shared with Posey, Cupid braced for disaster.

Curiosity piqued, Aphrodite leaned in, smiling. "Yes?"

"I'm a big believer in boundaries. If our bedroom door is closed, it would be in everyone's best interest if you would please knock before entering." With a relentless smile, Posey slipped out of Aphrodite's clasp and retreated to Cupid's side, where the two stood together with linked arms, a unified front.

Aphrodite studied the woman at her son's side, no doubt beginning to appreciate Posey's grit. Cupid tightened his hold on Posey, weaving his fingers between and around hers. He couldn't recall a time when a mortal had been returned to Earth, especially so soon after arriving, but if this were to be the first, Cupid wasn't about to let Posey go without him.

"Yes, I see your point," Aphrodite said with a sunny smile. "Old habits die hard, as they say, and my habits are positively *ancient*. Hmm, what if . . ." Aphrodite clapped her hands together as an idea struck. "I could cross-stitch a reminder to hang on the door!"

Cupid's guffaw dissolved into a coughing fit. Posey, meanwhile, was swift and gracious. "I think that's a lovely idea. Thank you."

Cupid stared slack-jawed at the two women in his life. He had the powerful sense that all his boring days were behind him.

"Now, speaking of needlecraft," Aphrodite went on, all business, "you'll both need something more appropriate to wear to the banquet tonight."

"*Tonight?* Must we go, Mother?" Cupid had serious, vivid plans for Posey involving that bed he'd outgrown, and those plans did not include a lengthy detour through a hall filled with gods.

"Well, of course you're going. You're the guests of honor!"

Teeth clenched, Cupid tried once more to spare Posey the spectacle. "Subjecting Posey to everyone at once is a bit overwhelming, don't you think?"

Aphrodite's hands found her hips. "Oh, fie! Your Posey does not strike me as the type to be easily intimidated."

"Indeed, she is not, but can't we postpone the celebration, say, for a few days?"

"Oh!" Aphrodite's hand flew to her chest. "Did you not want Posey to share your bedchambers tonight? I'm sure we can make other accommodations if—"

"Of course she will sleep with me, Mother," Cupid replied.

"Then, naturally, we'll want to begin the *proaulia* ritual as soon as possible." Aphrodite returned Cupid's glare with a cheery smile.

"*Proaulia?*" Posey asked.

Aphrodite answered before Cupid could find his voice. "It's the ceremony that marks the bride's transition from her childhood home before the wedding."

"Wedding!" the bride-to-be exclaimed.

"Yes." Aphrodite rolled on, seemingly oblivious to Posey's unease. "Traditionally, the day before the wedding, the bride would make certain offerings for a fruitful marriage."

Why hadn't Cupid thought this part through when he was making his demands? "Mother, surely you're not—"

She held up her hand to shush him. "*However*, I have persuaded Hera to merge the *proaulia* and the *gamos* into one night so the two of you won't have to be separated again. You're welcome!"

When the stunned couple failed to express their appreciation, Aphrodite waved her hands. "Time grows short as we stand here jibber-jabbering. Soon, my dear Posey, you will be whisked away for your purifying bath."

Cupid did not trust himself to read Posey's emotions, but her silence was not an encouraging sign. He needed to put some space between his beloved and this wedding cyclone that had overtaken them. "You've given us an awful lot to take in, Mother. Can we please have some time alone before the nymphs arrive?"

"Of course." Aphrodite sashayed toward the door. "And I'll be sure to advise them to knock loudly before entering," she said with a wink, then exited as abruptly as she'd appeared.

The apology was about to roll off Cupid's tongue when Posey's lips quirked into a grin. "Of all the conversations I anticipated your mother and I might have today, I hadn't once considered she'd propose marriage."

Cupid immediately dropped to one knee. "My darling Posey, would you—"

Sinking to her knees, Posey closed her mouth over his proposal. When she finished kissing him soundly, Posey pulled back, leaving him heaving for breath. "My sweet Q, do you not recall asking me—most eloquently, I might add—to spend eternity with you?"

A rush of relief blew out of his tight chest. "Of course I do."

"And here I am."

47

# NUPTIALS

*Deep breath.*

*I feel anxious. I feel the perspiration beading on my forehead. It is okay to feel this way. This discomfort will pass—eventually.*

"Having trouble managing the pig?"

Jolted from her mindfulness exercises, Posey regarded the goddess seated beside her. "Sorry. My stomach is a little rocky." And the saffron-dyed veil casting its mustard-colored tint over the dead zoo lying on her plate wasn't helping her appetite.

"Here, try a sesame cake." Artemis slid the platter toward Posey, who took one of the biscuits with a wan smile. The goddess of prenuptial maidens had been a constant presence by Posey's side during the preparation for the *gamos.*

"Thank you. You're very kind."

"You know, you're not the first nervous bride I've watched over." Artemis raised a meaty pig rib to her mouth.

"I'm only nervous about the pomp and circumstance of this event," Posey replied, "not my choice of groom."

Said groom, seated clear across the giant hall, hadn't taken his eyes off Posey for a moment since she'd entered the room. It was almost physically painful being so close but so far from his side, but the wedding feast was segregated by gender. A sumptuous dessert buffet set out on round tables divided the room down the middle like yellow police tape.

In another lifetime, Posey might have sent him a flirty text: *Feeling a sudden urge to gaze at the stars. Meet me on the balcony?* Not here, not now, not ever again.

Artemis followed Posey's gaze. "Only Cupid would return from banishment with a bride." *Ah, the classic he-always-gets-away-with-it trope. Posey knew it well.*

"Cupid suffered a great deal before he found me, you know."

"Did he?" *Was she impressed or just surprised?* "I'm not privy to that information."

"Yes," answered Posey, recalling her early conversations with Q. "In fact, his pain is what brought him to me."

"Whatever you did for him seems to have worked wonders," Artemis commented. "He appears much relieved now."

Posey felt her lips quirk into a smile because hadn't Cupid claimed the exact same thing? "Truth be told, he was the one who put his heart on the line and took all the chances. I was not the least bit interested in falling in love."

"No?" *Had a moment of kinship passed between the self-proclaimed independent woman and the revered virgin goddess?* "Cupid must have been very persuasive, indeed, since you left your whole world behind for a life here with him."

"How could I not?" Posey's eyes misted over, but she had no problem reading the devotion on Cupid's face. If only she could press the fast-forward button on this night, to the part where they would be alone together.

Artemis glanced at Cupid again. "Yes, our little Cupid has

undergone quite the transformation," she said. "Still, it might be a while before I stop seeing him as the little itch of Mount Olympus."

Judging from the electricity in the room, it seemed Artemis was in the minority. The assembled elite were quite enjoying their eyeful of New Cupid—not just the sculpted chest and shoulders holding up his custom-tailored *chiton* but a self-assurance blossoming right before Posey's eyes. She couldn't have said which thrilled her more, but she did know this: every eye on Cupid was an eye not on her, and for that, she was grateful.

"Was he really so bad?" Posey sipped at her water.

"He was like the tagalong little brother you need to ditch every now and then," Artemis said fondly, then grinned at some memory. "He made a terrible hunting companion—not that his bow skills are lacking. You see this olive?" Artemis picked an olive off her plate and propped it up on the table like a football set on its tip. "He could spear this right now from where he sits, no problem. But set an antelope here, and all bets are off." She picked up the olive and popped it into her mouth.

Across the room, Cupid's head tipped with curiosity. His extraordinary senses still caught Posey off guard, but she doubted even a god would be able to hear their conversation over the boisterous voices and the musicians playing at full volume.

"I still have so much to learn about his gifts," Posey said with a sigh. *How can you not know if the man you're about to marry can fly? Absurd!*

Artemis leaned in, waggling her eyebrows. "I'm quite sure he will enjoy enlightening you, beginning with your wedding night!"

Cupid had left his seat and headed for the nearest dessert table. Throughout the great hall, the din of conversation and laughter petered out as everyone paused to watch Cupid drag not one but two of the small round tables toward the two head tables.

"What is he *doing?*" Posey whisper-demanded of Artemis.

"I don't know, but he has definitely captured his parents' attention." That couldn't be good.

Sure enough, there sat the God of War, merrily pushing grapes into his mouth like popcorn as if the movie he'd been watching had just reached the car-chase scene. Cupid, meanwhile, had summoned one of the servers to clear away the desserts from the two tables. Now the musicians trailed off as well, all eyes glued to the God of Love's latest antics.

Posey's pulse galloped in concert with Cupid's, forever and fully his heart's partner now, even in crime. *Gulp.*

Not as quick as Mercury but faster than Posey could prepare for, Cupid crossed the giant hall and stood behind her chair. "Much better," he proclaimed.

"What are you doing? Have you had too much to drink?"

"Not yet," he said, sounding amused. He bent to whisper in her ear, his cheek pressing the veil to the side of her head. "You were way too far away. Would you please come sit beside me?" He offered his hand to Posey.

"Isn't that forbidden?"

He slid Posey's chair back from the table. "The custom stipulates only that the bride and groom may not sit at the same table."

Artemis shot out of her chair. "Brilliant! Go with your groom."

"Really?"

"Yes, yes," Artemis said. "I'll squeeze in next to Aphrodite."

Posey took Cupid's hand. Their fingers curled around each other's as if they'd been holding hands for fifty years. *I'm home,* realized Posey with a bright burst of happiness.

On Cupid's arm, she practically floated up the center of the room, inspiring awed whispers on both sides. "Everyone is staring," she murmured.

Without slowing his step or dimming his happy smile, he delivered his reply. "That's because they have never beheld such a beautiful bride."

They did, she had to admit, cut a striking vision in their traditional wedding garb: Posey in a floor-length violet gown trimmed in gold braids, her upper body adorned with precious stones in every color, a crown of gold set over the veil; Cupid looking every bit the prince of Olympus in his dazzling golden *chiton*, a wide cuff adorning his arm. They wore identical myrtle wreaths meant to arouse desire, as if any more needed to be aroused between those two.

"You make a stunning groom," Posey replied. "The gold suits you. Just sayin'."

Cupid rolled his eyes. "I look all too much like a certain stripper Pan dated for a time."

Posey giggled, happy to know he was still the same, guileless Q she'd fallen for on Earth. She squeezed his hand tighter, not just because her heart was suddenly too small for all the love she had for Cupid but also because they'd come face-to-face with Ares.

"Father, I'd like to introduce my bride. This is Posey." Cupid passed Posey's right hand into his father's. The God of War's resemblance to Cupid was even sharper at close range.

"*Chaîre.*" Bowing his head, Ares drew Posey's knuckles toward his mouth.

"Father greets you with 'rejoice.' Your response would be the same."

Posey tried the word, the resulting garble a further reminder of her otherness. "Forgive my pronunciation, please. I clearly need a lot of practice." A nervous bubble of laughter escaped her.

"No worries," said Ares warmly, closing his left hand over their joined right hands. "Your English will serve you fine here."

She gave him a nod of relief.

"Now, if you two would take your seat . . ." Ares gestured to the bench behind the two tables Cupid had arranged for them. "It's time for the groom's father to make a toast!"

They settled side by side into their seat. "Still breathing?" Cupid whispered.

"I think so."

Ares tapped his goblet with a knife, but he already held everyone's attention. "Gods and goddesses, welcome! Cupid's mother and I are pleased you could join us on *very* short notice"— scattered laughter—"to share not one but two joyous occasions this evening: Cupid's triumphant return to Mount Olympus and his marriage to the beautiful Mariposa!"

"Hear, hear!" Applause, applause.

"As you can see, my son has done a bit of growing up since that fateful arrow that brought him before the Divine Council."

Cupid's focus did not waver from his father though his Adam's apple did bob a bit deeper in his throat. *The "fateful arrow"? Do tell, almost-husband!*

"Of course I cannot take *full* credit for this dramatic metamorphosis." Ares turned toward Cupid for what Posey imagined would be a pride-filled, possibly tearful, acknowledgment of his son's hard-won successes. "Your *mother* and I spent countless, sleepless nights together"—*oh shit*—"wrestling for hours on end in passionate . . . debate."

A god seated about halfway down the table, a craggy-faced, red-haired giant who seemed about as comfortable in his wedding finery as a Rottweiler in fairy wings, brought his hand to his forehead and moaned.

Ares gained momentum. "Naturally, as parents are wont to do, we followed your journey with bated breath, rooting for you every step of the way. Of course, in our official capacity as overseers of your disciplinary action, we had to introduce certain course corrections."

Cupid flinched. Posey tightened her grip on his hand.

"Though it pained us greatly to inflict these punishments, I'm sure you understand they were necessary."

It took Cupid a beat to realize his father was waiting for an answer, probably because he was expecting a wedding toast, not a public castigation. He nodded grimly.

"While your mother and I strenuously hope we will not ever be in that *position* again, we would, of course, *come together* without hesitation to perform our civic duty if called upon. Isn't that right, Goddess?" Ares peered around a stoic Cupid and an increasingly wary Posey only to be met by a killer glare from Aphrodite.

Through gritted teeth, she replied, "Have we come to the part where we wish the bride and groom a long, fruitful marriage marked by love, forgiveness, and passionate make-up sex?"

Cupid whimpered. This meet-and-greet with the folks was going about as well as Cupid's waiting room interrogation. Posey reached for the glass of wine someone had kindly supplied, dragged it under her veil and straight to her mouth. The hell with waiting for the toast!

Ceding to Aphrodite, Ares raised his glass. "My son, you've been a bachelor nearly as long as I have." Awkward laughter. "I thought this day would never come," Ares said, slapping his hand down onto Cupid's shoulder, "but here we all are! *Na páne káto ta farmákya!*"

Cupid leaned in to translate. "Let the poison go down."

"Charming."

Cupid held his glass up, waiting for Posey to clink. Sheepishly, she reached under her veil and produced the remains of her wine. Cupid shook his head, chuckling. "Whatever will I do with you, my Posey?"

"I can hardly wait to find out," she answered, giggling when Cupid's eyes popped wide with surprise.

"Cheers, my beautiful bride!" He toasted Posey with a private wink that made her belly flip.

Helped along by several more glasses of Dionysius's finest, the rest of the wedding ceremony passed for Posey as it must for most brides—in a blur. Hera came forward to conduct the marriage rituals, something involving a pomegranate, two peacock feathers, and more than one mention of fertility. Posey could almost feel her uterus thickening. *More wine.*

Next up, the burly god who'd looked especially pained during Ares's toast stood and ambled toward their table. Posey tugged Cupid close. "Who's that?"

"That is Hephaestus, God of Fire and master craftsman—also my uncle, stepfather, and the truest father I've known."

Grasping one of Cupid's hands and one of Posey's, Hephaestus greeted Posey with a warm smile, his eyes dancing with joy. "I'm honored to meet the woman who won our Cupid's heart."

"It's a pleasure to meet you as well, Hephaestus. Oh! May I call you Hephaestus?"

"Yes, of course," he replied, "but I hope you will call me Father." Without waiting for Posey's answer, he plunged his plump finger into a leather pouch hanging from his neck and pulled out two gold wedding bands. "There was no way to consult you on the engraving, so I took a bit of poetic license. I hope you don't mind."

Cupid took the thinner of the two rings and read the engraving. "Yours says 'To my eternal love.'"

"Cupid's says the same," said Hephaestus.

Posey's eyes misted up. "Thank you. They're beautiful. Should we . . . or . . .?"

"Yes, yes," Hephaestus said, clearing his throat. "The bride and groom will now exchange rings."

Cupid grasped Posey's right hand and slipped the ring over her finger. "Mariposa Rey, will you be my wife for the rest of your days?" Raising her hand to his lips, he sealed his request with a kiss over the ring.

"Of course." Posey mirrored the gesture on Cupid's right hand, then began, "Cupid—uh, just Cupid—" Cupid snorted and Posey had to seriously repress the urge to stick her tongue out at him. "Will you be my husband for the rest of, uh, my days?"

With a gentle, intimate smile, Cupid replied, "Sweet Posey, I will be your husband for the rest of *my* days."

In her whole life, Posey had never felt so thoroughly loved and desired.

Still holding her hand, Cupid craned his neck to the corner seat at the head of the table, where quietly, minding his own business, sat a god in a taller chair than all the rest—a god who could only be Zeus. "Grandfather?"

A shiver rippled down Posey's spine.

Zeus rose from his chair. Robed in a weightier version of Posey's deep purple and gold costume and crowned with an intricate gold wreath, he ambled toward Cupid with unhurried steps, as if maybe he hadn't quite made up his mind.

Cupid held stock-still, barely breathing as the King of Gods reached for Cupid's cheek and brushed his thumb back and forth across his whiskers. "My grandson is a man." A wide smile stretched across Zeus's face as he patted Cupid's cheek. "Welcome home, Cupid."

Still cupping Cupid's cheek, Zeus turned to Posey. "Mariposa, is it your desire to fall asleep each night and wake up every morning next to this beard that will neither grow full nor entirely disappear?" Between her nerves and the wine, it took Posey a second to appreciate his attempt at wittiness.

"Yes, it is . . ." *King Zeus? Your Highness?* "Yes, it is, sir."

Zeus, serious now, stepped directly in front of Posey, his hand sliding from Cupid's cheek. "It is time to choose, Mariposa Rey. Will you live here as a mortal with your Cupid for the length of days appointed at your birth, to age as your human body will age, and to die when it is your time?" Cupid squeezed the hand he was still holding. "Or . . . will you live among us *as one of us*, an immortal, your eternal soul bound forever not only to Cupid's but to the body that now holds you exactly as it is and shall always be?"

Posey drew in a sharp gasp. There was so much she hadn't considered, and what a time to throw this at her, at the end of the longest, weirdest day of her human life! Who wouldn't choose to live forever with a permanently perfect husband, but how did one even contemplate immortality? Eternity?

"*Posey?*" Cupid's anxious voice jolted her attention to his even more anxious expression.

Posey's heart kicked into high gear. "Please forgive me," she begged. "I wasn't prepared for this."

Zeus held up his hand. "That is my fault. Call me old-fashioned, but before offering you a permanent place in our world, I had to be sure you and Cupid were thoroughly devoted to each other. Olympus is a small mountain populated by big personalities. I'm far too old for drama."

"Posey"—Cupid again—"do you need time to think? Grandfather, could she have some time to think about this?"

"No," Posey said before Zeus could answer. "I'm ready." Zeus raised his eyebrows in question. "Thank you for the offer. I accept. Enthusiastically. Please?"

Zeus's laugh crinkled his eyes into well-worn trenches. "Yes, by all means, let us do this, Mariposa . . . or shall we call you by your soul's name—*Psyche?*"

Posey felt the skip of their shared heartbeat, but she couldn't tell which of them had caused it. "I . . . I understand the reference, sir, but in this life, I have only been Mariposa, and if it is all the same to you, I would like to keep being Mariposa for the rest of my . . . time."

A familiar twinkle lit Zeus's expression. "Well, grandson, I can see we won't have to worry any longer about keeping you in line. This one knows her mind, and I dare say she won't put up with any nonsense from you!"

"I can promise you that is true," said Cupid with such sincerity, it left all three smiling.

"Good! Then let us make it so. Ganymede!" Zeus snapped his fingers. A flying creature—half boy, half eagle—deposited a silver chalice into Zeus's outstretched hand. "Drink of the ambrosia of the gods, Mariposa, and be immortal!" Zeus's voice shook the marble floor under Posey's feet. *Was it thundering right now in Connecticut?*

She grasped the chalice. Would this make her a goddess? Would she have superpowers? Could she start her own thunderstorms? Could she and Cupid make babies? Would sex be different? Would she be different? Would he still love her?

Cupid moved in front of her. "Grandfather, may I remove the veil?"

Zeus's reply came on a chuckle. "Yes, I think you'd better."

Gingerly taking her veil between his fingers, Cupid lifted the material in one fluid sweep. "*There* you are!" he exclaimed as if he'd been looking for her for hours . . . or eons.

She could only stare back at him, too overwhelmed to speak.

His hands closed around hers on the chalice of eternal life. "Do you want this, Posey?"

"I want *you*," she whispered.

He replied with a sober nod. "We'll figure it out together." It was no answer, and it was the only answer that mattered.

Together, they tipped the chalice and Posey had her first taste of ambrosia.

"Drink it all, my love." And she did. The chalice was swooped away by the fantastical flying creature.

Cupping Posey's cheeks, Cupid drew her to his lips. Joined now and for eternity, they kissed until the taste of ambrosia faded from their tongues.

Somewhere behind them, a drunken Ares boomed out, "You may now kiss the bride!"

48

# CONSUMMATION

Amid the crush of revelers spilling out of Ares's palace, Cupid faced his first challenge as a new husband—how to get his wife home from their wedding. The traditional mode of transportation, the groom's chariot, was woefully inadequate for a god whose own body had doubled in size, then doubled again by joining with his precious Posey.

"Take mine," Ares offered with a bawdy wink. "No chariot will get your bride into bed faster than my fire-breathing stallions."

"Due respect, Father, we've got this." Cupid turned to his wife. "What do you say, Posey? Shall we try out my new wings?"

Her eyes popped wide with delight. "I'm immortal now. What's the worst that could happen?"

Cupid shook his head, laughing. "You'll soon learn not to ask questions like that." He swept Posey off her feet and into his arms. With no more than a fervent wish to have his bride at home in his bed, his wings opened and stroked downward, easily lifting the two of them off the ground. Posey squealed as they rose high above the crowd, their long robes fluttering with the current.

"Are you cold?" he asked, snuggling her closer against his chest.

"I'm perfect!" Posey's arms tightened around his neck. "This is straight out of a superhero movie!"

Cupid had been called many names in his days but never superhero. "Hmm, maybe I'll forgo the new chariot and just carry you everywhere from now on."

"Works for me!" Peering around Cupid in all directions, Posey seemed intent on absorbing everything at once. "What's that trail of fire below us?"

"Our wedding guests are escorting us to our new home for the first time as a married couple. The torches ward off evil spirits."

"Evil spirits, huh?" Posey's amusement didn't surprise him.

"Nothing much scares you, does it, Mrs. Cupid?"

"I can't imagine anything evil getting past you, that's all."

"I'll never let anyone or anything hurt you, Posey." Especially grateful for the premature unveiling Zeus had allowed, Cupid managed a very sexy kiss—or so he thought until Posey started giggling. "My kisses make you laugh now?"

"I'm impressed you can kiss and fly at the same time."

"How about this?" He bent and kissed her again. With a slight dip of his left wing, he sent them into a roll, only pulling away from her lips after three full rotations. They were flying low enough to hear the cheers from the crowd tracking them below.

"What a showoff you are!"

Cupid laughed all the way to the soles of his sandals. "If you think *this* is showing off, wait till I get you alone, wife!"

Posey's desire flooded Cupid's senses. "Is it very much farther?"

"No," he said. "This is a small mountain—too small sometimes."

"Mmm. Then we'll be alone soon."

"Um..." Cupid glanced below to the crowd assembling outside Aphrodite's palace. "There are a few more customs yet to suffer."

"*What?* Can't you—"

"I'm afraid not." Dropping a soft kiss on her forehead, he glided to a gentle landing. "You might want to shield your head."

No sooner had he warned Posey than the two were barraged with the fertility *katachysmata* in the form of flying dates, figs, and coins. Aphrodite rescued them, as was her duty as the groom's mother, linking arms and propelling the couple inside.

"Welcome home—officially," said Hephaestus, standing at the hearth with his hands clasped behind his back.

Aphrodite picked up a large wooden bowl brimming with ripe persimmons. "May the season's fruit bring you prosperity and fertility."

Posey bowed her head and thanked them both.

Sharing a smile with his mother, Cupid picked one of the perfect specimens out of the bowl and presented it to Posey. "The first bite belongs to the bride."

Grasping Cupid's wrist, Posey drew both hand and fruit toward her mouth. Cupid watched, transfixed, as Posey bit through the delicate skin and caught the escaping innards with her tongue. Grinning broadly, Posey turned the exposed flesh toward Cupid. He completed the ritual, adding a wet kiss on his wife's lips for good measure.

Hephaestus cleared his throat and waited for the newlyweds to turn his way before revealing what he'd been holding behind his back, a red silk pouch cinched with a leather string. "My wedding gift to you."

"But the rings were—" Posey began.

"—obligatory," said Hephaestus. "This comes from the heart." He handed the gift to Cupid, who accepted it with a gracious nod.

"We are humbled," Cupid said. He pulled gently on the

string, and the pouch opened to reveal a round gaia glass more beautiful and unique than any he'd ever seen. The glass was set into a thick slab of wood with a distinct circular grain and handles reading "his" and "hers" on either side.

Posey gasped. "Is that aspen wood?"

"Yes!" exclaimed Hephaestus, delighted she'd recognized it. "Straight from your beloved Lake Tahoe."

"This is gorgeous." Posey skimmed her fingers along the telltale grain. "But how—?"

"Pan, Mercury, and three apprentices working at god-speed this afternoon," he answered with a wink.

Cupid, meanwhile, had been peering into the glass with no result. "Not to sound ungrateful . . ."

Chuckling, Hephaestus drew his arm around Aphrodite, who was beaming at her husband. "This glass works only when the two of you hold it together, one hand each."

"Perfect!" Grasping one handle, Cupid waited for Posey to take hers. "Shall we check on your father?" She gave him a grateful nod. "Here, just gaze through . . ."

Together, they studied the scene inside the glass: a man propped up in a hospital bed, laughing at something he was watching on TV. Posey's eyes welled as she whispered a teary thank you.

"You are very welcome, daughter," Hephaestus replied. A lump rose in Cupid's throat. "As for you, young man, now that you're home and . . . settled," said Hephaestus, his glance indicating Cupid's body, "come and see me when your bride is through with you, and we'll fit you for a new bow."

Posey answered with a flirty lilt. "I hope you're not in a hurry for that bow."

"It can wait!" Cupid replied hastily.

"So I figured," said Hephaestus. "Regarding your marital bed, I thought you and I might work on a new one together?"

A warm glow filled Cupid. "Yes, I would love that. I have much to learn from you, Father."

"Speaking of bed"—a grin tugged at Aphrodite's mouth—"yours awaits."

Cupid slipped his hand into Posey's. "Ready, wife?"

"Yes!" Posey's enthusiastic response drew laughter from Hephaestus first, and the others quickly joined in. Unabashed, Posey added, "It's been kind of a long day."

"Indeed," Aphrodite said, then gestured to the servant at the front entrance. "Let them in!"

The door was thrown open, and the throng of wedding guests streamed inside. Grasping Posey's free hand, Aphrodite ushered her and Cupid into the living quarters with all of Olympus on their heels.

Posey whipped her head around. "What is this?"

Cupid gripped her hand tighter. "Just keep moving."

Aphrodite led them up the stairs and into Cupid's chambers. The crowd gathered all around them, circling the bridal bed, which Aphrodite had decorated with a canopy of the same saffron-tinted fabric as Posey's veil.

The room quieted. Posey stiffened by Cupid's side, and he drew a protective arm around her waist.

Aphrodite addressed the guests. "And now, we rejoice together as our *gamos* ceremony comes to a close with the final tradition—the consummation of the marriage."

Posey burrowed in so close to Cupid as to be practically on top of him. "They're *staying?*" she whispered frantically.

"Absolutely not." Cupid spoke directly into Posey's ear, though everyone present had heard both her outburst and his reply.

With a knowing grin, Aphrodite concluded her remarks. "Presentation of gifts will begin at ten tomorrow morning. A very pleasant evening to you all."

A much-relieved Posey remained glued to Cupid's side as the crowd filed out with shouts of "*Eûge!*"

When the last of the guests had gone, Aphrodite took Posey's hands into her own. "Earlier today, you asked what to call me. From this point forward, I hope you will call me Mother."

Cupid might have wished for a different time and place for the offer, but he was beyond relieved that Posey had won Aphrodite's good graces and successfully averted the trials of Psyche.

Having prepared herself for the worst, Posey swiftly accepted. "Of course. Thank you, *Mother*."

Aphrodite leaned in to press a kiss to each of Posey's cheeks. The two locked gazes, and some great understanding seemed to pass between them. Cupid's thoughts spooled to the new mother and father he would never meet, huddled together along with his new sisters in a hospital room in a faraway world, no doubt missing their Posey.

Overcome with emotion, Cupid broke through the circle of Aphrodite and Posey's joined arms and pulled his mother into a hug. Aphrodite's frame felt small in Cupid's embrace, and he suspected his new stature was only part of the reason. "Thank you, Mother. For everything."

"Thank you for finding your way home to me, my son," said Aphrodite, shedding tears on Cupid's neck.

Hephaestus moved to his wife's side, slipped one arm around her waist and the other around Cupid. For the first time in Cupid's memory, they felt like a family.

With a hearty pat on Cupid's back, Hephaestus released him. Cupid, in turn, pulled away from his mother, his cheeks moist with tears.

"Come, my goddess," said Hephaestus. "Let us leave the newlyweds now."

Aphrodite nodded. "Hephaestus will guard your chambers

tonight . . . from a great distance." Twirling toward the door, Aphrodite waved over her shoulder. "Happy wedding night!"

Cupid took Posey into his arms and kissed her until the door closed behind them.

"Are we finally allowed to be alone?" Posey whispered.

"Mm-hmm." Smiling, he kissed her again.

Her hand pressed against his chest as she pulled back. "Do you still have your cell phone?"

He cocked his head. "Yes, but surely you know it won't work up here."

"I want a picture of my wedding day . . . before we get undressed."

"In that case, let me get the phone quickly!" His silliness set her giggling as he sped to his bedside table to retrieve the phone. "This feels so odd in my hand up here."

"Remember how to take a selfie?" she teased.

"I think I can manage." He tapped the appropriate buttons, then balanced the phone in his hand and reached his arm out in front of them. "Ready?"

In the camera screen, Posey's reflected image tipped her head. "Do I look different now?"

"Yes, of course. You grow more beautiful by the minute."

"I mean now that I'm immortal."

"Oh." Cupid considered her question anew. Despite the immortal blood coursing through her ever-beating heart, she was yet his same, beloved Posey. "I don't know. Do you feel different?"

"Actually, I don't."

He lowered his arm and turned his full attention to Posey. "Are you disappointed?"

"I don't know. Everything's happened so fast. I guess I have a lot of questions about how this all works. Like, am I a goddess now?"

"You will always be *my* goddess, but the answer is no. Becoming immortal does not make you a goddess." He couldn't read her pensive reaction.

"And our children . . .?"

*Children!* Cupid could barely contain his joy.

He stroked his thumb along her cheek. "You want to talk about children *now?*"

"Considering we've been invoking fertility spirits for the past three hours, and we're about to"—she glanced at the bed and smirked—"*consummate*, it seems like an appropriate moment."

"True enough. Our children"—he paused at the shiver that rolled down his spine—"will be demigods."

"Like Pan?" she asked.

Cupid huffed. "Pan's the only one quite like Pan. Our children will be immortal, half human and half god. And while I cannot say whether they'll have wings like their daddy or a stubborn streak like their mommy"—he grinned at Posey's adorable scowl —"I *can* tell you this for certain: they will be spectacular."

Posey's eyes drifted closed, and Cupid placed soft kisses on both. She drew in a breath and locked it inside closed lips, taking a moment to find herself.

Could he blame her? In a matter of a few short hours, Posey had fallen in love, nearly lost her father, confronted her sisters, left her home, her people, and her mountains behind. She'd accepted a one-way ticket to a world high in the clouds she wasn't even sure she believed in, to live the rest of her days—whose number she could not know—with a possibly winged man or boy, whose mother might impose impossible feats she might not survive. To top it all off, during the whirlwind wedding that immediately followed her arrival to this strange new place, she made the decision to live forever among—yes—actual gods.

That she was overwhelmed by the reality of her own immortality seemed like the first reasonable moment of Posey's day. The consummation could wait.

"Tell you what, Posey. Why don't we take this picture, then take off these uncomfortable costumes and sit down and talk until you feel more comfortable."

Her eyes blinked open. They were rimmed with tears. "You don't mind?"

"Of course not. Why would I?"

She grinned. "Oh, I don't know. I just figured a groom on his wedding night might have other things on his mind." It was nice to see her smile again—so nice, he wasn't about to point out that the bride had those same things on her mind.

"I won't deny it. But if we were to stay up all night talking, I'd be perfectly happy with that too."

She squinted just a little and studied him the way she'd done that day in the coffee shop, trying to figure out how much she should believe. "You really mean that, don't you?"

"Have you forgotten already, Posey? We have eternity."

49

# HAPPY ETERNALLY AFTER

"You promise it won't hurt?" Posey's hand met Cupid's shoulder just as he was about to release his arrow.

Target locked in his bow's gaia sight, Cupid replied, moving only his lips. "Promise."

He waited for Posey to remove her hand, but she only gripped tighter.

"This is my sister we're talking about!"

Lowering his bow, Cupid pivoted to meet his wife's gaze. She was never so glorious as when she was protecting someone she loved.

"Sweetheart, you've watched me launch a thousand arrows. Have you ever seen me hurt anyone?"

She shook her head, tossing her short, wavy locks across her bare shoulders. "No, I just . . ."

He cupped her cheek with a tender hand. "You know I won't do this if you disapprove, but I thought we'd agreed Tristan was the one." The Aussie ski instructor wintering in Lake Tahoe was the perfect match for Sofia. Had it not been Posey's sister at issue, the match would scarcely have required a second thought.

With her uncanny intuition and people skills, Posey had proven an invaluable sounding board and partner. She and Cupid would spend hours at a time, side by side in their rocking chairs, discussing prospective matches while sharing a pitcher of lemonade on their wraparound porch, a cherished reminder of Posey's childhood. Whether owing to Posey's good counsel or Cupid's newfound maturity, he had yet to misstep since his return. Even the Divine Council had acknowledged Cupid's improvement, as Ares was quick to boast during his most recent visit to their home.

"Tristan seems like a nice enough guy—for a ski bum," Posey added with a chuckle that quickly faded. "It's been just over a year since Sofia left Sebastian. What if she's not ready to give away her heart again?"

Her pout brought a smile to Cupid's face. "Then he will have to work a little harder to win her over. That's not such a bad thing, is it?" *Remember how hard you made me work, sweet Posey?*

Meeting his gaze, Posey relaxed, her expression easing into a grin. "Poor guy won't know what hit him."

Cupid slanted his head, amused. "We never do."

With a sigh, Posey fingered the white silk bunched at Cupid's left shoulder, sending tingles of pleasure buzzing under his skin. "Do your thing, Cupid."

He leaned in and brushed his lips across hers. "First, I will send these arrows, and *then*, wife"—he paused to waggle his eyebrows—"I will 'do my thing.'"

She gave him a playful shove and one of her eye rolls, but her desire wafted into the air to dance with his. Cupid was still smiling as he raised his bow and nocked the arrow in place. It took mere seconds to locate Sofia and Tristan on the chairlift above the snowy slopes. Swiftly, Cupid drove the first arrow into Sofia's heart, plucked a second arrow from his quiver, and sent that one into Tristan's heart. The deed was done, and just in time for Valentine's Day. Now to claim his prize!

Returning his bow and quiver to their stand, Cupid turned fully to his wife. A sunbeam caught on the heart-shaped garnet suspended at her throat, blinding Cupid momentarily with a spike of light and a jolt of pleasure at the memory of Posey's first glimpse of the necklace three months earlier.

The moment she'd awakened on their first anniversary, he'd steered her straight to the mirror. Stepping into view behind her, Cupid gathered Posey's hair into a twist on top of her head. "Hold this, please," he'd told her reflection. She'd obeyed with a silly grimace. "Now close your eyes," and she'd half rolled her eyes before shutting them, but that was just Posey fighting her romantic inclinations. He feathered soft kisses on her neck to throw her off—and because he so loved making her tender skin pebble with goose bumps—before threading the gold chain around her neck. The bright stone settled perfectly into the hollow of her throat. Posey's reflection started to smile but caught her lip between her teeth. "Happy anniversary, my love. Thank you for keeping my heart next to yours."

She'd thrown her eyes wide open, and with a teary gasp, pressed right up to the glass for a closer look. "Oh, Q!" Releasing her hair, she'd spun to throw her arms around her husband's neck and plant a kiss on his smile. He'd melted. He'd flared with passion. That was how it always was with Posey, everything at once.

And that was how it was now.

Her blooming desire forced the soft browns and gold flecks to the edges of her eyes. She licked her lips. Cupid lunged, a whimper escaping him just before their lips touched.

A wail rang out from inside the palace. The lovers pulled

apart where they stood, tensed, listening, waiting. The urgent cry blared again, bouncing off the limestone floors and gaining in determination and intensity.

Posey dissolved into giggles. "No need to look so forlorn," she said, patting Cupid's cheek.

"What? I'm not—" But even as he protested, Cupid could feel that his mouth had twisted into a frown. "Okay, maybe I was, but I'm over it."

And indeed he was, because headed their way, red in the face from crying, was the one creature in the cosmos whose need for Posey outstripped even Cupid's. For Eden, only for Eden, Cupid was glad to make the sacrifice.

Artemis scurried out to the terrace, straight to Posey's side. Despite the inconsolable bundle in her arms, Artemis was of good humor. "The princess requires her lunch."

Posey shook her head, grinning, even as she reached for the howling baby. "We really need to stop calling her that."

Artemis shot Cupid a conspiratorial grin. *I will if you will.*

Easing into her rocker, Posey slipped her chiton out of the way and guided her breast into the tiny mouth twisting frantically for the nipple. Posey let out a soft hiss, then relaxed again as Eden latched on to the breast and began drawing milk.

"*Ahh*, there she goes!" Artemis smiled brightly. "Just two weeks of practice, and this little one's an expert."

"She's a quick study," replied Posey, shooting Cupid a sly glance. "Takes after her father."

Eden stole back their attention with her greedy suckling and little baby squeaks and the way her angry fists punched the air around her as if fighting off some unseen foe. *Don't you worry, daughter. You will never want for nourishment or love.*

"The name suits her," Artemis said. "Look at this precious baby, pure delight."

Glowing with happiness and pride, Cupid reached his thumb to his daughter's chubby cheeks and swept away her tears. Eden glanced drowsily toward her father's adoring gaze, pulling a stream of baby-talk nonsense out of her father's mouth as she drew milk from her mother's breast. Sated and exhausted, Eden let her heavy eyelids drift closed. Cupid glanced up to find his wife's warm gaze waiting for him.

In all his life, he'd never imagined this kind of joy. What could he have known about fatherhood? He had been a mere child himself until Posey rescued him.

On their wedding night and so many times since, Posey had shared her reservations about bringing children into their lives. How does an immortal body create new life? Without her mother or sisters to consult, who would Posey go to with her questions, big and small? Would she know how to mother a demigod?

What Cupid couldn't answer, which was most of it, Artemis could and did, everything from pregnancy to childbirth to the mechanics of raising a child who would likely be very different from Posey. The two women had grown quite close over the nine months of Posey's pregnancy and had sealed their bond during the emotional delivery—a day Cupid would never forget. Artemis would continue to protect the baby through her childhood, right up to the moment Eden took her marriage vows.

A loud knock pulled Cupid from his tight family circle. "I'll get that." He brushed a kiss to Posey's lips on his way to the door.

There stood Mercury in Cupid's forecourt, grinning hard. "You know, this knocking trend your wife started is really slowing me down."

Though Mercury's objection to Posey's "trendsetting" ways was tongue-in-cheek, it was far from the first to reach Cupid's ears. Not surprisingly, her twenty-first-century ideas about gender equality had not gone over well with some of the more boorish divines, who'd been quick to report their grievances all the way to the top. After about a week of fielding complaints, Zeus made a great show of summoning Cupid to his palace, where the two swapped battle stories over many glasses of powerful drink and many belly-shaking laughs. "Be smarter than your old grandfather, will you?" Zeus had said with a giant wink. "Never disagree with your wife when she's right, and only in private if she's wrong!" Cupid had flown home wobble-winged but more hopeful than ever for the future of his beloved Olympus.

The changes began almost immediately. Not surprisingly, the female Olympians rallied around Posey, adopting her "simple elegance" as the new chic—minimal jewelry, spare makeup, natural hairstyles, and comfortable, utilitarian clothing—not that Posey had purposely inspired the revolution. A self-confessed "tomboy" whose Earth wardrobe had largely consisted of jeans, bike shorts, and ski pants, Posey had swiftly adapted the traditional chiton to her active lifestyle. Soon, the "skortunic" Rhapso had fashioned for Posey was popping up everywhere in a palette of heather-gray and denim, sand and soil, verdant greens and watery blues. To Cupid's eye, none wore it as well as his wife with her long, fit legs and firm rump carved by years of mountain biking, and he proudly told her as much on a daily basis.

Shrugging, Cupid invited Mercury inside. "Apologies for the hindrance, Uncle, but I must concur with my wife on the benefits of boundaries."

"Yes, you two do seem to be thriving since you moved out of your mother's palace," said Mercury, craning his neck to admire the newly painted ceiling frescoes. "It truly is remarkable what you've built for yourself here."

"With the help of Hephaestus and some very talented painters and mosaic artists." And if Cupid had drawn some inspiration from Ruthie's mansion, he was certain she'd be pleased to know it.

"Let me not delay further." Smiling hard, Mercury brandished Posey's phone tied with a pink "It's a girl!" ribbon. "From your favorite Earth couple."

Cupid gawped. "It's been three months already?"

Mercury laughed. "Time flies with a wee one in the house."

"Not between the hours of midnight and five a.m.," Cupid replied, taking the phone. "Thank you, Uncle. Posey will be pleased to catch up on her family's messages."

The Council had agreed to permit Mercury to pass the phone from Pan to Posey—"upload to the cloud," as Pan had joked—every three months. Posey was able to read and type out replies to emails while the charge lasted, and Mercury would deliver the phone back to Pan the next day. Pan would then connect to the network, allowing all the messages to send from Posey's account. No one on Earth was the wiser.

For Posey, the updates helped blunt the sadness of leaving her life behind. She'd followed her father's improving health with frequent checks through their gaia glass as well as checking in on her sisters and their children, but Cupid knew she felt their absence all the more acutely having just regained her family. At least now, she could share pictures of Eden with her mortal family—and with Pan and Reed.

"Please give my best to your bride," Mercury said. "Oh, and be sure to check out the videos before the battery dies."

"What did they do?" Cupid felt a smile beginning.

"I haven't seen it myself, but Reed recorded his first run with Pan." At Cupid's request, Hephaestus had fashioned a lightweight chariot Pan could strap onto his back so that Reed could have the sensation of running with him. "The two of them could not stop giggling." Mercury winked and was gone.

Chuckling, Cupid started toward his wife and daughter when another knock stopped him in his tracks. Spinning on his heel, Cupid returned to the door and peered through the peephole. There stood his mother, bouncing impatiently from one foot to the other, giving the door a hard glare. Beside her, ever patient, Hephaestus balanced a stack of tiny pink outfits up to his chin.

Cupid opened the door and stepped quickly out of his mother's path. Aphrodite barely gave Cupid a glance as she darted for the terrace.

"Is the princess awake?" Aphrodite's question trailed after her like leaves kicked up by the wind.

Hephaestus pulled up to Cupid's side and released a weary sigh in Aphrodite's direction. "That woman's been watching the sun all morning, cursing about boundaries."

Cupid stifled a grin. Poor Hephaestus. "Here, let me help you with all that." Cupid offloaded the pile of clothing onto the sideboard. "I didn't realize there was that much pink in all of Olympus."

"Oh, there wasn't," Hephaestus said with a laugh. "Mercury had to make three trips!"

"Mother's really embraced this *yaya* role."

"She'll calm down some . . . eventually"—Hephaestus scratched his beard—"maybe." The two men shared a laugh. "*Anyway* . . ." The old, wise eyes crinkled at the edges. Hephaestus wrapped his arm around Cupid's shoulders. "How are you getting along? A newborn is a huge change."

"Yes," Cupid replied. "I wouldn't have believed there was room in my heart for so much more love."

"Ah, the great and mysterious heart." Hephaestus glanced toward the terrace before returning his awed gaze to Cupid. "Fatherhood agrees with you."

"I truly could not be happier."

"Nobody deserves it more."

"Thank you." Tears welled. "Anything I've learned about being a good father comes from you."

Hephaestus answered with a firm squeeze of Cupid's shoulder. "Come, son. Let us join the rest of our family."

Lost to his thoughts, Cupid lay naked on the deerskin rug in their bedchamber. Hands intertwined beneath his head, he stared past his chin at the tiny miracle dozing on his chest, rising and falling with Cupid's breath as if they shared lungs. Skin-to-skin contact was ideal for bonding, according to Posey's books.

Her experts offered no wisdom regarding wings, but Cupid had not needed it. Instinct had taken over the very first time Artemis set the newborn in his arms. Cupid had snuggled his baby girl straight to his heart, and his mighty plumage had closed gently over the infant, kissing the downy pinfeathers at the top of her spine.

Wing-to-wing, father to daughter.

A soft click drew Cupid's focus straight up the bed's footboard, where Posey's camera clicked again before she moved it to meet Cupid's upside-down gaze. "I'm sorry I disturbed you," she whispered, her voice choked with emotion. "I couldn't resist. I've never seen anything so beautiful in my life."

She turned the phone to show him what she'd just captured. Their perfect Eden cocooned inside her father's wings, her miniature Cupid's-bow lips drawn into the sweetest circle below her cute button nose and thick, coal-colored eyelashes that were already the envy of Olympus.

Smiling up at his wife, Cupid lifted one wing in invitation. Posey set the phone down and tossed away her nightgown. Every fiber of his being vibrated with anticipation.

Eden didn't stir as Posey slipped in beside her and nestled into the contours of Cupid's body. Posey's cool, soft skin met his belly. He let out a soft moan. She slid her palm across Cupid's chest until it rested over his heart. Their gazes caught and held.

Since the beginning of time, his soul had yearned for hers without knowing she even existed. Now, she was here, and they belonged to each other in every meaningful way—mind, body, and spirit. He'd never tire of the miracle.

Cupid's wing closed again around his Right Love and the wondrous new life they'd created together. Who could say what their future would hold? Eternity awaited, and they had only just begun their own, private happily ever after.

THE END

*If you enjoyed The Quest for Psyche, please consider leaving a review wherever you go to find your next read. Just a line or two can make a huge impact on the book's future, especially for an indie author!*

# CAST OF DIVINE CHARACTERS

AUTHOR'S NOTE: The primary name (all uppercase) for each divine is consistent with the narrative of the "Great Syncretism," an invented departure from Greco-Roman mythology. The character snippets offered here are based on canon; where multiple stories exist within the classical sources, I have chosen my favorite version.

ADONIS: Aphrodite's young, beautiful lover.

AGLAIA: One of the three Graces (sister-nymphs), Aglaia is the goddess of splendor.

APHRODITE (Venus): Goddess of love, beauty, and fertility. Married to Hephaestus, bore four children to Ares, including Cupid.

APOLLO: God of light, music, prophecy, and medicine.

ARES (Mars): God of War. Son of Zeus and Hera, brother of Hephaestus, father of Cupid.

ARTEMIS (Diana): Goddess of the hunt, protector of new brides. Twin sister of Apollo.

ATHENA (Minerva): Goddess of wisdom and war arts. Sprang from Zeus's head fully formed.

ATROPOS: One of the three Fates ("allotters") responsible for spinning men's fate. Clotho spins the thread of life, Lachesis determines its length, and Atropos cuts the thread with her shears.

CERBERUS: The vicious three-headed hound of Hades, guards the gates of the Underworld to prevent the dead from leaving.

CLOTHO: One of the three Fates (with Atropos and Lachesis), Clotho spins the thread of life.

CUPID (Eros): God of erotic love. Illegitimate son of Aphrodite and Ares. The winged archer of Mount Olympus.

DIONYSUS (Bacchus): God of wine and ecstasy. Son of Zeus.

EUPHROSYNE: One of the three Graces, Euphrosyne is the goddess of good cheer, joy, and mirth.

GAIA: Goddess of earth. One of the primordial elemental deities born at the dawn of creation.

HADES (Pluto): Ruler of the Underworld. Brother of Zeus and Poseidon.

HELIOS: God of the sun. Crowned with the aureole of the sun, he emerged each dawn driving a chariot drawn by four winged steeds and descended in the far West at each day's end into a golden cup that bore him back to the East.

HEPHAESTUS (Vulcan): God of fire and forge, blacksmith and divine craftsman. Son of Zeus and Hera, married to Aphrodite, stepfather to Cupid.

HERA (Juno): Queen of the Gods. Sister and wife of Zeus. Famous for her ill temper.

HYPNOS: God of sleep. Rises into the sky each night in the train of his mother Nyx. Father of Morpheus.

LACHESIS: One of the three Fates (with Atropos and Clotho), Lachesis determines the length of the thread of life.

MERCURY (Hermes): Messenger of the gods, father of Pan.

PAN (Faunus): Demi-god of the wild, protector of the herd.

Satyr (half man, half goat). One of the only gods thought to have died. Son of Mercury.

POSEIDON (Neptune): Ruler of the seas. Brother of Zeus and Hades.

THALIA: One of the three Graces, Thalia is the goddess of youth and beauty.

THEMIS: Goddess of divine law and order, a prophetic goddess who presides over the most ancient oracles.

ZEUS (Jupiter): Ruler of the gods. Married to Hera, yet father of many, by many—divines and mortals alike.

For more information on the mythological
world of the Cupid's Fall series,
including full-color illustrations, timelines,
family trees and more, visit
www.bethcgreenberg.com/mythology

# ACKNOWLEDGMENTS

And so, Cupid's quest ends roughly where it began, even if he is a very different god from the one banished to Earth in book one. Sitting here at the very same desk where I first typed out my rough ideas for this series, I feel very much like Cupid—physically situated in the same place but seeing everything through new eyes.

With Q and Posey situated in their happily ever after, this is a moment to take a deep breath and express my gratitude to the many people who helped me move this story from a kernel of an idea to a published, four-book series. To every single person who believed in me and encouraged me along the way, to everyone who read the books and loved these characters, I appreciate you. To those who recommended the book to a friend or your book group or your social media following, thank you for lifting the voice of an indie author.

To Shelley and Michelle, two talented writers who both read this book well before the pages were presentable, thank you for asking the big questions. To Susan Atlas, I am forever grateful you reached out to me so long ago with an offer to edit my fan-fiction writing. I suspect you and I would have found each other anyway, but I'm so grateful to the stories that brought us together. Thank you for your expertise and keen eye and for helping me convey to my readers exactly what's in my head. Thank you for taking the writing seriously even before I knew how, and above all, thank you for your kindness and your friendship.

To Betti Gefecht, cover designer and illustrator extraordinaire, thank you for breathing life into my characters with your stunning drawings. Thank you for indulging my obsession with eyebrows and noses and generally allowing me to make a nuisance of myself. Thank you for sharing your many talents so generously, whether brainstorming title ideas or writing those dreaded blurbs or providing emergency tech support when my files go haywire. Thank you for surprising me on Zoom book chats in the middle of your German nights. You are a treasure, and I thank my lucky stars my soul found yours in this life.

To Domini Dragoone, thank you for working your magic on everything between the covers to seamlessly draw the reader into the dual worlds of ancient fantasy and modern reality. To Lisa Hollett, thank you for the professional polish on the final drafts and for bringing your experience and unique perspective to the party.

To my fandom family, words brought us together, but friendship *keeps* us together. To Maria, thank you for helping my characters occasionally speak and think in Greek. How comforting to have a native at the other end of the chat box! To Cecilia Rene and Jiffy Kate and Amy Argent and Melanie Moreland and K Evan Coles, thank you for sharing your wisdom and experience with a newbie author learning the ropes. I promise to pay it forward. To Karen Wilk, thank you for all your support, wonderful ideas, and encouragement along the way. To Kate, thank you for inspiring Mia and teaching me to write boldly. To Jayme, I so wish you were here for this leg of the journey.

To my ARC team and Suzy Approved Book Tours, thank you for making the book launches slightly less terrifying by having my back and getting those first reviews out into the world. To my flash fiction community, thank you for elevating writing and for teaching me how to recognize good critique.

To the team at Wellesley Books, thank you for your early and steadfast partnership with a local indie author. It's thrilling to find my books on your display tables.

To Lindsay, my strong and talented daughter, you fearlessly speak your truths, and you never let anything stand between you and your dreams. You inspire me every single day. To Jeffrey, my sweet son, I like to picture you hanging out with Cupid and Pan and having a ton of laughs.

To Larry, my real-life superhero, thank you for cheering the longest and the loudest no matter where my crazy ideas take me.

## ABOUT THE AUTHOR

BETH C. GREENBERG is a former CPA who stepped through the portal of flash (1000-word) fiction into the magical world of creative writing and never looked back. She lives outside of Boston, where she and her husband are occasionally visited by their daughter and grand-dog Slim. *The Quest for Psyche* is book four—and the finale—of the Cupid's Fall series.

To sign up for Beth's email list and get sneak peeks, special deals, and exclusive content visit: *www.bethcgreenberg.com/newsletter*

CPSIA information can be obtained
at www.ICGtesting.com
Printed in the USA
BVHW080726031221
622949BV00002B/14